Michael Pye, former
The Movie Brats (wit
Over the Water, *Eld*
he divides his time b

ELDORADO

'In *Eldorado* Michael Pye employs the classic ingredients of the modern bestseller – big money, both old and new, sex in some unusual forms, power, gold, vaulting ambition and catastrophe – and somehow stirs them into a mixture that is both original, well-researched and enthralling'
Daily Mail

By the same author

The Movie Brats (with Lynda Myles)
Moguls: Inside the Business of Show Business
The King Over the Water
Eldorado
Reckoning

MICHAEL PYE

Chaos

GraftonBooks
A Division of HarperCollins*Publishers*

GraftonBooks
A Division of HarperCollins*Publishers*
77–85 Fulham Palace Road,
Hammersmith, London W6 8JB

A Grafton Paperback Original 1991
9 8 7 6 5 4 3 2 1

ISBN 0-586-07470-8

Printed and bound in Great Britain by
Collins, Glasgow

Set in Century Expanded

This is a work of fiction.
Any resemblance to actual events, or
corporations, or persons, living or dead,
is entirely coincidental.

Only chaos, and the circumstances, are real.

The corridor was gaudy with sunset gold and acid green and the Rocky Mountains caught in mirrors; but the room itself had no windows. The light was manufactured, the comfortless blue-grey of neon. It stained the starched white of a high, narrow bed and the skin of the man who lay there.

He was learning to breathe; a machine ratcheted beside him. His body was overgrown with drips and valves. Apart from his name, all he had was a casing of dried flesh. But inside that husk, a will was practising, practising, trying to find fingers from memory and move them, to scratch or tap. The will was strong and furious, but it was held in flesh that was airless and motionless like ice.

He could hear, though.

'I hope he dies,' a man said. He had authority, like a doctor.

'Cost you a lot, did he?' The second voice sounded younger.

'The worst investment of my life. I need the charts, nurse.'

'I don't think they say too much. He's a dead man.'

'He can't even die right. Bastard.'

Inside the body gone to hopeless sleep, James Drake kept repeating his name. He made it sound in the vaults of his mind; he could not tell if his lips shaped anything. Thought was spasms with no way to tell the time between them, and when he summoned images, they formed no patterns. His memory was only pictures and headlines, like other people's newspapers glimpsed on a train. It was barely enough to make a world.

'I wouldn't wish this on anyone,' the second voice said.

There must have been life before this stillness. He wished he could open his eyes; the clues came through the eyes.

A little electrical current passed in his brain. He saw a city remade, modelled in clay and card, some huge ambition which bore his name.

He saw the same name on court papers. A courtroom, a bilious, tiny judge drowned in his own robes, struggling to his seat through a storm of black silk; but the judge had power enough to make him bankrupt. A judge, perhaps the same man, sending him to jail.

He was the saviour of the people's money. There were no details in this memory.

A long room, grey, with wire mesh tacked across the windows and a set of matched men in suits, expensive men and he was paying for them. There were guards. He felt great anger.

He was glorying in the sharp, sweet resin in the forest air, ambling on a high path and feeling damn fine. He was man enough to make a fool out of the judge and defy the world. He had come through.

Something about chaos. But not chaos as the dissolving of order; this was chaos that could be manipulated and used. It had something to do with maps, and oil and stocks and shares. He had been most concerned with chaos.

Then he remembered dying. Life went out like a slow, inexorable tide over wide, flat sands. Birds came down to bother what was left.

He had no way to tell the doctors that James Drake was still present. He was used to a body that did all he needed, when he needed, and now the effort of focusing an eye or raising an eyebrow was beyond him.

'The only question,' the older doctor said, 'is when. Does he have anyone who wants him alive?'

James Drake was dead. He was sure he had scores to settle.

1

Emma Griffier began to wake in a familiar place and in familiar arms, but she was not sure where. Her face felt cold, which meant an English bedroom. She could hear traffic which meant she was not in the country at Easterford, but there was birdsong which meant she was not in a hotel. She had a feeling she was home at last, which meant in David Taylor's bed.

He had turned his broad, black back to her, curled up like a muscled child. 'Bloody civil servant,' she said, softly. It was funny she'd settled with a museum man who would earn a civil service pension; but when he was not among the papers and the cases in London, he was out collecting ancestral spirits, or the feather capes of distant kings or the coloured filigree of island totems. She could wish for the same glamour.

He had opened only one dark eye. 'Ca-pit-a-list,' he said, and he pretended to be asleep again. She stretched like a young cat and curled away from him and the frontier of warm, used sheets between them was electric with waiting. Her skin was alive long before he touched her.

'I'm glad you're back,' he said.

Drowsy, friendly fingers shifted on the inside of her thighs, like down in a stray wind. He touched her at arm's length, so he could sense her body stiffen under the sheets, so he could see her respond; she had been away in Hollywood too long. He was like an engineer, checking for fractures in feeling or response, to be sure of her. He tugged softly at the reddish hair where her thighs met.

'They treat you right this time?'

She knew what he meant. 'I live like a monk,' she said. 'There's no time for anything else. We work seven days a week, fifty weeks a year – '

' – Mattins at the Polo Lounge,' he said, 'compline at Spargo – '

' – eight scripts a weekend, and every one of them a political minefield – '

' – living on freeways, living on the car phone – '

'I stopped them making *Invisible Man* with Eddie Murphy,' she said, proudly. 'And I have been polite to every single British director in town, personally.'

'Good, good girl,' he said. He tugged again at her hairs, a little less kindly.

'And I missed you,' she said.

He grinned, and most elaborately licked his lips. She was firm and young, and cunning and clever, and her breasts were like those early summer apples with a flush of red on the palest white and sweet, resilient flesh. And the best of her beauty was here, when she was animate and breathing hotly; she faded in cameras and the public record. She belonged to whoever was with her.

'Travelling lady,' he said, and he put down his huge head and rasped with his tongue where his fingertips had been, hot and wet. He found her lips and parted them, careful like a craftsman with a fragile medium; he pushed inside her, waking nerves and blood. He licked broadly like a dog, and he nipped softly with his lips and she rose from the bed like a conjurer's assistant, levitating into his kind face.

There was no more pretending about sleep. She sounded like a beast that senses blood in a forest, growling, seething, breathing like a wind. He was working furiously, and he stopped cold.

She had gone some distance beyond thought; she was

full of colours and abandon, and she was almost frightened. Her wide eyes were full of him, without seeing him, and he had the miracle of her attention.

She pulled him back into her and he licked up through the faint fuzz on her belly to those apple breasts, and he ended on her face, smothering her and bringing the blood to the very surface of her skin. He had painted her with a broad line of spittle that made her his. And he entered her immediately; she was slick and wild to resolve the cacophony in her heart. They made love and war all at once, layered white on black on white, and dreaming the momentary dream of being one, a dream like a harmonic over music in the bed, One, one, one, one, one; she was crying as she came.

Later, they threw luggage and threatened to leave each other, immediately. It was always like that when she came home. She fought and schemed to get to London, and she wanted respect: just being there was proof she was a woman warrior, able to finesse and sometimes bully the studio. Vice-presidents, even senior vice-presidents, needed to be there to survive, and every time she came to see David in London she took risks. Besides, Customs always stopped her nowadays, and she had no idea why.

But to David, each time, it was only ordinary and right that she had come home, and she should have come back before. They could rub each other raw with talk for days, and make it up with touch, and then it was time to plot the next meeting.

'You should come to Easterford,' she said. 'It's only overnight, and I have to go back on Sunday.'

'I need you,' he said, which he did not need to say.

On Saturdays, Simeon Ryder could visit Griffier Ltd with some of his senses turned down. The screens in the trading room were dark, the bank's corridors empty, and there was nobody in the partners' room. He could pull the dark rosewood of his office round him like a blanket, and do whatever needed to be done but was unthinkable to the Griffiers themselves. He was their steward.

But Saturday was also his day for walking, and he had to start early; in the afternoon, he was obliged to drive down to Easterford. He crossed the newly respectable streets of Soho, the frock shops bordered in the post-modernist pastel of the month, the ad agencies glittering with glass and chic neon. His London was a city with visual hiccups, a series of tiny shocks that suggested unease, but never quite required a doctor. The strip shows had gone, but kids still sold themselves, because they couldn't think what else to do; the sweat shops had been driven away from the heart of the city, but men and women slept in each other's arms and in cities of boxes. An old woman picked through the bits of leaf and squashed fruit that the street markets left behind. Simeon observed such things without passion or anger; they were the reality he was paid to manipulate. He was sure no politician would ever do what was needed.

He took coffee at Pâtisserie Valerie, curled anonymously in a corner. He felt like some senior civil servant, grandly giving up official cars and privilege for the day. He finished the paper, and he took a sepia photograph from his pocket and laid it on the table. His accidental companion, a shrill young woman in black, stared.

She saw the copy of a copy of a careful portrait: a woman in black against a cardboard pastoral, with shop-made flowers in an arc and a painted swan on a lake that was slightly bent. The woman was very dark, and lovely; even in her forties, her eyes shone. She very nearly smiled.

The girl sensed weirdness, but she was hooked. A little expertise told her what kind of picture this was:

the portraits made for newly landed immigrants, to make them seem solid and secure in a strange land and set them in a frame like everyone else. She wondered why a man in Armani carried such a picture.

Simeon registered her interest and pushed the picture back into his pocket. He saw strength in the picture, but also a woman who neither surrendered to her fate nor fought it, a peasant who could never be disappointed because she had no expectations. She wore black because that was the dress for a proper matron, but to him it seemed like a shroud for hopes and beauty.

'If you don't mind me asking,' the shrill girl said.

'I do, I'm afraid,' Simeon said.

He paid for his coffee, and he hailed a cab. He knew he was over-dressed for the address he gave, and so did the driver. But as the city began to lose definition in a scuffle of tatty shops and tenements, Simeon stared out, fascinated. He wanted to raise ghosts.

'Don't get much business down here,' the taxi driver said. 'You want me to wait?'

Simeon stepped out into a mess of dust and waste. There were fences of corrugated iron, scrawled over by kids; it was as though their frantic, overloaded eyes were trying to take away the hurt of blank space. There was an old market hall, being gutted. Otherwise, machines had bitten into the London clay for some new building and there was spoiled grass, little houses and tower blocks. Simeon had never been in such an empty place.

'You sure you want to be here?' the driver asked, being kindly.

'It's personal,' Simeon said.

He took out the picture again. He could give the woman a name: Sarah. The line of Sarah's street had been somewhere here. She had sewn for a living, when she had to, but she was not born to the trade; he imagined her long, easy fingers painfully cut when she started, and then toughened against the thread with time. She had walked somewhere here, wrapped in black. She had worked every hour there was light. To protest or fight was only a waste of the energy she needed to feed her children.

He felt connected to her, with all too little evidence. Her history was in the bed and the womb and in the heart; his was in prospectuses and deals, and as for the Griffiers, their past was all monuments, a public record. He had come past fifty without needing to know his own history, but now it was imperative, and awkward.

He was suddenly afraid. He was afraid of finding Sarah's passivity in himself. He was afraid of the emptiness of this place, and the tracks of an angular fury in the scribbling on the walls and fences. The past had been cut out here like a canker, again and again, so that nobody's memory went back more than a generation or two; in the name of improvements, better housing, social engineering, streets and families were shipped and stored like new products. History belonged to people who could afford it, now.

He told the driver to take him to Griffier Ltd.

'Quite a contrast, guv,' the driver said, conversationally. 'You work there?'

'I do.'

'Like working for the bloody Rothschilds,' the driver said. 'That some development of yours, is it? That place we went to?'

'No,' Simeon said. 'That's personal.'

The driver's eyes floated in the rear-view mirror like an accusation. But Simeon was half ashamed of having such a soap opera story, and not at all ready to explain. He was an adopted child who discovers, after fifty, the name of his real mother but little more about her. The only face and grave and street he could find belonged to

Sarah, his grandmother. There was no twist to the story to make it less banal. It was indulgent to go visiting, and worse to raise ghosts when he had no idea what to do with them. And, besides, he had other things to think about.

A deferential guard snapped to attention when he entered the bank. In his office, Simeon kept the phone very close to his hand. Enough of the morning had passed to start checking and teasing and finding out.

He had an agenda. The morning papers carried a stock-market rumour that someone was buying stock in Griffier Ltd, with intent. The Griffiers were august like the Rothschilds or the Hambros or the Barings, a fine City of London tribe, but they were not truly international, and for that reason they had sold shares and gone public two years before. The advantage was capital, and how much easier it was to find; the drawback was that the wrong people can buy and sell a public company. And it did seem, from the papers, that quite the wrong person was buying now.

Just under five per cent, *The Independent* reckoned, and they were usually right; and the buyer was – Simeon wondered how he would explain the buyer to someone who did not know the City. You had to imagine the motor mouth of the international trading business, the export-import king of the Western world with a passion for dealing anything from steel to influence to shares, a man with loud opinions and cold eyes. John Brown, in other words. He sometimes seemed to long for the attention that all his money deserved; he had bought a rather faded middle-market newspaper from its founder, and he went there to bully the editors on a regular basis. It was alarming, because Brown's interest in a share was enough to put a company in play, and start the various jackals and wolves about their baleful business of merging and taking over; baleful, as Simeon conceded to himself, only when your bank gets no commission on the deal.

It was also impertinent. Brown was new, brash, doubtful and foreign. The Griffiers had been new, brash, doubtful and foreign a hundred and fifty years ago, and now were gentlemen, if not aristocrats. They were certainly an institution, pillars of the court of the Bank of England, and Brown was just a trader. The two names did not fit together.

That meant, as Simeon knew, that everything Brown did would be noticed and reported. And it was bad enough steering an institution through the various revolutions that Mrs Thatcher's Government had decreed, without a rumbustious, rule-bending passenger whose motives were never quite sure, who might find it fun to run the ship on to the rocks or run up a flag of surrender at any time.

He might find some allies at Easterford that afternoon, with all the family assembled. But he was afraid their instinctive solidarity would keep him away from serious talk. It would be as well to have a sense of who stood where, to persuade at least one of the Griffiers that their situation was serious.

He would try Emma. She was a shareholder like the others, but she never came to the partners' room. She had spent her life running away from being a Griffier, while he had given his life to being an honorary member of the tribe; but that meant she would like to avoid trouble.

He liked to know things; so he knew she would be with David Taylor.

'I can't help you,' she said.

'I was thinking,' Simeon said. 'He fancies himself a movie mogul, I know. You could talk to a mogul. You know the trade talk. He's bound to be at the Cannes Festival – '

'I work at Cannes,' Emma said. 'I work from seven in the morning until midnight, and after, and then I take calls from LA.'

'Of course, my dear,' Simeon said. 'But you're the only one who can talk to him casually – '

'Nobody talks to him casually. He's either a shark or he's schizophrenic or he's a dealer who can't stop, and it doesn't matter. Talking to him is dangerous, whichever way.'

'We have to know what he wants.'

'Maybe he wants us to approve of him. Maybe he wants to come to tea.'

'You're not being serious,' Simeon said.

Emma felt the whole freight of the man's very quiet, relentless talk when she put down the phone. 'He's just a butler,' she said to David Taylor. 'He's a financial butler, an upper servant. He knows all the secrets, and he does all the deeds. But he has no damn right to give orders.'

'You sound very rich,' David said.

'Don't you start,' Emma said. 'You don't know what he wanted me to do. To talk to John Brown at Cannes, to sound him out about the future of the bank. Jesus, that's worse than oiling the Australian distributors.'

'You have to oil them?'

'Figuratively,' Emma said. 'I wish you could be at Cannes.'

'I couldn't,' David said. 'I'd frighten all the little old Jewish producers. Besides, you have to flirt at Cannes. I'd put you off your stride.'

Easterford, he implied, was quite enough.

Each thought had to be clawed for, a hold on a sheer wall. Together, they did not yet amount to a history. Old deals made a kind of fossil in James Drake's mind, scattered through blind clay; he wanted to see a map of all of them, to know who he had been.

All that was clear was grievance. The anger wrapped in these sterile hospital sheets was terrible; he felt it could corrode his flesh and burst free, vicious and autonomous.

He remembered the name 'Griffier'.

'Something's wrong,' Simeon Ryder said, persistent in the shade of the great cedars.

'You told me,' Emma said. 'Someone's buying shares.'

'I mean something more,' Simeon said. 'I knew you might understand. You're the one with the imagination. You won't just think it's indigestion or the mid-life crisis.'

'You sound like a minor-league prophet,' Emma said. 'You thought I'd believe in the doom of the Griffiers, is that it?' She had never thought before if she truly liked Simeon Ryder. He was sleek and dark, just plump enough to fill out the lines which duty and time should have brought him; now that he was annoying her, she thought he had a eunuch's face. He had been in the bank for as long as she could remember, a brilliant young man who was strategist and manager while the Griffiers went out to woo clients and represent the bank. The family did lunch, someone once told Emma; Simeon did business.

'I don't mean anything as melodramatic,' Simeon said. 'But you know as well as I do that the bank has problems. When Big Bang comes – '

'I've been away so long,' Emma said. 'I never had much to do with the bank.'

'You're much too modest,' Simeon said, which was what she expected. But then he said: 'You understand money so much better than either of your brothers,' and she was startled. Simeon was like a costly doctor, who reasoned his patients into health, never giving orders or taking sides; he was detached, whatever hurt or foolishness he saw. He never took sides unnecessarily, until now.

'I know things are changing,' Emma said. 'There are no more accepting houses, which ends our cosy little oligopoly; anyone can stamp other people's IOUs and make them respectable and tradeable. Soon, there won't be fixed fees for dealing in shares, and there will just be dealers – not jobbers to make the market and brokers to sell the shares retail. I know all that from the Sunday papers.'

'You can see it's the wrong time for things to go wrong,' Simeon said. He was worrying at the neat lawn with a long stick. 'And I have an odd sense of active malice, someone interfering in our affairs. More things go wrong than need to.'

Emma was lulled in the peace of the gardens at Easterford. The lawns were paper neat, cut and rolled for a steady century; they framed the brick of a grand Victorian palace, assembled, tower by tower and stair by stair, from a catalogue of tourist views of the châteaux of the Loire. Beyond the woods lay the new suburbia of Essex, a jigsaw of leaded windows and red roofs, brought here by the railway, just as the Griffiers had been in Victorian times; but the woods were deep and wide enough to buy quiet. Besides, this place – every hill, valley, stream, pool – was built to the design of a Griffier, in those fine days when the Hambros could simply drown a village to make a lake. Here, the tribe was in perfect control.

But there was a shiver of breeze under the cedars, enough to remind her how conditional an English spring can be.

'I might need some help,' Simeon said.

'I have my own life.'

'But if it was a family matter, if it affected the Griffier name – '

'I know about the Griffier name,' Emma said. 'When I'm at studio meetings, people still ask me if I'm a real Griffier. It's the bear at my shoulder, whatever I do. It puts me in the freak show.'

'It's who you are,' Simeon said. He knew there was a risk in saying such a thing, because he had made a life without knowing who he was. But he had made her cross, he could see it, and he packed away his difficult intuitions, and he watched her stalk towards the house, an angry gazelle, her hair like red gold. He thought how alive she seemed among the other upper-middle-class ladies, with their lapwing voices and their long print frocks that barely grazed their tiny breasts, and their defeated names like Patience. She was their hope, and she had chosen to go away.

Of course, he thought, she won't escape.

'They are very, very polite,' David said. 'It's uncanny how polite they are.'

'I think they're surprised. They'd be as surprised by any intellectual.'

'Any black intellectual.'

'Thank God they're in shock,' Emma said. 'It makes them much easier to deal with.'

'Is that why I'm here? To shock them?'

'You're here because I love you.'

David said: 'But we have separate rooms.'

'It's a house party tradition,' Emma said, 'changing rooms at midnight. It sounds like mice stampeding. In any case, everyone has separate rooms. You know that. At least they didn't put you in the bachelors' wing.'

He stood at the mirror, tying his black tie deftly.

'You're the first lover I've ever had,' Emma said, 'who could tie his own tie.'

‘Trading up,’ David said. He decided he had done enough of being nervous. ‘You ought to show me the house before dinner.’

‘I didn’t know you’d be interested,’ she said.

‘It’s heritage, isn’t it? Treasure houses of England, all splayed out in grand museums in America. And nobody mentions where the money came from to build the houses and stuff them full.’

‘It isn’t heritage. It’s furniture,’ Emma said. ‘And it isn’t a treasure house, we live here. You don’t have to clean so often when you live there.’

‘And the money – ’

‘We were Dutch when there was slavery. We only became rich and English later.’

‘You think that’s an alibi?’

She rushed him, with a pillow in her hand, and she beat him round the head.

‘Heh,’ he said. ‘The defence of class interests – ’

‘Shut up,’ she said. ‘Come exploring.’

She was intimate with the house. It was the skin that had held her childhood, from the dark, mossy smells in the fruit cellar to the high dormer windows that gave on to the slate roofs, and the curious Italianate, gilt and majolica church that her great-grandfather had thought proper for an embarrassed and stringently Protestant village. She led David there by the hand, and stood in the quiet and the smell of polish. Any light that crept through the high clerestory windows was kept frantically busy, colliding with shiny things. There were a pair of grand tombs, with marble and pilasters.

‘I feel like a tourist,’ David said, and his voice echoed off the pale blue tiles.

‘So do I,’ she said, ‘almost. I’ve been away so long.’

Their heels sounded on the gravel path back to the house.

'I mean,' David said, 'I feel like a tourist somewhere like Blois, on the Loire.'

'We stole the towers from Blois,' Emma said. 'And the circular staircases, either side, but Great-grandfather glassed them in. He did it when he was building the hills.'

'They're very fine hills,' David said.

She showed him the stone hut, in the perfect shade of the woods, with shelves for blocks of ice. She let her hand brush against him, for the sake of the warmth and hardness of him; she was reassured. She led him back towards the house, and she pointed out the bachelors' wing, and the kitchens that were ranged beneath it: the pastry-cook's kitchen, the bread-maker's kitchen, the kitchen proper for roasting meat, the kitchen and still-room for jams and coffee and tea. The system fascinated him, she could see; he was trying to fathom what they meant, like the doings of some distant, painted tribe.

'It was very, very grand,' he said.

'The Prince of Wales played tennis here,' Emma said. 'The fat Prince of Wales, that is; we have a picture. He's ambling around in a blazer with a squared-off racket in his hand.'

'You fit here, don't you?' He sounded accusing.

'Here, and other places.' She had been thinking, briefly, of Simeon Ryder's warnings, and how embarrassing they were: like a clerk having visions. She was ashamed of the thought, but democracy had a hard time climbing the driveway to Easterford.

'I mean, you really fit here.'

'I wanted to show you my great-grandfather's room,' she said.

They climbed the circular staircase to the east of the house, and walked a gallery of bland, ancestral faces hung against a very modern white wall. Some day, she thought, she would specify their names for him: the

Victorian banker, big and pompous in mutton-chop whiskers and morning dress, in a rosewood room; the uncle in a too-snug Army uniform, an oddly sensual picture, who was now retired to a garden in Barbados; her own father, Sir Alistair Griffier, in shirtsleeves on a veranda, done in light, bright colours, the proconsul being enlightened in his last colony.

They pushed through curtains into a room that was full of sunset. For a moment, David could see no reason why this particular room had stayed in Emma's memory: it had the usual plush, the usual reds and woods. The wall was lined with pictures in carved, gilt frames. After a moment more, he became aware of eyes.

And then his glance skipped from frame to frame. In each one was the picture of a woman, always a lovely woman, sometimes a girl-child, sometimes a matron, but a company of beautiful friends.

'It was his harem, I suppose,' Emma said.

'He had taste,' David said.

'He did,' said a woman's voice from the doorway. It was a dark American voice, fit to be scoured down with booze and tobacco, but not yet. It embarrassed both David and Emma in their shared thoughts.

'I didn't mean to interrupt,' said Lady Griffier, Emma's mother. 'I expect the boys are boring you both, and I didn't want to be bored, either.'

David thought he knew the type: an angle of flesh in a flurry of silks, a woman pared down by sheer social effort. In every other way, she might be an Englishwoman – horses, a little expertise in Alpine plants, headscarves from Hermès, a practical way with dogs, a valiant indifference to which of her husband's pictures was truly good and how his business ran – but she stayed defiantly Manhattan-thin, like a new arrival. A second wife, she said with every bone, needs an identity.

'The boys can't entirely help it,' she said, brightly.

'Maternal genes. You'd be dull if you were bred to the Griffiers to give them aristocracy, and so would your children be.' Florence Griffier never had forgiven the shadow of her husband's inoffensive, and long-dead, first wife.

'We haven't talked to Maurice,' Emma said, 'or Rupert.'

'Close the door, and draw up chairs,' Lady Griffier said, shifting the gold at her wrists purposefully. 'Let me fill you in.' She looked at David pointedly. 'Of course, this will probably bore you –'

There was no offence in her eyes or talk, he could see. She meant only that he was not a husband, who must tolerate a mother's talk, and so he had a chance to escape; and she also meant she wanted some time with her daughter, without outsiders. For the moment, David was an outsider.

'I might take a shower,' he said vaguely, and strolled out.

'What a very clean young man,' Lady Griffier said, watching Emma watching David. 'You'll have to be careful with Maurice. He won't approve.'

'David's a bureaucrat, as well,' Emma said.

'God!' Florence Griffier said. 'I have to tell you that Maurice is no longer content with being a Conservative MP. He has discovered political thought, or what passes for it in this country. Twenty years ago, he'd have sat there believing in sound money and a strong defence, but now he has all sorts of fine ideas – the power of free markets, privatizing, deregulation, family values, libertarianism except for the queers and the blacks, the core of Englishness. You know the kind of thing.'

'It's why I live in Los Angeles,' Emma said.

'Maurice,' Lady Griffier said, 'brings in Parliamentary bills to take the dirty bits off television although I have to say,' and now she was examining her daughter's bare arms, fretfully, 'I have watched British television for years and longed for something truly offensive. Even rape looks polite in this country.' She sighed. 'You have absolutely none of the six telltale signs of skin cancer,' she said. 'You're a disgrace to cosmetology.'

Emma said: 'I expect Maurice is nervous. He'd have been a proper Cabinet Minister under Macmillan – sound name, good manners.'

'Manners are always a problem with Maurice. He occasionally tells us the whole Government is Jews and builders now, and he honestly can't understand why it is offensive to say so in quite those terms. They don't much like him, of course, and he's always trying to be more Thatcherite than Thatcher. I can't think why she keeps him.'

'He tries to keep the true faith.'

'He thinks he's shedding the skin of a good merchant banker, like a snake does. The trouble is, he's too much like a snake. The skin that grows back is just the same as the one he sloughed. I haven't the heart to tell him.' The words bustled out of her with awful energy; she took Emma's arm, and guided her out into the gallery and along to her dressing room. After the long months and years of her exile, she was at home when her daughter was with her.

'You didn't tell me about Rupert,' Emma said.

'He's not in jail,' Lady Griffier said. She truffled among her various condiments for a pot of certified miracles, in cream form, and she said: 'You need this in California.'

'There must be something more than not being in jail.'

'You wanted news. It is news that Rupert is not in jail.'

Emma settled on a *chaise-longue* that was stacked with papers and magazines, the demanding ones that Lady Griffier allowed herself in this sanctum of frills and indulgences. Being serious was an indulgence for a wife of her generation. 'And you?' she said.

'I don't have news,' Emma said. 'I don't have time for news.'

'You have David,' her mother said.

'Not in Los Angeles,' Emma said, 'unfortunately.'

'I suppose that's not easy. On the other hand, it gives you both time to be other people when you want to. You can be the studio executive without having to be David Taylor's lover.'

'It's not easy.'

'Couldn't he be a professor at UCLA or something? Follow you to the ends of the earth?'

'It isn't like that,' Emma said.

Lady Griffier looked quite disagreeably shrewd.

'I mean, I don't want it to be like that,' Emma said. 'We're independent, adult people – '

'The sheets are still cold, though.'

Emma said: 'It won't be for ever. It's a dead end, talking. If talking was going to solve things – '

Florence Griffier put her bone-thin arms around her daughter; she had a skimpy frame, but ample sympathy. 'Of course,' she said blithely, 'if you had children – '

'Mother,' Emma said, and the word lay like frost in the air.

'It might be difficult here,' Florence said. 'They do like to have precedents here.'

'I'm going to my room.'

The maid had left a fuss of tissue paper in the wardrobe, and a faint smell of Boots' cologne that prickled Emma's senses, disagreeably. She was furious at the competition her mother could rouse. She faced the mirror like an inventory: she wanted reassurance that she still had time. And it was not time for children that she wanted, as her mother might have assumed; she wanted time to find the settledness that was missing in the siege economy of her life.

She thought of David and her head filled with blood like a blow; it was everything, and it was not pleasant. She went to find him. She was half afraid she would catch him unprepared, not being David at all; that he was David only when she would see him.

In the side corridors, she saw that Florence had exiled the stuffed heads; she said the portraits of partners had the look of dead moose and she was campaigning against those, too. The walls were an austere white, like sanatorium walls. Emma found the whole gaudy contrivance of this beloved house had gone cold around her.

She took the backstairs up to the east tower. It had been like a private lane when she was a child; her brothers had a life out of the house long before she was born, and she was the indulgence of her parents, a luxury too sweet to be corrected. So she could have private ways through the house that nobody else would use; she could have territory like the tower room. She went there sometimes when she was full of fears that must not be spoken out loud, tiny fears that levered her world out of kilter; she sat like a princess at the window, looking out beyond the woods to the Essex flatlands and the marshes. She felt high and safe.

She could hear talk from the room while she was still on the stairs. There was the smooth cream of Simeon Ryder, insinuating his points, and the crash and boom of her father objecting.

' – it had better bloody well be friendly,' her father was saying. 'He owes us everything.'

She was ashamed to stay and listen on the stairs like a tricky maid, but she wanted to know more. She wanted clues to this trouble Simeon Ryder sensed was coming. At the very least, she wanted to know what had stirred his imagination after all these purposeful years.

'I don't think,' Ryder was saying, 'John Brown has ever bought into a company without putting it in play. If he buys, it means he wants to sell – soon and for a profit. He may tell the market he's simply making a long-term investment, and he may believe it at the time, but he's not capable of meaning it.'

'Does he have to make a statement at all?'

'It's in the papers already. He's dangerous and we're famous and it won't go away.'

'I can't quite think of Griffier Ltd in play,' Sir Alistair said. He tasted the words 'in play' and found them sour, like old cheese. 'My own brother started him in business, after all.'

'John Brown is not a sentimental man.'

'And can we fight him?'

The silence spoke for itself. A chair scraped against bare boards. Emma was stock still; she could smell candles and smoke, like a church. She made her footsteps sound out on the stairs deliberately.

'I didn't know anyone was in my room,' she said.

'Darling,' her father said. Simeon Ryder was clearly not happy to see her. 'Should I be changing for dinner, then?'

He had taken her tower room and stripped it to white walls and bare wood. A cross of gilded wood hung on the wall opposite the windows, and a prayer stall before it, without cushions. There was a rack of candles, unlit. Nobody would ever disturb her father here; prayer was far more embarrassing than any bodily function. It was the perfect room to talk with God, or a confidential servant.

Ryder said: 'We have to talk later. By Monday, everyone will know.'

'I don't think we need to talk at dinner,' Sir Alistair said. 'We do have a guest.'

Emma left them. Stairs she had known for thirty

years now seemed steeper; the house had lost its easy familiarity. Her father had need of a sanctuary, just as she had, once, and he needed magic. Things were no longer sure.

Something had crept into this place, something very like doubt.

Sometimes he struggled not to fall back into sleep, just when he was close to seeing something new. At least, inside this withered chrysalis of bone and skin, he thought sleep was what he was fighting. It might also be something final.

He was very faintly aware of the nurse. He sensed warmth, softness, a faint perfume; but he was entirely passive, unable to test what he sensed. Once, he heard her say: 'Poor old boy.'

He had to own his mind before he could rule his body. He needed to knit all the traces of memory into some kind of sense.

The name Griffier. He saw manners, unscrupulous English manners; it was an honour to be invited by them, and then they knifed you, and the honour was such there was no way to complain. If the Griffiers asked you to defend the mutual fund business, to prevent a huge failure, you were grateful for the chance to do something impossible.

He had been betrayed, that was it; tricked and ruined. But he remembered his past as full of networks and agreements and intelligence and deals and complications. He needed to know what made the Griffiers different, and why the name hung before him like a banner.

He struggled with how to know things. He faltered into sleep.

The men of the family were neat in evening dress, a black and white uniform which drew unkind attention to the histories Emma read on their faces.

Rupert had been somewhere exotic, long enough to bronze carefully; he dealt with people who put their trust in tans ('must have money,' they said, thinking of Bermuda). Maurice shook David's hand, awkwardly. Now he was into his forties, the veins stood in his face, pumped up by whisky – not too much, but too often, an oil to slip him through the day. He fussed about time to finish work on his official papers; as a junior minister, he had become a dull weekend guest, ostentatiously working. And Sir Alistair looked like a drinker of water, a careful man. And Simeon Ryder's face was too smooth to take an impression of his life, like a gigolo.

The outsider was obvious. He wore an artfully crumpled Paul Smith suit, wire-rimmed spectacles to look Sixties, but in a large, bifocal size, and penny loafers on his feet; usually, he affected a day's stubble. He was the youngest goddamn doyen in the business, that was obvious; but Emma was not at all sure what his business might be.

'This is Mr Porter,' Sir Alistair said, 'who will talk to us later.'

Emma leaned across to Simeon. 'What's all this about?'

'Corporate image and entering the Eighties,' Simeon said, very quietly. 'Your father has decided to be modern.'

'Oh God,' Emma said. She looked about desperately for David's reassurance, but he was talking about South Sea islands to Maurice's angular wife. She was glad he had charm and intellect, but someone else was getting the benefit.

Mr Porter seemed pernickety and defiant; he held his hands close into his chest, like a killed chicken, and he fidgeted with words. He was used to love and respect, even from clients.

'Your new friend works for a museum, Emma?' Maurice sounded sceptical.

'Virtually a member of the caring classes.'

'I see. Where's he from?'

There was a certain pleasure in delaying the answer. 'York,' Emma said.

'I see,' Maurice said.

Mr Porter sucked on a fat white stem of asparagus, like a scared child at the nipple.

'Mr Porter,' Sir Alistair said, maliciously, 'tells me we have too many ascenders and we lack descenders almost entirely. Isn't that so? Our name is very difficult to design.'

Mr Porter nodded. 'It's very interesting,' he said. 'A challenge.'

'We don't have to become Griffbank, do we?' Rupert asked. 'Or Griffco?'

'I remember,' Emma said, 'a print designer who asked me where the Nazis would have been without the swastika, or the Christians without the cross. I asked him about Buddhism.'

Mr Porter would have liked to say: 'Look here, mate' in those vaguely Cockney vowels he had so strenuously preserved from the heyday of the King's Road in the Sixties. Instead, he played missionary. 'You'll find,' he said, 'when every bank has a brokerage house, and every broker has a bank and you're all making mortgages and selling gilts and nursing mergers – when everything is in flux, then the bank with a sharp print image – '

'A sharp print image,' Maurice said. 'And what was all that about ascenders and descenders?'

'A "g" goes below the line, so it's a descender,' Emma said, helpfully. 'A "d", on the other hand – '

'I'm not a fool,' Maurice said. He blossomed at times into a florid kind of flower: the unregenerate squire. 'Sounds to me like we prepare for the revolution by buying a new suit of clothes.'

Lady Griffier made that tiny motion which would bring meat to the table after a while.

'Mr Porter,' said Emma, with malicious kindness, 'Daddy says you're making a new corporate image for the bank. A new logo – '

'Yes,' Mr Porter said, pulling at his wine. He felt very far from shore with these offhand, disrespectful persons. He who had brought the concept of rebirth to a traveller's way through national airports, plane to kerbside; he who had understood, first, that white bread was about home and fireside, that a man's virility was at stake when he bought anti-perspirant. He knew the soul of simple things, he thought.

'Distinct,' he said, 'but not eccentric. Functional, but attractive. The contemporary aesthetic climate – '

'I suppose Mr Porter will lift the Griffiers,' Maurice said. 'With a flourish of his pen, we will be Citibank, we will be Nomura. The loveliness of our notepaper will keep our clients, even when the Japanese seduce them and the Americans woo them. God be praised for Mr Porter!'

'Amen,' said Rupert, slyly. 'The better the image, the better for all of us.'

Mr Porter sat through the very potent silence looking furry and baffled. Everybody else knew that Rupert loved his surname like a lure to bring in stooges and gulls. They would buy bothersome companies, suspect shares from an old name; they were sure of him, right up to the moment their money was gone. Everybody was far too polite to explain all this to Mr Porter.

'I am sure,' Lady Griffier said, rather late, 'Mr Porter is very talented at what he does.' She heard herself make that perfect little English sentence – lifeless, patronizing, faintly bitter – and she was absolutely delighted. Her protective colouring was perfectly in place.

Mr Porter declined an Armagnac, and a bed for the night. He prayed that his nice, red shiny Porsche would behave itself this evening, and carry him back magically to the dancer wife and the house in Kew, and respect. He made the engine roar in the quiet of the park, to show them.

But he was only a curious sideshow to the Griffiers, who wondered why he had been invited.

'Father,' Rupert said, 'likes to show he is still in control. In modern times.'

'Father likes to make trouble,' Emma said. 'If I'd had a week talking seriously to that man, I'd want to annoy him back.'

Simeon Ryder was not so amused. He tried to cut out Sir Alistair and take him aside. 'We have a very serious situation,' he said.

'Thank God that man Porter has gone,' Sir Alistair said. For a mandarin he attached some importance to style, his own style; he resented being advised on style as a commodity by a man in over-wide trousers.

Simeon Ryder caught Emma's eye. He was miming despair, and asking for her help, and she only shrugged her shoulders.

'I really think we must talk – '

'Don't be dull,' Sir Alistair said.

'We are a public company like any other. Anyone can buy our shares if someone is prepared to sell, and someone is buying now. Someone we don't trust.'

Sir Alistair said: 'Bring me some ice, Ryder. Don't fuss.'

'Chinese walls,' Simeon said. 'We're going into an era when everyone knows there could be clashes and corruption even within the bank – the take-over people and the investment people and the traders, all knowing different things, all playing different games with the same information. We build Chinese walls inside the bank so those friends can't talk to each other. Imagine what would happen if those walls weren't real. Imagine if the corruption came from outside the bank, and had no interest in doing things decently or properly.'

'I can imagine many things,' Sir Alistair said. 'I need ice.'

Emma went up to bed very early, and David followed soon afterwards. She was home, and she was always hurt by how much this home had shaped her; she belonged, too easily.

She turned out the lights, and listened. There was a full, cold moon in her window and a prickle of stars beyond. She listened for footsteps, for David coming to her; she heard a faint tap on her door.

He said: 'I was afraid you were one of the wives.'

'I'm not one of the wives,' she said, and she threw off the covers. The moon and the starched sheets and her body were enough to dazzle him.

In the white room, the nurse passed with water and cloths. She wiped his body respectfully, but without interest, like the old women do for a corpse. She left him neat on his high bed. He was still cool to the touch; his eyes were slack and empty; his great limbs had been arranged as neatly as an effigy.

She said: 'Sleep well.' She closed the door.

James Drake closed his eyes against the hurt of a whole kaleidoscope, splinters and stabs of light. He had his will; he had a moment's lucidity. He tried to force his whole body up off the bed. He tried to imagine and sense where he was, and how he could kill someone for putting him here.

They had left him for dead, or a fine imitation. He concentrated painfully. He would retrieve sensation in some outer limb. He would make himself move, when he wanted, as he wanted.

There was no witness in the room. He had believed he could move before, and been wrong. But this time, the little finger on his right hand moved when he wanted. He could tell because it touched the cold chrome of the bedframe, very lightly.

The finger shrank away from the cold. It was a start.

2

All along the corridors at Griffier Ltd, there was dust and the racket of drills and hammers; the polished floors were up and tunnelled for miles of computer cable, black, thick-skinned stuff, like a pudding. The dealers had claimed their territory down below, with the barks and shouts of howler monkeys, and now they were reaching out for more screens and keyboards, new jungle.

On important matters, Simeon Ryder was not conservative. He was glad the outsiders had come inside the castle; he was glad that something worked, unequivocally. The business helped Griffier survive, and survival was very much on his mind.

He thought most things were urgent; but he knew that too much urgency would be dismissed as neurotic. He bustled to the secretaries' room, where faint yellow lights on an ancient panel of stained glass showed which of the partners might require attention. He nodded to the women there. He composed himself as he passed the final guard of messengers, stiff and fading in their cardboard Burton's suits. He tapped on the glass of the partners' room and, where the messengers would have waited to be recognized, he pushed his way in. By now, he was almost casual.

Sir Alistair Griffier said: 'Time for my lesson, I suppose?'

'I think we may have more important matters to discuss.'

'It is important that I understand everything the bank does. Everything.'

'Nobody understands everything any more,' Simeon

said. He stopped a sigh, with difficulty. 'And the real issue is talking to John Brown.' There was no point in sidestepping what was on his mind.

'Brother Edward made him. Brother Edward can keep him under control.'

'That was a very long time ago, in another country. I'm not sure that John Brown wants to be reminded.'

'I don't see,' Sir Alistair said, 'that he has any choice in the matter.'

It was the right room for such a fine, patrician sentiment. It smelled of wax and leather that has gone to powder; the smell had come, quite mysteriously, with the panelling and the brass lamps and the partners' desks when the room was shipped to this bright glass tower from the old offices. The room had come on careful rollers, like a shrine in a procession.

'We should at least know who sold,' Simeon said.

'Someone will tell us,' Sir Alistair said. 'That kind of news travels well.'

Against one rosewood wall stood a tantalus on a stand, a cage of bottles which made it hard to reach the whiskies inside. It had been installed in 1891, after the Griffiers nearly collapsed like some summer marquee and smothered the City of London to death. It was meant to imply that drink was expensive; it said drink was often also necessary.

'I think,' Sir Alistair said, 'that you might begin the lesson.' He had a most infuriating smile.

'We have made a speciality,' Simeon said, 'of interest-rate swaps. They're a rather abstract idea – '

'I'm not a technician, but I am a banker.'

'You have to think of the bank as a broker,' Simeon said. 'Then you apply calculus.'

Sir Alistair looked eager. Simeon could imagine the old man in his colonial days, looking eager when some bright technician proposed action or improvements, a drain or a canal or a bridge or a school; like a schoolmaster, he would encourage but finally he would judge, grade and dismiss.

'A client wants more interest than they can get on their money. Someone else wants to pay less interest than they're being charged, or else they want to pay it in a different currency that they think will cost them less. But both sides are locked into their particular deals, and so, without us, they can't escape.

'But the deals exist. They're on the ledger. Someone has already done what a banker does: thought about risk, looked at collateral, followed an instinct about the chances of repayment and so forth. When our boys come along, they deal in ledger entries.'

'I cling to the idea of lending on a man's credit,' Sir Alistair said, 'although I suppose that, too, is an abstraction. Everything grows more abstract all the time.'

Simeon did not feel inclined to argue. Instead, he said: 'Suppose we have a client with a few million on deposit, and he's getting the London Interbank Interest Rate on that, which is good for a customer, but he wants more – say, LIBOR plus an eighth of a point. On a few million, that could be significant.'

Sir Alistair nodded.

'Now, we have our own books and we happen to have – say – a Eurobond that pays eight per cent and matures in ten years and naturally we've paid over par for it. The reason we bought in the first place is that it's sound, we don't have to think about the assets, and so we can trade it. We bought to sell.'

'My occupation,' Sir Alistair said, 'divides nowadays into barrow boys and theatrical directors – the ones who buy and sell, and the ones who tell others how to. Barrow boys and theatrical directors.'

'So,' Simeon said, 'our greedy client takes the Eurobond off our hands, but still pays us the eight per cent interest it earns. We pay the client LIBOR plus one-eighth of a point, which of course can go up or down. We gamble, so far, it will be less than eight per cent.'

'The client could take that risk.'

'But he won't,' Simeon said, 'because he doesn't have all the choices we can offer him. Besides, he may think interest swaps are arcane and alarming. He may want someone else to do the work.'

'I don't suppose you could put all this on paper?'

'I may as well finish. We're not taking chances with that eight per cent, of course, because we know that the going rate for a ten-year swap is under eight per cent and we do another trade – we pay out that lower rate and we get LIBOR back.'

'It sounds as though we buy above par and sell below it. That affects some very settled instincts.'

'We do take a loss at first,' Simeon said. 'But over ten years we make a profit, which is the difference between the interest we get and the interest we pay. Discounted, we make maybe £34,000 on a ten-million swap. We make that £34,000 with an hour at the most on a terminal.'

'It sounds – insubstantial,' Sir Alistair said. 'We're a kind of matrimonial agency, aren't we? Finding money and friends for clients when they're in need. We preside when companies marry, and when they divorce and when other men lust after them. And I suppose when their family expands.' He pushed a bell for coffee. 'But I don't mean to be sententious.'

Simeon said: 'We build relationships. The new thing is that we trade in them.'

'But we buy and sell loans, we don't simply arrange them or make them. Bits of mortgages, bits of the messengers' car loans. We sell company paper which is debt, and people value it as highly as equity. I remember when debt and equity were very different things. I remember when there were speculators on the foreign exchanges, but now the men who speculate are the cautious ones – they manage corporations, they want to save themselves by betting which way the currencies will move.' It was a good mind, but sometimes it relaxed and showed its age. 'Sticking to a deal, that's the greatest risk of all,' Sir Alistair said. 'Risk is caution, caution is risk.'

'And we need calculus,' Simeon said.

Coffee arrived, borne in Georgian silver.

'And we need friends,' Simeon said, more urgently.

'Brown won't find sellers,' Sir Alistair said. 'He'll be stuck with his shares, or he'll sell them on.'

'He could sell to one of the big American banks. Or the Japanese, or even the Swiss. They'd love to be in London under our name.'

'We're talking less than five per cent. That can do little harm.'

'The very fact that John Brown has those shares – '

He could never quite bring himself to tell this man that the Griffiers had a name, and their address books, and a hunger for capital that the markets were never likely to satisfy. They had to be sold. The Americans would come buying, but they were terribly vulnerable to their own mistakes: in oil, gas, real estate and the Third World. Buying London was another one of their evasions; they were hardly secure. The Japanese would offer a kind of sushification: slicing, moulding, displaying and digesting. The Griffiers had to choose their buyers, and they were selling reputation. The name of John Brown did not help.

Simeon Ryder picked his way back through the dust, a sheaf of papers in his hands. It was obvious that he had to decide for himself who should buy Griffier Ltd.

He heard the roar of the traders again, raising up barrow boy voices to consummate their deals. He wondered how long they would be happy as outsiders and when they would want their share.

Sometimes he could hear only the hisses in words, and tried to make sense from them. Sometimes, he knew exactly what they were saying. He was angry the outsiders tried to interest him only in nursery food and bodily functions, as though that was miracle enough. A man like James Drake wants proper miracles.

He wanted them to see anger in his eyes, the anger and authority that had made him a fortune once before. He wanted them to remind him about the world, read him the *Wall Street Journal*, relay the contents of a Qotron screen. What appalled him was the gap between what mind could want, buried and bound in flesh, and what body could perform. He bridged it only sometimes.

'Tap if you understand me,' the older doctor said. He had it on his conscience that, when he expected John Drake to die, he had wanted John Drake to die, and said so. He liked to indulge the old man with talk of the markets, just in case he understood, and he kept the process of his recovery very quiet.

Drake tapped. It was a little spasm in a broken hand. It disgusted him.

'Your friends the Griffiers,' the doctor said, not thinking the wrecked body could cope with an ironic statement, 'they're in trouble, I see. Someone has five per cent. You'll get revenge yet.'

Drake tapped, twice for 'yes'. Would they realize that two taps meant 'yes'? He listened very hard. He wanted details: who bought, how and when, how the Griffiers reacted, how the market reacted, where the advantage lay. Nobody told him such things; even when they tried to amuse him, they treated him like a child.

He could think with clarity, sometimes, and clarity had been unfamiliar for the past few weeks. That was a start. But it hurt his fragile mind to wait any longer for simple things like reading or moving. He could feel his ideas beating at the border of his brain, like a bird trapped at a window.

Suppose the Griffiers had a hostile bidder. They would already be stirred and worried. They would have a problem of image: the august bank, with all its stolid institutional investors like pension funds and insurance companies, and one of those investors loose.

He had to think of something more, something worse. To make his revenge personal, he would have to do something extraordinary.

He tapped for attention, without waiting for the doctors to ask a question.

'Involuntary spasm,' the younger doctor said. 'You don't think the tapping could have been arbitrary, do you? Just coincidence?'

Drake tapped once, for 'no'. He felt the doctor's breath, minty-sour on his face.

'Nobody at home,' the doctor said.

Drake wanted to scream, but instead, he had to hold all the force of a scream inside his useless body. He felt he would burst with fury.

The doctor said: 'Poor sod.'

Emma settled in the cup of soft leather, and pulled her long legs under her, and the lights went down. David sat beside her, but he kept his distance; she was working. On her other side sat a man of medium height, with an unremarkable moustache; he seemed weathered, and his smile came all too easily. In the only hierarchy that could bother Emma Griffier, he was the boss.

'I love London,' said Fred Garrity. 'I even like going to the movies here.' He beamed myopically like a cartoon uncle, his way of showing he was far too preoccupied to focus on any single person. A few fools took this for charm.

On the screen, they watched seven versions of a lunch. Emma held her breath. Even when she watched hard, she could still feel what she wanted: the conspiracy of feeling between the women on the screen. And it was her movie. She had talked this project into life, and now there were dailies to show. It made worth while the awkward transition from being producer and part of the team, to being the studio executive and the Money – disliked, essential, the target. At least she had made something happen.

Garrity leaned back. 'Heart, Emma, real heart,' he said. 'You're coming down to Cannes with us, aren't you?'

They watched the dailies from a comic strip epic now shooting in Britain, oddly empty images waiting for painters and computers to put in the action, and a murder done eleven times. At the end, David escorted her up the basement stairs to Wardour Street and the faint spring rain.

'I feel restless,' she said.

'You want a drink?'

'I think I want to work out. I have all this energy.'

They worked furiously at the gym, and they worked together. He cared for her body, for the specific sinews of it. She felt his touch helping her blood and muscle work against the machines; she fought the weights more strongly because he was watching. He watched her eyes, as though he was working with her and for her; he watched her willing herself to lift more, push more.

It always started innocently, with an almost brotherly care, and very soon she was something else: a white doll, legs parting and closing like a lovely automaton, her breasts taut under her bright T-shirt, her long legs first defined and then tight. She opened her mouth to force down air, and it was as if she was making love: and he could stand back from her, see what she must be like. Her legs rose and fell rhythmically on the hip and back machine; he stood by her, encouraging, and very slightly mimicking her actions. Without touch, their bodies sweated and co-operated.

He concentrated on what she had to do; it stopped him flustering. She came down from the machines, slick and hot and tired, and he wanted to hold her; but she was too sly for that. She still kept her distance; she slipped away to the showers. He had changed in minutes, and he sat waiting for her. It was painful to wait.

She came out gold and glowing, the blood singing in her, and he said, 'I got to get you home.'

They found a taxi in the rain, and it went slowly, slowly. The city had gone grey like a blanket; they were the only light in it, safe in the haven of the cab. They did not dare touch.

At the door of David's house, there was a man stooped under an umbrella, a black figure in the splash and echo of the rain.

'Who the hell – '

'I can't guess,' Emma said.

'I wasn't expecting anyone.'

David dashed for the door, unlocked and pushed Emma through it. He turned to the man under the umbrella.

'I don't suppose this is convenient,' Simeon Ryder said.

'It bloody isn't.'

'I couldn't reach Emma at the office, and I couldn't reach you at home.'

'Come in, dammit,' David said.

Simeon Ryder shook out his umbrella, and walked in.

'What do you want, Simeon?' Emma said.

'I came to ask you to talk to John Brown. I can't make sense of what he's doing, and nor can anyone else.'

'If I can,' Emma said. 'But my time at Cannes – '

'I'm afraid you are my only hope.'

David said: 'I'm soaked. I have to change.' He stormed the stairs, and they could hear him walking heavily around the bed- and bathroom.

'Maybe,' Emma said, 'I'd like Griffier Ltd to be in play. Maybe I want to sell and be free of it all for ever.'

'It won't be that easy,' Simeon said. 'If Brown's involved, people won't want to buy. A bank isn't a refrigerator. Even electricity isn't enough. It only works if everyone trusts it.'

'You ought to clean up your aphorisms.'

'We can't get Brown out unless we know what he wants. And if we don't get him out, the bank's value declines. That means the value of your shares, too.'

'I have enough.'

'Besides, your father – '

'I don't work for the family firm.'

'But you only have to talk to Brown. None of us can do that officially.'

'You're afraid he'd bully you into something.'

'He'd use the meeting.'

Emma could hear David upstairs. A board was singing under the weight of angry push-ups.

'I can't talk, Simeon.'

'Then you'll help?'

'I'll help.' She almost pushed him to the door, and out; he shimmered away until he seemed to dissolve into the rain. She went running at the stairs, and slipped, and howled for her knocked knee. On the landing above, David stood; he was grinning.

'If there's one thing worse than the wages of sin – '

He came down to the crook of the stairs, and kissed her.

And out in the cold rain, Simeon Ryder went walking. The long river of municipal gardens was full of rose shoots and forsythia leaves, and the schemes for summer; he had it almost to himself. He let his mind stray.

There were aristocrats like Sir Alistair, and then there were the traders, and the traders made big money for the bank; only the major merger business made more. The barrow boys mattered just as much as the pinstriped operators with their burnished connections and their thoughtful care for slowly maturing clients; banking was also the instant, nerve-end reaction, the exact eye for taking a turn on the difference between one price of cabbages and another. The cabbages might be gilts or equities or some exotic financial instrument; it hardly mattered. The point was the difference, and the profit it spelt.

And how they were hated, the brash, raw people who made that profit. They had stamina and shrewdness; they did not need to understand anything except the gap between prices, and the life they could build there. Upper-class parties were beastly about their social gaffes; Cockney was chic in the 1960s, and now it was only nouveau. The caring classes patronized them, worrying about burn-out, suspicious of the passion for work, resentful that working-class clients had escaped and made fortunes; and, with the fortunes, were making other lives. Burn-out was planned for and expected; work was intended for a dowry when the kids, at thirty, married for the rest of their lives. And bureaucrats fussed that they did nothing serious; their short horizons shocked the lifetime civil servant, who had been guaranteed authority and probity, without risk. Trading was only an expedient. Making cars or teapots or ingots was the only real thing.

Their anger made Simeon sure there was a real change

happening, for better or worse. He gloried that the boys went drinking too much good champagne; he was glad the wrong people were gouging out brief riches. He was only sorry to see the politicians talk as though Britain were still tight as some offshore drum, and not a link within a market that would choose its home by calculation, not sentiment. Phone lines were the real rainbow now; at their end, there was gold. Money was in the minds of the dealers, perhaps up among the pulses from satellite to bank to satellite; it was not to be counted and weighed like rations.

Sir Alistair, the proconsul and gentleman, was out of his depth, but at least he realized the obligation of change. Probably he would miscalculate, left to himself. But he offered an institution which could be changed, and that was what stirred Simeon. The house of Griffier was his life, his interest; when he cared about changing things, he had first to care about changing the bank. Other new men were bored now; Simeon was fascinated.

He thought: the boy traders and Sir Alistair have at least one thing in common. Neither truly understands what they're doing, only how to do it. Such a situation suited the man in a fine suit, tramping through the spit of a London evening, in the sallow lights. He never said he was uninterested in power.

The nurse was hiding. She had gone quite suddenly out of his field of vision; but she still said: 'Look at me, Mr Drake!'

She was teasing him. 'Can you see me, Mr Drake?'

There would be no more love, no more adventure. He formed the thought quite unexpectedly. Women in white would bother and tease him and vanish behind some wall of his mind, untouchable, invisible, not to be had.

He tried to turn on his back; she began to prop him with pillows, to throw him off what he thought was his balance. He tried to protest; he whimpered, when he meant to roar.

She took his hands and tried to make him clasp them together. She tugged, to make one arm pull the other into the air; she wanted to fool him he was helping himself. She turned his head and his arms followed; and then, patiently, she pushed his back and his buttocks and his legs, so he was resting on his side.

She came very close to his face, her breath as sweet as plums. 'Spasm, Mr Drake,' she said, as practical as a cook turning pancakes. 'We must avoid spasm.'

He was alone, unless she was hiding behind the wall in his eyes, and he wanted to say: 'Why, why, why, why, why?' He did something he had never done before, not consciously, which was to doubt himself. Perhaps he had brought all this on himself; perhaps he had deserted others by this brutal event in his brain.

And then, he was angry again. His doctors said it was a natural phase – guilt, and then anger. They sent someone to ask him dumb questions – is this a watch? is this for writing with? is this a pencil? is this for writing with? what is your name? It was like catechism as a child in a prairie church. My name, he wanted to say, is N or M.

We are in Denver. We are in God's care. The President is Reagan. The Lord is good.

This is a pencil. This is a pencil. This is a pencil.

'How do you think you have done in the test?' they asked.

On the fifth day, she had time for family business at Cannes. She checked the neat, small scrawl in her diary; she lunched the Far Eastern distributors; she took meetings on the half-hour; she saw a single movie out of competition, and one at the grand, black-tie evening shows. She missed the days when she hunted some new

Russian movie out at the Maison des Jeunes, or giggled through the cult film of the market – *Attack of the Killer Bimbos, Surf Nazis Must Die*; now she pushed through the rush hour Croisette like a commissary queue, under a bought-and-paid-for sun which simmered like arc lamps and by the irrelevant beaches, which were only for lunch. A pair of matched paparazzi from Britain took her picture, several times, and seemed glad when she spoke to them.

And on the fifth day, the royals came. The festival which had been too busy to have shape was suddenly defined, as a magnet defines a pile of iron filings. The studio execs could put aside movies and have dinner, as they liked, and the Press had their first real stars. The boys and girls of the Majestic bar, the finest flesh in town but already spoken for, prepared to make memories for their mothers, too: the sight of a prince and princess, after dark.

Emma Griffier would be there, naturally; she was a senior studio executive. John Brown would be there. He could never resist a royal occasion; he liked to speak for the people at royal occasions. It was an unremarkable time for them to meet.

She sat in her big, soulless room at the Grey d'Albion, and she answered a tithe of her messages. She checked through the various hand-delivered memos, and called Garrity's room at the Majestic. Usually, her boss found it hard to imagine that anyone disagreed with him seriously; he made discussion into a game, droll but not useful. Tonight, he was distinctly flustered, and uninterested in business. Tonight, he would welcome the royals on behalf of the industry.

'We'll see you there,' Emma said. 'We're going to the movie.'

David had happened to be in Nice, talking to museum officials, and he had happened to be free that night, that one night. He said he did not want to cramp her style. He would wait for her in the lobby, like a gentleman caller. She drank a half-bottle of Evian and went down.

'I used to see movies at Cannes,' she said.

'That was before you worked here,' he said.

They walked down to the Croisette through the pack of onlookers, and turned right for the blank, shopping-mall walls of the bunker: the Palais du Festival. Up its side steps were a rank of guardsmen, helmets shining in the evening light; Shirley Bassey shrilled through huge speakers, the theme from *Goldfinger*. The crowd had been artfully packed to look like a mob.

The cards in the hand were everything: at least a pink card, God forbid a blue card, best of all a white card with a discreet gold star. Tiny men from the basement market, who sold shares in posters for which a film might soon be made, asserted their dignity. People recognized people on the helpful side of barriers. The photographers jostled out of habit for a traditional flash of thigh, but it was older women, keeping to traditions, who supplied it; Edie Adams was, for once, dressed. The crowd expected royalty and, later, Elizabeth Taylor.

Hand in hand, they passed the various bottlenecks and had the red-carpeted steps almost to themselves. Cameras followed assiduously, not liking to judge between potential employers. In the Palais, they took their seats in the huge, plain vault of the auditorium.

The lights died, the movie opened; what happened on screen had some impact. A street chase made the matrons talk about dinner ('Of course, we'd have gone to the royals but the Moulin gave us a table'). The wider landscapes led to a hiss of reminiscence. Close-ups that flattered any female star produced a distinct click of disapproval. And a look of beamish neutrality stayed on the clever faces of the studio chief who made her name selling toilet tissue, and the one who liked the reassuring bite of leather under his tuxedo, and the one who had danced with Mickey Mouse. They had no opinion here, for fear of being wrong.

The movie was wrapped in a soft, loud wave of applause and put away.

They walked from theatre to casino by way of a corridor which had been paved with drifts of rose petals, sweet and dead like the victims of some special effect. They settled at their tables, discussed how bored and sullen the princess looked, gossiped reverentially. When the royals were seated, the dinner opened like a flower.

And John Brown entered, a little late, a huge square man who trumpeted for attention and moved through the room like a blind beast that everyone knows to avoid. He was seated at Emma's table, which had taken seven phone calls and finally a bribe.

The enemy said to Emma: 'What a pleasure to meet a fellow countryman who has been so successful in this demanding business.' He finished all his sentences, in a flat, dark voice that was faintly robotic.

'Mr Brown,' Emma said.

'My newspaper supports the British industry,' he announced. 'I am most concerned with the future of the British industry.' He glared at Emma. 'We must hear from you on the future of the industry.'

He paused elaborately, head cocked. She realized that everything was force with him; his flirting was like other men's assault.

'I think it has one,' Emma said.

Brown's entourage looked disconcerted. A cue from John Brown required performance at least long enough to be interrupted.

'I mean,' said Emma, in the awkward quiet, 'I'm sure it has one.'

John Brown stared at her. 'I don't think I understand you.'

Unease went round the table like a wind in corn.

'My dear,' he said to Emma, 'please do explain what you mean.' His voice, like his manners, had been pasted together out of a book.

Emma said: 'The fish is terribly good, isn't it?'

David said: 'I don't recognize it. It's one of those obscure Mediterranean fishes – '

One of the Brown entourage, a man who had once been a Fellow of All Souls, said quickly: 'Of course, the old studio system – ' He knew the script for the evening and he could read any part.

John Brown beamed. 'Irrelevant,' he said. 'Only a fool thinks otherwise. The future lies with video – thousand-line video, high-resolution video in every home. Why, only today – '

He insisted that others listen to the catalogue of prophecies and deals, but Emma had an odd sense that he did not concentrate on himself. The bombast was meant to stop others distracting him; the mind was working, but not at this table.

If the talk was only a screen, she had to watch most carefully; and she realized that he, too, was watching. He was trying to make a player out of her because, once in his game, he could use her. She was trying to invade that private mind, where the schemes were made.

'My dear,' Brown said. He had noticed her properly, and marked her down as trouble.

'This is a pencil. This is a pencil.' He could hear the lilt of the words, and understand them, but he could not say them. He knew, from the look of patience on the therapist's face, he was drooling and mumping the words, a bagpipe sound.

'This is a pencil.'

They had given him a pencil to tap out the rhythm on

the table top: dum dum de dum dum. Dum dum de dum dum.

Dumb like Drake, as much voice as a dead man and the tongue curled back on itself the same way.

Dum dum de dum dum.

He said: 'Thi is a pen seal.'

'Very good,' the therapist said.

'Read me,' he said. 'Read me Gliffer.'

The therapist said: 'What is Gliffer?'

'Gliffier,' he said, teeth and tongue conflicting with the word. 'Ge-li- fer.'

'I don't know Gliffer. Is it a book you used to know?'

'Ban,' he said. 'Ban,' and he seemed to spit at the sound of a 'k'.

'A bank,' the therapist said. 'I think it's a little early for that.'

Later, she made a brief report to the doctors, and they read it in conference the next morning.

'He can think. He can see. He can almost speak,' the older doctor said. 'Soon he'll start walking and stealing. Are you sure we're doing the right thing?'

The younger doctor sat on his ethics like a throne, and talked of the duty to conserve human life. His colleague did not seem convinced.

On the seventh night of Cannes, she should have worn a long frock to the evening movie. Instead, she cut through the unofficial back streets, past shops that blared out, co-ordinated Muzak in the open air, and across the grey sand by the plane trees where the fishermen played boule. Overhead a little plane made its last pass of the day, trailing a gnomic banner: POURQUOI FILMEZ-VOUS?

The tender was waiting in the Old Port, and John Brown's yacht lay out beyond the bay. It was not the grandest of yachts, but its decks of chrome and white clung to the water like an insect, and it was odd he moored it out of sight. He seemed to think it was a convenience, not a boast.

He sat in the cool of the rear deck, beached like a whale, his hair suddenly darker than it had been the night before; out of the fine engineering of Savile Row, he was a fat man with a gift for being still.

'You're late,' he said, graciously. 'I said seven-thirty.'

'You invited me for seven-thirty,' Emma said.

'I suppose your family sent you to talk to me? That it?'

'I'd like a kir royal. And I would love to meet your wife.'

'I intend to hold the shares as a long-term investment,' he said. 'That's all.'

He fell silent. He did not feel the need to notice other people, even Griffiers; he had exhausted his snobbery on the royals. He'd simply had no experience, for many years, of other people saying 'no' or anything else of substance.

'A kir royal,' Emma said. 'Do I shout for a servant?'

'I won't sell,' Brown said, 'and I won't trade. Not until I'm good and ready. You can tell them that. This is business.'

'When people say that, they usually mean it's much more.'

'You have a lot to learn,' Brown said. 'Nobody's grateful. Nobody stays grateful for forty years.'

'You have no reason to be grateful to the Griffiers.'

He was still again, absorbed in himself so that he needed no extraneous sound or movement. And soon he would lumber out to the attack again, rushing his great weight at the world like a huge rogue beast, lethal at speed.

'I thought it was kind of you to invite me here,' Emma said. 'I imagined we were going to talk about movies – '

'Your family must be nervous,' he said.

'I haven't talked to them.'

'I'm a bigger shareholder than you.'

'I don't doubt it.'

'You can tell them,' he said, expanding grandly like the frog in the fable, 'the shares are safe in my portfolio. You can take that message to London.'

'I won't pretend I'm not interested,' Emma said. 'I didn't think anyone would buy such a small part of Griffier Ltd. I like to know what's happening.'

'I like the stock.'

'You like stock to trade. Anything. I could give you a price for shrimp in China or an airline in Hawaii or coffee in Ghana and you'd be interested.'

'You should be happy I think Griffier Ltd is worth buying.'

'Obviously,' she said, smiling, 'you expect the value of your shares to rise. Obviously, the bank is doing well.'

Brown shouted for servants and finally conceded a drink.

'It could do far better,' he said. Perhaps she was here to sell her shares, too. 'A great London name, out of the history of England – '

' – and Holland,' Emma thought, but said nothing.

' – a great name in banking and trading, full of history. But in the hands of stuffy Victorian managers – '

'I thought the Victorians were in favour,' Emma said.

'Not with me. I believe in socialism. Socialism is good for business.' He meant traders, Emma thought, and it made some sense; he could buy low in markets that were bound by rules, and sell high elsewhere. But then, it did not need to make sense to other people. It was simply another belief among a selection that he held in parallel, like plants in a border.

He stood up and he was tall like a bear. He moved like some Russian party boss, expecting nothing in his way; for a moment she was instinctually afraid of him. He had broken her balance for a moment, as he did with everyone to frighten them.

'That bank won't exist in a year or two,' he said, 'you'll see – unless things change. There's a revolution coming.'

'It was kind of you to give me some sea air. But I have to get back to work – '

'Banks will buy brokers, brokers will buy banks. The high-street banks will sell gilts and the Swiss banks will make a market in ICI. Nothing inflexible will survive.'

'That has a biblical ring.'

He massed himself at her side, and glowered at her. 'Our future,' he said.

'Does your future contain Griffier Ltd, then?'

'Griffier Ltd will be glad of my help.'

'You don't think you could do things under your own name, perhaps?'

He said: 'The name of John Brown is a fine name.'

She wanted to say it was not his name; he had picked it up on a battlefield somewhere, or on the streets of Berlin in 1946, and put it on like a coat. But instead she said: 'A very fine name. But now I've had my drink, I need either a boat or a swimsuit. Could you help me to get back?'

'You'll be lost,' Brown said, with very quiet reason. 'You'll be victims of history.'

She noticed movement in the water. As they were talking, the yacht had slipped anchor and was moving in the soft, luminous evening. From the side, she could see the lights of Cannes slip very slowly into view, a string of glare and crystal.

'I'm making an announcement tomorrow,' Brown said. 'Going into the movie business. Top projects, top stars, international market.'

'Far too many people say that.'

'We have all the money we need within Brown Trading, of course. The bank facilities we need – '

'You know I have nothing to do with the bank.'

'I hate to see cash tied up in film accounting. It takes so long to make a film, and then to sell it, and then to make the distributors send you money, and then to make the distributors send you the right money.'

'You bought five per cent of the bank just to get a loan?'

'It would be perfectly sensible. Shares you can buy and sell, short-term, but a loan is a loan; it stays on a bank's books for ever. I use short-term money, you give me long-term money.'

The yacht had begun to turn on a wide wake of water, towards land.

There was a cough at Emma's side, and a middle-aged woman stood there. She was quite absorbed in John Brown; she was fascinated. She said: 'You've finished your business?'

John Brown said: 'My wife. She has a PhD in the history of art and she is the world authority on the life of Vasari.'

'You shouldn't mention it here,' Mrs Brown said.

Emma heard the separation in the phrase, the sense that these two lives should not be muddled together; she could see a whole, cold marriage. Since she and David had so much of it, she was growing afraid of separation.

'It was very nice to have met you,' Mrs Brown said, as Emma stepped down with her into the tender, and John Brown followed, making the little boat wallow in the still harbour. There was some ceremony, and the proper British ensign flew, and they set out for the town.

On shore in the Old Port, past the yachts and among the working fishing boats, Emma saw unusual figures: not fishermen, not lovers. As the little boat settled alongside the quay, there was a clatter of light and flashbulbs.

John Brown had spread his face into a smile. Emma

Griffier looked startled. Of course, the man owned photographers from his one dowdy English newspaper, *The Reporter*; she should not be surprised.

She thought briskly, but helplessly. Tomorrow morning, these pictures would be in the trade paper pushed under every door in Cannes, and it would make at least one British paper. Movie men would think Brown's movies were coming through Emma's studio. City of London men would wonder if Emma was selling to Brown, or the family cutting some deal behind the back of other shareholders; suddenly, there would be a market for John Brown's shares. Both ways, Brown had an advantage for the price of the gas and the film.

'You have to know what you want,' he said, as he stepped ashore. He shut down the mechanical smile for the photographers, and Mrs Brown trailed him to the waiting limo.

'I do not understand the pictures,' Simeon said.

'I was set up,' Emma said.

'The pictures will be embarrassing.' Simeon always made the family believe he was clearing their wreckage; nothing was ever his fault. But he had wanted her to see John Brown in this most public and recorded marketplace, and she had done what she could.

She was almost sure it was dumb to think Simeon expected all this, maybe even organized it; but he did have a thesis to prove, that some malicious force had turned against the Griffiers. The fact was, Cannes was a time for paranoia: all the smiles and deals, and convenient, casual meetings. With Garrity, who loved division, it was two weeks of scurrying for position; the whole studio was concentrated into a small town, with no home to go to, and only rivals or clients around. It made for unkind thoughts about everyone's actions.

And David had gone back to London from Nice,

without calling; it was what they had agreed, but it infuriated her. The last time they talked, his mind had been away somewhere called New Ireland; he talked about the fascination of malangaan, and she realized that if she asked what malangaan was or were, she would be lost.

She went walking among the dressed, anonymous crowds on the Croisette. The gougers on the Carlton Terrace took cups of coffee to their clients at no more than the price of Château Petrus; the James Bond girl as usual framed the Carlton entrance, legs apart. Security at the Majestic looked more than ever like doormen from a 1970s discothèque. She thought a great deal about façades.

Simeon Ryder, for example, had no history outside the bank; she had no idea what else, who else he was. John Brown the mogul, for example, who talked about not being grateful to the Griffiers. Of course he did not mean to convince anyone with his copybook Englishness; he only needed to stop questions. But what in the history of her family made him think he should be grateful?

She could make a story of it all; that was her trade. But, this time, she needed to deduce what was precise and true. Aside from anything else, her independence was not just a name: it was three per cent of the bank. It was only sensible to take care of her independence.

She saw herself, as if in a seaside snapshot. The lady is between palms and cannas and the sea, in the middle of the movie souk, fussing over family history. She had come so far not to be just a Griffier, and what could the history possibly matter?

What she did next seemed like waking up.

'No stick,' James Drake said. 'No frame, no chair. Nothing like that.'

'It will be important to reduce stress,' the younger

doctor was saying. 'Stress could set you back at any time.'

James Drake stood himself up like an awkward box, swaying at first and then settling as though his shoulders and body were a great weight that held his legs locked upright.

'I expect to be busy,' he said.

The bright new life in his eyes was cold and fierce. The doctors acknowledged they had nothing more to do; they stepped back. They had remade a man, which was enough miracle for them; they did not want to know the consequences.

'You can go now,' James Drake said. He was feeling across a narrow table for the telephone.

3

There was a squall in Hollywood the day James Drake went to war: a cross, brief wind that turned the jacaranda into stained rain. In a script, Emma Griffier would have blue-pencilled the storm: too easy, too ominous. But she was not to know.

She was working a storyline like algebra, making sure it had the right terms, the right puzzles and the right solution; her plotting was neat as embroidery. She allowed no excess of mystery. Like Garrity, she liked stories out of headlines, with a theme the critics might find grand, and something to care about; it took time to make a movie, and it was easy to waste.

Her secretary, a deliciously imperfect Californian with a taste for cake, brought in the weekend scripts. One about Wall Street, one teen movie proposed as an oddity now the movie audience had grown up, one off-key epic set in a prison camp in the first years the convicts went to Australia. Knowing Garrity, there would be one in the pile he truly wanted to pursue; the game was to know which, to be right.

Her secretary announced a call from Rupert Griffier.

'Yes?' she said, like prosecuting counsel.

'I thought you might like to come to Denver for the weekend,' Rupert said.

'You're in trouble, are you?'

'You'll be amused. We could go up into the Rockies, blow the smog out of your head.'

'I don't have time.'

'There are some things we could talk about.' She rolled

her eyes; her secretary looked sweetly and truly concerned.

'If I don't come,' Emma said, 'tell me the consequences on the Beaufort scale. Twelve is death row, one is you have to bounce a cheque.'

'About nine,' Rupert said, and he sounded almost sober. 'Strong gale. Branches break from trees.'

She scribbled her secretary a note about Denver flights.

'Can you tell me about it?'

'Face to face. You never know who's listening.'

'Nobody wants the movie rights,' Emma said. 'And nobody here hangs on your investment advice.'

'That's not at all kind,' Rupert said, irritatingly uninsulted.

He fired the doctors suddenly.

'I doubt if you can do that,' the older one said. 'Legally, you're still certified dead.'

'Then I can't pay you, and you can't sue me,' James Drake said, with sweet logic. 'Ain't no great point in you staying around.'

'Our responsibility – '

'Your nurse is staying. Little Helen will look after me.'

'I've no doubt she will. But the position – '

'I think I can still use a gun, gentlemen. And being, as you say, certified dead, I have very little reason not to.'

'We do not respond to threats.'

James Drake wheeled himself laboriously to his desk. From the upper drawer he took out a 9mm Beretta, a solid, military gun; he could hardly hold it in his weak hands, but he pointed it at the older doctor.

'I truly think you do respond,' Drake said.

They left in some confusion, and he asked the nurse to

bring the piles of photocopies she had been collecting in the public library.

'Sort them,' he said. 'Griffiers there, James Drake there. The others in alphabetical order.'

'And if they're on more than one – '

He glared at her: angular, skinny creature, with a kind smile and just enough skill to keep him alive. He said nothing.

'I never realized who you were,' she said.

He had been surprised by the cuttings, too. The images he had fought to recover only weeks ago were recorded here, most of them; his memory was public knowledge.

He found his wife. His wife of thirty years, it said; but he had no sense of warmth towards her. She was dressed in a new fur coat on a front page; the text said James Drake had just been declared bankrupt, and bought this birthday present for his wife. He knew he had wanted to spite that tiny, angry judge; he must have loved his wife enough to use her and not some other broad.

There was an extraordinary scheme for a Rockefeller Centre in Los Angeles, fifty years after the New York version, all towers and wonders; his name was on it. He must have had money, but he knew that. He must also have been believed by many people. The scheme was respectfully reported in the *New York Times*.

In the usual way of business, there were only occasional mentions of his name. He had prospected for oil on every continent, and often found it; he was one of the few independents with the knack. The hunches, the calculations, the finds were not in the cuttings; but the parties were, and the politics. He had run for the Senate, it seemed, on the Republican ticket, and been narrowly defeated. The profile said he made his first money staking a wildcatter with all he'd earned, and for once the well was not dry. The profile said he was an excessively lucky man.

He was awkward with his big hands still. His fingers caught at paper and pushed it when he meant to pick it up. When he was excited, he was more awkward still.

'You don't need to read them all, not now,' Helen said.

But he needed to read them all, at once. It was his past on these faint sheets, waiting for him to decipher it.

He was reluctant to tackle the pile marked Griffier, at first. He had such pure and terrible anger against the whole company of Griffiers. To have evidence for his anger might compromise what he felt. But he was hungry to know things.

For some reason, he expected his own name in the Griffier cuttings, as though they only mattered because they had offended him. But there was gossip, as well as substance, and there were stories about the younger Griffiers.

He had never met Rupert, but Rupert was here, working some bucket-shop share deal out of an Amsterdam basement. That was not the proper occupation for a Griffier; it seemed to embarrass them greatly.

He made a note about Rupert. Almost anything he did would take time, and he was not at all sure how much time he had, but he could easily start with Rupert.

She was adrift in a wild but kindly crowd. They had lizard boots and huge hats; sometimes, a big man stood still as though in some wide open place and not an airport lounge; there were cowboys, rufous like paunchy foxes, elegant as taxi dancers. She liked the long, serious looks they gave her, and the smiles. She liked them off balance.

She called Rupert, so he would have time to clean up his life before she arrived – if, that is, he could be bothered. Maybe there'd be the usual, wide-eyed blonde who could dress in a moment and he'd be sluicing himself sober with cold water; he was an old-fashioned kind, the ones who organized a fine confusion of a life but who were never actually without. The name, of course, didn't hurt.

Her limo ran between mirrors and needles of towers, past pale, post-modern Byzantiums and down to a block by the railroad station. She stepped out into preserved memory. The buildings were brown brick, low and with their frontier pediments in place; at the end of the street was the railroad station and its grand sign; but the streets were unused and clean, like a set. Rupert had found himself a small hotel, pleasant enough, with a Forties cab outside to make sure the world knew its virtue was being old.

He said: 'They think it suits an Englishman.'

Emma checked in. The girl at the desk had no reaction to her name; it was just a strange name to pronounce. She tried it once, twice and then smiled very broadly.

'I guess they don't know you here,' Emma said.

Rupert, perfectly predictable, winked at the girl until she shifted on her seat.

At the bar Emma tried to get down to business.

'You can't have been here long,' she said. 'You haven't borrowed a house yet.'

'This is not an international centre,' he said. 'The ones that could afford to go to Gstaad don't know how to pronounce it.'

Emma said: 'You're a snob.'

'I met a woman from Kansas City,' Rupert said, 'who felt chic here.'

'You only sneer at towns that are likely to jail you,' Emma said. 'You were beastly about Larnaca. You hated Amsterdam.'

'It's a middle-class city.'

'Buying or selling?'

Rupert looked carefully around the empty room, as

though the barkeep, assiduously polishing bottles of sweet spirit, were a likely spy from some grand bank or the fiscal cops.

'You can tell me,' Emma said. 'You called me because you need money, I guess, and I was closest. And you must think nobody in London would be sympathetic, or else you need the money very fast. Well, I'm here, but I have seven scripts to read and – '

The fact of her career grated on him. 'If you're too busy to listen – '

'I'm here,' Emma said. 'Do you need a lawyer? Do you need money?'

'I need something more specific,' Rupert said. 'I need a way out.'

She sighed. 'Is it like Amsterdam?'

'I don't know what you mean.'

'You put twenty kids in a basement, and you had them cold call the world. They used your name. They sold shares. And the shares were worthless. I call that a bucket shop but I expect you call it an investment consultancy.'

'I do.'

'And Larnaca, too. You went to Cyprus and the only difference was the phone bill and the fact that the new kids were above ground. The shares still weren't worth the paper or the postage.'

'IBM can go down, too.'

'IBM can go up,' Emma said. 'IBM can stay steady. IBM can be bought and sold, for God's sake, which is more than your shares ever could.'

'It isn't like that,' Rupert said. 'This time it's more – complicated.'

'I'm listening.'

'I was offered an investment opportunity,' Rupert said. 'I'm not sure now it was entirely legal, what I was doing. It's going to look bad.'

'You put your own name on it, of course?'

'I'm not that stupid,' Rupert said. 'But it doesn't matter. All the people involved know I'm the one.'

Emma said: 'Then it's worse than the others. Do they have photographs or fingerprints or what?'

'Kind of a confession,' Rupert said.

'A confession,' Emma said. There was a time when she was very young, and Rupert might have been her hero, that he took up the luge, hurtling in an ice corridor, flat on his back; she thought he liked risk. But he was never good at it; she came to the conclusion he simply liked disaster. 'I'm going to my room to have a shower, and when I'm feeling fresh and strong, we'll have dinner there. We can talk.'

'They like me here,' Rupert said, his face as frank and open as a guilty child. 'They like me in the oil business and they've been talking about property deals. I have friends.'

'Can't your drinking buddies get you out of this shit?'

'I don't want anyone to find me,' Rupert said.

She said: 'You're afraid, aren't you? I mean, afraid of something worse than embarrassing us all and ending up in jail.'

'I'm not sure,' Rupert said. He was a sack of worry; anxiety had unknotted the carefully kept muscles.

Emma said: 'I'll come back.'

She went to her room. She tasted one of the pile of scripts. It was a delicate study of academic middle age in which love was nervously attempted and set aside, like a tricky recipe for cake; its brief best-sellerdom had been confounding. Emma reckoned Americans confuse professors with their fathers, and are fascinated by the faintest signs of their humanity. She was sure there was no movie. But she wanted to be able to argue the point, and she read on, for longer than she intended.

The phone rang and, almost before she could focus, he

was shouting at her against the sounds of a bar. 'If you want me to keep out of trouble,' he said, 'come and get me. I'm in the Slant Hole.' He let her hear the talk and the tills; he put the phone down.

She called him a bastard, and she asked reception about the bar.

'It's kinda – kinda masculine,' the man at reception said. 'I mean, a lady wouldn't usually just go there, except maybe lunchtimes. Lunchtimes, the secretaries go, in groups.'

She put on her executive armour, the least arousing she could be. The cab driver said: 'You looking for someone?' and Emma didn't say. 'I mean,' he said, flustered, 'are you looking for one person in particular?

'My brother.'

'He's drunk?'

'He said he was in trouble.'

The cab slid quietly into a side street, low buildings left like old wood in an orchard of brand new glass and steel. The driver spat from the window, reflectively.

'I don't think you ought, lady,' he said. 'Not without help. Not in your nice suit.'

'It's just a bar,' Emma said. Then she wondered precisely how risky and embarrassing Rupert wanted to be. 'It's not a gay bar, is it?'

The cabbie laughed.

She stood alone in the soft dark, watching the neon in the window. The sign above was more of a diagram; it showed how a wildcatter drills at a diagonal to siphon the oil from his neighbour's land. At least, that was probably what it showed, the street being public.

She pushed the door.

'Sweet thing,' a voice said, automatically. A tiny, bouncing man was standing in a casual light, ready to want a woman like a demon; 'Sweet thing,' he seemed to think the words were a courtesy, 'you want to lay some casing where the piping's bin?'

There was a wall of backs at the bar, used and practical bodies, and the girls bringing beer had the sane, hard smiles of girls who hear it all in the course of business; they could be raucous as parrots when they had to be, and as gaudy.

One thin, exuberant blonde cut out Emma. 'Honey, you lost? Or you working?'

'I'm looking for my brother,' she said. 'He's English.'

The blonde said: 'How did I guess that?'

'Big man, blonde, tan. English accent.'

The blonde raised her voice like a glass. 'You mean big, honey, or Texas big?' and she winked elaborately at the next table. 'You're unsettling the boys,' she said, quietly. 'Stand back by the bar, where we stand.'

Emma said: 'It sounds absurd to collect a grown man, but – '

'If he's big enough to look after himself, he can stay. If he's big enough to look after me, he can stay longer.' She hollered at the line.

'You don't have a public address system, maybe? To get the boys to go home.'

'We have guns and we have pussy,' the blonde said, archly. 'That gets them home.'

Emma said: 'I don't need the act.'

The blonde dipped under the bar, into her own territory. 'I know that,' she said, very serious. 'Just don't spoil it for the boys in the bull run. A game like this takes work.'

'My name's Griffier.'

The blonde shouted down the bar to a persistent, horse-faced man; he liked her sharp. She said: 'You sure the name ain't Morgan or Rothschild, hon?'

The tannoy broke between waves of talk. There was movement at the back of the bar, and Emma could see

Rupert elbowing the amiable crowd a little too hard. He put big hands on her shoulders.

She said: 'Time to go home.' He could read the anger in her eyes.

'Have a drink on me,' he said.

But the tiny, roaring man was back at their side. 'You really Griffier?' he said. 'Griffier like the bank?'

'Sure,' Rupert said. 'I just don't have money on me – '

'Griffier? For true?'

'And this is my sister, Miss Emma Griffier. But I don't think I know your name.' He had summoned back his most patronizing English manner.

'You shit,' the little man said, jabbing at Rupert. 'If I'd known what kind of shit you were – '

Emma tried to mouth to the blonde that she needed help, but the blonde had special senses; the management rose like a wind and began to steer the stranger, Rupert, to the door.

The little man had wound himself into fury. 'You bastards killed James Drake,' he was shouting. 'You killed Jimmy Drake, who was a better man – '

The air outside was comfortingly soft. 'That's enough games for tonight,' Emma said.

'The rodeo's in town,' Rupert said. 'I could go and drink with the rodeo boys. They love me there. I could go up to the Petroleum Club, any time. They love me. Everybody loves a banker in hard times, when they don't owe him money.'

Emma said: 'What the hell have you done to be so scared?'

The day's drink was tight under the skin of his belly, like a new and essential organ; he was grateful, tearfully grateful, for its help. 'I didn't kill a man called Drake,' he said. 'I know that.'

The street was clammy with moonlight and hot neon, where even the colours had colours for shadow. Rupert had put back his head to roar, but thought better of it; he leaned towards her, confidentially. 'Maybe,' he said, 'it was you.'

She looked away. Her embarrassment saved their lives.

The car came on in a grand corona of light, but with no unnecessary sound. The fact of the lights made Emma think it must be on the road; it was almost too late when she saw that the car was aimed. But the lights had burned out her sight for a moment, and she couldn't outrun the machine. She felt her heels catching in the sidewalk. She felt Rupert teetering against her. She knew in a cold, sick second that she was prey.

She couldn't throw herself away from the car, only towards it. She tried; she pitched out from under the wheels and against the rasp of a brick wall. The pain from the graze seemed to wake her, to start time moving again. The driver scraped the wall ahead of them in a brilliant spray of sparks, and went off into the city like a twister.

She must be as white as Rupert looked, down on his knees by the wall. She tried to lift him, and had to settle for holding him.

'They found us,' he said, and he passed out.

'The whole story,' Emma said.

'You should have called the police.'

She said: 'Rupert, I don't have much time.'

'It's about the penny market,' he said. 'You know about the penny market?'

She had heard of it – penny shares, sold through the back of comic books to people with almost no money, who dreamed of miracles that would make them a future, if not a fortune. Once it had been a miners' market, in Spokane, and when it was shut down there, it moved to Denver; you could buy a bit of a gold mine that was probably worked out, a silver claim where title was in dispute, a casino with a record or a pizza parlour with too little record or a bit of an unmade movie. Sometimes, the company amounted to a man and an idea; you paid to applaud him by buying shares. It was the market of last resort, for the kind of entrepreneur who can't get a meeting in a bank, and the kind of punter who'll never raise the cash to be secure; a toytown version of investment. She knew because she'd read a script.

'Overcooked books,' she said. 'The ruin of widows and orphans.'

'It's a perfectly legitimate market. People make fortunes.'

'I guess the people who sell the shares do,' Emma said.

'There's a market in all the shares,' Rupert said, 'nationwide.' He ran his fingernails along a line of the pad before him, deep enough to cut.

'And what did you do?'

'Stagged an issue. The whole issue. It seemed like such a simple thing – in and out the same day. I did it all on margin. No money down.'

Emma said: 'You didn't lose money?'

'I made it. I simply bought all the shares from the bank that was issuing them, and the brokers sold them for me to investors, the same day, and I took a profit. That's all. It was ordinary trading.'

'Then what is the problem?'

'There is a problem,' Rupert said, 'of perception.'

She went to the window. There were frontier buildings there, kept in developers' aspic, garnished with decor shops and designer coffee houses. She ached to see living things. She said: 'Tell me.'

'Some reporter, and some bureaucrat from the Securities and Exchange Commission – they wanted to make trouble,' Rupert said. 'Damn the SEC,' he said, as though the words were a spell to protect him. 'It's all unconstitutional, you know. Outside the powers of Government. Everyone knows that.'

'Except the cops,' Emma said. 'And the courts.'

'It'll be tested in court, in the Supreme Court,' Rupert said. 'It's pure Star Chamber – harassment of the public. They wouldn't dare send anyone to jail.'

'They just might,' Emma said.

He paused a beat. 'They're alleging conspiracy,' he said, 'conspiracy to defraud. They say I conspired with the bank.'

She was grateful for a little war of sparrows in the gutters opposite. It was accidental life in a landscape where man had planted every tree.

'It was a video store franchise,' he said. 'Just starting out, not much record, but a sound idea. The SEC say I got the shares cheap because the bank issued them all to me. So the company didn't get what they were entitled to. But because the issue was bought out, the punters thought it was a wild success. The bank had its salesmen cold calling all day and night. People came flocking in to buy, at prices way, way above what the company got.'

Emma said: 'Did you take a risk? A real risk? Or did the bank buy back the shares so it could dump them on the widows and orphans?'

He said nothing.

'Did you kickback any of your profit to the bank?'

He stared at her. 'No,' he said.

'Did you know the profit you were getting before the shares were issued?'

'I invested.'

'Or did you just lend your name so the bank could give less to the company and get more from the punters?'

'You sound like the man from the SEC.'

'You said you gave someone a confession.'

'I signed a paper for the bank. Just to say I would buy

the shares through nominees and give the bank first option on them; it was just a formality. It wouldn't have mattered if the Gestapo hadn't started asking questions.'

Emma said: 'What about the nominee names?'

Rupert shifted on his hams. 'One name,' he said. 'Not my name on the shares, you see. I was George Youngson on the shares. It almost looks as if I was hiding something.'

Her face was impassive, almost lifeless.

'Nobody cares about financial crimes,' Rupert said. 'They know it's all a matter of interpretation. It's not like mugging an old lady.'

'A Griffier rigging the penny market,' Emma said, 'is like a mugger called Rothschild.'

He said: 'Maybe – just maybe – I made a mistake.'

'I don't think anyone cares when banks steal from banks,' Emma said. 'But they make themselves care when some Brit with privilege wipes his boots on people with nothing, and that makes them very loud. Besides, you're spoiling a dream of instant riches. They'll have your balls.'

'I know a lawyer.'

'I'll talk to him.'

'You can't simply walk in here and take control – '

'Somebody has to be in control,' Emma said.

She sent him out like a school brat. She had four scripts more to read; she had to be back in Los Angeles within forty-eight hours; she had to stop a scandal. She sifted through the fall of documents he had left on the table, the prospectus, gaudy in several colours, and the numbers of the share certificates: he didn't have a copy of that awful confession, but he did already have his cancelled cheque for the full amount, payable to Hope and Prospect Investments. It was drawn on a Denver bank account; she had to hope he hadn't opened the account in cash and then been reported to the Internal

Revenue Service. That would make sure the Feds already had a copy of the cheque.

She felt she owed it to the family to get this one right.

She called Rupert's lawyer. He offered her lunch on the sound of her voice, and promised to collect her. He drove a Porsche, trimmed with a special compartment for his .357 Magnum Smith and Wesson; he said the opposition sometimes got testy. He was a big man, full of blood, and she liked the joke.

He squired her, with great attention, to a glassy building and up to the Petroleum Club. She was shown the crystal oil well in the foyer, and the wall of company logos cut on glass, like trophies and coats of arms in a cathedral. He sat her down before a window filled with the mountains, a horizon of white and iron.

'Think of all the gold and all the uranium still in the Rockies,' he said. 'Think of all the future out there. Awesome, isn't it?'

But that was not the point.

'Rupert has friends,' the lawyer said. 'We don't stop drinking with a man in this town just because the Feds are after him.'

'He needs more than that.'

'He still has his credit cards and his passport.'

'But the scandal – '

The lawyer shrugged. 'You do know what's happening, don't you? The local SEC office has been sweating for years on the penny market and they need something big. Your brother's friends at Hope and Prospect have thrown him to the lions, because he'll make headlines so the Feds look good. It takes the heat off old Moe Hope and who cares about a passing stranger, anyway?'

'But Hope and Prospect look bad, too.'

The lawyer sipped his drink of seltzer. 'It depends,' he

said, 'when they told the SEC what they were doing. Maybe they told them before Rupert signed up.'

'It was a sting?'

'Possibly,' the lawyer said. 'In which case, Moe Hope will be denying nothing. He's buying time.'

'We can't go up against him?'

'You got nothing else to do before 2000? The problem is that men like Hope don't have to rig their markets; they are the market. You'd need Moe's help to get the dirt and Moe won't be volunteering.'

'Then there's nothing I can do?'

'I could show you the town,' he said.

He'd stood behind her at the window and been appreciative; she was smooth and tight and full as a tulip glass.

'I need the phone book,' Emma said.

There was one obvious thing that she could do. She looked up 'Y' in the book, and she wrote down some addresses and numbers. She said to the lawyer: 'You don't happen to know where these places are?'

He looked down the list. 'You don't want to go there,' he said. 'Black area. And that's way, way out of town. And that's a sharp address – country club territory.' He said: 'Why do you want these numbers anyway?'

'I don't like the story we've got,' Emma said. 'We need a new one.'

For an empty hour, the lawyer waited, parked around the corner from the hotel. The streets were slightly south of where people shopped, and lifeless. Then a taxi went past to the station, at a time when there are no trains, and Emma Griffier walked out of her hotel.

He felt protective. Truth to tell, he felt horny. He also felt curious. He wondered what she had seen that he hadn't.

She didn't take a cab; she must know there was no chance of finding one in these dead streets; she could not be going far. She turned left, towards the grand arch of the railroad station. She was purposeful, but she had a spicy walk; that was the word for it.

She crossed into the high, airy temple of the station, set about with empty pews; a bird was scrambling frantically at the glass in the roof. One inquiry window was open; behind it, a man typed letters, very diligent. There were signs for the ski train late that afternoon and for the Los Angeles express expected around seven. An arcade of drab shops opened off the hall, their windows like women who no longer bother with appearances.

He could see nobody, but she must be meeting someone, and there was no train expected. She went out of sight for a moment, and he was bothered; the place was so blank that if something happened, anything could happen. He had to watch over her.

And she walked around the walls, listening carefully, looking at the sepia pictures of high-toned passengers stepping down into Denver, of cattle moving out and working men in scuffed leather chaps; but always listening. She heard a water closet boom, and a door slam. A wire of a man, shoulderless and dungareed, came out, his rubber shoes squeaking against the marble floor.

She didn't know him; she could not go to him. She was the exotic one, who wanted the favour; he had to approach her.

The lawyer fretted on the threshold of the main hall. The other man seemed edgy, maybe looking for a special kind of assignation, not the kind of man Emma Griffier should know. He had a puzzled look, and he sat down suddenly behind the high back of one of the pews.

Emma went to stand at the end of his row. She turned away from the photographs on the wall and stared at the newcomer. He shuffled his feet. She said, distinctly: 'Mr Youngson? George Youngson?'

The lawyer heard nothing more. When the man stood up his blade of a face looked alarmingly grateful, and he shook Emma's hand; his other hand stayed firmly in his dungaree pocket. He slipped and danced out of the station. The lawyer's presence didn't faze him at all.

Emma brushed down her skirt, and left. She came out into the bright light, and she blinked; the mile-high sun and the fouled air stung her. Her eyes began to water; she seemed to be standing alone, crying.

Softly, she called the lawyer's name, and then she called it more loudly. Of course he had followed her. It never crossed her mind he wouldn't.

The gentlemen from the SEC had the dreams of a G-man, of one day bringing down a public enemy to universal applause. Their pain was to uncover crimes that almost nobody understood, on moral judgement calls that a cynic might think marginal. When they found a villain as grand as a Griffier, guilty of stealing from the poor, they were blind keen.

They wanted an arrest for Monday, in time for the nightly local TV news, which meant finessing the paperwork for a warrant over the weekend. That, in turn, meant hoping they could push the rather ineffectual Rupert Griffier into one final mistake; he was only an animated tan with credit, after all. The last thing they wanted was plea bargaining when the whole thing came to a judge; this time, they had a straightforward fraud, a paper that could clinch the charge. Griffier was going down for just what they said he did, not for what he chose to admit.

At the door of the hotel, the investigator set his suit neatly on his shoulders and felt proud. It was a dangerous feeling.

Rupert came down to the assorted Chesterfields of reception, leathery and fake; he sat with the investigator in a timewarp of stuffed pheasants and chintz and an open fireplace. The hotel had an odd, economical charm.

'We'd like a full statement, Mr Griffier.'

'I'll need my lawyer.'

'You know we have documentary proof that you bought these shares to sell them back to Hope and Prosper. We can show Hope and Prosper loaned you the money to do so.'

'Doesn't your broker lend you money?' Rupert said, with an irritating display of naïve surprise. 'I thought it was called buying stock on margin.'

'A bank that did that thirty years ago,' the man from the SEC said, 'would be a closed bank.'

'You must long for the old days,' Rupert said.

Emma joined them and, since there was still no warrant and the man from the SEC was on foreign territory, there was no way to prevent her.

'I don't think Rupert has anything to say,' she said. 'Not until Monday.'

'I don't know who you are,' the investigator said.

'Rupert is leaving now,' Emma said.

She goaded him through the revolving door like a difficult heifer, and opened the door of the hotel cab for him. 'There's a good chilli place four blocks away,' she said. 'Green chilli, local girls, good beer. They even have jazz. Reception couldn't recommend it too highly. You go there, and you stay there until I call you. Is that understood?'

Rupert almost dared to be cross, but not quite.

'You don't move from there. You don't tell anyone you're there. Someone tried to kill us last night and I'm not going into the firing line for you again.'

'You've found something, haven't you?'

Emma said: 'I have a date with Moe Hope, your banker.'

'Be careful,' he said. The cab drove him off to his evening, and the lawyer's Porsche arrived for Emma.

'Moe Hope will see us,' he said. 'He lives over the shop, as it were.'

'And Mrs Hope?'

'She has a big house on Staten Island. She's kind of retired from marriage.'

'We can talk business, then,' Emma said.

'I wish you'd tell me what you've got.'

'I'm going to appeal to Moe Hope's better nature.'

The lawyer laughed hoarsely, like the bark of a seal. 'We're talking a man who started out shipping meat and filling vending machines,' he said. 'Stocks and shares is a retirement job. Less violent.'

'Watch me,' Emma said.

She tried not to be startled by Moe Hope's shop, which was a lush brick of mirror glass that captured the span of the Rockies, a foyer of Carrera marble with a plaque to say so, a bank of TV monitors to keep out the unwanted and a coppice of ficus to comfort the wanted while they waited. At one end, the brick rose in a stubby tower that was topped with glass battlements; the elevator rose through fifteen storeys. There, a perfect girl presented them with a plastic card; a polished, bulky black man watched their moves. They were expected, and the card allowed the elevator to go one floor higher.

The smell, unmistakably, was brownies fresh from the oven; it compromised all the fleshy flowers and the grand teak of the penthouse. They were announced; they waited; the lawyer said to the desk girl that it had been a long time, hadn't it?

Grand mosaic doors opened automatically. Emma strode in, and almost stumbled. The carpet was deep as summer grass, but it stopped at a cliff. Each new arrival had to walk down and rise again to a fortress on the other side, up steps to what looked like a circular altar of stone. From the doorway, she could see Moe Hope's head and shoulders behind the stone.

'Enter,' Moe said. 'Enter.' His voice resounded in the dome above his head; when he stood up, it was obvious why he felt the need of amplification. 'I'm sure you'd like to see my place.'

'It is,' the lawyer said, encouragingly, 'remarkable.'

And it was. Above his empire, where he hardly ever expected to be visited, Moe Hope had built himself a suburban ranch-style home, in the sky. The furniture wore artificial fur, all the levels had been split and split again, and in the home gymnasium there were posters signed by two vaudevillians and a woman famous, among those who knew, for losing her virginity five consecutive times in sexual films. There was also a vast kitchen, and a vast woman cooking there, a latter-day Butterfly McQueen who glowed and trembled at the thought of someone liking her poor cookies ('those tings . . .').

The tour was mechanical, and, like some machines, almost unstoppable; but when Moe stopped boasting, he ran out of small talk, and he settled his tiny body on an office throne. The sun was always behind him, his visitors always on a lower level; Emma was duly reminded that nobody said 'No' to Moe Hope.

'I was very glad to meet you,' Moe said. 'Now tell me why you're very glad to meet me.'

'There's an extraordinary story going round,' Emma said. She sounded half apologetic. 'I didn't want any misunderstanding.'

'Go on,' Hope said.

'The SEC have got it into their heads that there are banks in the penny market who rig the first day of a new issue. They lend someone money to buy out all the shares, cheap, and they sell them on to the masses the same day, expensive. The SEC are very worried about this.'

'They worry too much. Bastards.'

'Now the gentleman from the SEC seems to think someone called Rupert Griffier was involved. Only, for some reason, he was called George Youngson on the books.'

Moe said: 'You tell such interesting stories.'

'Which,' Emma said, 'is a surprise to the real George Youngson.'

Moe Hope was concentrating furiously; he had a curious, tortoise movement of the neck, very slowly to one side, which proved it.

'The real George Youngson,' Emma said, as though she was reading from a brief, 'is a school janitor with a crippled daughter who needs an operation he can't afford. He's got the money now.'

'I'm very glad,' Moe said.

'He's signed a statement that he is the George Youngson mentioned in your files and in the SEC papers. And, of course, it does make sense. He had nothing to lose, whoever loaned him money could dictate what he did, he'd take any risk for $20,000. That was unimaginable money to him. It could change his child's life.'

'Touching,' Moe said. 'But we have a paper where your brother Mr Griffier confirms in his own fine writing that he's the one that bought and sold.'

Emma said: 'My brother would hardly need – '

'He's done deals before,' Moe said.

'When it's so clear this poor janitor – '

'Your brother took the profits,' Moe Hope said. 'You can't get away from that.'

'And where are they now?' Emma crossed her fingers and hoped that Rupert had the sense to wash the money, fast; given his history, she couldn't be entirely sure.

'And where are the janitor's profits?' Moe asked.

'Oh,' Emma said, 'he took cash, of course. He couldn't put money like that through a bank account without attracting attention. People would think he'd done something illegal.'

Moe Hope stuck out his neck, very straight, inviting execution; he looked blank.

'I don't have to spell it out, do I, Mr Hope? If the SEC persist in their absurd story, we'll have to produce Mr Youngson. The moment we do, and we'll do it immediately, the heat's off Rupert Griffier and on you. It looks like you told the SEC you'd set up my brother, and actually you just did a deal for yourself.'

'This Mr Youngson, he has friends? Good friends?'

'You think you'll win the love of the Feds this way?'

'They never liked me,' Moe said.

All the way down, Emma was tempted to feel sorry for him, a man with no experience of defeat; but the elevator was out of order, and they had to walk to the ground, and on the way, she saw the rows and rows of trading desks, their computer screens shut down for the weekend, and the piles of glossy Hope and Prospect brochures ready to be mailed out, and she knew there was no call for sympathy. The worst that could happen to Moe Hope was that he lived on a knife edge; and, for him, that was also the best.

On the ground floor, the guard waved a phone at them.

Moe Hope had to take his time to lose his temper nowadays. For charity, he had a heart big as his clients' hopes, but the pump itself was suspect.

'James Drake used to tell me the Griffiers were bastards,' he bellowed at Emma. 'He's right.'

In the car, Emma said: 'Just like Rupert, only more professional.'

The lawyer evidently did not yet know the full story of his client; he looked interested. 'You were good,' he said.

'Yes,' she said.

Her hands were balled up in her lap, and full of sweat.

She had never done anything quite like that before. She thought it was not too much of a risk – the SEC visit showed they were unsure, and if Moe would forge a paper for a few months' peace, he would surely lose it to avoid a few months' questioning.

'But Youngson – he'll remember a lady with a British accent,' the lawyer said.

'He has cash. He gets the rest in two weeks, if nothing goes wrong. Besides, he thinks I talk like a New Yorker.'

The lawyer stared.

'One thing you learn in Hollywood,' Emma said, 'is how to tell what they just don't know in Denver.'

His foot slipped on the pedal and the Porsche began to hip-hop between the speeding cars.

Simeon Ryder took her story most matter-of-factly; he expected more and worse from Rupert.

'I'm very grateful,' he said. 'Usually it falls to me to sort out Rupert. I've always thought it should be a family task.'

'Something does bother me,' Emma said. 'Rupert was invited to Denver for this deal, most specifically. They went out of their way to get him in particular interested, and not just another gull.'

'I suppose he needed the money?'

'He said they mentioned taking him into the business – making him the distributor overseas.'

'He doesn't have the right background. Useless with an Uzi.'

'They set him up, Simeon. Why him in particular?'

'I told you there was something wrong,' he said.

He remembered distinctly drinking Jack Daniels, liking the sour sweet taste of the mash. They forbade him Jack Daniels. Even Helen, who would do anything, refused to bring him a drink.

Friends like Moe Hope came to visit, bringing their scraps of news for him to set into the wreck of his memory, to dress up what he had forgotten with what they knew. Most of them seemed embarrassed, even horrified by the wheelchair. Moe called to say they hadn't caught Rupert Griffier, as they hoped; his sister had interfered.

Let him go. There would be another place, another time. It was only a preliminary skirmish, to help that grand family understand they now had an enemy. But he wanted to know more about the sister. He would let go, but he would not let anyone interfere.

Everything was simpler now. His wife was rioting like a widow down in Houston, without credit; let her go. He was glad that the friends who took custody of his money had mostly returned it; as for the rest, let it go. There was enough of everything. The house had long since gone, with the garages famously carpeted to bring comfort to his various cars, and the rooms full of what designers thought would go with horses and the West. Let it go. He needed only the apartment. And he had Helen, bright, sharp-featured, dark-haired, and she gave head like an angel, and a dead man had no need to feel shame. He only wished he could respond to her kind attentions.

His life was wonderfully simple, but he found he could never quite explain the engine of it. Too much talk about the Griffiers sounded like a sick obsession; and he must sound like a man who was worth help and support. Yet he needed every scrap of detail he could find. He would fight like a judo fighter, use the Griffiers' own weight against them – their vulnerable name, their particular fears and desires and ambitions. He could never know too much.

He would kill and spoil, steal and tease, break up their pretensions like his had been broken by their schemes.

And then, he would take his profits, because there must always be a design beyond revenge.

He wheeled himself from table to table, stirring the piles of copied cuttings. Emma Griffier, studio executive, one of the new women in Hollywood, long-distance affair in London; she seemed to rest on that love like a boat on water. He could use that, somehow. Some nonsense about how each of them could keep an identity apart, without being smothered, how his being black was not an issue because of that. He worked in a museum, it seemed.

And Maurice Griffier, too old to be a young Turk, too stolid to be a member of the new and lurid Right, too eager to be a hero. Something there.

He enjoyed the melodrama. He enjoyed the idea of reaching out into the world he once knew from touch and smell and sight, and breaking it. He was even sure that his plans were somehow a reasonable form of investment strategy, one that stopped at nothing.

Chaos. He had asked sharp little Helen to find anything on chaos. She had brought back a bundle, tied together with red string. The knot defeated him; he had to call her.

'Here,' she said.

He turned the pages. CHAOS IN GILT MARKET, he read. CHAOS ON FREEWAY. WHITE HOUSE CHAOS THREATENS TRADE BILL. SUBWAY CHAOS TONIGHT. It was all chaos as metaphor, nothing precise. He knew there was something precise about chaos.

'Can't you do anything?' he shouted. He picked up the pile and held it awkwardly over his head and threw it down so the papers slid and scattered to every corner of the room. Helen ran out of his range. She stood in the corridor, worrying her nails and crying.

The first thing he needed was something to trade. Something to make him a player again so he could play rough. He would have to trust his memory of some greater and more lucrative purpose.

'One by one,' he thought. 'For the moment, one by one.'

4

John Brown was not the problem; but the Griffiers were not to know that. There was insult in the very idea of the man owning Griffier shares.

'Edward will deal with him,' Sir Alistair said flatly. 'Edward can control him.' He could not manage a great deal of conviction.

Simeon Ryder said: 'The longer Brown is a shareholder, the greater the risk.'

'He is a businessman.'

'Of a very special kind. He knows enough about death not to worry about trivia like bankruptcy.'

Sir Alistair snorted. 'We don't have to worry about Mr Brown's psychology. The issue is Mr Brown's money.'

'His money,' Simeon said, 'is as good as anyone's. That is the problem. His name, on the other hand, puts us at the top of every City page. Did we ever have another shareholder who could do that?'

'It will draw attention to the quality of the shares.'

'Just at the moment we might be grateful for less attention. We're in a kind of limbo until Big Bang, you know that. We lost our core income when the Government opened up the accepting house business. We haven't found anything yet which is quite as easy as guaranteeing other people's paper when they want to lend or borrow.'

'We do business. We have our specialities – '

'Anybody else can have our specialities,' Simeon said. He used his privilege as the most established servant.

'There will be too little business and too many firms and nothing will make us special then.'

'You do think we have a future?'

'I think we could live without surprises, just at the moment.'

Sir Alistair brushed the issue off the leather of his desktop with a literal hand. 'You should ask Edward's advice,' he said. He was not in the habit of calling his own brother, not to ask for help.

Simeon Ryder tried to place the call to Barbados, but Edward Griffier did not dash to take it. He was told that London was calling, and he stayed in the damp of the orchid houses among the fine, white blossoms. If it was Alistair, the old imperial bore, he could wait. Rupert would want money; Edward barely acknowledged that he was in the family. Maurice was strangling in his own propriety, and Edward had made a life of his own, with no desire to be reminded what he might have been. Emma would never be in London; she got out, as he had done.

He loved his exile here, his orchids, and the sharp fall of land that went down to the pulse and glitter of the great Atlantic. He walked quite deliberately away from the house into a grove of short banana trees, their leaves broad with the sheen of a good knife. He stood very quietly.

In among the trees was an elegant creature, lanky, silken and silver-gold, watchful but never sudden. Edward watched the green monkey sample his way through the fruit, bush by bush, until he found the banana ripe enough for his taste. He admired the epicure for his grace and his taste; he saw an image for himself.

He wished he was carrying a gun.

Emma walked soberly from the conference room, but she went dancing down to her office, holiday in her moves. So Garrity wanted her in London to scare the shit out of some epic-makers who were over budget; so she would have to look stern while they exercised their luscious, Sachertorte charm on her; so what? She could be with David unexpectedly, without the usual planning and conspiring.

She sent away a goose-like gaggle of producers, honking and waddling, and declined to meet a director who, now he accepted he was unemployable, wished to be known as a genius. She asked her secretary to apologize to the secretary of a man who looked exactly like the doll Ken, boyfriend to Barbie, and also to the secretary of a man who was drunk on words that ended in -ize. She forgot them at once.

She spun the car out and down through Santa Monica Boulevard. She wanted to wave at the brown bodies and the pastel flags of West Hollywood, to help out the old mahogany joggers toiling through Beverly Hills, to beam at her furious fellow drivers caught at the boulevard stoplights like fish in a net. She was ready to think of the studio as a fine machine, not just a slip-sliding matrix of deals and contacts and schemes for personal survival. She felt joy.

Across town, assorted producers cursed her for a hard-eyed bitch, child of privilege, who knew nothing about their struggles or their needs, not one of them; but she lived for the high moments when something was achieved not, as they did, for the humdrum continuum of being in development or turn-around. They would never have understood the ebullience in her, wild as a child and utterly without side or self-consciousness. It was the excitement of nerve ends, not comfortable at all. She was, after all, a wage slave freed by corporate duty.

She took a single glass of champagne on the London flight. She looked down on the endless carmine of the sunrise. She smiled at the kind, green patchwork of fields down below, and the scraps of mist. She could almost believe the land below contained those tourist pictures in the magazines – orderly country houses full of labelled Titians, thatched cottages with cream teas, green hills and churches which spoke history as a second language.

It also contained the Customs officer. He was a middle-aged man whose body slumped from his bull neck. He looked at passers-by as though he knew things. He knew about sin, and its first manifest sign was leaving the country.

'Resident in the United States are we, miss?'

His sermon would be preached with prying fingers and interrogation. He required, like some Puritan minister, the submission of the congregation.

'I am,' Emma said.

'Miss Griffier,' he said. 'What line of work are you in?'

'I make movies.'

He judged her with every ounce of his roadblock body. 'Please open the larger case,' he said.

The search took a full half-hour. Her anger amused the customs' men, confirmed them in all the quiet pleasures of their authority. She was sure it had not always been so.

'I control every aspect of your admission to this country,' said the customs man, reading her passport like a cheap novel.

'I enter my own country as of right.'

And so the search had been prolonged; they waited until she had to hide her anger. She was only a headline waiting to be written, a grand name to be attached, if possible, to some ordinary crime.

In the limo later, she found herself rehearsing everything that had been said. She was no longer private; her sense of self had been burgled. And it was not the routine business of any customs' official, and God knows it was not the lack of deference that offended her. It was the glee, the autonomy and the malice. It was the sense that authority didn't have to listen any more.

She told herself she was being absurdly sensitive, and probably tired from the night flight; but she had the energy that comes out of love, and fuels you for anger as well as joy. She felt she had dangled for a while from the will of a fat man. The washed and sleepy look of London was no longer a pleasure.

She went directly to the studio. She might as well use the anger that was welling in her. She thought to call David's house, but a machine answered, very formally. She called the Museum.

'I'm afraid,' a thin, plain voice said, 'Dr Taylor is away this week.'

'Away?' she said.

'He's gone abroad.'

'Could you tell me where?'

'Papua,' the thin voice said.

'And when do you expect him back?'

'He's gone for ten days,' the thin voice said. She did not seem inclined to develop the point.

It was like braking very suddenly on a fast road: she felt breathless. All the giddy hopes of the past thirty-six hours ended and she was just away from home, working in another town.

She did not bother to summon the producers she was meant to reprimand. She sat in her studio office, and she waited for rumour to bring them; it took an hour.

They were gentlemen of middle years and middle European origins, and they smiled and fawned, and when that failed, they summoned their long years in this fine industry and then they tried to imply that some snip of a girl from the studio could not possibly know what they knew. They ganged up, they argued with each other, each tried to stop the other saying what he meant;

Emma watched them like a Punch and Judy show. They knew when they had to leave.

She stretched in her office chair, and yawned uncontrollably. At least she had tasted a little blood.

Edward Griffier came in from the garden at dusk. His back, at seventy, was soldier straight, although now it began to look like an actor's posture, carefully kept. He was trim still, almost dapper; the islands had not coarsened him with drink or loneliness, as sometimes they do to strangers. He was happy in a place without news or events.

He had evaded the London call. He took the next call, thoughtlessly.

'I thought I'd phone first,' John Brown said. 'I was sure you'd be in touch.'

'Where are you?'

'In Bridgetown. I'm coming to dinner.'

'You're sure we have anything to discuss?'

'Your family think we have, I'm sure.'

Edward could not argue. He surrendered the bank to Alistair long ago. He was not made to be a king or a front; Alistair had at least been the right kind of Governor General, who did not feel absurd in uniform and cocked hat. Alistair could give independence to a colony like a gift, and be thanked for it, and keep a straight face. He had gravitas, and Edward was the light-footed one; but that left Edward with an odd reputation for magic. He could tame beasts.

'At eight o'clock,' Edward said.

He breathed the thick and female sweetness of the frangipani. He looked down on the coastline, at the last gaudy rowing boat jousting with the horizon, after barracuda, and the brown, shiny cows coming home. He loved the sense of order. He seemed very far away from the compromise and muddle of London, that perpetual sense of half-clean thinking.

He walked into his library, and called for tea. The library was where he kept the past: ledgers, letters, files and share certificates and the papers which made sense of what the bank had been. Alistair had wanted to give all this to some institution, but to Edward it was a kind of talisman; if he kept the records, he would never have to live them again.

Besides, it was intelligence. He had always dealt in intelligence, for interest, for a career and for influence: economic information and what to make of it. He had been clever with intelligence when he first met John Brown. He took down a file and some documents, not to confront Brown, but to remind himself.

At eight, the lights were lit in the driveway and the cicadas sung their numb song, and the sprawling house was glamorous in its coat of bright, white stucco. The lights picked colour out of the dark gardens; the scents were heavy. Edward had a starched shirt and a careful white dinner jacket for evenings like these.

He did not hear John Brown arrive. Somehow, the man had equipped himself with a Rolls-Royce and a driver able to slip it through the narrow lanes between the fields of sugarcane, across the six-way unmarked cross-roads and into the sharply angled drive. Edward expected Brown would say he made a point of driving a British car. He did.

They shook hands like diplomats, and not from friendly countries.

'I see Mrs Brown isn't with you,' Edward said.

'Of course she isn't.'

'I didn't know you liked the Caribbean?'

'After New York,' Brown said, and, in the same breath, 'You never married then?'

Edward had a wonderfully silly image in his mind:

John Brown like a great ape, sailing the Caribbean and picking the islands like fruit.

'We should have a drink,' he said.

They sat on the terrace, each uncompromising in his own style: the gross Brown, the needle Griffier, on either side of a small table with a servant attending them discreetly. They shared such a history they could hardly speak.

'Fine house,' John Brown conceded.

'I remember the movies we showed in Berlin,' Edward Griffier said, abruptly; he had to remind the man what they had in common. 'They loved *Henry V* for some reason, they hated *Rembrandt* and they didn't understand *Brief Encounter* at all. They didn't understand why the wife and the man didn't just go to bed.'

'I remember a room full of Madonnas, hundreds of them, painted Virgins. They were stacked there, by century of origin.'

'The nightclubs shutting at ten. The girls wearing their stockings inside out. The way the Staatsoper wasn't damaged at all – broken streets, but the chandelier and the gilt and the plush were still there.'

'They took a thousand tons of rubble a month out of Cologne, and you still had to walk on boards.'

The two men looked out into the night. They brought out their common experience carefully, afraid it might rebound. Each waited for the other to show how much had still to be said.

'Silk dresses,' John Brown said. 'The girls had silk dresses, and there were dresses in the shop windows on the Kurfürstendamm. You couldn't buy them. You brought in the material and they made them for you. Everyone had the material.'

Carefully, Edward Griffier said: 'Of course you'd know about that.'

'I remember things.' He stood up abruptly; for a big

man, he was surprisingly quick. He seemed to think memory had gone quite far enough.

Edward said: 'Of course I'm intrigued by your plans for the family business, if you have plans, that is. I don't suppose a dinner is pay enough for that information.'

'You never did know about prices.' Brown laughed. 'You weren't born to be a trader.'

'You might say we were almost friends once,' Griffier said.

'The Allies,' John Brown said, sententiously, 'owe me a lot.'

They ate efficiently and quickly, like soldiers in a barracks who have no reason to be social. After soup, John Brown lit his first cigar. He was in control here, and he wanted Griffier to know it.

'It was a good dinner,' he said, at last. 'All that spice can't be good for you, though.' He beamed; he seemed to expand with goodwill and drink. 'You have rats here?'

'By night,' Edward said. 'By day we have mongooses which were supposed to destroy the rats. Unfortunately, they just divided up the day.'

'Rats need shooting,' John Brown said. He heaved himself up, less steadily than before. 'You have a gun?'

'We have guns,' Edward said.

'Don't have to stand on ceremony,' he said, taking a remarkable swig from the decanter of port. 'Old soldiers together.'

The two men clattered out to the back of the house, alerting the servants. There was a porch like an English house, with boots and a smell of wet dog and a rack of guns chained together. Brown grabbed at a lightweight Purdy shotgun, and tried to pull it from the rack.

'You'll need a key,' Edward said. 'We're careful with guns here.'

'You'll need a gun,' Brown said.

They walked softly in the warm night, down to where

the cliffs fell into the sea. Nobody moved; the cattle were in shelter. It was no longer a quiet island; their path led them, half drunk, back into Berlin. It was 1946, the DDT powder thick on the ground, the girls in their dull stockings and the bones of the city all jumbled still together.

'Over there,' Brown said. He had seen the long, sleek shape of a mongoose on an untimely prowl; he aimed and he blasted. The fire from the barrels seemed to fall away like stars.

'Won't see anything now,' Griffier said.

'Rats everywhere,' Brown said. 'Damn rats.'

'I never carried a gun. You always did.'

'I wasn't English. I wasn't sure the soul of Germany was healed.'

'What were you?' Edward asked.

Brown grinned. He turned his gun towards Edward, and because he was a soldier, it was not a careless gesture. 'Useful,' he said. 'You burned the files I was so useful.'

'Did you ever think you'd get out?'

'If it hadn't been you, it would have been someone else. Talent is talent. You want to remind me what you did for me, I suppose?'

'You obviously remember.'

'Ruins. People trading for their lives. Shooting rats in an office. A Rembrandt for a cigarette, is that what you want me to remember?'

Edward shrugged. He put out his hands for the gun, and Brown surrendered it. He stood quite still for a moment and then his exact eyes sensed movement. He fired, and the movement was over, though whether because of terror or a sharp shot, he could not tell. Something small and furry lay under the vetch. It did not seem a worthy victim.

'I don't expect gratitude,' Edward said. 'What's past is past.'

'You started things for me,' Brown said.

Edward said: 'Other people helped in Berlin.' He handed the gun back to Brown. 'I always did wonder where the rest of the money came from. You'd got rid of your German identity, of course, and just to have hard currency was something.'

'Some people were very tired,' Brown said. 'They no longer wanted to be responsible, even for keeping themselves. They handed me their burdens.' Arbitrarily, he let loose one last shotgun blast into the underbrush. Nightbirds flew up screaming.

'I know things, too, of course,' Edward said. He had no wish to say more; he did not know how to use what he knew.

They settled themselves companionably on a rock which overhung the sea. There had once been a railway that beat sluggishly along this coast and some of its girders and props were left along the way, sometimes on land and sometimes out among the rocks. The sea played around the ruins and settled like lace on the tables of the reef. There was a moon.

'They used to stop the potato trains,' Brown said.

'Wait until they were going slow on an incline. Then they jumped aboard and put on the airbrake. It took them five minutes to strip the train.'

'They robbed the potato trains,' Brown said.

Both men had before them a kind of diorama, the three-dimensional picture you find in old-fashioned museums, but this one was personal. It reeked of cordite, piss and fear. It showed a city broken like teeth and still smoky with gunshots and dust. The Russians left flesh behind them like a papertrail and the Americans were dividing the spoils that they found and it was moral night.

'I didn't have to help the British,' Brown said. 'I could have gone to any one of the Allied powers.'

Without the bark and spit of the ocean, there would have been silence.

'Griffier is an interesting situation,' Brown said. 'I buy steel stockholders and plastic fabricators and graveyards for the same reason.'

'You think we're arrogant to imagine we might somehow be different?'

'I don't need respect like you need respect. I'm good enough to own you.'

'Would you bid for the bank?'

Brown had a look of startled virtue. 'Then I couldn't possibly tell you before the other stockholders. That would be improper.'

Both men looked deep into that city of memory, and neither could quite bring himself to laugh at the idea of impropriety. They had done so much worse.

'You gave me a gun,' Brown said. He rose from the rock and put out a great paw to help Edward, who chose to get up by himself.

'It's getting cold,' Brown said.

'If it came to some kind of war,' Edward said, 'about the bank, would you be on our side?'

John Brown strode off into the bush, slapping aside the sea grapes and the vines, and left Edward Griffier to scramble after his huge bulk. He stopped suddenly, and turned.

'All that history,' he said. 'It's a game. It's decoration. It doesn't matter a damn, not to me and not to you.'

It was not the answer Edward Griffier wanted.

'I can't imagine what you mean,' Maurice Griffier said, meaning that he knew full well.

'I'm suggesting a little caution,' Simeon Ryder said.

'Emma imagines that brother Rupert was seduced into

doing what he can hardly be stopped doing. That is her problem. She spends too much of her time inventing stories.'

Simeon heard the growl of every judge who ever faced a writer or an actor, unreasonable and inventive people, in the witness box: the established man's distaste for imagination. 'There is,' he said, 'a certain amount of evidence.'

'If you mean the man Brown – '

'Brown is a professional.'

'Exactly. He makes his money as we do. We can hardly object.'

'Your friends are sure of that, are they?' Simeon stressed the word 'friends'.

'The gossip is absurd,' Maurice said. 'The man was valuable to British Intelligence after the war, that's all.'

'Is he still of interest to your friends?'

'My friends in the market?' Maurice said, with fake innocence. But he was flattered, and he could not hide the fact. He fancied himself a friend of right-thinking men, and of the intelligence agents who thought more right than most. He accepted the faint drip of innuendo and suggestion they offered, and converted it to the steel in his speeches. He was their honorary brother in his mind, fighting a just war.

'I worry,' Simeon said, 'for a very simple reason. I don't see the profit in harassing Rupert and Emma – trying to trick Rupert and driving a car at the pair of them. When I do not see profit, I see irrational behaviour. I get scared.'

'Very well,' Maurice said, dismissively.

Simeon allowed himself a brief surge of temper, more than he had allowed himself for many years. Maurice could be a blimp or a Bulldog Drummond or a sensible man; as he advanced into the thickets of Government, and met the wilder fringes of the Right it became harder and harder to predict which he would be. Someone else, as usual, would have to pick up the pieces when he broke.

'This is going to sound very odd,' the voice said.

Emma said: 'Is this Patience?'

'Yes, dear. I'm sorry. Maurice's wife.' The woman had become wonderfully self-effacing. 'I could not think who else to call. And I really did not know where to find you. I thought you might be at home, or with David or in your apartment – '

'I'm here,' Emma said, thinking the obvious was the only way to get her to the point.

'I'm sorry,' Patience said. 'I heard about you and Rupert in Denver. Maurice doesn't seem to think there is anything to it, but these days – I mean you can hardly get on a plane wearing jewellery, can you? Not that I would, of course.'

'No,' Emma said, guessing wildly what Patience might mean.

'And in Britain, too. I think of going down to the country and being safe there, like in a nest. All the doors open, and people calling. But Maurice has these electronic devices absolutely everywhere – everywhere. The cats can't go for a pee without the police of four counties.'

'Maurice is careful.'

'Yes,' Patience said. She was quiet for a moment. 'I mean, no, he isn't careful. Not at all.'

Emma remembered the young Maurice Griffier once in the divorce court, listening to the story of how he had been pleasured on the Washington beltway by an adulterous wife, while speeding in an over-powered Jaguar. But Patience was a provider and a practical wife; she simply organized around such matters.

'He's not safe,' Patience said, 'and we're not safe. I heard about the car in Denver.'

'It might have been an accident.'

'Maurice has gone away to an EC meeting, and then he goes to Zurich, for this most peculiar meeting, and I don't at all know what he means by it.'

'A meeting?'

'It isn't one of his usual Parliamentary groups. It's full of rather young men who just bristle with certainties. He was only invited last week.'

'It's a talking shop, just another talking shop.'

'But he is a junior minister, and if it's at all dubious – I mean, if someone is trying to embarrass the Griffier family – '

'What makes you think it is dubious?'

'Of course, they send the women out while they plot over their coffee; they're thorough young fogeys. But they talk at dinner, too. They talk a lot about direct action, helping the forces of freedom, volunteering for a war. They're far too sensible to be guerrillas, but I don't know what they might not do in Zurich, with a clean bed to go back to and a good dinner.'

'Has Maurice ever gone away to one of their meetings before?'

'He never does public things. He never wants to look a fool.'

'You never worried before?'

'I worry all the time, dear. He wants to be a hero. He wants to be thinner and less grey and livelier. It's so natural, but it's so inconvenient.'

'What do you want me to do?'

'I don't know, dear. But you were so clever with Rupert's little problem, and you do seem to realize there is something very odd happening. Somehow the people who stay in Britain, they take it all for granted, you know? They don't think anything is odd. But I don't really see what you could do.'

Emma asked if Patience knew how Maurice would travel – flights, train times, hotels.

'His private secretary would know. Ever since they buried the poor darling in some bit of the Department of the Environment, he has to go to talks in places like Amsterdam. He's going there before Zurich.'

'Could you find out for me?'

Patience was suddenly ruffled. 'That would seem very odd,' she said. 'I don't want Maurice to think that I'm interfering.'

'Tell me when he goes to Zurich, at least.'

'At the weekend,' Patience said. 'So you'd have a little time, dear,' she added wistfully.

In the dark of the morning, under the vault of the Amsterdam Centraal station, the Rhinegold Express was a line of light, of pale golden wood and gilt, lovely as a toy; and the cops watched the platform. A pair of German businessmen clambered aboard like weighted, nodding dolls. An impossibly neat family, with broad open faces and shiny blond hair, captured their compartment like a fort. And Emma found her seat in the coach for Zurich and Chur. From the reservation slips, she was not travelling alone.

She kept looking for Maurice. His private secretary said he was travelling out of Amsterdam very early on Friday morning, and there were no other grand trains. The Etoile du Nord to Paris was too late. The Rhinegold went directly to Zurich. It seemed a curious use of a full day, but his staff were sure he was going by rail.

She had business in Rome on Monday; she told the studio she was travelling overland. They took it for a sign of eccentricity and sent the inexorable scripts. She took up the bulkiest of them: wife discovers family are Soviet spies, not Naval architecture buffs at all. How can she save her child and herself? How can she live with impossible, intolerable knowledge? By page twenty, Emma had a sense of real horror. She had always been young, strong, bright and rich enough to change the story if it seemed to be going wrong; but what if she could not?

The train had moved out gently as she read. There were dark suburbs, cut with the glint of canal water; there were flatlands, glistening like marsh in the grey white dawn. There were woods, wet and tangled, as the sun came up and at Emmerich, at the German border, the train stopped short in a soft wrap of fine, grey mist. The blue-suited border guards were out working the train.

She learned her police work from the best sources – Hitchcock, and the films of Jean Gabin – and she was not sure what to do next. She was on this glittering procession of a train, but should she skulk in her compartment or risk Maurice knowing she was following him? Should she present herself brazenly at his door, assuming she could find him, and surely he should be in this coach or the next, the two for Zurich. What if he did not catch this train at all? What if he claimed the seat opposite her?

She turned to page twenty-one of the script. She was indulging herself, and there was no time. The border guards were not *Stamboul Train* or *Shanghai Express*, she was not travelling *North by North West*; she was on a glamorous but functional train, going somewhere on business.

The world had come down to a sheen of pearly light against the windows, a mist that seemed to grow perversely thicker with the morning. She drank her coffee. She fancied secret police at a Balkan frontier, some spectacular and unfortunate travelling companion; the journey ahead seemed very long.

She watched a tall man wrapped in black run down the

platform, drenched in a fine rain that was made mean by a chilly wind. He threw himself into the Zurich coach and with him came two heavy black bags, like doctor's bags. He shook his hair, dog-fashion, and began checking the compartment numbers.

She was furious with David for being absent. She acknowledged, intellectually, their separate lives, and was mortified by each reminder. She was in a mood for company.

'I hope I don't disturb you,' the man said. He was curiously formal.

Emma smiled. 'I did know the seat was taken,' she said. 'I was expecting someone.'

He was young and lean, and he laid out his coat with military neatness. He had an open face, but a cage of careful manners which stopped him seeming as clumsy as he really was, unsure of his strength and reach. He seemed overgrown.

'I won't disturb you,' he said. He tugged files out of one of his bags, and then he thought that perhaps he had been too abrupt. 'I hate to fly,' he said.

She nodded. She could see a Sotheby's catalogue inside the file, for a sale of model trains.

For a while, they travelled in silence. She sensed that he was looking at her from time to time, discreetly; if she caught his eye, the look prickled his skin. He liked the look of her.

The sun had begun to burn away the mist, and the Rhine had become a narrow force as they moved upstream, and not simply a wide stain of water between green fields. The train announcer named each town, each castle now they were in Germany. She could see that he wanted a chance to explain to her, to help her.

She dropped the script and looked out of the window. The hillsides were green and verdigris from the vines and the sulphur sprayed on them. In the middle of the water long barges coasted round a black and white folly, regular reprimands to whatever trivial mind wanted to build an allsorts castle in the useful river. She was bored.

When she stood up, she thought for a moment the man opposite would do the same, click his heels with Junker manners. Not Junker manners, she corrected herself; German landowners, like English squires, were famous for being unclever and red-faced. But then, she had no particular reason to think the young man was German. He had the lifeless, metallic accent of any European who learned his English from the movies and an army of occupation.

She said: 'Excuse me for a moment.' She meant him to follow, but he was absorbed in his catalogue and the pictures of big, square trains that once belonged to a king.

She walked towards the club car, checking each compartment. She tried not to attract the attention of the under-occupied businessmen from Köln who were only too ready to be intrigued. She could not find Maurice in the Zurich coaches, but there were unattended bags and papers.

She found him in the club car sitting with a coffee, a brandy and the *Herald Tribune* spread out before him; she settled beside him and ordered mineral water.

'You can have your postcards stamped on the train,' he said, quite unsurprised that she was there, 'if you are a tourist, that is.'

'I didn't think Tories travelled on trains,' Emma said. 'Mrs Thatcher doesn't like them. Too collective.'

'Ah,' Maurice said, 'but on a fine day and in another country – ' He flourished a hand at the valley rushing by, its rocks and lushness. 'I thought this might be pleasant.' He finished his coffee. 'Is there a lot of film-making in Zurich?' he asked, politely.

'I'm travelling to Rome.'

'But in the Zurich coach,' Maurice said. 'Are you with that man?'

'Alone,' Emma said. She had not reckoned on being observed before she could begin observing. 'And you?'

'With friends, otherwise I'd ask you to lunch.'

Someone else entered the car, and she knew who it would be: the exactly polite young man from her compartment. He acknowledged her only briefly, but he thought hard. Nobody coincided with a friend on the train; she must be more ready to talk than she allowed. So why would she not talk to him?

'It's almost as though you're following me,' Maurice said.

'Don't be absurd.'

'You called my staff earlier this week.'

'I wanted to surprise you. That is, if it was possible to travel together.'

'Then you won't mind if I say it's not possible. I am not having an affair, it has nothing to do with my tax position and I shall not appear on television. I am doing something serious.'

She saw how he wanted to boast, and how he made himself keep quiet. Both factors made her think he had found significant mischief.

His tone was brusque. He patted her on the shoulder patronizingly, and her travelling companion could not bear it.

'I am sorry,' he said to Emma, eyes big and worried behind the steel frame glasses. 'Perhaps I might join you.' He glared at Maurice.

'No,' Maurice said.

'But this lady seems to be – '

Emma looked from one to the other.

'I mean,' the young man said, 'you should not trouble this lady.'

'This is quite unnecessary,' Emma began.

But Maurice was a man of substance, and he balled his fists. 'I have no idea who you are, young man,' he said, chewing on the word 'young', 'but I think you ought to leave.'

Her travelling companion clicked out words like a hurdy-gurdy plays notes, as fast as he was wound up. 'It is my opinion that you should leave. Sir.'

'There is some misunderstanding – ' Emma tried.

'As it happens,' Maurice said, grandly, 'I do not have the time to teach this young man a lesson in manners.'

The young man had squared himself, ready to be taught, and ready to answer in kind, but Maurice walked away. His mind was, he implied, on far more important matters. The young man was left posing in the middle of a moving train; Emma, and the jolly girl behind the bar, took pity on him.

'I think,' Emma said, 'that was kind.'

The young man's smile drowned in the adrenalin he could no longer use. 'I am most sorry,' he said, 'if I did not understand that situation.'

'He's my brother,' Emma said. 'Brothers and sisters always fight.'

'I expect they do.'

This time, he did click his heels, and he withdrew.

Emma sat with her mineral water. The Rhinegold had seemed a glorious game only hours before, but now it was claustrophobic like a corridor. She had nothing to say to Maurice. Her compartment was infested by an over-careful young man. She wanted lunch to go on for ever, but she wanted nothing to eat. She picked at a plate of smoked salmon with some horseradish cream.

Maurice came to lunch with his associates; he was playing the cool, confidential executive, but sometimes his voice took on a politician's boom for a phrase or two. She heard 'valuable property of this kind' before he mumbled again into his bottle of hock and his fried pork, and 'freedom of information' which seemed an unlikely phrase. As she left the car, Maurice was saying: 'We shall give him the chance to choose.'

She walked the corridor carefully, back to her seat. Maurice was drunk on slogans, which was not new; but he had in mind some particular valuable property, which was curious. She found the Zurich coach.

The young man was there, and he pitched himself obviously back into his seat as she appeared. She could not remember how she left the pile of scripts; she had a wild dream that he was the spy from UFA come to steal Hollywood scripts for the Volk. She wanted to giggle, but her companion looked startled and abashed.

'Welcome back,' he said, and buried himself in a book.

She looked out at the pipes and fires of industrial cities, and then at the dead spikes of the Black Forest. The train had seemed an exhilarating private world, a moral universe to itself where she was allowed any move, any want. She was not sure any more.

They ran into Basle only a little late. 'The coach won't go through,' he said, authoritatively. 'The Swiss always leave on time and our connecting train is gone.'

'Oh,' Emma said, blankly. The Swiss disdain for German inefficiency was new to her.

'You should take the first Zurich train,' he said. 'I'll have to help you.'

On the platform, she said: 'I don't know your name.'

'Adam Heller,' he said. He was disconcertingly close; he was thinking that he wanted to be her cat, to run a rough, industrious tongue – but he knew there must be preliminaries.

'I don't know your name,' he said.

'Emma,' she said. You could never be too careful.

* * *

Maurice bought papers ostentatiously in the underpass between platforms at Basle: *Die Zeit*, *Libération*, *Le Monde*. If Emma was a coincidence, she was a bore. If she had chosen the train deliberately, it could be worse. He finally had his chance to do instead of talk, and he would not let her spoil it.

He saw her on the Zurich train, still with that tall absurdity of a kid who was following her before. Evidently, they had made friends; evidently, she had forgotten David for the moment. Probably as well, Maurice thought, full of prurient visions.

Since everyone was meant to think he was heading for Zurich, he went there. Emma would be a useful witness. When the train stopped, he brushed through the kids standing like cattle in the cold and stormed down the platform. He scattered the polite commuters with the swing of his overnight bag. He ignored the taxi rank to the right, and went straight ahead, past ticket office and left luggage and the first-class restaurant.

He slowed down. He had moved fast enough to shake off Emma, he was sure; she had luggage, and obligations to be polite to her companion. He did not want to attract unnecessary attention. He knew he was to meet a steel-grey BMW at the side portico of the station; his companions would not follow. From now on, Maurice was the solo and the hero.

The car was waiting. He tossed in his bags and took the back seat. The driver turned and said, with a little sarcasm: 'Mr Griffier?' but he did not wait long. He turned into the traffic, and made the turn back to the Bahnhof Bridge and along the line of the Limatquai. It did not occur to Maurice to look back.

He had been waiting a lifetime for this. He had been just old enough to go when Hungary blew, but somehow he did not go. He had met the undergraduates who smuggled out refugees, and envied them their legend.

He had heard about the pipelines that brought people out of East Berlin, but the operation sounded too professional. He told himself he was not sure what he could contribute. When the Russian tanks rolled into Prague, he had been confused for a moment; socialism with a human face was still socialism. It might even be worse, since it had to be answered by argument as well as force. Somehow, until now, Maurice Griffier had never volunteered.

This time, he had been called. He was told a Soviet geophysicist wanted out, a specialist who had toured the world to make energy maps. He knew where oil and gas lay in every country, on every continent; his maps were strategic documents of enormous importance. More than that, his absence and their absence would seriously embarrass the Russian energy programme, including the part of it the West called expansionism. This man knew which wars would pay.

This man – they called him Pavel – had asked for the protection of an MP when he jumped. Maurice's friends had thought of Maurice. He would use his authority in the cause of freedom and, after a decent interval, be thanked for what he had done. He expected applause.

He was full of certainty, the kind that lights up the eyes and films the hands with sweat, a bit like lust. He watched the lake sweep by; he scuttled briskly into a nondescript concrete apartment block in the suburb of Kusnacht. Security was vital, from now on. It was like all the wars he had missed, a credential. He even thought that it might be reasonably safe.

The story on Pavel sounded right. He was forty-three, malcontent, without a Ziv to drive, low on the privileges of the nomenklatura, the Soviet ruling class; he could go to the hard-currency stores, but with too little to spend. His marriage was over but sticky; he needed to run away. And besides, he had spent five years of his life, jungle by jungle, mountain by mountain, infection by infection, on a survey which, short of the triumph of world communism, was at least two-thirds useless. He knew prospects where nobody guessed there were prospects, where the spirit of Marx might never penetrate; but dollars and AMOCO might.

Maurice had read the right spy novels, listened to the decent, rational paranoia of the security services. He believed in information, that there was always something definite to know, and he set aside the problems of whom to trust and whether everything was fraud and treason. Besides, Pavel had to be the one. Mornings, his muscles no longer stretched as easily as once they did, and in the afternoons, alone with a pretty friend, he was sometimes breathless before she was. There were teeth that might need to be replaced. He did not have much time.

At Kusnacht, he was told the details. Pavel would come across the East German border, close to Bayreuth. He would come over to Maurice, and it was Maurice's business to get him safely to Munich Airport and out to London; he would need all his MP's clout.

Maurice was proud to hear his heart like a jazz club: syncopated and too loud. Perhaps he had been too generous to himself on the train, but sometimes drink filled unoccupied moments gratefully. He was introduced to his driver and his minder, and he sat up front in the car, bolt upright, sent out like some mercenary guard to the cheers of the young men left behind. They had twenty-four hours to bring back a defector, without creating diplomatic fury. There was nobody to protect them, and nobody knew officially what they were doing.

'But that,' said one of Maurice's friends, a philosopher who had outgrown his training, 'is what makes it real.'

Maurice nodded. He pretended the cold sweat trickling between his buttocks was an illusion. He could hear

Patience quite absurdly telling him to be careful, and as the car lapped up the black night like a cat, he would have liked to be careful.

Like the man who does the orchestrations, James Drake missed his credit and he missed the show. His friends brought him gifts of contacts, rumour, information. He could walk now, but he chose to have Helen drive him. She was a determined, reckless driver.

The world was his files: the smear of black and white on copying paper. There was Maurice Griffier cleaning up TV, a long piece in the *Daily Mail*; and there he was, covering his face as he was bundled out of some London meeting to send support to the Nicaraguan contras (but James Drake wondered why he should be ashamed). The man was about to give up a strong body and quick mind without ever having used them; he was that age.

Of course he'd go, and he would bring back the asset James Drake needed. There will be scandal, and Maurice will be precisely what he fears he already is: a shell, misplaced. He will be ashamed, because in his heart he senses some authority – his class, his elders, his club – with the right to judge what he does, and what he is.

So Maurice will go silently, covering his tracks, and nobody can catch him in time.

She saw Maurice barging the crowd like an out of season football player, through the narrows by the ticket office to the lost world beyond the first-class restaurant. She panicked. She thought he was coming to a meeting; she had booked a hotel, but not reserved a car. She thought she would simply shadow him to a destination, and keep him out of trouble by her presence.

Adam Heller was close to her, still. He refused to separate himself from the smell of her, the taste of the air she walked through. He was ruthless, because infatuated, and he was very nearly a perfect nuisance.

'I have a car,' he said.

She made a smile out of bones and patience.

'We could follow him,' he said.

He must have registered how Maurice was eager to lose her, and how keen she was to keep close. She was alarmed at this early flourish of lover's intuition.

'We'd better move,' she said.

Maurice was lost in a press of greeters and travellers. Most likely, someone was meeting him. That someone would have to negotiate a tricky junction out of the side road by the station; if only Adam's car was waiting, ready, they had a chance of catching up.

By the taxi rank, the driver surrendered a Porsche to Adam, with something like a little democratic, Swiss salute. Emma expected a Porsche: as eager and easily damaged as the man who was going to drive it.

'Do you know which car we should follow?'

She had nothing to say.

'If he comes out by the bridge, and he's going across the Limat, he'll have to wait. There's two lines of traffic to cross, at least.'

He spun the car to the start of the bridge. A little side street let him wait until the cops passed by.

Emma stared at the cars, willing Maurice into focus. One by one, they filtered into the main traffic. There were too many neat Fiats and Alfas; he would have something more solid or more flashy. Look for something fast and German.

Last of all, a silver BMW pulled out. Emma thought she had seen every face in the car; she assumed Maurice would ride at the back. But as the car pulled away she saw him, by the driver, and the car drew away into the old town.

'That BMW,' she said.

Adam slipped out into traffic. The silver car ran ahead of them at the first lights, but Emma could see it streaking out along Limatquai; they knew its route. At each set of lights, they had a chance to catch up; by Kusnacht, they were almost embarrassingly close. Maurice's car turned off by some new and low apartment blocks, and Adam deliberately overshot.

'How far do we go?' Adam asked.

Her only possible answer was quite unreasonable: as far as it takes, wherever he's going. She didn't know how to break in and demand information, but she did know how to follow.

He might not leave in the silver BMW. If he did not, she could be sure he had some melodrama planned, expecting opposition and pursuit. She thought he was a man with an obvious taste for meat he could no longer quite chew.

A car came out of the cul-de-sac. Emma nudged Adam, and he drew gently from the sidewalk, careful to seem as though he was unsure of the way and staring at signs. They came up close at the first lights. Maurice was not there.

She said: 'It isn't him.'

In the time they had been away from the cul-de-sac, some other car could have crept out and away; she knew it. Perhaps Maurice already knew this aggressively visible Porsche was following him.

'We go back to look?' Adam asked. He made an alarming U-turn.

After a long half-hour, the silver BMW appeared again.

In the car, Maurice asked: 'How many hours to Bayreuth?'

'Five, maybe four,' the driver said. 'Get some sleep.'

'There must be an airport.'

'Nuremberg. One flight a day, and you think they wouldn't notice a British MP?'

The suburbs ran out, and the world narrowed down to a strip of roadway unspooling. He slept fitfully, but his neck bothered him.

'The Wagner house,' he said.

The driver, a solid and thuggish boy, said: 'Wahnfried. They have stage sets in the basement and the old boy buried out back under a marble slab. Usually, there's a guilty little section in the library about how Wagner really liked Jews.' He laughed.

'Pavel goes there once he's across the border?'

'He has some privileges. Besides, the Bayreuth University specializes in Africa, and he has some old associates there who might help him with maps. Apparently the geophysical survey gets less detailed, the more unpleasant the terrain, and where the terrain is brutal – ' He put his mind back to the road, and skirted a dinosaur lorry, long and iron-clad. 'Pavel's good,' he said, 'but every man has his limits.'

The driver wished he could catch Maurice in a mirror. The man seemed slow, and a little excitable, and neither was an advantage. But he was paying. The only trouble was a red Porsche just behind them. There was nothing odd about a Porsche screaming out of Switzerland into Germany at night, and no rule that Porsches shouldn't take the autobahn, far from it, but this particular car had held their tail for almost a hundred kilometres. Porsche owners, the driver thought, never tailgate; their ego forbids it.

'We might have dinner early,' he said.

He turned off the motorway and climbed to a small village. There was a gasthaus with, on the first floor, a restaurant that smelled of wood and sugar and frying; there were rough veal sausages and a crisp, brown cake of rosti. After dinner, Maurice had the look of a middle-aged man who has eaten well, a tendency to sag.

No Porsche in the village, the driver saw. The old man – the driver thought Maurice was an old man – could sleep.

'But after Wahnfried?' Maurice asked.

'We get out to Munich. As we discussed.'

'As we discussed.'

'Which is where you use your Parliamentary privilege, if there's the slightest trouble, and Pavel takes the next plane to London.'

'Of course,' Maurice said. 'Yes, yes, of course.'

He began to snore like a broken thing.

Twenty kilometres along the road, Emma and Adam waited in a lay-by.

'You know where he's going?'

Emma shook her head. She wondered why Adam was still stuck to the chase, how he made sense of it. And Adam was sorry they had a full hour to sober up from the chase. He liked the shared passion.

'You want to tell me anything?'

The lights of the cars came up like a sunrise every minute, dazzling a little stretch of road into life before fading away. If the BMW went past on its own, with no following car to spotlight it, they might miss it altogether.

'Do you usually take strange women for rides the day you meet them?'

Adam said: 'I like to help people.'

'I don't even know your nationality. I give mine away every time I open my mouth.'

'American-Swiss, by origin. Now, I'm Swiss. They make you choose.'

'You live here?'

'New York. Zurich, sometimes. London, sometimes. I deal in things.'

'Like model trains?' she said, remembering the catalogue.

'Nobody has sex now,' he said, 'so everybody needs a hobby. The trains are the new dirty books.'

She was afraid to take her eye off the stream of trucks and cars, but she did not like his talk. She was fretting when the car jolted forward and out into the road.

'We almost missed it,' Adam said. 'Check the number plates when we get close.'

'They'll recognize us.'

'We overtake, we stop for gas. I just have to be sure.'

'I didn't even see them.'

'We all know how to do this,' Adam said. 'We read all the right books. There'll be a moral question or a human dilemma along, any minute.'

But there was only the curtain of rain and lights and night, hour after hour, and the risk that they had lost the car ahead. The BMW was elusive and silver as a trout in storm water. It went off the road very suddenly, down the road to Bayreuth. They twisted after, through narrow streets. The town was dead and small, but it was full of all the myth and godheads of Wagner. It was the perfect place to fool people.

The silver BMW was by the railway station. The station hotel was full, but while reception thought again (Adam had shown a collection of large denomination notes) Emma looked carefully at the register. There were no new arrivals that night, under any name; Maurice most likely had settled in the Königshof, across the way.

Emma expected Adam to offer her protection, in the same room, but he did not. She slept until bleak, very early light began to cut into the room. She had morning thoughts: she wondered how she ever thought she could protect Maurice from himself. He would be whatever kind of fool he wanted.

Coffee helped, a little, but it was still a cold morning. She dressed, and when she was almost ready to face the world, there was a furious beating on the door.

'I've paid the bill,' Adam said. 'They moved out.'

'You don't pay my bills,' Emma said. 'You don't know who I am, even.'

'I can read the etiquettes on cases like anyone else. And you're under no obligation. It would take millions to put you under an obligation.'

'Where did they go?'

'I don't think we can catch them. But we can't just stay here in the hotel.' He thought he might seem too eager to start the chase again and set her heart racing.

'We can't,' she said. 'It's a trap, you see,' she blurted. 'I know it's a trap.'

But Adam was not the man to talk about traps. He had too modern and vague a face and body, a steel-rimmed, benevolent, not entirely serious face. He was made to talk about chocolate or tickets or shoes.

'Of course,' he said, 'we could go for a trip. There is a palace encrusted with sea shells and the Festspielhaus. We could go to Wagner's house – '

'Where the hell did he go?'

'His driver went with him. I couldn't ask the driver.'

Emma put her hands in her lap like a schoolgirl. 'I guess we wait,' she said.

There was always drizzle and mist when such things happened, Maurice knew it: nature conveniently shrouding the odder things men do. It should be cold at a border, cold and irrational. But they were fifteen kilometres towards the border and the only sign was the lack of traffic. He could, for God's sake, see rolling hills.

A little Ford rolled past like an omen, quick as its straining engine allowed, with pockmarks in the paint.

'Bullets,' the driver said.

'They fire at the border?'

'Sometimes.'

Maurice huddled in his seat, grave as a soldier. He tried to remember his all too brief time in national service; he had never shot at anyone in anger. He had met people with different accents, and muddled class and habit with an officer's authority; nothing else had happened.

'Pavel will be at the border, then?'

'He should be. There are guards, of course. They know how valuable he is.'

'And yet,' Maurice said, 'they let him visit the shrine of Wagner.'

'They have symphonies, too. And they want information, and it's only twenty miles to the border. Twenty miles, twenty minutes. He talks to his colleagues at the university, and then he's back before the first sign of trouble.'

He was uneasy in these hills. He knew who came from here: the Protestants with Bavarian politics, the grim elect of the Nazis. Julius Streicher, the cook of hate, was born here, and went forth to slander whole peoples to death. It was not a time Maurice could be casual about; he lacked the New Right's easy dismissal of a history in which they had no stake. He still thought the past was not always a game.

'What do we do?' he asked.

'We wait. We don't know exactly when they come across. We just know they'll take Pavel to Wahnfried. We'd be too obvious waiting there.'

'The Germans aren't watching us.'

'Everyone gets edgy near the border. They get paid

more, too. If you have three men waiting by the door of a national monument – '

'We know about that, from Ireland.'

'It's why we need discretion and an MP.' The driver turned full body to Maurice and said: 'You're really very useful.'

He was being patronized. He wasn't pure like his younger colleagues; the past tainted him. He was there to be used. He wanted action so he could prove that he was one of them, by right.

On the narrow road, a pair of cars came roaring into Germany in official lockstep.

'Them,' the driver said and he lit off after Pavel and his escorts. In the centre of Bayreuth they saw the cars parked outside an eating place. The group in suits were unworried by the smoke; they had ordered dumplings and ham hocks and cucumber salad, and a queue of beers. They had hard currency, but unchanging tastes, Maurice assumed. There seemed to be too many guards for a single academic who knew how to read maps.

Maurice said: 'Which one is Pavel?'

'Blond. Short. Neat. The human one among the gorillas,' the driver said.

'We should wait for them at Wahnfried.'

'Only when they go. They may go to the university first.'

'They wear very good suits,' Maurice said, vaguely.

'There's no reason why they should come back,' Emma said.

'I could show you the town,' Adam said. 'The Festspielhaus, the pictures of divas, the sets. The statues – '

'I have to call the studio today,' Emma said.

She owed him the journey here; she could give him a day. He was warm, breathing company that did not want to compete and she was grateful.

They walked around the great Wagnerian theatre, and she thought of soundstages and temples all at once. They contemplated the severed heads of Cosima and Richard Wagner, fearful things set on plinths with eyes incised so they seemed to follow passers-by, judgementally. The bombast began to seem absurd, and Emma was tired enough to laugh out loud. Adam did not approve.

She thought the whole inoffensive town had a cardboard look. The villas distilled all the suburbias she had ever seen. The squat, busy figures on the main street went on errands that might require confession. The rivers ran in concrete beds, the churches were blank houses, the sausage shops and hardware stores began to seem less real than the Wagnerian fantasies of gods and dragons. When they walked into Wagner's own villa, Wahnfried, Emma had a sense of relief. It was only a square suburban temple, pompous and inscribed, but it had some connection to a world of feeling.

She walked into the red of the main hall. The house smelled of polish and respect. Through double doors, by busts and pianos, she could see a grand drawing room lined with books. Chairs were set out in rows, facing two huge black speakers; and beyond that, the wide windows, a stretch of grass, and a marble slab that lay among trees. As she stood there, the music began: the great carpet of the Siegfried Idyll, lush and splendid. She was caught in a sense of ceremony, hopelessly invoking the spirit lying under that marble, a hi-fi resurrection to make her shiver.

Adam said: 'You're cold?'

His voice startled her; she had felt alone. The speakers, the windows, the pale trees, the black marble slab; she turned away gratefully.

'They have models of the stage sets in the basement,' Adam said. 'Like children's theatres. They have more swimming holes for Rhine Maidens than you can imagine.'

She let herself be led. The basement room was dark and the only light came from model sets that were ranged in rows like fairground games. There were corridors of Valhallas, under enormous theatrical skies, and grottoes of Venus with row after row of cardboard trees, vistas of heaven and metal gods and heroes. Once through the single door, the basement became a maze of illusions.

There was a slight commotion at the door, the unspeaking kind an official party makes when it arrives, expecting attention. The room was too dark to see precisely, but Emma could feel there were others present now, maybe six or seven. They talked reverentially in German, and they shuffled steadily, the pace of a group that takes its cue from one important person. Emma turned a corner and she could see two men before the earliest of the model sets, their faces lit like children at a peepshow, and dark, disinterested bodies behind. Two men, five escorts; or five guards.

Adam had come close enough for her to feel his warmth. The seven men had spaced themselves so nobody could approach; she knew Adam would push them aside for her sake, and she was horrified at the very idea. She would like a little less adulation. She wondered how often medieval ladies really wanted the protection of their knights; it was the knights who told the stories afterwards.

The house had seemed empty moments before. Now, other people arrived; they seemed to seethe with purposeful movement. She would have much preferred to be in one of the lit rooms, but the easy ways out were blocked by two parties of men. She tried to concentrate on a Venus' Grotto from the 1920s, an intricate fantasy with a Gothick forest leading into the distance, too delicate for the steel and paint of a stage.

She thought she heard Maurice's voice, very low; it was more a sense of vibration than real recognition. It made sense, she supposed; he was seen at Covent Garden in the bank box and sometimes stayed beyond the smoked salmon sandwiches. She wanted to take Adam's hand, and tell him she must get out of this room, because it was a trap.

The guards were broad, static men, like oxen; but they, too, were restless now, almost skittish in the way they drummed their fingers and scratched and turned. There might be a problem: the new group might obstruct their easy escort of their party out into the light. And the other group were no longer together. That was ordinary enough at a museum, but it disturbed Emma to see them pass one by one, at either end of her little corridor of lights. They were moving with exaggerated care.

There was a shot, or something very like it.

Upstairs, the schoolma'am at the door heard the noise. It made no sense in this tranquil place, and she ignored it. It seemed to have no consequence; no glass broke.

There was the quiet of still men checking each other for movement in the faint light, but the shadows began to move again at the corner of Emma's eyes. She was tempted to stare straight ahead and lose herself in stage pictures.

Someone said softly: 'What exactly is happening, please?'

Emma was sure the prowling men must have collided; there were just too many intentions for a small room. She was unwilling to move, and afraid of being trapped.

She smelled a lack of air. It carried no smell of smoke or chemicals; it was only airlessness. Adam pushed her down to the floor. Her eyes were open so wide they hurt.

'Move,' he said.

They scuttled, crab-like, over the floor, making for the doorway. There still seemed no reason for the way their own bodies were short of air. At the lintel of the room they came up against the little wall of fire that had been sucking out the oxygen behind them.

'Don't think,' Adam said. 'Throw yourself.'

She rolled through the fire, and she came out on the other side with a lung filled with hot needles.

'Get out,' Adam said. 'Slowly.'

She had no interest in taking orders.

'Please,' he said. 'There'll be cops and all sorts of people.'

'I feel as though I'm covered in soot.'

'Maybe you could wash your face – '

'Nothing has happened,' Emma said. 'That was special effects fire.'

'It was some kind of fire.'

'We're going to listen to the music,' Emma said. 'We are going to be shocked like everyone else at whatever happened downstairs.'

She walked proudly to the drawing room, puzzling about the false fire. The sound like a shot had not disturbed the nine people sitting among the neat rows of chairs, rapt as visionaries: a pencil of a man, with a silver-topped cane, and a woman like a spread of cake dough hemmed in with silk, and students, scrubbed and blond, and a middle-aged man who seemed to be willing himself to be worthy of the music, the tendons of his neck stiff with effort. All of them drowned in the music from the speakers, and looked out through the wide windows with blind eyes.

Across the windows ran four men. Emma saw a nondescript man who kept running, through the bushes, past the marble tomb of Richard and Cosima Wagner, out into the gardens beyond. She also saw Maurice, a thuggish youth and a flustered, flailing man who did not want to be with them. The man was protesting, but not stopping on open ground.

The trio came to the grove around the tomb, and the prisoner made his stand. Out of the house came more men, broad and quick men, one at least of them with a handgun. They were the oxen from the basement, the guards who were right to be restless. Emma watched them barrel into the trees.

The Wagnerites watched an opera in their minds. They saw no chase, and nobody on the run. Anything in the garden or the sky had been conjured there by the music, and it would be more terrible than thugs or guns.

Between the trees, Emma could make out the symptoms of a fight: men moving, and then fists flickering, a man falling.

'I have to see what happens,' she said.

'There will be cops.'

They made a very public progress across the lawn, but it did not matter; the Wagnerites were off dancing with the gods. They found a man measuring his length against the huge marble slab; he had a bloody eye, but he was breathing. Somewhere beyond the trees, a siren wailed and wailed.

Emma sprinted over the marble and out into the formal gardens beyond the grounds of Wahnfried. She could see Maurice and the thug running together, the other man between them, awkward over the rough ground. They reached a road, and she shouted after them; they did not pause. Adam had gone loping ahead, and he was a stranger, enough to alarm them.

She reached the roadway. Maurice was arguing with the flustered man, an Englishman trying in uncertain German to make a foreigner see sense, an important person trying to reason with a heckler. When the man grabbed at the air as though he could pull himself out of trouble, refusing to bend to step into the waiting car, Maurice pushed. The car was away before the police arrived.

Emma watched the cops come out, bandbox neat, and go headlong into the formal gardens, ready to block an escape that had already been made. Mostly to herself she said: 'What the hell did we just see?'

She was wondering still as Adam drove towards Munich on the autobahn. She was also angry. If there was a trap for Maurice, she had watched her brother rush into it, with enthusiasm.

But if there was no trap, then her brother had voluntarily kidnapped a man under guard, in broad daylight, in a small, secure and rather edgy German town where the border is a constant and unfriendly presence and where everyone knows everybody else's business. She had thought Maurice pompous, an ass, a cultist when it came to politics and ambitious for ends she would never understand. She had never before considered him a fool.

She watched Adam drive. He seemed unworried by the violence that broke around her like lightning breaks around a high tower. She wondered if she should be taking him for granted. She lived in a business where you never gave markers, least of all to strangers, and she very nearly owed this man her life. At least, she thought she did. And he was still there, persistent as skin.

'I really don't know anything about you,' she said.

'You don't particularly want to know, do you?'

'I didn't pick you out of the crowd,' Emma said. 'We won't grow old together. But we saw some things – '

'You're not interested.'

'You expect me to say I really can't believe what

you're saying, don't you? Well, after twenty-four hours, it doesn't surprise me at all.'

'At least I can make you angry.'

'Not angry,' Emma said. 'Petulant. I don't think that's much of an achievement.'

There were two hours before her flight to Rome. Adam suggested lunch; she could hardly refuse. She saw, for the first time, how airport corridors are like a hospital: the same gleam and uniforms and confusion, the tyranny of big, painted numbers and the same faint smell of disinfectant and tired people in extremis.

She saw Maurice along one of the shiny corridors. He was not quite being bundled along by large men in uniform, but they were certainly not listening to him, and his face was crimson with anger.

'I am a British Member of Parliament,' he was shouting. 'Ich bin ein Member of Parliament. Abgeordnete. Britisch!'

She caught up with the outer man in uniform. She asked, in her most authoritative manner, what was going on.

'I can't say.'

'But this man is a British Member of Parliament – '

'So he says.'

The cops wanted Maurice out of sight before the arrest made other passengers nervous; now they were sure he should be buried.

'They say I kidnapped someone,' Maurice shouted.

'I can vouch for him. I'm his sister.'

But the cops had gone through the walls at one of those seamless doors which hide the workings of airports. Emma tried to follow.

'I'm going to call the British consul,' she said.

The last of the men in uniform shrugged.

'You will give me a phone, please.'

'Your deputies don't have diplomatic immunity,' the man in uniform said. 'It's a police matter.'

'Do you want to keep your job?' she asked, dangerously.

The indifference was more than she could bear. It was painful, like some Third World woman begging to have her rights noticed at a British immigration desk; here, the British had become the troublemakers, the suspect ones. The Germans told Polish jokes, Irish jokes about the British.

The man in uniform pushed through the seamless door.

She ran to a public phone and called the consulate. She half hoped there might be no answer, in case Maurice was in the kind of trouble that could not become official. But there was an immediate answer, a quiet and practical voice. She explained there had been some misunderstanding. The junior minister Maurice Griffier MP had been arrested.

'God,' the voice said. He was a good consular man, put out by the threat of action. 'The consul will be furious.'

Emma stormed back to the police offices. She asked to talk to Maurice alone, and he had the wit to ask to talk to her; the cops were considering now that their prisoner might indeed be troublesome.

'They bug these rooms,' Maurice said. In the struggle, the plastic handcuffs had rubbed his wrists and his mind felt almost as raw within his skull.

'You can tell me what's going on. What do I say in London?'

'You shouldn't have followed me.'

'Thank God I did,' Emma said. 'I seem to be the one friend you have.'

'I don't think I need your assistance.'

'I have to know what happened. You need a lawyer – I've called the consul and he'll be here soon.'

'If you must know,' Maurice said, and his look was

stubborn, 'I helped a Czechoslovak scientist defect. He was here to talk to scientists at Bayreuth, we outwitted his guards. We carried him to freedom.'

'Except,' Emma said, 'he didn't want to go.'

He was truculent; he had his own doubts. 'Of course he wanted to. He had to put up a show of resistance. We knew he was going to do that.'

'I saw the argument by the car,' Emma said.

'It was a misunderstanding.'

'What's he going to say when the cops ask him?'

The blood no longer coursed in Maurice's cheeks; he was almost sallow.

'You mean he's gone? You don't know where he is?'

'He ran at the airport. He ran for the taxi rank, and we didn't have time to stop him,' Maurice said.

'He's a defector, fresh over the border, and he had enough deutschmarks to pay a taxi?'

'Obviously,' Maurice said, 'I wasn't there when he paid the taxi off.' But he had to make explanations. 'We couldn't chase him, you see; we were caught in the traffic lines.'

'You'd better get a story ready,' Emma said. She thought afterwards that she should have spoken her mind.

Helen could hear James Drake down the corridor, laughing until he was in pain, cackling until she was frightened for his heart. She came to stand in the doorway like a health warning.

'They really arrested him? At the airport?'

'He couldn't explain anything. Couldn't say what he thought he was doing and couldn't understand what had really happened.'

'And Pavel?'

'Easy. He'd gone to Bayreuth to talk to the university, as Griffier thought. But he'd gone with his sponsors from

Mammoth Oil; it's wonderful how oilmen in dark suits look exactly like the Czech KGB, if you want them to. Same build, same passion for security, same watchfulness. And when Pavel finally got away from Griffier, he took a taxi to the hotel we'd arranged and I met him there. He just wanted a bigger offer than Mammoth were prepared to make.'

'How long's he been over the border?'

'Six weeks. He knows he needs a lot of money for the lifestyle he wants. He wants to meet William F. Buckley at the Playboy mansion and talk about Plato.'

'He has the US visa?'

'Mammoth fixed that weeks ago. In fact, they've done all the work for us. They didn't think to take his passport because he told them he might get accidentally separated from the group and then he'd need identity papers.'

'And Griffier, Esquire?'

'Being questioned by the cops, told off by the consul. The story will not make him popular, I think. Member of Parliament assaults company executives, tries to set fire to Wagnerian shrine, kidnaps and menaces scientist, evades arrest. Maybe he even broke the speed limit.'

'You did very well.'

'You should have called me before. Mother talked of you.'

'How is your mother?'

'She's dead,' Adam Heller said.

James Drake said, vaguely and softly: 'You don't say.'

5

He was there again in Rome. When she came back from Cinecitta in the evening, it was very nearly pleasant to have company in a warm town, without strings and without studio politics. She did notice the sad concentration that comes with puppy love, but she also thought he must have nothing else to do. She acknowledged him; he hung around.

She worked as furiously as Rome allows. The studio's demands were the spine of her life, and she could not throw them aside because of Maurice's troubles. Maurice would no doubt get bail; Maurice would no doubt go back to London and face the headlines.

As for Adam Heller, she had dinner with him in Trastevere. He was funnier than the robotic voice suggested, but he was uncomfortably intense. She would be grateful to be without him in London or Los Angeles.

She couldn't imagine him touching her life, not ever.

Maurice Griffier never felt ill at ease in the House of Commons, not even on his first days, until now. He crossed the lobby floors and looked, for the first time, at the ornate and patriotic mosaic glistening above him. He looked to see how the specially soft policemen were regarding him. He went to take coffee in the tea room with the Chief Whip; he thought the invitation might be kind. But he was expecting some brutish gesture, and the brute might well be from his own party.

The Chief Whip was brisk. 'We'll have to discuss all this later,' he said. 'Mrs T. is not thrilled, you can imagine. Either we have a diplomatic incident or you have a criminal record or, just possibly, both.'

'The man was choosing freedom.'

'He seems to have done a lot of choosing,' the Chief Whip said. 'I think this kind of affair is like zoo-keeping. You have to bring the animal back to be believed. Otherwise,' he tapped at the cigarette case in his pocket, 'people wonder if you really saw the beast at all.'

'I would be grateful for some support.'

'I know what it takes to say that. I'm sure you would.'

'Some official approach to the Germans – '

'Mrs T. doesn't like to ask too many favours. And, of course, we need your letter of resignation. Once you've dealt with all this, no doubt you'll be welcome back.'

Maurice's features seemed to hang in wax from his bones. 'You said we would discuss this privately,' he said.

A tweedy, rumbustious Labourite passed, and grinned where Maurice at best expected a scowl. 'Bulldog Griffier,' he said. Two members of his own party, with decent fortunes and connections to titles, cut him dead.

'I expect the letter within twenty-four hours. An hour would be more convenient, frankly. Mrs T. will do the decent thing, of course. Nice letter in return. Brief vacation on the back benches, that kind of thing. Of course, if it gets to court – '

'Of course.'

'It will look better if your letter gets here before the German warrant.'

Maurice left the bill to the Chief Whip. He wandered slowly down the corridor between the ornate wood wardrobes. He opened his, and took out a coat that seemed to weigh him down. In the lobby there were clusters of schoolchildren and five of his own constituents, tied like parcels in the faded colours worn for smart in the Midlands, eager to see the Commons at work.

'I won't be speaking myself,' Maurice said, signing their passes.

They didn't pretend they cared.

James Drake took delivery of his new asset, who was cross. Pavel expected everything from the West: decadence he could despise, women with breasts like cantaloupes, uncensored works of Ronald Knox, Christian endeavour, ski-lodges with real fireplaces, evenings with French brandy and videos. He knew about the evils of capitalist life; he was eager to transcend them all.

He had a room with a view of very distant mountains. He did not have a CD player, or satin-type sheets as advertised in *Playboy*; James Drake was not interested in Kierkegaard and a more personal relationship with God. Pavel, yet again, was made to set the personal aside and concentrate on the professional; but there, at least, he found James Drake was worth talking to. He was another man who could read land like a scholar reads a book, for what is in the depths.

'Chaos,' James Drake said, thoughtfully. The word was bothering him; it was a word without a history in his mind, and he could not remember why it mattered.

Pavel said: 'Kolmogrov in Fifties. Russian work on chaos first.'

'I didn't know that.'

'Americans come to ask about chaos,' Pavel said, brightly. 'Chaos Russian discovery. Americans think this is new.'

Drake said: 'You use – chaos?'

Pavel shrugged. 'Useful,' he said. 'Ordinary mathematics only give average, trend, not particular. Chaos you can predict the difference from average and trend. You understand the order where everyone thinks there is no order.'

'I see.'

'Geology,' Pavel said. 'You map geology without chaos, you get straight lines. You look at rock, seashore, edge of sea, infinitely complicated line, not straight at all. Straight line is lie. You use fractal geometry, you study the line as really is. See geology as really is. Find oil.'

'Without instinct, without smelling it out?'

'Who can go round world everywhere smelling landscape? Mathematics better.'

'In America – '

'In America, have stock exchange,' Pavel said. 'Price up, price down. Price up and down same day, same hour. Nobody know why or how. Everybody look for underlying trend, average. But everybody know reality no trend at all. Reality jump and peak and splutter. Like wet fire. Study reality, use mathematics of chaos, see order where everybody see random movement. Someone will do this very soon, I am sure. See what happen next, like crystal ball.'

When Drake began to remember, it was like a dam breaking.

She spoke to Simeon Ryder first. He knew the bank and its workings; he managed the family like a firm. She leaned on his knowledge as on a summer tree, and it was good to have one sure thing.

'It's not a coincidence,' he said.

'I didn't think we had enemies like this,' Emma said.

'Banks have enemies, but usually they don't have the money left to fight back. That's the advantage of being the banker.'

'They knew enough about Rupert to set a trap, and enough about Maurice.' She held herself very straight to stop a shiver. 'I suppose they know enough about me.'

'You're visible. We know they can organize in Europe and America, anyway. They must have cash and knowledge. And I presume they have a real grievance, something personal. Money can be very personal.'

'It has to be something recent,' Emma said.

'Recent, or obsessional. I don't know the psychology of these things. I suppose it might be an old grievance that suddenly came to life again. I suppose it might be some irrational man – '

'If it's rational, it must be something in our history.'

'Edward Griffier knows about that. Ask your uncle.'

'Perhaps,' Emma said, 'somebody else could do the asking. I have a career in Hollywood. I don't have much time.'

'It depends,' Simeon said, heavily, 'how important you think the family is. I don't know how you feel. In fact, you go to so many places and you do so many things, I wonder if you know how you feel yourself.'

'You could do this. It's your job.'

'You wouldn't have to come back,' Simeon said. 'The answer doesn't have to be in England.'

'I have a studio to run,' she said.

But he was right of course; it was coming back that frightened her, being mired here. She had the habit of travelling; she was immune to airport lounges. She liked to imagine something new every day.

She called David Taylor's number. She expected the answering machine; he was in Papua, after all. But he answered.

'You got back quickly,' she said, tartly.

'Ten days,' he said. 'I couldn't find you to say I was going.'

'What was it this time?'

'Haus tambaran,' he said. 'I'll show you. They've fumigated most of it now.'

'Could I come to see you?' she said.

'You don't have to ask.'

'I wasn't sure if you were working.'

He knew she was feeling guilty. He said: 'I want to see you, bad.'

She felt so at home in his arms that she was flustered by the fact, but it was impossible to talk about her family affairs.

'Maurice was in the papers,' he volunteered.

'I was there.'

'People keep asking me what really happened, as if I'd know. What did happen?'

She told him, briefly.

'He's a fool,' David said.

'He's a fool and a victim,' she said.

'A victim of society? You're trotting that out for merchant bankers now, as well as black kids on estates?'

She dropped the subject. She never did get to tell him that her family was at risk, and so was she.

'It was tough in Papua,' he said. 'Five years negotiations, and then they nearly gave up because a truck went down a mudslide.'

'I'm glad to be back,' Emma said. She wanted him to say the same.

'But you've got to see the haus tambaran. It's extraordinary. Painted in ochres and browns – all drying, of course, it's got to be fixed. It'll take years to conserve it properly. They make them so they'll fade and die in the forest; they made this one specially for the museum.'

'You'll have to explain it all.'

'I'll take you down to the warehouse,' David said. 'Tomorrow morning. There won't be anyone about except the guards.'

They were awkward in bed at first. Usually, they had time to set aside business and obsessions, and anticipate being together. Being together was a surprise this time, and they had to slip around the surprise to find each other. The studio called at midnight, thinking the world ran to Pacific Standard Times.

In the early morning, she clung to him as though he was going away for ever, and it was her fault.

* * *

James Drake had specific questions now for Pavel. He spread out the maps around the apartment; Helen kept her distance. He kept asking about a stretch of West African territory.

'Good,' Pavel said. 'It'll be good.'

'And what did they say about it at Mammoth?'

'What you'd expect. They'll have to buy up their neighbour company to have the whole field.'

'And it's good?'

'They'll even say so in public soon. Up goes share price so easier to buy small neighbour with shares.'

'You have a fine grasp of the system,' Drake said, without sarcasm. 'You like Las Vegas? Go to Las Vegas, we'll get tickets. Tall women and tall drinks.'

'Very interesting,' said Pavel, doubtfully. He had dreamed of meeting the editors of the *National Review* first.

When the defector had gone, Drake shut all the doors and took up the phone. He knew exactly what to do; the scam was almost too simple. He now had information which would move the price of two quoted shares on the New York market: one, because of a major new oil find and the other, because it would be bought to make sure the whole of that find could be exploited. He knew there was going to be a brilliant success, and a bid, and the knowledge was worth more than money. It was worth attention.

He had been reading the papers carefully for signs of genius, the kind of brokers' genius most easily explained, when a man is almost always right. Whoever knew where the merger kings would strike next had to be more than a prophet; he was likely to be a friend of the players.

He had three names: one in Los Angeles, two in New York, all in the same firm. He had to cold call, but that hardly bothered him; the phones of such men were always open. Besides, he was a fellow undersider, not quite proper. Nothing is less official than being dead.

And when he had their attention, he would offer information and expect help. When they knew first about deals that were coming, they could not deal in their own names; but a man like Drake could deal, pay for the chance, and cut them in for part of the profits. He could give them a useful front. It could not, of course, be his own name; there were those on Wall Street who had announced, ironically, that James Drake would come back to the Street only over their dead bodies.

He fancied the name Jude Klein. Somewhere between Thomas Hardy and the Lower East Side. As Jude Klein, he could be a player again. He could suggest which London merchant bank might co-operate a little, and be reluctant to ask the right questions. He could push the interests of the Griffiers, push them deeper and deeper into the game until they were too far gone to surface.

Helen slipped into the room. She wanted to calm his pain with syringes; she did not understand his obsession had already done the job. He was not like a sick man at all.

'Get me Adam in Zurich,' he said.

She misdialled the first time, and he snatched the phone away from her. He dialled three times, and there was no answer.

Adam must be about his own business. Drake didn't like that, at all.

The limo left her in a narrow street that wandered like a line drawn without a ruler, from Shoreditch to the start of municipal housing, through factories and low warehouses. The limo left her at the wrong door.

It was a pale morning. She had taken a breakfast meeting, thinking only how much she wanted to be inside David Taylor's life and not just his bed. She had come down to this dead street where the storehouses of the Museum stood, the encyclopedic overflow of a collection to which every missionary, soldier, teacher, traveller and passing merchant seaman had felt entitled to contribute. It was the memory of an empire, full of freaks and wonders, piled on shelves which rose to the ceiling.

She came to the desk. A middle-aged guard took her name. After a while, David was found. She felt a fine thread of nerves working in her belly.

He walked down from the Oceania floor, past the floor for Africa and the one for the Americas. He walked softly; he wanted to see her first, not just step out of the elevator into an awkward hug under the guard's prissy eyes. He paused at the turn of the stairs by the shaft of the elevator. She was reading off the nonsense notices on a board, the variegated orders of a bored administration. She seemed a little tired. She seemed wonderfully exotic in this hall of civil service grey and green, like flowers.

He ran the last few stairs and stopped short. 'I suppose Miss Griffier has signed in?' he said to the guard. 'Come on,' he said to Emma.

They took the elevator up to Oceania. He unlocked the door in a partition, and they were in the stores. He had become so used to the curiosities that he no longer pointed out the Maori skulls, tattooed blue-black, or the skeleton of a mermaid, part trout and part monkey, which had been most embarrassingly presented by royalty.

'I missed you this morning,' he said. He watched where her long legs parted under her short fur coat.

'I can't just say you've got something to show me,' she said. 'Not with a straight face.'

He grinned and he held out his hand. She slipped out

of her coat, silk against silk; she was smooth as a cat and as mischievous.

'We got the last of them out of the cyanide yesterday,' he said. 'They're wonderful things – our very own. Hell's own job to get them down to the coast. I told you we almost lost one lorry.'

Her skirt caught against a box that had been put back carelessly. David tugged her down the narrow spaces between high shelves. He stopped only once, for a box that his quick eye told him must be out of place. He pulled aside the tissue paper and there was gilt and red lacquer, colour rich as silks.

'A drum,' David said, 'even if it looks like some king's canoe. You remember the drums?'

She had seen them before. She was always surprised by him in this place: the strong, just past athletic body was inspired by the soul of an antiquary. He seemed at home in the dust and the dim lights. At the end of each stack, he pulled the cord to turn out the light behind them, and the stores filled up with shadows.

'You don't get nervous here, do you?' he asked.

'We must be almost alone.'

He looked at his watch. 'Alone,' he said, 'except for the guards downstairs.'

'It's very quiet.'

'Nothing moving. They've all gone home, all those old men with their biros and their bent shoulders and their querulous voices. And no spirits. We fumigate for spirits, girl – bugs and snakes and spirits, all the same.' She bumped softly into him. He stroked her breast. He pinched the nipple, quite sharply.

'Come on,' he said. 'No dawdling.'

There was an open space by windows at the end of the maze. Outside, the clouds had thickened and the light was the black-green of storm. Against that darkness, she could see the silhouettes: tall and gaunt, poles of carved wood, rank after rank of them in a grand parade. Her hand slipped from David's hand. She felt the presence of a council of the dead.

The lights flickered on.

'Haus tambaran,' David said, bustling keenly. 'Spirit house. They build these houses for each funeral, company for the dead man, and then they leave them in the bush. Paint, you see.' He stroked the stem of one ancestor, blue and ochre and brown; the colour stained his palm. 'They're meant to be ruined. It's quick, with the humidity and the heat and the termites. This one they built for us, and these are the ancestors, visiting London.'

He always trusted her reactions; she was always interesting. But she was silent.

'Fifty of them,' he said. There were tarpaulins over the back rows; he tugged the cloths down and she stared into more of the big-eyed faces, with their line of sight on some inaccessible time. The faces were history, she thought.

'They're very fine,' he said. 'Aren't they?'

The faces were impersonal, but not unlike the stairs at the old Griffier bank, with the standard portraits of partners, each a cliché of top hat and probity.

'Their past,' she said. 'Do they try to keep it away from them – at a distance?'

'They revere their ancestors.'

'But do they want them to stay away?'

He held both her hands. 'I didn't think they would disturb you,' he said.

Sometimes, she found it hard to remember their treaty which said she must not explain her Griffier past to him, or tell him when it impinged on her. Perhaps there was no treaty at all, only her own reluctance to face how much it mattered.

'Some things happened,' she said. She must not eat

into the brief time they could have together. 'Just things.'

The rain had started.

'You're tired,' he said, shocked at how fast the life could seep out of her. He put back the tarpaulins and cut the lights; the back ranks of ancestors went into shadow, and then the front ranks.

Emma made herself stay with them for a moment. She could like the idea of a house where the ancestors congregated, to be tamed and put away.

David was already out of sight on his zigzag path to the door. She could hear the very faint stirring of draughts and objects settling into place, the illusion that brings even an empty library to a little life. She said, very distinctly: 'I love you.'

She heard a door slam shut.

She waited for David to answer. She felt uncomfortable between the drab boxes with their freight of memory. At eye level, a shelf held gaunt, spiky birds of wood.

'Where are you, David?'

There was a glassed case of head-dresses, long falls of feather and bone, and she was looking at her reflection against their reds and burned browns. When she moved, she caught her foot against a box on a lower shelf. She was almost grateful for the sound as the box tumbled out beans of styrofoam and coloured, shiny figures. The next step, she skidded on tin and styrofoam. She caught at her balance like a ball that someone else has thrown. She told herself it was daylight, and there was nothing to fear.

David never made jokes like this. He would never walk out.

Her hand brushed against some dried, embossed and natural thing. She shivered. She thought she heard a cough. It was absurd to summon demons out of these boxes, she told herself. The shadows were animate with awkward, unknown things.

She walked to the windows. She heard her heels tick briskly on the metal floor. At the door, the mermaid sat in a pool of spilled light that was not intended to show it off.

Outside, by the elevator shaft, she thought she heard movement. She could sense on her skin that someone was coming closer, and she was no longer sure it was David or the guard.

David would never go away like that.

She pushed open the door that led out of Oceania to the stairs and the lift. She could take the stairs, but the stairs had dark places. The elevator would take her directly to the ground floor, and there could only be one risk of shock: the moment when the cage arrived. She pushed the button and waited.

It came down out of the roof, sighing on its cables, with the light inside. She pulled open the awkward metal gates and jammed them back into place. The elevator began to go down. She saw herself in a movie: a woman in silk and fur, her face in deep shadow, in a cage.

The elevator shuddered and stopped. There were still two and a half floors to go.

She tried the controls. She looked for 'door open' and 'door close', but it was an ancient elevator, mostly meant for freight. The doors would only open at a floor.

Suddenly, the elevator lurched down to one side, and then only one of its four corners was suspended, and then it was falling. She knew to jump just before the elevator landed, a drill she'd feared she might one day use in a building of forty storeys, not four. The cage stopped abruptly.

She forced the doors open. She had cut her hand very slightly, a little line of blood.

The front hall of the storehouse was empty. A little

wind tugged at the papers on the noticeboard, even the ones stained with time and damp. There was nobody at the desk by the visitors' book. The door was open to the street, rocking back and forth.

She shouted, one last time: 'David!'

She was mystified. She was ready to be furious if he had played a trick, but it was quite unlike him.

Some odd sense of propriety made her sign out in the visitors' book. She imagined she should report the failure of the elevator, but nobody was there, and her limousine was waiting at the door. It was usual and comforting, after the shadows inside; she stepped in gratefully. She could leave the store to its guards and ghosts, and go back to her world where anything could be organized.

She picked up the car phone. She was peevish that David had simply disappeared, and she did not understand. It must mean something. She left a message on his answering machine: 'Where the hell are you?'

She was still angry at Heathrow. She was grateful that the police waited with discretion.

'Miss Griffier?'

She said 'yes' to the pleasant-looking man in a blazer.

'I'm a policeman. I wonder if we could have a word in private.'

She put boarding pass and baggage slip into her passport.

'What is this?' She was curious, and not alarmed.

'I'd rather discuss it in private.'

In the office, he said: 'I think you knew Dr David Taylor?'

She stared at him.

'Mr Taylor was found this morning in the Museum warehouses at Halisham Road. He was badly injured. He lost a lot of blood.'

'Where is he now?'

'Dr Taylor is dead.'

She held the edges of the desk for a moment. She did not know quite what to ask, but she said: 'Where did you find him?'

'At the foot of the lift shaft. It seems the cage fell and crushed him to death.'

She remembered the sickening lurch of the cage, hanging in the shaft and then crashing down; and how the cage would not settle straight. She had brought the cage down on him.

'I suppose I killed him,' she said.

She was very still. The policeman thought she was brittle with horror, ready to snap.

'I don't know if you're ready to talk,' the policeman said. 'I don't know how close you were to Dr Taylor – '

'Very close.'

'I see,' he said. He couldn't quite approve, black man, white woman, and he couldn't quite show the fact: she was so coldly sad. 'I'm afraid I have to ask some questions.'

'Of course.'

'It was a very old lift,' he said.

'It must have been sabotaged.'

'Those old lifts sometimes slip,' the policeman said. 'What we don't understand is how Taylor came to be under the cage.'

'I don't know. He just walked off the Oceania floor and I didn't see him again. The lift fell, I was all right, my car was waiting. I waited for him to call.'

'He didn't have any reason to kill himself?'

She stared at the cop. 'Who would kill himself by waiting under a lift cage for the cables to go wrong?'

'He didn't – er, black out?' The words were too close to what he was thinking.

'I don't think so. He was in good condition.'

'You were there, Miss Griffier. You tell us how he died.'

'I can't go to Los Angeles,' she said. 'Why did you let me check in?'

It was evening before she could reach Simeon Ryder.

'They killed David,' she said.

'I don't understand.'

She told him the story. He had nothing to say. He had been anxious because his world was unsettled; if it was going to become a melodrama, he was terrified.

'Something is terribly wrong,' she said. 'They came after me, and they got David.'

'Unless,' Simeon said, 'they killed David precisely to get at you. There seems to be real malice in all this.'

'I don't want to believe you,' she said.

'They got Rupert through avarice, Maurice through pride –'

'And me through lust? Is that what you're thinking? You're lucky. You can walk away from this at any time.'

'I can hardly walk away from you, or the bank,' he said. He wanted to say he, too, was part of the family, but it was too strong a claim.

'You wouldn't be a target.'

'It makes the problem of Mr John Brown seem quite minor,' Simeon said. 'He may be unpredictable, but he's not quite mad. He had the nerve to call me and say he personally kept the story of Maurice's arrest off the front page of his wretched paper. He sent me various editions, to prove the point.'

'There must be other people who have grievances.'

'They have to know how to hire hit and run drivers in Denver and killers in London. Not our sort of client.'

'You could check the books.'

'Banks have enemies, that's all. Those are the terms

of business. I don't think I can help you; I'm no detective.'

She called her mother.

Lady Griffier said: 'You'll come here, of course.'

'I don't know what to do. I can't stay away from the studio. It's like a garden; you turn your back and weeds grow and pests devour what you've nursed to life and the loveliest beds get choked.'

'You can't avenge David,' Florence said, sagely.

'I could make sense of things, somehow. I could see what his death meant.'

'Death doesn't have to mean anything.'

'I'm so afraid it was an accident,' she said. If it was an accident, then she killed David. If she had taken the stairs, he might still be alive. Without her weight, the cage might not have done such damage. If the lift had never moved, it might never have fallen. If she hadn't been there, he would not have been at risk.

There was no sense in what she was thinking, but she kept seeing the dim-lit cage of the elevator going down like a great hammer on his curled body.

'I don't think I want vengeance,' she said, unsurely. 'I just want it all to make sense. I just want to see why he died, what it means.'

'Poor Emma,' her mother said.

6

The furniture turned against her in the house in Westwood. When she was alone the edges of tables cut her, the phone cord tangled in her hands. The coffee machine, which had never been good or mysterious, now spat hot water and dissolved filters. She did not cry or shout at all this. She even denied herself time to feel grief.

Her colleagues said she was cold at meetings, but they never said she was preoccupied. She held herself straight. She wondered if she could ever again feel enthusiasm. She had a terrible lack in her life, and fear for her future.

Her secretary came in, pussy-footing like a kind nurse, with sushi from the place on Santa Monica. Emma looked at the tray: split shrimp, the roe of sea urchin, a piece of octopus, a lovely rose purple. She ate slowly; she tried to let herself be delighted by the tastes. It was a start.

She had buried David in a Birmingham suburb, in a green churchyard. His parents seemed bruised with sorrow. His mother was torn between polite deference and the pain of arthritis, and she could hardly bear to be touched. His father was warm and rueful, and not sure if he should be happy to see Emma. They threw damp, rich earth on to the coffin and walked separately away.

She lost her bearings for a day. She was too shocked to know she was in shock. She drove quickly through the Severn Valley. The fields were lush with green and the day-glow yellow of rapeseed. The trees were canopies of peace. In the villages, the houses nestled low around churches far too great for so few people. She went home by way of postcard country, abbeys and old bridges, and she felt as remote as some foreign postmaster handling the pictures of prettiness and Oxford towers.

As long as she was conscious, it was tolerable. When she tried to sleep, she was besieged. She had some duty to David, and a duty to her family; but the duty was to confront an enemy still shapeless and nameless. If she was to know more, she had to end a lifetime of deliberate indifference; she had to know the history of the Griffiers.

She grew eager for clues and omens. She could find lessons in a change of traffic lights, or the late arrival of the morning mail. She read everything for its hidden meaning, like a cop, like a historian, like a paranoiac.

She told her mother: 'If I get back to work, I can get all this out of my mind.'

'I buried two husbands. You never get it out of your mind.'

'I have to be here.'

'You stay there. You'll never quite believe that he has gone.'

'That's what I want.'

She had ridden the cage down on to his unguarded body. She was not likely to forget.

It took another death to make her think clearly. Her sweet secretary brought in the mother of a studio runner, who had died very quickly, from AIDS. Emma remembered the boy: he was bright and scared. She liked him, and she wanted to reassure his mother that he had worth, which was not easy for her to believe; her fellow Chicanos thought they knew everything when they knew the cause of death.

Emma said the boy had such promise, which was true and she said she was sorry. But the mother sat, sweet and silent, as though she had not been given permission to move. She was blank with her grieving, uncomfortable inside the grand fortress of the studio; it was not her place to speak. She had lost, and the loss could not be repaired; she must suffer because it was ordained. She smiled too much.

In comforting the woman, Emma grew purposefully angry.

She had the name: Griffier. She had the will, the credit and the influence. She thought she might be capable of killing, a thought she had never had before. She did not have to hold her tongue.

She, at least, was qualified for revenge.

Sir Alistair's mind was clean of dreams. He had prayed and tranquillized himself; he had no more need for thought.

That very day, he had lunched with perhaps the Griffiers' most important single client, the Emir of Timor; who was a leather-skinned humming bird, a tiny, brilliant man, whom Alistair had once patronized and now admired. The Emir's fortune rested on oil, in enormous quantities, and in a tiny population; since the British Government guarded his luscious palaces and his grand cars and there was no Timorian tradition of sharing with the people or masquerading as their father, the Emir was rich beyond responsibility. Sir Alistair was his guide, his conscience, his financial father; to Sir Alistair, it seemed a most natural relationship.

The Emir had been on his way to Rowlandsons, to play. He had a hard, spoiled look, a special kind of concentration for the casino tables; they were the only risk in his life, and he loved them. He had evidently not bothered with the silly story of Maurice in Bayreuth. Rupert in Denver was something nobody talked about because almost nobody knew. The sudden death of Emma's lover had been dealt with in a wonderfully circumspect fashion, not least because various newspaper Editors in Chief were among the Museum's trustees.

Sir Alistair had not asked directly, which might sow doubts, but he knew the Emir had perfect confidence in Griffier Ltd. Sir Alistair could sleep easily with this lack of news. He was like a Maharajah's secretary, there to indulge the man and make sure he had what he wanted: a grand hotel, an electronics company, a village in Switzerland. He was also the guardian of the Emir's interests, the one who made him reasonable.

His certainties paraded like tin soldiers, until the phone rang. He woke so suddenly his head ached, and the tranquillizers left him unsure of his tongue.

'Please hold for John Brown.' The voice was steely.

Sir Alistair pulled his consciousness around him like a coat, hoping it would keep out the cold.

'Griffier?' Brown sounded ominous.

'Mr Brown. It is three o'clock in the – '

'I have a proposition.'

'I don't think I can possibly do justice – '

'I am one of your most substantial shareholders. Your other shareholders will be happy to sell to me. I want you to agree to a bid.'

The wind was out of Sir Alistair; he could not make a sound.

'Terms in the next few days. I want an agreement in principle.'

Think. 'There can be no agreement in principle,' Sir Alistair said. 'We would need to know terms.'

'Would you fight me?'

'Griffier Ltd is an independent bank, not part of a group. Naturally, we value our historic independence.'

'Value. What value? What price do you put on it?'

'I mean,' Sir Alistair said, 'if you want to make a proposal, we would naturally consider it – '

'Consider it. You'll do better than that. You'll consider it,' and Brown only pretended to search for the word 'favourably.'

'It is three in the morning – '

'Great financial institutions never sleep, Sir Alistair. We shall talk at a more seasonable hour.'

The line was dead.

Sir Alistair had heard it said that John Brown had to be occupied on Sunday afternoons, in the long lulls between lunch and tea and dinner, because otherwise he would try to buy a company. It was, of course, unthinkable that John Brown could buy Griffier Ltd. Unthinkable.

Sir Alistair did what gentlemen naturally do: having been disturbed, he disturbed the servants in turn.

'A nightmare,' Simeon Ryder suggested. 'Perhaps he was having a nightmare.'

'I depend on you,' Sir Alistair said.

'You can deal on my account,' James Drake said. 'It is a little difficult for the dead to deal.'

'The dead vote in New York,' his companion said. 'I can't see why they shouldn't buy and sell shares.'

His companion was a globular man, with a huge head, like some turnip creature made for Halloween; but in among all the flesh there were little, dark eyes that could burn glass. He was the first broker Drake had called, and he came willingly to talk; Drake's crash was one of those rare Wall Street memories which lasts more than a month, a name not to be spoken out loud for fear of raising ghosts.

'It's like a nominee account,' Drake said, reasonably. 'Except we give the nominee account a name. And in time, perhaps the name will have a reputation.'

'People like reading about arbitrageurs,' the broker said, 'I'm glad to say. Lots of money going into arbitrage funds. They really think there is some magic foresight which lets a man see when a share price is going to move, and act accordingly. Fundamental research, market technicalities, all that sort of thing. Chartists and elves. Anything at all but the simple truth that to get it right, you have to be told.'

'This new arbitrageur,' Drake said. 'He could become quite famous. And if anything went wrong, which God forbid, he doesn't exist. The man to blame is dead. The brokers just acted on instructions.'

'Ingenious,' the broker said. 'No doubt the ghost will find backers? Fine merchant banks and their clients? Excitable foreigners who want their share of the fashionable "arb"?'

'Oh yes,' Drake said. 'Remember the oddity of the days we live in. People have come to think that arbitrage is a sure thing – that if a man knows how to buy in one market and sell in another, he'll always get it right. Of course, it helps that underlying share prices are all going up all the time. It would be quite hard to be totally wrong.'

'They even think what you're proposing is arbitrage,' the broker said.

'It is. I buy information cheap and sell it dear. I buy where it's secret and private, which is one market, and I trade it where there are lights and buyers. That's a kind of arbitrage.'

The broker laughed. He had screwed himself tightly into a small hotel armchair, and now he extricated himself carefully; he did it, somehow, with no loss of dignity.

'We do understand each other very well,' he said, pumping Drake's hand. 'When you went under, years ago, I was still a cub trader. I never did think it was your fault.'

'External factors,' James Drake said, 'that was it.'

'External factors,' the broker said, respectfully.

Helen hovered at the door. James Drake had told her to put away the clippings; the Griffiers were in trouble enough with John Brown and he had other fish to fry. She could come to New York if she wore the nurse's uniform, starched and white, and kept her manners to match. She had walked into the Pierre like a doll, expecting to be caught out.

'It's time for your nap,' she said.

The broker looked at the thin, bright girl in white and at James Drake, who seemed hearty and healthy. He thought he saw the point; old devil, he thought. He winked, hugely.

The helicopter was a theatre to John Brown. He loved the way other people looked nervously out, with only thin steel between them and vertigo. He loved having to bellow; it was hard for counter-arguments to carry through the noise of the rotors. A mid-air decision reminded him how valuable, how useful was every moment of his life.

'The people,' he said, 'must speak. We must speak for the people.' It was hard to quarrel before he made clear what he meant; but it might be necessary. By the time Brown became specific, he had usually won.

His aide-de-camp was a severely intellectual man of middle years, eternally promising and very briefly a politician. His attitudes were mandarin; he could never quite believe that John Brown mattered. But he had worked outside the mandarin class, and the effect was rather sad: the perfect senior civil servant, perpetually otherwise engaged.

'Do we,' the aide-de-camp bellowed, 'prioritize this?'

Brown scowled. He loved the word 'prioritize'; but he hated to share plans. He liked to unsettle people, surprise them with the next great move. He shook his huge head, all oiled and dark, he said: 'Prioritize.'

'Everything,' the aide-de-camp shouted, 'about the Griffiers.'

'A book,' Brown said. 'No point in owning a paper if you can't get information. Everything there is.'

In his mind, this was simply strategy. Behind that, he had felt insulted by Sir Alistair, and the insult gave him energy; but he remembered nothing particular. He only knew he had to win.

He sat down abruptly when the pilot announced their imminent arrival on the London plantation, among the wage slaves.

The trouble was time. She had none of her own, and usually she was grateful for that: the studio filled the days. But to visit Edward on Barbados, she needed an excuse.

Remake *High Wind in Jamaica*. No, that would be blasphemous. Remake *Island in the Sun*. Pointless. A pirate movie; no trend. The island drug movie was no longer high adventure, not with the Jamaican Yardies ensconced in neighbourhoods, and for the same reason people didn't feel as kindly about soca as they once had about reggae; in any case it had been six months since anyone proposed a script. The assembled executives would, with great regret, acknowledge the public had some problem with too many black faces in a single movie. They blamed demographics.

Garrity himself, the great boss, saved her. For months he had been nursing his 'wrinklies' picture', in which he proposed a roll call of old stars. Their comebacks were meant to make palatable a vaguely political story.

'At twenty-two million,' Emma grumbled, 'it's worth more to *People* magazine than it is to us. It's a great cover story, that's all.'

'The budget is exactly right,' Garrity said. He could almost be passionate when the project was his.

'Besides,' said Emma, stuck on a cool, inexorable roll, 'which stars do you want? The ones that work do two TV movies a year and a soap opera on the side; people get bored with them. The ones that don't work are gaga or uninterested or much too rich or out of their minds on Geritol and gin. Where are all these great stars who want to make comebacks?'

'You tell me,' Garrity said. 'By tonight. I want a memo from each of you.'

In payment for her doubts, he made her spin a story out of air, and the others listened hard because they were meant to disapprove of it. It became a game: the more they liked what they heard, the more they knew they had to reject it for the sake of Garrity's heart. But she wanted to be hard to reject.

Garrity dealt with the story without words. He produced a curious, Arctic mooing sound, like a walrus disturbed.

'On serious matters,' he said, dismissively. 'Emma, you could at least do some errands on wrinklies – if you're not too occupied with personal matters, that is? No? Good. Then there's Nova Aston. You get me Nova Aston.'

Miss Aston had no agent, he said. She could not be approached by telephone; it would take a few days of the time of a senior studio executive. And Miss Aston long ago retreated to sugary beaches and emerald seas, to a long, wide house under palm trees, and a little light tropical gardening: in Barbados.

'God,' Emma said. 'Do I have to?'

No reason why Garrity should know she had what she wanted.

Nova Aston hardly knew when she was wooed; that was how the world treated her, always. She lived on a delicate estate, in a gingerbread house, where nobody crossed her.

'I've met your uncle Edward from time to time,' she said. 'Of course you must come down.'

Emma found, very quickly, that everything was the present to Miss Aston. She understood only two hierarchies: the Hollywood 'A' list of the 1930s and 1940s, and the pages of *Burke's Peerage* into which she had briefly married. One servant still used her title, but it was the only trace the marriage had left. As for Hollywood, Miss Aston remembered gossip like movie plots like memories, muddling the three. She would calmly say it was Barbara Stanwyck who slept her way to the top of a bank, floor by floor, when really it was Barbara Stanwyck's character in *Baby Face*.

Emma had a fearful sense of this white, white woman's mind wandering aimlessly on her perfect beach, scavenging bits of memory like shells and making them into a picture. Miss Aston chose to live in the picture.

'Your mother is from Baltimore,' Miss Aston said. 'Just like the dear Duchess.' The fingers held their Perrier like a wax mould, a shop-window hand. Miss Aston lived on a beach where the sea was too dangerous to swim because of the undertow and the sun was too violent to be borne. She was a creature of the shade.

'My mother admires your work so much,' Emma said. She knew any past tense would sound in Miss Aston's ears like gunshot.

Edward was not happy to be invited to dinner. He had chosen the east coast of the island deliberately, away from the stars and the exile life of the West. He was immune to flirtation, and very bad at it, and he was far too rational still to deal with the pretensions of the ageing stars.

But he smiled when Miss Aston was late, in her precise way; her entrance was modest, assuming attention and not demanding it. The other guests dealt carefully with the Griffiers; outsiders would soon go, and they were barely acknowledged in the rockpool. It was easy for Emma to make an excuse after dinner and walk on the beach with Edward.

The moon was high and the water rustled against the sand.

'I've done my favour for today,' Edward said. 'Coming here is quite enough. So if you want anything else – '

'Miss Aston is rather splendid, don't you think?'

'Mad,' Edward said. 'If she was in some tiny row house in Baltimore instead of a grand plantation in Barbados, she'd be certified. She has no sense of time or place.' He was especially offended; his own intelligence officer's mind was full of cabinets and categories.

'She's always been loved in public and much too rich to cross in private. What do you expect?'

'I want to know,' Edward said, 'what you want.'

Emma scuffed at the sand with her immaculate city shoes.

'If this is about John Brown,' Edward said, 'there's nothing I can do. He will do what he wants, as usual.'

'It's not about John Brown.'

They walked on for a while in silence.

'I came down for the studio,' Emma said. 'They want to put Miss Aston in a new film.'

'Extraordinary,' Edward said. Emma could taste a little tang of jealousy in his voice.

'I need your help,' she said. 'Not with Miss Aston, and not with John Brown. With the family, and our history.'

'For a film?'

'Of course not.'

'I could show you the night-flowering cereus. There is always a night-flowering cereus at dinner parties; it gives middle-aged couples from England an excuse to slip into the groves.'

'I'm serious.'

'When you went away,' Edward said, 'and made your

own life in Los Angeles, nobody was more keen than I. I cheered. You don't have to turn back now. I never turned back.'

'It isn't that easy any more,' Emma said. 'Someone is trying to destroy us. I don't mean upset the bank or make Father cross or bring down the share price. Some of it may have to do with money, but it's personal, too.' She gulped a breath of the salt night. 'They killed my lover in order to get at me,' she said. 'For example.'

Edward stopped, and he leaned back, arching his long back; he seemed preoccupied with the order of the armies of the stars.

'They killed David,' she said. 'I will not let them get away.'

'The police are not giving satisfaction, I take it?'

'How can they? They don't see the connections. They might find the people who pushed him, but they could never see why they should be looking for who paid to have him pushed.'

'You loved him, did you?'

'Of course I did.'

'I always thought love was comfort,' Edward said. 'Without comfort and rest, what's love worth?'

'I think the same people tried to set Rupert up. They succeeded with Maurice. They've hurt me terribly. The next target could be you, or my mother, or my father – or the bank.'

'And who do you think would do such things?'

'I have no idea,' Emma said, 'because I have no idea who has grievances against us. A child isn't told that sort of thing.'

'There are so many stories.'

'They will take whatever is dearest to you,' Emma said. 'If they came after me, they must be after the whole family, not just the bankers. Rupert and I don't do anything with the bank, except cash the dividend cheques.' She was impatient for him to react. 'You're not safe,' she said.

'I never was,' Edward said. 'If ever you get time off from Miss Aston, you could come and see me. I know some things.' He bent down easily and skimmed a stone over the moonstruck sea. 'It's not for Alistair, though.'

'I thought you loved my father.'

'Brotherly love,' Edward said, 'has its limits.'

She knew better than to ask. She had a thousand stories already, jumbled in her head; only one story was killing them. And most likely, only one person; the campaign was very knowing.

She had lost count of the people with a grudge. Even Edward had a grudge, it seemed. She excused herself that evening and was lulled to sleep by the sea; and dreamed of interlocking cages, each with anger in it, sometimes furry, sometimes feathered, once a white harpy eagle with wide wings.

John Brown had wanted something to use, not just a history lesson. He listened impatiently to the reporter. He was simply filling the vacuum of the hour.

'What people forget,' the reporter was saying, 'is that if you said Griffier in the 1890s, people threw things. Vitriol, as often as not.'

Brown raised his great head like a judgemental bull. He liked his employees to be very careful on the subject of capitalism and the established order.

'They were one of the great Victorian banks, of course. They were like the Barings or the Hambros or Natty Rothschild with his own pillar in the Exchange. They were Dutch, originally. There was an artist called Griffier in the seventeenth century, painted flowers in London and Amsterdam. Rhine Valley, nude maidens extra, sold a lot to the Duke of Beaufort; made the world look manicured. He might have something to do with them.'

John Brown did not allow gaps in history, unless he had put them there. 'I pay you to know things,' he said.

The reporter knew the interruption had exactly the value of his contract. 'They made grand Victorians,' he said. 'Built Easterford in Essex, grand house, meant to rival the Rothschilds'. Big involvement in South America, although it was never as great as the Barings, and they never did get into North America properly. They were decorous, they were conservative, so naturally they were the first to fall.

'It was called the Griffier crash. It very nearly broke the City of London in a week.'

'Ah,' said John Brown.

'This isn't exactly hot intelligence,' the reporter said. 'There are PhD theses.'

'Then make it into a very good story,' Brown said. 'A very good story indeed.' He was both benevolent and menacing, a father out of nightmares.

'The trouble was South America. The Griffiers built the tramway systems of a half-dozen cities. They funded ranches. They were the best hope of the gauchos and the cariocas. They dreamed of gold and steel and a new United States of their very own, at the other end of America. Then, one week, they didn't have the gold or cash to back all the bills they'd casually issued, or all the ones other people had cashed just because the Griffiers guaranteed them – "accepted" them, as they say.'

'I know what an accepting house is,' John Brown said. 'I own large parts of an accepting house.'

The reporter went back to his notes. 'Natty Rothschild refused to bail them out. The other big merchant banks couldn't. The Bank of England didn't have the gold. But if the Griffiers went down, who was going to trust any bit of commercial paper issued in the City of London? It didn't help the Griffiers had been so damned self-righteous all this time: proper little Dutchmen, always moderate, quite insufferable. So the unrespectable banks took over, the ones that actually had branches in the High Streets, and millions from the savings of doctors and hatters and butchers. They were the ones who saved the City and from that day on, they were the ones with the power.'

'Of course,' the aide-de-camp put in, snatching a rare chance. 'It's the high-street operations that keep the big banks solvent now. On their fancy trading and their foreign loans they'd be in terrible trouble.'

'Banking 101,' sniffed Brown.

'If you're planning to make a film,' the reporter said, 'you ought to know about the gold. There was a weekend when the Bank of England ran out of gold and it had to be brought from Paris and from St Petersburg. There were great sealed trains of bullion crossing Europe, five million pounds' worth, rushing to save the Bank of England.'

'Anything else? Anything that was not in the PhD theses?'

'Only one story. The senior Griffier at the time of the crash seems to have been leading a double life. He had his family at Easterford, of course, just like the books say, but he had another family. Another woman, children by her, another house. And when the bank was on the point of crashing, it all stopped. It looks as though he dropped her because he couldn't risk scandal, and he never went back.'

'What happened to the children?'

'We're looking,' the reporter said. 'We have some clues.'

'Then find me answers,' Brown said. 'I am not to be put off like one of your – ' he searched for a truly dismissive word ' – readers.'

When the reporter had gone, he said to the aide-de-camp: 'Check if he comes up with anything else. When he's finished, fire him.'

He smiled, and asked for tea.

The roads to Edward's house at Avalon looked like a ball of tarmac strings, twisted through the tall sugarcane, with sudden cross-roads and sharp turns. In Miss Aston's car, Emma lost herself in memories.

As a child, she had come to see Uncle Edward, and bicycled through these lanes; then, they seemed almost English in their order, with churches that were rough-cut versions of the ones she knew in Essex, with brushed and quiet children out of Metroland and a lovely sense of decorum. In winter, sugarcane seemed as ordinary as brambles in the fields. She could let herself imagine things, because it felt safe.

She counted on Edward, when she was very small, to be the story-teller who could conjure talking fish and flying cats and hiccuping dragons who burned their friends without meaning to; but Uncle Edward also calmed her, and made her sure the dragon only lived in stories. Nothing changed, she thought.

He was waiting for her at the door. 'We've got a very great deal to get through,' he said briskly. 'Better come into the library.'

In that cool, high room, there were books and papers scattered around the tiled floor, and huddles of print on high shelves. There was a bad, sentimental oil of Easterford – fat cows, oak trees grown impossibly broad as though they were holding up the picturesque clouds like banners. There were two good pictures, painterly and bought in New York in the past year, and a Carrington which ought to have been in some Bloomsbury biography. The rest, the ledgers, the closets full of files, was memory.

'Of course, the vital bank records are in London,' Edward said. 'What I brought here was the story of the bank, if you understand me. The things that mattered, and the proof of them.'

'I understand,' Emma said. The story could so easily get lost in the facts; that was their situation now. They had all the hurt of their enemy's campaign, a sense of what he had done, but not the slightest fix on who he was.

'Start at the beginning,' Edward said. 'I suppose it's possible that there is some ancient feud that goes back to selling wine and giving credit in Amsterdam. Maybe someone has hated us for centuries. But then why should they strike in this year, now? They have chosen a good time, of course, when the bank is confused about its own future and the Big Bang is ominously close and John Brown is fooling with the shares. But that suggests business timing. If you want to kill the man who ruined your great-great-grandfather, do you really wait until his share price is lower than usual?'

'All this is personal,' Emma said.

'I agree. It's as though they started at the edges of the family, forgive me saying so, and worked inwards. Rupert is such a damn fool, he's easy, although it's unusual for him to go along with someone else's schemes.'

'They offered him a whole new collection of widows and orphans to defraud.'

'Irresistible,' Edward said, 'to a man like Rupert. Of course, if Rupert was set up as part of this campaign, then we're looking for someone with American contacts, Denver contacts, perhaps even rather criminal contacts.'

'Does that suggest anyone?'

'Oh, yes,' Edward said. 'You're really too young to remember what the collapse of Mutual of Mutual meant – the greatest fund on earth, money collected by special plane from powerful generals in Argentina, money taken penny by penny from hopeful investors in Oshkosh, Nebraska, money taken anywhere, any time, and in huge quantities. Mutual of Mutual was the grandest mutual fund of them all.' Edward seemed to be hunting a paper in the scatter on the floor. 'Various European banks had thought it was a great way to democratize investment. No absurd small punters wanting to buy and sell a share at a time, because the mutual fund did all that, but access to the money of the grafting class. It was when everyone had just discovered the working class were paying tax, not just surviving. If they could pay tax, they could invest.'

'I remember it going wrong,' Emma said. 'People wrote books about it going wrong.'

'Lots of books,' Edward said, 'because it was truly a wonderful story. Everyone involved was a promoter, so they knew how to promote themselves; they had the right houses, the right girls, the right chums. The trouble was, as you no doubt remember, Mutual of Mutual paid widows and orphans huge amounts of money; the return was formidable. But they paid out of the new subscriptions from the next generation of orphans and widows. You simply couldn't make that kind of money in the honest stock market.

'When it fell apart, the obvious idea was to stuff it full of assets so the balance sheet went on looking all right. The banks that had loaned their names in earlier years – their names, you understand, and nothing more – now looked around for someone who had a vast portfolio of possibilities, and a desperate need for cash to realize those possibilities. It couldn't be industry, or TV networks, or even stockbroking firms, because the return had to come fast – Mutual's money, somebody's prospects, the prospects come good and all is well. You needed a top man in oil and gas and uranium and anything else that came from the ground for a profit.

'I regret to say that Sir Alistair Griffier found a man called James Drake. I regret it, because Drake was a substantial man who came in with Mutual because of a slight cash-flow problem; but there were problems with the substance. Technical, you understand. There were vast areas of oil prospects in East Timor, perfectly feasible at the time, but later covered over with civil war and massacre. There was a whole Antarctic field which Drake had put together with great ingenuity, and it still may yield, but the cost of starting was far greater than the potential profit; every single government with Antarctic rights was happy to take some cash for drilling, terrified of authorizing a start because of their environmentalists, and insistent on such vast taxes that crude had to stay above $40 a barrel to make the exercise profitable. Drake was brilliant, without a doubt. He was just wrong.'

Emma's skin prickled, as though the storymaster had named the enemy. She busied herself with notes on a legal pad.

'Drake went under. Went to jail, for a bit. Busted. You have to understand this was a man who could dream of rebuilding cities; he had a whole plan for the Drake Center in downtown Los Angeles which was a modern Rockefeller Center, towers and all. He had grand political friends; he was going to be a Senator at last. And he lost everything, because Sir Alistair asked him to take over a derelict idea at the wrong moment.'

'Motive,' Emma said. 'Isn't that what convinces juries?'

'Motive, yes,' Edward said, 'but hardly opportunity. James Drake was killed in a hunting accident, a year ago.'

Emma said: 'I'd like a drink.' And then she said:

'Maybe he has family. Friends. People with vengeance on their mind.'

'It's almost twenty years since Mutual of Mutual went down. Why did they wait?'

'They're avenging his death.'

'He died because he tangled his neck in a tree. They might shoot the horse.'

Emma sighed. 'Then where do we start?'

'He has a lovely Caribbean home,' Helen said, buried in glossy magazines that smelled of clashing perfume cards. 'His home was exclusively featured in *Town and Country*. Not for him the tourists of Mustique or the colonial glitz – '

James Drake said: 'Thank you.'

She had adopted the Griffiers like a soap opera; she knew the back story from the clippings, and bits of the history from books where she chased the name in the index.

'He was a war hero, decorated for secret work in France and Yugoslavia, but he never married.'

'Fag? Or not interested? Or lucky?'

'It doesn't say,' Helen said. She said it most innocently.

'Career?'

'I don't think he had one, not really. He's older than that Sir Alistair whose,' she ran her finger down the column, 'whose second marriage to the lovely Florence – '

'Yes.'

' – was the talk of Baltimore in 1958,' the girl finished. She knew the rules of soaps: accentuate the weddings. 'Now,' she said, 'they have a lovely English country house whose treasures were featured in the Washington exhibition – '

'But what matters to him?'

'It doesn't say. He seems to spend his time in the

garden. He looks very thin and distinguished.' She screwed up her eyes. 'Very English,' she pronounced.

There was something wrong with a man who found peace so young, and kept it; Drake was sure of that. It insulted all other men, who moved like water, perpetually. If what Edward had was paradise, then he would be expelled from paradise entirely.

Drake had sat for a while, and the blood had stopped in his legs. He hated anyone to see that he could not move. He sent the girl out, to buy oranges.

When she had gone, he puzzled over quite how she'd lodged in him, deep and irritating, like a splinter. She was only a waif, biddable out of habit. He shouted at her when she came back for letting him run short of oranges. She simply took it, no tears or anger; he could scribble on her like a piece of card.

'I never stayed still so long,' he said.

'I could take you for a drive.'

She went to make juice for him. He called the brokers while she was away. He asked about the fortunes of their brilliant new arbitrageur, Jude Klein.

'He's going to have quite a reputation,' the broker said.

'Call me, won't you? Don't be a stranger.'

'When there's news.'

'Get news,' Drake said. He thought it was time to show a little claw. 'I mean, disappointed customers might get gabby. When they're dead, they have nothing to lose.'

'Jude Klein would go on trading even if you died again,' the broker said. 'Don't sweat.'

'Get back to me, real soon.'

He could see the reputation of Jude Klein inflating itself and rising above the city, obvious as a big dirigible. He had arranged an embarrassment for Edward Griffier, too, and perhaps a catastrophe later. His body might be poison in a shell, unable to support him half the time, but his mind was mobile and he could go anywhere his malice would carry him.

Helen came back. He told her to raise her skirt above her pin-thin legs. He looked at that tender little badge of fur. He remembered when the faint smell of fleece on a hot beach, among the oil and sweat, would make him weak. She was willing enough to come to him, but it was a matter of pride that he should tug himself forward, pushing each numb leg, one by one, until he was close enough to touch her.

'Be careful,' she said.

Impossible resurrections he could manage; the ordinary resurrection, a hinge of flesh made hard, was now an event worth a saint's day. He wanted to be alive again.

He slapped her across the face, as hard as he could. She did not move. He tumbled down at her feet, his eyes staring. His breathing was violent and loud.

She looked down at him, and smiled.

'I never knew history,' Emma said.

'It makes a hobby,' Edward said, but he meant it was his life: patching together a reality out of reports and memories.

'We must have made enemies all the time,' she said. 'Refusing loans, or calling them in, or not accepting someone's paper or winning some bid – or losing it for a client, I suppose.'

'Not enemies,' Edward said. 'Ex-clients. And what we are looking for is passion.'

'You're very vulnerable here.'

'I don't have Miss Aston's wire and walls. She needs to believe people long to see her and if she keeps them out, she is never contradicted. All I need is some good dogs, and some good friends.'

'You have to be careful,' Emma said.

'The only thing they could take from me is my life,' Edward said. 'In any case, I've very nearly had enough of that.'

His words persisted, like dust in a summer street.

'There must be something else. Not James Drake. Someone else.'

'You're the one who knows about character and plot. You imagine it.'

The wind was tousling a tree outside, a poor man's orchid, and its shadows flickered on the library wall. She was almost sure the enemy was at the corner of her eye, always there; she had only to picture him. And she was good at pictures, at how to stage and where to put the camera; she watched movies with her mind on.

Imagine.

'There's the Griffier Crash, of course,' Edward said. 'But you know that story, don't you?' Emma did not, and Edward rehearsed it.

Imagine.

A raw night at Calais, cold and sodden air, and a tall man standing there in a top hat with the rain running down him like a glass coat. He is watching bundles, small but heavy enough to bend the backs that support them, as men unload them from a line of carts and swing them slowly on to the ferry deck. He is being watched, by Rothschild detectives. He is intent on this cargo, which is bullion, from the Banque de France and the Imperial Treasury in St Petersburg, masked with black tarpaulin. He feels a duty to be there.

Emma could feel the pain in this man; he died only four years after this shipment, leaving her grandfather as the head of Griffier Ltd. She sees him walking decks that are slick with sea and moonlight, as though he was the pilot. She can understand his resentment, his humiliation, his anger, his sense that the kingdom of his name has been infiltrated and compromised. He cannot control his world any more; he cannot demand. He was a lion of the City, a pillar of the Court of the Bank of England, broker to governments and breaker of governments, if need be. Now, he has to compromise, use cunning; what was once just a matter of his will is now politics.

He has to be seen to remake his life and his bank, answering to others. He is beginning to understand what that will mean. The ferry slips into Dover, as into a recent and more tolerable past; torches flare, and there are only a handful of passengers stepping ashore. The paddles of the ferry come to a halt.

Edward said: 'I suppose you could say the balance of power changed for ever between the merchant banks and the high street banks, but that is hardly a motive for murder. Not after a century.'

'Nothing happened then, did it? Nothing else?'

Edward went to a low shelf and picked a small black ledger book from a pile. The writing was copperplate neat, against elegant lines of red and black. The edges of the pages had begun to burn with age.

'He kept this in the partners' room,' Edward said. 'Usually, everyone knew everyone's business in that room, but this was a different matter.' He turned through the pages. 'From 1884, he starts a section called "Sarah", written in Greek. There are payments every month, generous payments. After eighteen months, they go up; after another fifteen months, they go up again. After another twenty months, they go up again. They don't change on quarter days, like rent might; they don't change annually or at regular intervals. But every time they change, there's an extra expense which he's labelled "Aesc.".'

Emma said: 'Sarah was a woman?'

'I think that's a safe assumption.'

'And the extra payments?'

'I think "Aesc." is for Aesclepius, god of medicine; it's the doctor's bills for confinements. For the time, they're high; Sarah can't have found childbirth easy.'

'But if he maintained a mistress, that's quite ordinary, isn't it? I thought that was why every house in St John's Wood used to have a canopy – so nobody could be seen going in.'

'The payments stop in 1891, on the weekend the gold came back to London. They simply stop. Of course, these were his private account books; he knew why they stopped, and he didn't need to put down an explanation.'

Emma said: 'How do you know they stopped that very weekend?'

'Because that was the due day. He was punctilious about due days. And that was the last time he paid.'

Imagine.

She saw that tall, distinct figure hidden in a cab, driving into a leafy suburb to visit a dark woman and abandon her. Her, and the children.

'He could have stopped writing down the payments in case the new bank overseers found out,' Emma said. 'Perhaps she left him. Perhaps – '

'You didn't know him,' Edward said. 'My father used to say he changed appallingly that weekend. It was the first time he fully understood that he was no longer in control, that the bank was not truly his. It would have been easier to handle a collapse, but of course the Bank of England couldn't allow that to happen. The moment they knew there was trouble, the humiliation of rescue was inevitable.'

'You think he dropped Sarah without warning, and with three children? Is that it?'

'It could give someone a grievance, I suppose,' Edward said. 'In any case, I only meant to show that even the Griffier Crash hurt people in unexpected ways. There must be unexpected motives.'

Emma fancied she could catch the face of Sarah in her mind. 'Poor woman,' she said.

She drifted back to Sarah's face even when the stories had reached the 1940s, and her eyes were red from the light and the reading. They had stumbled forward through the history of bad loans, the Great Crash, the pre-war years and refusing to do business with the Nazis, the property boom of the 1970s.

'That,' Edward said, 'was when we acquired the new headquarters, of course. Property firm on the verge of bankruptcy sold at a realistic price. Of course, they thought it was cheap.' He sighed. 'You cannot imagine the sheer communal foolishness of those years. Everything was going to be worth far more in a minute than ever before. Every last square inch of a North Country graveyard.'

'If you know the history so well,' Emma said, 'why didn't you want to be part of the bank?'

He said: 'Then there was the deal with Moscow Narodny, but everyone was doing business with them; they virtually started the property boom, trying to be more capitalist than the capitalists. There was an oil deal in the late 1970s; Griffier pulled out and it very nearly ruined five senior brokers. That contested merger we refused, which turned so dirty.'

'You didn't answer me.'

'It's my income, too,' Edward said. 'And besides, I take an interest in the City. In economic news, you might say. Some of my wartime friends are very interested.'

'I see,' Emma said. She liked to think of him as a kind of spy, a significant man even in his long, remote retirement. He had the whale's temperament: able to filter an endless stream of minimal information and be nourished by it.

Late in the afternoon, Edward said: 'You're the one

with the imagination. You tell me what sense all this makes.'

Emma said nothing.

'There's the dead James Drake, the invisible children of Sarah. It's unthinkable John Brown would kill to get control of a bank, though he might play games.'

'The least likely suspect,' Emma said. 'Agatha Christie Rules.'

'The killer always strikes again in Christie, have you noticed? And again, until Miss Marple and Hercules Poirot have all the clues they need.'

'I expect he will strike again.' She sounded very sober.

'He knows a lot, too. He knew about you and David Taylor, for example, and setting up Rupert with a simple crime, and what kind of derring-do Maurice would fall for.'

The outline of the orchid tree was soft and diffuse now; the sun was almost gone. It was the twilight when a grown-up cures the story he has told with hugs and kisses.

'We're in the headlines,' Emma said.

'I only wonder,' Edward said, 'what else this man knows?'

'Your Jude Klein,' said the broker, reasonably. 'He has to have a voice, a presence. He's an arbitrageur who makes famous deals. People want to talk to him, touch the hem of his robe. People who might invest with him. He ought to write a book or go on lecture tours or – '

'He's reclusive,' James Drake said, inventing as he went along. 'Brilliant but reclusive. Since so much of his success depends on technical analysis, he's out in the Painted Desert with a computer. His own brokers don't know him well.'

'Lovely,' the broker said. 'And when we get calls from people like Sir Alistair Griffier – '

'News travels fast,' Drake said.

'They have to know how the game works,' the broker said. 'They know it's contacts and information and socializing. They're never going to fall for some Howard Hughes rerun.'

'Let me talk to Griffier,' Drake said.

'But you've done business with him before. He'll know your voice.'

'He won't recognize it. He won't let himself. He'll be far too excited at talking to the wave of the future. For him, I'm instant profits with virtually no capital – just what a fading merchant bank needs.'

'What number do I give him?'

'I'll call him,' Drake said. 'At my convenience. Let him sweat a day or two; he'll be all the more grateful.'

'You sure you need him?'

'You tell me half our funds ought to be from legitimate overseas investors for tax purposes, right? Then I have to get out there and bring in the money. Since that's a little difficult from the grave, and since I'm still quite well known on Wall Street – '

'You're a health hazard on Wall Street. Everybody has a heart condition.'

'I'm glad I'm not forgotten,' Drake said. 'In any case, someone has to hustle money for the Jude Klein Benevolent Fund. I can't think of a bigger name than Griffier who needs us more, can you?'

'You're enjoying this too much,' said the broker.

'I enjoy life,' Drake said. 'I know about the alternative.'

When the time came to call London, he had wisps of caution caught in his mind, like wool on a fence. Griffier might know the voice; but Griffier thought James Drake was dead. Jude Klein might seem too eager; but Griffier had shown he was more eager still. It was a fine, steely trap, with cutting jaws, and Griffier was begging to be let into it.

Even so, Drake held his breath while the call went through. He was close as a whisper to the man he would destroy. He had the man's attention; he could tell him how best to wreck himself.

There was the inevitable wait while they found Sir Alistair; in a leather armchair, Drake thought, with his gin and his cigar and his dreams of survival in a malevolently changing world.

'My dear Mr Klein – '

The familiar voice of the enemy: dry, amiable, frank.

'We've heard about you, here in London,' Sir Alistair said. 'You have a most impressive record. Almost the gift of second sight, it seems.'

'Sure.'

'And now you find yourself in need of overseas funds. I'm sure you will have no problem attracting investors; everyone is starting to know your name. But you might find it helpful if an established European name were sponsoring you, hunting the money for you. Do you think, or not?'

Drake was silent. Let the bastard sweat. Let him give away everything.

'Of course, we, too, would be interested in backing you. We have a number of high quality investment funds which we market to very well-to-do clients. They would benefit from the kind of excitement which your name could bring.'

Drake could almost be sorry for the man – ponderous, serious, needy, using too many words to hide the note of supplication, trying to do equal business with a phantom. He was selling a ramshackle house, insisting on its finer points, trading on Englishness and fame, like some lord who lets the tourists into the castle for their shillings. But when the tourists come, life goes; curators rule where the family used to muddle its muddy boots and occasional treasures and sporting prints. Lords behave as the paying public expects, and demands. It could happen, also, with a bank.

'You could send me a proposal,' he said, with proper arrogance.

'Perhaps if we could meet, whenever it is convenient. In New York, or in London or – '

'I don't travel,' Drake said.

'But it would be so helpful,' Sir Alistair said. It would be a development to offer to his board, a sign of the family's ingenuity and resilience; even in the newest markets, their contacts still brought business.

'I would be personally most grateful,' Sir Alistair said.

'Perhaps,' James Drake said, 'something could be arranged.'

For a living man, that moment might almost have been enough.

7

Emma was swept back into the comfort of Miss Aston's estate, where time and reality were shut out by everything that surgeons, razor wire, a competent cosmetologist and a private screening room could provide. It was intolerably agreeable, and planned; no flower of unmannerly beauty grew, the light on the sea had its schedule. It would terrify anyone who, like Emma, had seen the chaos which follows when too perfect a system cracks.

Perhaps the old woman was right to stay here, and never to work again. If she took one chance, the whole of this lovely, lifeless case might shatter, and it could never be repaired. It had taken Emma time to realize such things. She was older, of course, and she had lost a lover to someone's malice and the fall of an elevator; she had seen her studio runner buried, very young; she was no longer sure that everything grew back in time. The name of Griffier could also die.

She dined alone with Miss Aston, in sensible state. The talk was difficult, and usually Emma was fluent and easy; at first she thought Miss Aston was calculating when it would be proper to refuse her offer. But that was not the problem. Miss Aston had read the script, and found it admirable, if a little racy; but distinctly modern. That was already a great concession from a woman who never made a movie outside the Hayes' Code. There should have been cause for modest celebration, a Perrier-with-lime raised to their new venture (Miss Aston, being an earlier generation, did not yet know that studios drink only Diet Coke). But there were handcuffs on their talk, and Emma did not understand it.

When the fish and the fruit had been taken away, Miss Aston sighed very deeply.

'This isn't my business,' she said, 'and frankly, I don't imagine it is yours.'

She took from her neat evening purse a sheet of that grey, shiny paper that comes from old-fashioned copying machines, or else a fax. The letter had been sent to someone Emma did not know, evidently of a firm of accountants or attorneys in Los Angeles. The letterhead belonged to some old-fashioned London solicitor, all mock-copperplate and lists of tiny names; but instead of that, it said Bank of Roseau. And the Bank of Roseau was touting for business, offering unspecified special services and 'tax advantages' in nudging prose. It stopped a very little short of saying: 'Anything considered.'

'I don't know anything about them,' Emma said.

'I think you know one thing about them, dear,' Miss Aston said, 'and I am sorry to bother you with it. You should read the names of the directors.'

She would not have been surprised to find Rupert there; but she found Edward. There was no doubt about it; the initials were right, and the military decorations.

'I told my man of business you were coming down,' Miss Aston said, 'because I thought it would impress him. I like to make him think I am a practical woman. He asked me if I would find out about – this. He wanted me to be discreet, but I think we know each other well enough for me to be direct. Darling.'

'It seems so very unlikely,' Emma said.

'I think we call this a laundry, don't we, darling? For washing dirty money, and packing it away in neat piles. That, at least, was what my man of business seemed to be suggesting.'

'Edward would never be associated with something like that.'

Miss Aston said: 'Of course, dear, we all know your uncle has done sterling work for various Government bodies; I mean, we all assume, for some reason, that he is some wonderfully senior kind of spy.' She was looking for confirmation, Emma realized, but she could offer none. 'We wondered – I wondered – if this might not be entirely legal, some Government scheme to trap people. Dope-pushers and terrorists, one hopes.'

'It seems a bit brazen.'

'My other thought,' Miss Aston said, 'was this. Does your uncle even know about the Bank of Roseau and being on its notepaper? Perhaps someone is taking his name in vain.'

'I could call him – '

'It might be better, darling, not to use the phones. You see, something like this can be terribly embarrassing in a very small country. We all have to mind our p's and q's.'

'Uncle Edward has been here for ever,' Emma said.

'Of course. But they keep saying Barbados will be a great financial centre one day, and you know how they are. The last thing the authorities want is anyone with – difficulties.'

'I suppose not,' Emma said.

'We are all here on sufferance,' Miss Aston said. She sounded curiously sad and careful.

She might be Edward's ally. She might have some unobvious link to this plot that engulfed the Griffiers. Or she might be an actress, always watching how people react, studying the fear and shock so rarely seen in her cocoon of light and flowers.

'You must tell Edward, of course,' Miss Aston said. 'And there are planes to Roseau, several a day; Mary will arrange the bookings. But I'm sure someone would lend a plane.'

'You're very kind,' Emma said.

'And I shall accept the role in your little film,' Miss Aston said. 'You need waste no more time on me.'

Guilt was one thing Miss Aston managed like a mother.

'I do understand that names must be protected,' she said. 'I have my name above the title, after all. Do you need to call your uncle?'

Edward understood the emergency; he drove himself across the island, and he even seemed glad to see Miss Aston. She understood that his life continued on the islands, and was not simply drifting to an end. He liked the woman, but he was fidgety when he felt required to perform around a star.

'You know the islands so well,' Edward said to her. 'Please don't go.'

Emma put the paper before him.

'I don't know this lot,' Edward said. 'Usually I hear when the pirates come ashore.'

'I'm so sorry,' Miss Aston said. She was watching like a cat watches the dance of a bird in the air. 'I know you've done such good work keeping track of the – pirates.'

'I'm interested in such things. But not as a practitioner, you understand.' He took an empty pipe from his pocket and gnawed on the stem. 'They're clever to use my name. It makes them sound respectable or official, or both. I am going to have to answer some very awkward questions.'

'My man of business was surprised,' Miss Aston said.

'He didn't happen to know if the bank was active yet, I suppose? They have a post-office box in Roseau, but they must have some kind of office in London or Los

Angeles or New York. They build offices where the money is.'

'All I know,' Miss Aston said, 'is on that sheet of paper.' She was a player, Emma realized; she had set a puzzle and she wanted to see it solved.

'We go to Roseau, then. There is nowhere else to start.'

Emma said: 'What do you think it's about?'

'There are dozens of these banks, if bank is the right word. Sometimes they come into an island and offer to set up a free port and a bank and a harbour – a bank with no regulations and no tax, naturally.'

'That is why it seemed so odd to try Roseau,' Miss Aston said. 'I don't think they would get away with things there. Somebody tried before and they were chased out most unceremoniously.'

Edward said: 'It doesn't need to be quite so official. Sometimes these banks take in money and wash it, and sometimes they just take money in and when people want it back, in a year or two, they've disappeared or they've lost the account number. Since you don't put clean money in the Bank of Barracuda, you can hardly hire a lawyer to get it back. Besides, you first have to find the bank.'

'Do they have to look respectable, at least?'

'Not at all,' Edward said. 'The same people pull the same trick again and again and again. People always want to believe in some new, untested tax haven; people don't like tax. And, of course, if the proprietors do get a local politician to listen, and build that freeport, they've got a kingdom of their own. They might want something simple, like gambling at Grand Bahama, or they might want drugs and guns.'

'I can see,' Miss Aston said, 'that you appreciate the problem.'

'I'll go tomorrow morning,' Edward said. 'If they took

the trouble to set up a post-office box, they may have visited the island.'

'May?' Emma said.

'May,' Edward said. 'Some of these bankers never move outside Dover Street or Third Avenue. They say they have banks on atolls off the coast of Belize, or islands in the Grenadines that wouldn't carry five people at the same time.'

'I will ask Mary to prepare a room,' Miss Aston said.

'I think Edward should go back to Avalon,' Emma said. The sharpness of her tone was surprising.

Edward drew himself to his martinet height, stick stiff. 'That is very kind, Miss Aston. I should be delighted.'

'But you should be at Avalon,' Emma said. 'It means so much to you. You have to protect what matters most to you.'

Miss Aston watched. Anxiety was energy, and she could live from the energy of others nowadays.

'I should be grateful to stay here,' Edward said. 'Tomorrow morning, we can make an early start.'

Miss Aston marshalled the household for another guest. She sat with them on the cool, screened porch, looking out at the dark and the sea: a pale and lovely face, acknowledging only a little of its age.

She was glad about what she had done.

She was always Miss Aston, the star; they were always trapped in their name of Griffier, publicly known, exciting reactions they could not predict or control. She was secure now in her accent and her posture, the grace that comes from living to your own timing; but she had learned these things. She wondered what it would be like to know nothing else, from birth.

She remembered the brick of her Midlands school, how she had walked there each morning, how she had been the scholarship girl who left at fourteen when there was no more money for repairing shoes, let alone the middle-class changes of clothes the school deemed essential. She remembered the copy of *Tatler* that a schoolfriend brought: the ovals and the ornate frames around the pictures.

They showed a garden party during the Henley Regatta: straw hats and silks and strawberries and a river that lay unnaturally still, tame as jade, and champagne glasses and women with jewels so fine, and so many of them, they did not need to show off. She remembered the party given by the Griffiers.

She had sighed over the pictures, like the other girls, and that same day she walked home from school for the last time. The party danced in her head. She would be like the lords and ladies of creation; she would learn. And when she was as good as them, she would know far, far more, because she would remember the years before.

She tried to imagine Emma Griffier by the lawns and trees; it was not difficult. Edward Griffier would fit, escorting – an actress, perhaps, famous on the London stage. She could taste the strawberries.

'Quite an adventure,' she said to her guests.

The worst of it was the patience of the drivers all around. Crawling north through contraflow on a wet motorway, Simeon Ryder wanted speed at least to take him away from the low, lifeless lands.

Beside him sat Maurice, stiff and patient as a prisoner, who had finally screwed up the courage to go north to face his constituency committee. He had left it too late for the meeting to be easy. He was alarmed, too, by Simeon's head prefect air of having something important and hurtful to say.

The traffic cleared at last, and Simeon began to ask questions. 'You've news from Germany, I suppose.'

'No,' Maurice said.

'Surely they have to issue warrants or drop the case, don't they? What does your lawyer say?'

No point in claiming this was no concern of Simeon's. Men who did business with Griffier Ltd wondered what Maurice thought he was doing; there were calls to the bank, accidental encounters in club bars. Nobody quite withdrew, but three lunches had died on Maurice in a week, with apologies. He was gossip now, reduced from being a power.

'I suppose my lawyer talks to them all the time,' Maurice said. But he worried more about the laughter he could hear collecting in the corners of rooms.

'Any news at all is bad news at the moment,' Simeon said. 'We don't need any more trouble.'

'It's hardly in my hands, old boy. I expect I shall pay for what they say was a mistake, but I can't stop people talking.'

Simeon smiled faintly. He was preoccupied with slipping out of the motorway and into a knot of roads piled one on another, and lit from high above by industrial lights in a bitter orange haze. It was like the edge of some forbidden technical zone.

'Your father's getting far too keen on Wall Street and arbitrage,' Simeon said. 'He's putting money with a man called Jude Klein and he's offering to sell Klein's funds over here.'

'Nothing wrong with that. If we can't get to Boesky, we get Klein. People know the name.'

'Klein is too lucky,' Simeon said. 'It is, quite literally, criminal how lucky he is.'

'I expect his information is good.'

'It's illegal to have information that good.'

The town began around them in self-effacing lines of brick, cut with rail lines; after a dizzyingly low bridge, the road dipped to an empty, limelit High Street. Young people in a doorway had eyes like eggs. Maurice gestured to turn left.

'Nobody goes to jail for being well-informed,' he announced.

'Things are changing. There is a moral low pressure system coming, and examples will be made. We cannot possibly afford to be the example.'

'You're becoming quite nervous.'

'If John Brown not only had shares, but controlled the management of Griffier Ltd – have you thought what that could mean?'

He thought for a moment that Maurice might huff with fury, but instead he evaded the subject. 'Welcome,' Maurice said, 'to my constituency. We need to find something called the Vintners' Hall. Known locally as Vimto Hall.'

'Give me directions.'

Maurice shrugged. 'They change things so,' he said. 'Years ago, I lobbied to get them what they wanted, which was an old-world leisure centre, shopping mall and tourist attraction. I never went after the opening.'

'Then we'd better ask someone. You only have an hour before the meeting.'

'Oh God,' Maurice said. 'Constituents. Salt of the earth. You'd better do the talking.'

There was a middle-aged couple, in tents of grey and beige wool, stooped by a bus stop in the rain. They watched the sleek car draw up, without interest.

Maurice, from the passenger's seat, said: 'Excuse me!'

The couple saw polish, money, nicely spoken men in fine suits; it was remote as television. 'It's Mr Griffier,' the woman said, and the man said: 'He wouldn't show his face here.' The woman said: 'We ought to be polite. Where's your manners?' The man said: 'What did he ever do for me?'

'It's absurd,' Maurice shouted through the splash and

echo of the rain, 'but I seem to have forgotten exactly how to get to the Vintners' Hall.'

Simeon looked down the street. He thought of some closed concrete frontier in middle Europe. There was an air of lives abandoned as not worth the effort.

'Well,' the man said, wondering if he should leave the shelter for the sidewalk. He seemed quite blank, with no purpose beyond the next bus, a nice fire. He shouted the way to them.

Simeon leaned across. 'Can we give you a lift?' he said, disingenuously, knowing the couple would refuse.

As they drove away, Maurice made a face. 'Unwashed coats and plain soap,' he said. 'Probably on social security, too. Workshy.'

They made a right turn. On the far side of a wide road, there were sketches for black and white buildings, with cutely angled roofs and lanes, and windows faked with diamond panes and half-timbers painted on the stucco. The buildings were too low, too thin, too mean and the walkways had been cobbled with artificial stone.

'You opened it,' Simeon said.

'People must like it,' Maurice said.

'It's convenient history. History with plumbing, and all people can remember of history from school. It never surprises you. It is never more than you know already.'

'Development,' Maurice said.

Simeon leaned across and opened the door on to the sodden pavement, as though he was dismissing a rider. 'I thought you liked school history,' he said. 'Battles won, civilization brought to savages, march of progress, triumph of Christianity. I thought that was what the schools taught nowadays – nothing to surprise the governors, nothing more than you know already.'

'Nothing wrong with children knowing the date of the Battle of Trafalgar,' Maurice said. 'Or being proud to know who won.'

briefcase in her hand, but the postmaster talked about the confidentiality of the mails. He could not say who owned a particular post-office box, or allow any outsider access. Access was by a combination; if you didn't know it, the contents of the box were none of your business.

Emma retreated. She stood in the shade and counted the boxes; she knew which one mattered, and where it was. She had only to watch.

The breeze off the sea was pleasant enough, but the day grew sticky. She had to keep the post office in sight, and that meant she could only walk the few yards left to the gents' loo or the few yards right past the Venezuelan consulate and the Green Parrot Club, still shut, to the edges of the fish market. The sun caught her on the seawall, and there was nowhere else to sit. It was going to be a long day.

The sun was enough to make her reason like a child. Probably, nobody would come, and therefore it couldn't matter if she slipped away to find a seat in the shade, and perhaps a drink. Probably, the Bank of Roseau did its business in some LA walk-up, as Edward had suggested; she was keeping watch on a name, nothing more.

A pair of young girls in starched white came walking by. They climbed the post-office stairs, the sea wind catching at their skirts and lifting them above long, black legs. Tellers at the Bank of Roseau, Emma decided sarcastically. The boys playing by the empty lot became the messengers; a lawyerly man in a lightweight suit became the vice-president of the bank. She had staffed the whole operation in her mind before she grew bored. She imagined some bank tower standing among the low, companionable houses, a vision of glass up by the white cathedral.

She was tired of standing, but cautious about the midday sun. She felt sure she would be suspect, staying still as she did; two very neat, very young policemen had already passed by, and stopped to make notes in little books. Sooner or later someone was going to ask if they could help, meaning something quite different.

She remembered the real island ginger beer, the kind that catches the back of your throat with fire. She was interested in almost anything but the slow procession of careful, sensible, anonymous people who pulled their letters out of the wall of boxes and went more or less happily away. And since Edward was gone for an indefinite time, she could not expect to be relieved soon. She would decide for herself. She would walk up the hill to the restaurant there, *La Robe Créole*. It had a reputation across the Caribbean; she deserved a break. She dusted down her skirt and swung her briefcase like a little girl going home from school.

She turned the corner just as Adam Heller, loping along, head back to catch the sun, crossed on to the waterfront and made for the post office. At the wall of boxes, he had a ritual, punctilious as always. He looked around; when he was sure he was not being watched, he flexed his fingers and worked the combination of the lock. The mechanism was sometimes not as precise as his fingers. He found this hard to forgive.

Emma was in sight of *La Robe Créole* when she thought of turning back. But there was lunch ahead, and a chance to rest out of the sun, and that was what she most wanted.

Adam Heller pulled out the mail for Bank of Roseau, a clump of papers that he stuffed into a canvas shopping bag. He felt around for anything that might have wedged in a corner. To his surprise, some sorter on the other side of the wall slipped an envelope into his hand. 'This for you,' a cheerful voice said.

He took the letter. After a beat, he said: 'Thank you.' He slid his long fingers under the seal.

'I am on the island and I would be most interested to

meet my fellow directors,' it said. It was signed, with exaggerated clarity, 'Edward Griffier'.

On Saturdays, Simeon Ryder took a taxi to go walking. He was in the red brick of Earls Court, where London looks like a drab in her fifties that everyone would still like, very much, to respect. Arab women passed in bird masks, and men wrapped in leather and cross Sloane Rangers trying to park, bits of a city trying not to cut themselves on each other's oddities.

He had bought the best roses he could find, and he crossed through the high, grey gates of the cemetery. He liked the coolness of the place, the trees and the smell of damp ground, the proper mourning notes. He kissed the roses, first.

There was a statue of a weeping Virgin; he laid the roses there. The inscription read: Sarah Huissier Adams, died 1934. There was no other detail; mostly, this woman was still a document to him, a death certificate which tied him to his mother and his name. He was alarmed at how sentimental he could become in this place, before her memory.

There were too many unfamiliar things in his life. He had recovered his name, and he wondered if that was the same thing as finding his identity. He knew who his real mother and grandmother were, but not if his feelings for them were more than a passion to have feelings at last. He thought the bank was his family, and that was under siege.

Each Saturday he mourned, and then he had sex, of a kind. A big woman put him in ropes and handcuffs, and for a precious, paid by the minute half-hour, he was not responsible any more. He did not want to be hurt or punished; he wanted to be free. Just making love, he lost himself only for a moment, and even then he felt responsible for someone else's pleasure. Tied, he had no duty to be in control.

Maurice was side-lined, Sir Alistair making a mistake. He had so much to control. He had to worry if John Brown could truly take a bank like Griffier Ltd, or whether he was too much the newcomer.

That was ironic, of course. Imagine the Griffiers landing in London, upstart Dutch, smelling of genever, full of ambition, not our sort; now they could patronize others who aspired to act like them.

'Hell,' he said, out loud, 'whenever you have two Englishmen, you have irony. They think it's enough for a civilization.'

'What you say?' the taxi driver asked.

Edward was unsurprised that Emma had left her waterfront watch for the cool of *La Robe Créole*. She was brave and generous just to be here; probably, she would unmask no villains in the midday sun.

She had settled in the dark room, before a bowl of fat crayfish; she shelled them carefully, and clipped the white flesh with neat teeth. She reminded him, only a little, of the child he had known and loved: a kind, serious, wilful child.

He smiled at her, and she wiped the cream and peppercorns from her mouth. 'I ought to feel guilty,' she said, 'but the crayfish are too good.'

'They have a river for every day of the year on Dominica,' Edward Griffier said. 'The crayfish feel at home.'

She said: 'The crabbacks looked awfully good. And the callaloo soup. I was just being sensible.' She picked apart a particularly succulent fish. 'I don't suppose you found out anything?'

The boy waiter faded from Edward's side with an order for mountain chicken; Edward looked around. There were some tourists eating pizza, and a local family at the far end of the room.

'Nothing,' he said. 'At least, we've established that the authorities here don't even know the Bank of Roseau is in business. They certainly haven't licensed it.'

'And they'd tell you, would they?'

'Oh yes,' Edward said. 'We helped them with their last problem. They always help us.'

Emma wanted to ask precisely who 'we' were. She decided against it.

'So we have a rogue operation,' Edward said. 'The only oddity is this post-office box address, here in Roseau. It's an elaborate cover when you think about it; it means having someone here, at least from time to time, to clear the mail and make the whole operation look plausible.'

'Then someone must come back and forth. The immigration people – '

' – were very pleasant,' Edward said. 'But they don't keep special note if someone keeps coming back; they only want to know if it's all right to let him in. We don't even know how long the Bank of Roseau has been giving this address. It could be some local secretary or lawyer or anyone who could remember the number, collect the mail and forward it.'

'Someone on the island has to know,' Emma said. She picked at the long, elegant beans and the cooked christophene that came with the crayfish; she pushed the bowl of sauce and shells aside. She was sure it was an impasse, that they had made the only move they could, like the end of a chess game. The advantage still lay with the nameless enemy.

'You're wondering if we should even defend ourselves, aren't you?'

She stared at Edward. 'Yes,' she said. 'Yes, I am.'

'You think the name is nothing, that you can go anywhere and be anything. You think it's none of your business to fight for Griffier Ltd; they should look after themselves. You think – '

'I think the Griffiers are where I come from, my home,' Emma said. She thought for a moment, because there were things she hesitated to say even to Edward. 'And I want to kill the man who killed David,' she said, softly.

The door to *La Robe Créole* flew open. A gangling man, dark and forceful, expected attention at the bar.

Emma felt Edward's hand on hers. She looked around embarrassed by the passion that had spilled like tears, and she saw Adam Heller.

She thought of a studio rule: coincidence can only work to your characters' disadvantage. Zurich, Bayreuth, Roseau; that was too much coincidence. She caught Heller's eye across the room.

He stopped barking at the bar; he smiled a boy's wide smile. All morning, he cursed the discomforts of a bagman's lot; it was not what he did for a living, after all. He thought this long, long favour to James Drake was tolerable only when Emma Griffier was there; then, it was hot. She stopped his breath and melted him. He knew he should be careful. He checked the bag of letters with the bar.

Emma said: 'What a surprise.' She was neither welcoming nor dismissive; she almost seemed to expect him. 'Edward, this is the man who gave me a lift from Zurich to Bayreuth. His name – '

'Adam Heller,' Adam said. He wanted to be definite in her memory.

Emma said: 'He seems to be there, providentially, wherever I go.'

Edward looked at Adam with an unkind uncle's glare. 'Extraordinary he's here, too,' Edward said.

'But a great pleasure,' Adam said.

Edward said to Emma: 'He'd better sit down.'

For an hour, they were polite, which is to say: they avoided every possible issue. They talked about rivers, boiling lakes, rain forests, sulphur springs, the attractions of the island. The menu came, and Edward discoursed on the hunting of the giant frog eaten as mountain chicken ('it's very good,' Emma said, remembering it from childhood, in beer batter, with its strange Airfix bones). They were all just travellers.

'I get the plane back this evening, I regret,' Adam Heller said.

'Then we'll take you,' Emma said. 'We have a small plane waiting.'

Adam said: 'It would be most convenient.'

On the plane, he clutched at the canvas holdall. It seemed very flimsy suddenly, and all too likely to spill its contents. There was no room to put it under a seat, and he was terrified of leaving it, or tipping it. The more he tried to stop them knowing, the more he telegraphed the importance of that bag. He was distracted by her, smelling the musk of sun and sweat on her skin, but he was clear that both of them must have an idea what he was carrying. But he was almost sure they had no idea what to do about it.

James Drake's orders had been awkwardly vague. These letters mattered, Adam thought; so he must keep custody of them, and keep them private. But if he was left to his own initiative, he would simply plant them on Edward Griffier, make a fuss at Customs and see that the Bank of Roseau was for ever linked to his name. It would be so easy; Adam Heller, the honest Swiss, could pretend to be the accidental witness to a major financial scam. Edward had been outside the system so long that nobody could assume he was honest.

Easy, but forbidden. Adam Heller's head was spinning. Duty and body were warring in him, and he also had hopes; Emma was at least tolerating him. It could get better.

'You've been to St Lucia, of course, Mr Heller?' Edward was as sociable as marble.

'I don't think – '

Emma wanted him to stay. Some other time, he might have satisfied one of those wet night itches in a strange town, when company and comfort matter more than anything; but that was not why. She wanted to know all that he knew, now. She was prepared to be friendly.

Edward detected sex, and he was sorry.

At Bridgetown, the plane came in gently among the 747s. Adam stood to help Emma, bent almost double, the canvas bag lodged under his arm. She kicked him, deliberately, and the bag slipped. With a surprising agility, Edward went down on his hands and knees in the aisle.

'Bank of Roseau,' he read out loud. 'Bank of Roseau, Bank of Roseau – this one is just to a post-office box, but it's the same number as the Bank of Roseau.' The two men glared at each other. 'Explain yourself.'

Adam Heller looked at Emma, but her look was fearsomely detached.

'You were collecting mail for the bank?'

'You can see what I have,' Adam said. He barely avoided sounding sulky.

The engines of the little plane cut out and, with them, the air conditioning. Under the sun, the little metal craft grew stiflingly hot. The pilot was not inclined to come back and talk with them; he always awaited orders. Adam shifted awkwardly, his tall back bent by the low roof of the plane.

'You know who the principals of the bank are?' Edward was prosecuting counsel, full of wrath and short on patience.

'I believe, sir,' Adam said, clipping his words, 'that you are a principal of the Bank of Roseau.'

For a moment, Emma thought that Edward would strike him.

'Don't waste my time, boy,' Edward said. 'Who are the principals? Who sends you out to Roseau to collect this stuff, and where do you send it?'

Because of the plane's small body, Adam could not help seeming to tower over Edward. 'That is confidential,' he said. 'I am Swiss and I care about confidentiality.' He smiled as though the words really did amount to an apology.

'Besides,' he said, 'I think it is better for you that I carry the letters, don't you? You are the name on the letterhead. It will make perfect sense that you went to Roseau to collect these letters. They are on your plane. You don't have permission to fly on, so you could either admit everything at Customs when I denounce you, or wait for the plane to be searched. Or you could let me go through, and say nothing.'

This much, Adam thought, he must be allowed to go beyond orders and improvise. He felt liberated.

'Sarah Huissier Adams. He visits her grave every Saturday, leaves flowers. Then he goes off to some dominatrix in a basement. His naughty day.'

John Brown was never a patient man and the reporter had brought him far too many unusable facts. The aide-de-camp could see him next time.

'*The Reporter* will not engage with the trivia of a man's private life,' Brown intoned, 'unless it is in the public interest. Get on with it.'

'Sarah Huissier Adams, it seems, is Ryder's great-grandmother. It's an old story – grandmother died in the 1930s, daughter looked after her to the end, five minutes after the old woman died, the daughter was pregnant.

She was in her forties by then, no money, so she put the child up for adoption. That's Simeon Ryder for you, and Sarah is where his family tree begins, as far as he has one.' The reporter beamed. 'I got the adoption people to help by saying I was from "This Is Your Life".' There was no smile to reward this ingenuity, only silence. 'And Sarah Huissier Adams came down in the world very suddenly, the month of the Griffier Crash. She lost her house in St John's Wood. She and her three children moved into a pair of rooms above a tailor's shop in Aldgate. She made a living as a seamstress until she died.'

'You think she had stock in Griffier Ltd?' Brown said. In his way, he was truly innocent; he found it hard to imagine passions greater than money.

'She was the mistress of the head of the bank,' the reporter said, triumphantly. 'She bore him three children out of wedlock. And when suddenly everything he did was under scrutiny and the bank was in trouble, he dropped her. She was penniless. She went back to the East End and worked her fingers to the bone for her kids. And in time, her grandson became the man who runs the Griffier bank, all unknowing.'

'He doesn't know the connection?'

'No proper birth certificate, except in the parish records. I guess he assumes his mother was born out of wedlock, too. Granny called herself Adams, you see, because she did belong to a man.'

'And "huissier",' John Brown said, 'is much the same word as "greffier". A huissier is a court officer. A greffier is a registrar.' He looked, even for John Brown, exceedingly pleased with himself. A vowel here or there was nothing to such a man.

'I didn't know that,' the reporter said.

'It seems to me,' John Brown said, 'you have an irony more than a story.' He smiled the smile that had turned the hearts of ambassadors and ministers to stone. 'People don't want to know these things. They want men they can admire, bigger than life – men they can emulate.'

The reporter felt himself trapped into the final, intolerable flattery, by a desire to stay in work. His immortal soul, bought and bargained for over the years, was at its most dreadful risk.

'Men,' John Brown said, patiently, 'with a record of achievement. Of charity and concern. Of – '

'You don't want the story written?' the reporter said. He had avoided the compliment. He had a glow of moral courage, but no hope of survival at all.

The doors to the office flew open, and two of the John Brown women entered, coiffured and manicured like steel flowers. John Brown said nothing more to the reporter who, not being dismissed, was not sure he was allowed to go. He edged into the deep sofa which was a social disadvantage in itself. He tried to edge from the room, but as he did so, the doors flew shut again.

'This gentleman,' John Brown said to one of the women, 'is fired.' He smiled. 'Take his pass.'

And the reporter went out into the light of day, free and fragile as a bird, leaving John Brown what he liked least: a puzzle. He had the key to the managing director's soul, and it did not seem negotiable.

He asked for Sir Alistair Griffier's number, thought better of speaking to him, and left Sir Alistair blank. 'Mr Brown does not need to speak to you, after all,' the woman's voice had said, with only the faintest hint of apology. Brown decided the greatest mischief must surely lie in telling Ryder his own secrets.

His call came at the end of a fraught day. Simeon Ryder was exasperated with the Griffiers, and with their refusal to think or speak about what must be done.

There was always some reason or some hope why now was the wrong moment; they were Micawber and Co.

He was interested when John Brown called. There was a final meeting where he hoped to persuade the board what must be done, but if that failed, he had almost had enough of bailing out a small and foundering ship. John Brown might offer something more interesting.

He could always have a life of his own. He was learning.

Until they cleared Customs, Adam held the canvas bag of letters like a trophy; it was his protection and confession, all at once. He deferred to Edward, and he was unsure of himself with Emma. He was only the bagman, scuttling here and there on instructions, and all he had done was save his skin.

'You have to tell us what happens next,' Emma said.

He sweated. James Drake had his nets of influence, his old friends from bank chairmen to roustabouts: he could fix a beating-up, a burning, a false prospectus or a loan. What Adam could do was use his hands, as he was told; or, sometimes, a little more.

Miss Aston's car slipped between the green fields and came up beside them. Emma and Edward waited for Adam.

He was meant to bring back the letters on the New York plane the next day. He could do that, and he could also spend the evening close to Emma, if he simply entered the car. He settled, comfortably. The car and driver sailed sweetly off, along a still sea dazzled by the start of sunset. Adam was miserably absorbed in Emma, in the grace of those long, fine legs, and the salt of her after a day in the sun.

And Emma calculated. This man was either infatuated, or acting. She thought of kiss and tell: she would kiss, he would tell. She had the first connection to the enemy that was not simply hate.

She turned a little on her haunches, let one leg go softly against the other; Adam's eyes were caught on her. She liked the heat. She would be grateful for a brief escape from mourning and the memory of a lift cage coming down. It was pressure to be a victim, too; she could lose herself with another body.

She told herself to stop. She brought down the window and closed her eyes, abandoned herself to the breeze. Her long hair streamed past her smile. Adam Heller had the strongest sense that if he touched her now, exactly as she wanted, they would be lovers, but he was afraid to try the wrong touch. And the ramrod back of Edward Griffier was a reprimand.

The grey limousine passed the electronic gates of Miss Aston's estate and came to rest among scents and shade. Emma broke out of her dream. The erotic, she knew very well, was not convenient.

'The driver found you, darling?'

Miss Aston bustled like a tea-room owner sometimes, before she fell back into the waxy, scene-stealing stillness of a true star. It was something Emma had not seen before, something intimate.

'Miss Aston,' Adam Heller said.

They knew each other, and Miss Aston was deciding whether or not she should recognize the boy. That was obvious.

'We met very briefly,' Adam was saying, 'when you were in Switzerland. I don't suppose you remember.'

Miss Aston was allowed to recognize him then; she was relieved. 'I'm sure I do, darling,' she said. 'How is your father?' She realized at once that she had said quite the wrong thing, so miserably wrong it could not be covered or taken back.

'Well,' Adam said, 'as far as I know.'

Emma heard distance in his voice, quite different from his usual mannerly deference to the older woman. She had to listen for the words that neither Miss Aston nor Adam would say out loud.

'You must encourage him to come back to the islands.'

'If I speak to him,' Adam said, 'I will tell him.'

Emma made herself take control of her suspicions. There were too many connections, but among people who travelled with money, there were also casual links, without significance. Yet Miss Aston produced the letter from the Bank of Roseau, and now she seemed to know the bagman from the Bank of Roseau. She was douce, tiny, careful with a kind smile; Emma scoured her with a look.

'How long have you known Adam's father?' she asked, sweetly.

Miss Aston looked away, as though her old senses were not quite sharp enough to catch the words. 'The trees are so lovely at this time of year,' she crooned, 'and you must all need a drink after the journey.'

Emma said: 'I've never met Adam's father.'

But the old woman had returned to the wax of her white star's face, which showed only what the script required. 'You must ask Adam,' she said. The words drifted as though she lacked the strength to push them into the full stream of the conversation.

In her room, Emma remembered the heat in Adam's eyes. She belonged to David, still. Her hands went like feathers down between her breasts to her belly.

This was war, the enemy was close, and the only weapon she had not yet tested was her own body.

8

The machine of the bank ran smooth as milk, from the sharp doormen to the bellowing traders to the directors' floor; it was galvanized by the shrilling of the phone, and kept in motion by a hundred ambitions. But the future of all this lay between the rosewood panels of the partners' room, where the family met.

'There may be legal implications,' Simeon Ryder said. 'This is not a meeting of the full board.'

'You are here to take the minutes,' Maurice said. 'Be sensible. The law couldn't stop us meeting for dinner at Easterford to talk like this.'

'Law,' Sir Alistair said, 'is not really your strong point at the moment, Maurice.'

And Rupert Griffier smirked.

'There is no possibility of a binding vote on anything,' Simeon said. 'This is not even a quorum of the directors of the bank.'

Rupert counted out loud, with great elaboration. 'Close thing,' he said.

'The important thing,' Sir Alistair said, 'is to present a united front.'

Simeon took up his notes. He had never felt so separated from the Griffiers, so much the professional among those he advises and not at all an equal.

Lady Griffier said: 'As far as I know, I can vote Edward's shares. I have his proxy.'

'Voting is not in question,' Simeon said.

'Very well.' Sir Alistair drew on deep wells of certainty, like a headmaster. 'Simeon has a proposal to put and I want it discussed. I think we owe it to Simeon to discuss it, at least.'

Simeon cleared his throat. He would sound reasonable, practical and not at all apocalyptic, if he could. He only wanted them to know what was at stake: whether the Griffiers would keep their power and position in the bank which bore their name, or whether they would be tossed out. Simeon Ryder would, this one last time, try to salvage them.

'You know, of course, that John Brown is now sitting on slightly more than seven per cent – '

'Five, less than five.' Sir Alistair sounded bland. 'We do have his word on it.'

'His yesterday's word,' Simeon said. 'I've been talking to the brokers. The market for Griffier shares is pretty tight – hardly anyone buys or sells. They can tell when there's interest.'

'No doubt,' Sir Alistair said.

'At any rate, John Brown has taken a view on Griffier Ltd, and we don't know what it is. Now he is a volatile man and a difficult man but he is also extremely acute. He makes dealing profits out of firms other people have forgotten.'

'I hope you don't mean people have forgotten us,' Maurice said.

Simeon ignored him. 'We have to assume a strategy, or at least tactics. I thought at first he might just want respectability, or a cut of what happens after Big Bang. He might just want a profit. When he bought, our share price was not exactly elevated, and since the market knows he's interested, the price is much more interesting. A very little good news, or the whisper of a bid, and he might be able to place the shares.

'I say place, not sell. His slice of Griffier Ltd is too big to be dumped on the market without a prearranged buyer, but it's too small on its own to interest anyone who wants to take us over. It doesn't carry control. If Brown tried to sell all at once the price would crash; people just don't sell Griffier stock. We're still trying to calculate exactly who gave Brown his seven per cent.'

'The only reason for telling us what Brown might be doing,' Rupert said, 'is because you think you know what Brown is doing. Get on with it.'

'I can guess. My guess is he will huff and puff and look influential until someone – some Japanese bank, some American bank, maybe some German or Swiss bank – decides they want a slice of London. They'll pay a premium without noticing it for the shares, because they can't get in otherwise. But they won't be quite as dismissive about Brown as we are. They see that he does get money from institutions, and he is a serious player. They'll assume Brown has influence enough to persuade other shareholders to sell, once there's a respectable, viable buyer out there. They won't even feel the pain, paying in deutschmarks or yen.'

'Not dollars,' Florence said, with feeling.

Simeon said: 'The process has already started, just because John Brown bought. We can't put the clock back. We know there are buyers who fancy the idea of a known name in London – especially if London stays the hinge of the world market, half-way between New York and Tokyo and English-speaking, and such nice houses in the country. They'll want to be here.'

'Very interesting,' Sir Alistair said, 'but only theoretical.'

'Brown has to sell on,' Simeon said. 'By selling on, he sets the rules for the auction, and we're on the block. The family has less than fifty per cent of the bank, for tax reasons among others; we could lose control overnight. Now the game's started, we have to decide who we want to win.'

'We can change the business,' Maurice said. 'Some of

the Hambros are talking about starting a kind of boutique – dropping all the expensive trading, and concentrating on big corporate deals.'

'We're a public company with a duty to shareholders,' Simeon said. 'We're a public company in need of capital, too, so that we can compete after Big Bang. Can you suggest where the capital is going to come from after the past few years? Or do you think we should mortgage ourselves so we're no longer worth buying, in the fine old tradition of American corporate suicide? We need money to survive while we're taking risks, and to buy other firms, and we're going to find it very tough as a company in play. People want to buy us.'

'We've had some bad luck,' Rupert said. 'Some bad PR. If Maurice does have to go to jail – '

'Better,' said Maurice, mumping his words, 'than being tangled in a major SEC investigation. Especially when the Feds are looking at how actual widows and orphans lost their money.'

'That's political,' Rupert said. 'All those SEC things are political.'

'There is no point in wrangling over circumstances,' Simeon said. 'The point is we need money, and the prospects for a major rights issue are zero. We need a friend.'

'The very idea of Griffier Ltd losing its independence – ' Maurice had nothing else to say; he spoke, expecting a rabble of agreement to end his sentence.

Into the quiet, Simeon said: 'A buyer might only want the name and the institution. A buyer might not care to keep the family on the board.'

'And what if John Brown is the buyer himself?' Lady Griffier asked.

'I can deal with that,' Simeon said.

'He's not influential,' Maurice said. 'He's clever, but he doesn't have the ear of the right people.'

'Anyone can buy and sell shares,' Simeon said. 'You don't need a police certificate. But persuading the Bank of England you should influence the workings of a great bank – that's something else.'

Sir Alistair did not enjoy disagreement. 'I think we should vote,' he said. 'Is Simeon to put us on the auction block, or do we continue as we are? That seems to be the issue.'

Simeon sat back in his chair.

'Of course,' Sir Alistair said, 'if we decide to continue as we are, Simeon will not find it necessary to inform the full board of his concerns.'

'I really – '

'I insist,' Sir Alistair said. 'This bank is Griffier Ltd, after all. It is not Ryder and Associates.'

They voted to stay as they were. Maurice did so, out of anxiety to keep one certain thing. Sir Alistair did so, out of faith. Rupert did so because for once he was not the cause of the trouble; but he could use that moral advantage only with his family. Florence did so because she saw a family consensus, because Edward liked to keep his distance by agreeing, and because the vote was not binding.

Simeon Ryder, after a moment, voted with the others. They had not even listened to the idea that they could be exiled from their own place, and he could not bear to be wholly excluded from the family.

'There,' said Sir Alistair, in the satisfied tone of a doctor who has stopped a child's whining hurt.

In his office, Simeon began to shake. They did not grasp, and he could not tell them, one simple point: only if a friend bought Griffiers would the family keep their easy hold on power. He sifted the letters in the file before him. He wanted distraction.

There was a Museum letter, reporting a talk with Maurice Griffier MP. The partners' room, the letter said, could be lifted into history at the Museum, an image of the old City of London before the coming of tubes and wires. Perhaps Mr Ryder would investigate how this could be done?

Simeon tore up the letter from the Museum.

He would make one last attempt. He went directly to Sir Alistair's private room.

'Don't be pompous,' Sir Alistair said. 'It's all decided.'

'I have a duty to the shareholders. We can't simply form a cabal and decide what the main board will discuss.'

'You lost, Simeon.'

'We have to protect ourselves.'

'John Brown seems perfectly friendly. He might hold those shares for ever. He did keep that story about Maurice out of his paper, didn't he?'

'He has started a game that cannot be stopped.'

'I do realize the world is changing,' Sir Alistair said. 'You seem to forget that I have helped change the world, over the years. I don't think that is too grand a claim. But now I am out of public service and I see opportunities. The small, sharp-witted merchant bank will sail through. People never like these big machines.'

'They will outsell us. They will undercut us. And it will not be because we lack talent; we lack capital.'

'There will be new things. Things I can't even discuss with you yet, Simeon.'

'We are a public company – '

'I really don't have time for this, Simeon. Your arguments are becoming obsessional.'

The partners' room connected to the outside world in unobvious ways. A partner could not simply be telephoned; he had to be summoned, if he chose to notice the beckoning figure at the door.

Simeon heard: 'Mr Jude Klein is calling again. From New York.'

It seemed Simeon might block Sir Alistair like a football player. He controlled himself with obvious difficulty.

'We cannot afford to be associated with that man,' he said.

'He is a very successful investor.'

'He is criminal.'

'You need rest, Simeon. As for Mr Klein, it would be most unmannerly to keep him waiting.'

Simeon reeled down the corridor. He had never before felt his body betray his feelings in this way; he had never felt quite so angry. He was the Griffiers' servant; their destruction was his destruction. Their identity was his identity; he was nothing outside the bank.

He would go, while the going was good. He would find some other berth, and look back on the bank as an apprenticeship for the rest of his life.

He could hardly believe he thought such a terrible thought.

She stood before the mirror, proud in her long, firm body, ready to begin the game. She could trust Simeon to manage the family, she thought. It was up to her to hold Adam Heller here until they had the name of the enemy.

Between the trees, she moved like grains of light, sifting. The sun had risen on the other side of the island, and the sky was suffused with white; she could see the last stars. A mongoose crossed her path. An early humming bird hung at a flower that had not yet opened.

She was a very physical shadow in the garden. The kaftan caught her body here and there, like some flicker-book image of a woman walking; she drifted into the mind of anyone looking towards the sea.

The servants were stirring in the house but they would stay unseen and unheard. Adam had nothing to fear; he was on friendly ground. She was the kind of woman who was never alone, but now she was alone. He was bound to come down to her.

At the blue, curved sides of the pool, she slid out of her kaftan and stood naked. She would swim until she had no more clear idea of where she was, only the workings of lungs and heart and limbs. She could lose herself. She lowered herself into the bright water and she struck out from the sides. The chlorine caught her eyes; the water was all she could see or feel or hear. She turned, smooth as a seal; she slashed at the water to race to the other side, and she came leisurely back and she jack-knifed down to the bottom and came up with her lungs roaring and her mind blank, but clear.

The idea of Adam had almost washed away. She no longer worried whether to play him coldly or indulge him. She had been a little mad to think of him like a man, when he was something to the enemy, maybe even the enemy's son. She romped in the water, her blood up, and she pulled herself out, hair and light blinding her eyes.

He was too close. She could have touched him as she came out of the water. He said nothing. She was full of life in the bright morning, but he was serious; she had wanted to bring him to the pool, and now she had no idea what to do with him. She could not read his mind.

'Come in with me,' he said. 'I wanted a swim.'

'I need a towel.' She did not want to give this proud body to this man's eyes; she could feel her shoulders curling in to mask her breasts. She felt like a rabbit on a table.

'Please,' he said. He could smell heat and chlorine.

To push him aside, she had to touch flesh. She was afraid to start the wrong tides with something as simple as the touch of a warm body. She did not even trust herself.

'I love the water on you,' he said. 'You go into the

water, you shimmer. You lose definition and there's just the ghost of you. Then you come out, and you're there again.' He would not look away. If he would move, she would know how her body would respond.

She straightened herself, and marched to the chairs. She wrapped herself in a robe. The rough cloth made a welcome shield.

'I need a shower.'

'I saw you in the garden.'

'I needed a swim. I've been doing too much thinking.'

'I want to talk,' Adam said.

She sat down on the edge of a pool chair. He sensed, rather than saw, the dark gold hairs between her legs; they were never quite out of his mind.

'I run the errands,' Adam said. 'That's all. I felt it was my duty.'

'Your duty to your father?'

He did not say 'no'. 'It's my duty. So you see, I'm not allowed to want you.'

'You want to talk about your father?'

He shook his head furiously. 'It isn't possible, not to you. I could complain or I could confess to anyone else. Even if I made love to you – '

She stiffened, and he noticed it. She saw obsession in his eyes, the kind that sees no alternative and ends anywhere, even in rape or killing. She was the sum of all his fantasies of her, as well as the particular woman sitting by the pool.

'I would have a duty to find you out or to hurt you,' he said.

'You could tell me your father's name,' she said.

He skinned his teeth, as though he was in pain. 'It's not Heller,' he said. 'That was my mother's name, and she's dead.'

'If you really liked me – '

'I do not like you,' Adam Heller said. 'I need you.'

From his bedroom window, Edward Griffier looked down on the shadows and blossoms of the morning. He saw Emma and Adam by the pool; he saw them close. He wanted to warn Emma, but an old man lacks the authority; every warning seems like jealousy.

He opened a little attaché case which travelled with him. He took out a screwdriver, a broad knife and a small silvery disc. He began to prise open the plastic case of the telephone extension in his room.

He was glad he had friends, and that sometimes he took their advice.

John Brown rode a Rolls as though it was a horse in need of breaking: he cheered to himself, puffed a little, put his body into the power steering. Simeon Ryder did not like to complain.

He had not expected a car trip. They had swept through the East End, almost like the first miles of the way to Easterford, but John Brown offered no explanation until the traffic thinned out and there were no more lower marques to nip anxiously out of his way. Then, he was an almost ordinary driver again.

'You'll wonder why I wanted to talk to you?'

Simeon said: 'You're a substantial shareholder. I'm always available to shareholders, when possible.'

'You drive out of London with shareholders when they want you to? Ordinary shareholders.'

'Of course,' Simeon said, 'you are not an ordinary shareholder. Not at all.'

'I make you nervous, don't I?'

Like some huge sea creature with a talent for mathematics, Simeon thought: like a thinking manatee.

'I like to make people nervous,' Brown said happily. 'But of course I'd deny ever saying that.'

'It might help,' Simeon said, carefully, 'if I had some idea of what you wanted to talk about.'

'Oh yes,' Brown said. 'You wanted that on the phone, didn't you? I thought you were a man who thinks on his feet.'

Simeon said: 'I'm sure you can find that out for yourself.'

'Beautiful evening,' John Brown said, maddeningly.

The low fields scudded by, flat and colourless.

'Most people,' John Brown said, 'try to impress me.'

'I'm curious about where we're headed.'

'Tell me about yourself,' John Brown said.

It was something like a job interview, although Simeon had to compete with every chance of a truly spectacular manoeuvre on the road. He said: 'I suppose I am the manager of Griffier Ltd. I make things happen. I make sure the right things happen, for the most part.'

'You've had a run of bad luck recently.'

'Every reader of a tabloid knows it. The trouble with family businesses is that you have to contend with the family.'

Brown turned to stare at Simeon, and for a moment his snake track on the wide road was alarming. 'You don't approve of family businesses?'

'I've spent my life in one,' Simeon said.

'If someone wanted to take Griffier Ltd,' Brown said casually, 'where is the greatest weakness?'

He must know he could not ask that question of a loyal manager. He must think he was buying Simeon Ryder, for something. Simeon would have been happier if Brown would say so, in front of witnesses.

'Come on,' John Brown said. 'The best way to manage is to know your greatest weakness.' But then, as Simeon thought but did not say, John Brown was a dealer and a chancer, not really a manager at all. 'We can be frank,' he said.

'I don't think I can be frank,' he said. 'I belong to Griffier Ltd.'

'Lock, stock and pension plan,' Brown said. 'I suppose you'd never think of leaving?'

It sounded like the start of a proposal. Everything hinged on Simeon Ryder's guess what John Brown meant, and Brown was well aware of the quandary he had created. His gamble was that Ryder would guess wrong.

'On the bad days,' Simeon said, 'everyone thinks about leaving, if not doing actual bloody murder.'

'Would you leave Griffier Ltd for another bank, maybe?'

'Griffier Ltd is one of the great banks of London,' Simeon said. 'I don't think any of the other banks could offer me the same sense of – belonging.'

And John Brown chortled. To Simeon it was a curious reaction in the middle of a seduction; but then, he did not know what John Brown knew. John Brown was enjoying himself hugely.

'I expect,' he said, 'you feel like part of the family.'

'I feel like part of the bank,' Simeon said.

'Is that not as good as being part of the family?'

'You are born where you're born,' Simeon said. It was curiously personal for an interview, but perhaps Brown needed to know reaction and emotion before he worked with a man. He certainly did not know where to stop.

'Family still run things, don't they?'

'They are directors of the bank. Of course they run things.'

'But you're a director, too. You feel like a junior director? Not one of the charming circle.' Sometimes John Brown lost control of his English for a second, and a dictionary mistake showed through the usually seamless language. 'We could change all that,' he said.

He was coming to the point, at last, Simeon thought, and he was grateful. He knew the Griffiers were the structure of his life, but he wanted to be offered a choice.

'We could certainly change all that,' John Brown said.

He stopped the car suddenly in a familiar lane, between butchered hedges, with high grass verges.

'This looks like the road to Easterford,' Simeon said.

'It is the road to Easterford,' John Brown said. He shut down the engine, and left the great bulk of the car wedged between a muddy gateway and a tangle of brambles; he was not inclined to move for other traffic.

Simeon said: 'This is a rather awkward place for a discussion.'

'You'll want to go directly to Easterford when I've finished,' John Brown said. 'You'll have to talk to Sir Alistair.'

Simeon said: 'You're very sure.' He was distinctly edgy now, as though John Brown must have some mesmerist's trick that he planned to use, some infallible device; it was true that he charmed or paid or alarmed the most unlikely people into working for him.

'Imagine,' Brown said, 'if you were in control of all this. Really in control of one of the grand and noble banks of London. In control, in your own right, and not because you get on with a family that's accident-prone.'

It sounded like the devil tricking the innocent to the mountain top, and showing the powers of the world on a market stall. John Brown boomed, but Simeon noticed the fine-sounding offer was inexact.

'Do I understand,' Simeon said, 'that you expect control of Griffier Ltd to change very soon?' It would amount to a declaration of war, or at least of bid; it would make it impossible for Simeon to listen to any more. John Brown must know that.

But Brown only snorted again, his inexplicable laugh.

'Listen,' he said. 'Every Saturday you go and lay flowers on a monument in Brompton Cemetery; don't you? Before you go to visit Wanda with a Whip or whatever she's called.'

'You have extraordinary information,' Simeon said. He was rattled.

'And you know that lady, Sarah Adams, was your great-grandmother, as far back as your family goes. You don't know your great-grandfather, do you?'

Simeon said: 'We don't know his name.'

'We? You don't have brothers or sisters. You only have adopted parents and the name of your great-grandmother. You hardly have a plural at all.' John Brown softened. A dirty, battered Mini had come up behind the Rolls, and was squeaking for its right of way. The driver was an angular woman, with a fair sense of her own importance. John Brown ignored her.

'Your grandfather,' he said, 'was Sir Alistair Griffier's grandfather. The same man. He kept two households, two worlds, and when his bank was on the point of crashing, he had to choose between them. He chose home and heirs. He abandoned your grandmother. He had found her when she was a new immigrant in Aldgate, and that is where she went back.'

Simeon Ryder looked at John Brown with wide, startled eyes. 'You can't think I could possibly believe such a story,' he said, abruptly. 'You've owned a sensational newspaper for far too long.'

'I can prove the story, of course,' John Brown said.

The driver of the Mini had abandoned the usual signals of the road, and was out of her car, tapping like a furious bird on the window of the Rolls. John Brown turned and glared; she froze. She was afraid of the man, but quite unable to retreat.

'You are a Griffier,' Brown repeated. 'Easterford is as much your inheritance as theirs. And if you've felt a special loyalty for the bank over the years, it's hardly surprising – '

Simeon said: 'I am loyal to myself. I helped construct so much of that bank as it now is. I could never walk away from it.' So there was no offer; he had come all this way to be confronted with mischief, and at the gates of Easterford. Anyone who passed would see him in close talk with the man likely to make an uncomfortable, untenable bid for Griffier Ltd. He had to get away.

John Brown noticed the thin woman still standing in the lane, the Mini bouncing lightly on its worn suspension. He was suddenly furious. He flung open the car door, and stepped out. He rose to his full, and even monstrous height.

'I must insist,' the woman said.

Amiably, almost, John Brown said: 'You have absolutely no need to insist. No need at all.'

'Your – vehicle is blocking the road.'

'I am aware of that.'

'I need to get through.'

'I have no interest in that.'

'I shall summon the police,' the woman said. 'We shall see if they have an interest in all this.'

'Fah!' said John Brown. He lowered his huge face to meet the woman's tired, cross eyes. 'Fah, madam, is all I have to say.'

He left her shaking, and settled back comfortably into his seat. 'Country people,' he said. The woman had crept back to her Mini, and she sat there, a fugitive tear on her cheek.

'Are those your management techniques?' Simeon asked. Suddenly, he was sorry John Brown had made no offer; he was denied the honour and glory of refusing a bidder. As a plain shareholder, the man had some right to courtesy.

Brown turned to him. 'The facts won't go away,' he said. 'I shall take you to the drive to Easterford. You can decide what to do.'

At the gatehouse, he said: 'You should be glad I told you. You're somebody now.' And with that simple, insulting dismissal of a life and a career, he swept away, the Rolls catching the grasses on each side of the narrow lane like a cat in a tunnel.

Simeon Ryder stood between the brick gates, with their grand and Gothic construction, and their non-specific saints carved in soft stone. Brown was right; the facts would not go away. They unravelled a whole career of mild deference, of being the supporting player and the *éminence grise* all at once. They also hurt him. The Sarah who had become his only link with his past, his people whoever they were and their tradition, had been betrayed. And he had never needed to defer. He grew angry.

Half-way through a thicket of rhododendrons, he stopped. He wanted to know why John Brown took so much trouble with a melodrama. It sounded almost like those other pieces of elaborate mischief: the murder of Emma's lover, the framing of the dishonest Rupert, the adventure invented for Maurice to make a fool of himself before at least two police forces and a consul. He had been wrong to think John Brown was a rational man.

He was in sight of Easterford now, and the great lawns were welcome only as a delay before he reached the door. He had been home all this time, he thought, without knowing it; but what kind of home left him only a cold, professional son?

He had perhaps three minutes to decide what he could do about these impossible facts.

'Adam seems to have gone,' Miss Aston said. She had a sweet smile, but she was masked again, acting untroubled.

'You mean he left the island?'

'He came without luggage. I can't tell. Darling,' she said, almost as an afterthought, the smile still sweet like sugarcane.

'Did he seem disturbed?'

'Men feel these things so much more than we do,' Miss Aston said, obscurely.

'Do you know when he left?'

'He can look after himself, dear. Even if he was upset, he'd come to no harm.'

That smile was a brake on honesty. Emma wanted to shout that she did not give a damn about Adam's well-being, mental or physical; she only wanted him accounted for.

'It's going to be a lovely sunset,' Miss Aston said. 'Splendid for your last night on the island. Mary found you a seat on the afternoon flight to New York.'

'How very kind,' Emma said, although the kindness amounted to diplomatic expulsion.

'Mr Griffier has been such a pleasant guest, too. So interested in things. He will stay to dinner, of course.'

There was not a trace of irony in what she said. She should have been knitting today: a tabby cat lady in a rocking chair, soft and kind. Instead, her hands were bone still.

'We'll have dinner early,' she said.

Edward was restless while they ate; something had broken his usual calm and his fine manners. He wanted to be back at Avalon. It crossed Emma's mind that he would not have wasted the day, that he would have tried to make sense of the links between Miss Aston and Adam Heller and Adam's damned, lost father who could pull such malign strings. Good information set his blood racing, as a woman or a horse can do for other men.

But there was no chance to talk about such things and, when he left, Emma drowned in the peace of the place; there was a silence fit to make the ears ring with pain, a silence like a shroud. If Edward knew something, she was jealous of his advantage.

She was drowsy on her bed when the gatehouse rang.

'Mr Griffier sent a car,' the voice said. 'He wants you at Avalon, soonest.' There was a little sidebar of talk, and the voice continued: 'His phone's down. He couldn't call.'

Emma was out of bed already. She pulled on jeans and sweater and skidded down Miss Aston's grand, ornamental stairs like a child expecting Christmas. For a moment at the door she thought of other calls that had come to her family: the calls to Rupert, to Maurice, offering what they wanted. She was glad to recognize Edward's driver at the front door. He was a crisp, neat man, but there were smears of black on his boiled white shirt.

'What happened?' Emma said, throwing herself into the front seat.

'You has to see,' the man said.

'Edward is all right, isn't he?'

The man shrugged and he raced out into the lanes. The faster the car went, the more the cane leaves thrashed and danced in the light, like a pressing crowd; they cut the night like knives. They could have been shouting to drown out explanations. She was suddenly afraid.

She had lost the ease she once felt on this island. The childhood afternoons, the beach at Bath and the fishermen's boats at Martin's Bay, bicycles down to St Peter's Church: that was wiped memory now. Instead, the car lights were spotlights and the cane mobbed the road and the leaves hacked out an ironic kind of applause. The star was coming home to Avalon, and everything was wrong.

The light, particularly, was wrong. There should have been a vault of perfect black, blown with stars; but there was a faint, smutty red up ahead.

'They don't burn the cane at night,' Emma said.

'Long time to harvest,' the driver said, grimly.

The familiar shape of St Peter's Church, the tower of

stone and the shade trees, was cut out against a sky that was sore with light. Something was burning, towards Avalon. The car bounced ominously over the crest of a little hill, and went fast down a steep avenue of tall trees. The breeze that should have been full of the gusting Atlantic was carrying something acrid. Shade trees and bananas had shadows like the red of stained glass windows. It was bright enough to see the quick, silver shadow of a monkey slip away.

The driver wrenched the wheel to take the sharp turn into the driveway at Avalon. He had to stop. 'Mr Edward wanted you, particularly,' he said, and his huge brown eyes looked wet and apologetic.

He set out again with grim care, as though the solid driveway was really mountain scree or sinking sand. The garden, and then the house, rolled slowly into view like a filmed dream. There was the familiar parade of soldier palms and the roses and hibiscus, but they were blackened by shadow. The garden reflected fire.

Avalon crouched on the hillside, its comfortable ranges bright with light. The heat had bitten into the old pitch outhouses, and they were ready to flame like torches. A palm tree caught suddenly and its leaves cracked along the black spine in brief, golden fire. Emma choked, as much on memory as smoke.

She could see Edward Griffier at the library windows, stripped to the waist, the fire's light and shadows mottling his old man's flesh. She remembered Edward on the wide lawns here, explaining how the mongoose came to Barbados and how orchids are propagated. Now he was sooty and desperate, tearing at the shelves, finding all the strength in his pencil arms to salvage books and papers.

'I didn't have the words,' the driver said. He opened the boot, and pulled out a jerry-can of water and some clean, thin towels. 'For the smoke,' he said. 'If you go close to the house.'

'Can I get into the library? If I open the windows, the fire will just get more air.'

'You might get through the house, Miss Emma.'

Edward was up against the windows with piles of books, slick with sweat. He was close to exhaustion, his body like a rough suit of skin and bones that hung from stooped shoulders. These books had been brought laboriously from England to feed his exile and now they were the enemy, more fuel to burn down Avalon. He was turning in the heat and the fire, despairingly.

She wrapped the wet towelling around her mouth and nose, and she went in through the kitchen quarters, into the main hall. She could hear and smell, but not see the fire; it seemed to surround her. She went low to the door of the library.

He saw her there, a ghost beyond the flames. He beckoned her. She saw his hands worn down to bird claws, crusted with filth and smoke; he rubbed them together, and she realized it was an old man's gesture to save the circulation. He beckoned her again.

The least she could do was help. It was a life in flames around him, not simply papers and timbers and a house.

He had piled books by the huge windows that gave on to the lawns – ledgers and record books and sometimes the novels he most valued. He wanted help to carry them clear of the house, when he dared to open the windows.

The first journey, they stumbled on to the cool wet crabgrass with their load. The second, the heat in the library was close to unbearable. The room was full of pots of flame. Emma put out a hand to steady herself and pulled back on the point of blistering; the fire was greedy for oxygen, and it smothered her senses.

The sentimental oil of Easterford, with its cows and

broad trees, shone like a hot face and then crumpled inwards, blackening and shrivelling and flaming inside its gilded frame. A shelf came down in a storm of feathers of fire. The windows were framed in fire, and the tiles dark with smoke and carbon. She knew they had to get out, for good.

She missed Edward, and then she caught sight of him, deeper in the room, closer to the heart of the fire. He had a huge book in his arms, and its weight seemed to pull him slowly and deliberately to the floor. He lay still, and she dived down to him, choking on the vacuum at the fire's roots, tugging at his ragged pants. He was locked on to the great book; it was a painted atlas that she remembered. She dragged him by the arms across the tiled floor, grateful he could slide without harm. She cannoned into a table behind her, and for a moment she panicked.

Inside her mind, she was sure. She had to pull Edward clear of the fire. In the dew outside, there was hope of cool rest. She was half afraid his bony body would splinter before she could make him safe.

She wanted him to walk. She could not simply drag bare flesh across the paving stones. But his eyes were blank. She rolled him, still clutching the great book, until he was safe in the cool grass. The soot and the bruises looked the same.

She pulled the atlas out of his arms. He had tried to stop it burning by holding it tightly against him, but it had singed his flesh, and it still smouldered. She knew the book: the painted continents, the flecks of humanity on deserts and forests and mountains. She had spent hours looking for other places and other people to be.

She dropped the book and it spread open. A flicker of fire from Edward's trousers had to be snuffed out, but it caught at the book's pages. It cut across the horn of

South America to the mallet of Spain, and the checker-board USA; the fine paper curled. Pages floated out like leaves on a black stream.

She slapped Edward's face. She needed his attention now. She could hear the fire brigade at last in the lane, engines roaring, bells ringing. All he had to save was himself.

She could see China floating against the stars and burning still.

He breathed suddenly, like a man waking from ordinary sleep. His eyes were a mirror to the fire. He said: 'I ache, rather.'

'Someone set the fire.'

'I know. I know who gave the order.'

Emma cradled his old head like a treasure. 'Tell me in good time.'

'Time,' Edward said, contemptuously. 'This is James Drake. Drake. The Aston woman called him to say we'd seen the Bank of Roseau letter; he asked her to show it to us. She sounded very friendly.'

Emma sat down on the lawn. The cold and the fall jarred her spine. 'He's dead,' she said. 'Everyone said he was dead.'

'Ask Heller,' Edward said. 'You should be careful of him. Too intense. I sent him packing this afternoon.'

He turned his head to look at Avalon. The fire had taken the skin of the house and cracked it open. The old storehouses, which once held sacking and sugar, were already down to the bone.

He said: 'It was like a friend.'

'You have to tell the authorities,' Emma said.

'You can't indict a dead man. You can't count on a dead man to do the decent thing. We picked the wrong, wrong enemy.'

Emma stroked his forehead. Suddenly, Edward felt a kick in his chest, a blow from within his own body; his heart shunted and broke into a chaotic dance. He opened his mouth as though he had something to say that would save him.

His face seemed torn in different ways, like a copy that has slipped in the machine; his fine hands crooked. Emma pounded on his chest, and breathed deep into his lungs, but his life went briskly.

Certainty went with it. She looked at the fire like a fine cinematic effect, but without mercy or intermissions. She looked at Edward Griffier, whose heart had revolted only just before it broke.

She had to find and kill a dead man, before he took her life, too.

9

Miss Aston took the stairs carefully, as though she knew something terrible was waiting. It was after two in the morning, but she had dressed.

From the doorway of the house, Emma said: 'Edward came back with us.'

Miss Aston paused, while she still had the advantage of the stairs. 'Where is he?' she said.

'He is waiting in the car.'

Miss Aston could smell old smoke in the air. She allowed Emma to lead her, not quite kindly, to the door. She was reluctant and brazen, like a child.

'Go talk to him,' Emma said. She pointed to the car, whose length gleamed in the house lights.

Miss Aston was fragile like the very old. When she was unprepared, the air could seem a challenge and she half expected to trip between the chips of gravel. For a moment, Emma thought of stopping her.

She said: 'The back door.'

Miss Aston pulled the door open. Softly, suddenly, Edward Griffier fell sideways from the car, face up and forward, sooty and half naked and twisted.

Miss Aston fell to her knees. Emma could feel the rush of the old woman's heart, the cuts from the gravel. She put a hand gently on Miss Aston's shoulder, and the old woman leaned forward to kiss Edward Griffier's forehead.

'While we were here,' Emma said, 'your friends burned down Avalon.'

'The wickedness of it all,' Miss Aston said.

'James Drake,' Emma said. 'Or perhaps Adam Heller. He's Drake's son, isn't he?'

'We must take him indoors,' Miss Aston said. She was not escaping the question; she could see only Edward's broken face, and the proper ways his death must be honoured. 'We must call for a priest, an undertaker,' she said.

Emma steadied her. Inside the house, it was Miss Aston who could offer comfort because she knew closely about matters of death. 'I have the habit of people dying,' she said. 'But it's never sudden now, never. You live in its shadow, or they take you into a hospital and it takes months with tubes and machines. Death's never surprising. It is survival which seems the miracle.'

The servants had brought a low table and covered it with fine linen cloth. Edward lay there, in an improvised kind of state.

'It was an unpleasant joke, I suppose,' Miss Aston said. 'But it was only meant to be a joke. Drake sent me the letterhead from the Bank of Roseau, and I was to show it to Edward when I had a chance and then Edward would have to defend himself against a charge that didn't even exist. That's all.'

'They burned Avalon,' Emma said. 'The library had gone, and the outhouses, when I got there.'

'It was such a peaceful, lovely place,' she said, and Emma knew she was in mourning for her own calm. 'I never knew Mr Drake very well, only like some rich people and some Hollywood people know each other. I used to think of him as an explorer. He was really a lawyer, I think.'

'James Drake died,' Emma said, flatly. 'So they say.'

'I never heard that.'

'He died in a riding accident in the Rockies. We checked the death certificates.'

'But he called me. I'm sure it was his voice. And why should anyone pretend to be a man with such terrible troubles?'

'Edward said you called him today. Where did you call him?'

'A New York number, a hotel. The Pierre. He said it was amusing you'd gone off to Roseau.'

'And you didn't know what else he had planned?'

'I promise you I knew nothing.'

'He had my lover killed,' Emma said. 'He tried to ruin my brother Rupert. He succeeded with my brother Maurice. He tried to kill Rupert and me. He burned down Avalon, and that killed Edward; morally, he killed Edward.'

'To me,' Miss Aston said, 'he only proposed a little joke. I know it was malicious, I know. Sometimes the sheer ease of some people's lives – ' She thought of the pictures in *Tatler*, the immaculate Griffiers, and the more human, more terrible reality here.

'Do you have any other number for James Drake?'

'He must have a Denver number. I can't imagine he lives at the Pierre; he never liked New York. I did hear his wife was in Houston. She was spending like a widow.'

'And Adam Heller?'

'I was surprised to see him,' Miss Aston said. 'I don't know why I feel responsible for him.'

'I think he worries people.'

'You shouldn't tease him.'

Miss Aston looked down at Edward's body which had stiffened into a parody of a soldier, muddy from the battlefield. 'I would like to wash him,' she said. 'I know how to wash him.'

She brought out soap and cloth, and she kneeled beside Emma. They washed the old skin gently; they uncovered the bruises that had blackened before he died. They shared the work like old women do in a village, in companionable silence.

Cleaned, the face and the heart were still broken.

'. . . and arrived quite unexpectedly at the gates of Easterford,' Sir Alistair was saying, 'with some extraordinary story about how he was the long-lost great-grandson of Ralph Griffier. It was rather difficult to know what to say.'

'We shouldn't be talking in the partners' room,' Maurice said. 'Ryder comes in constantly.'

'I have given orders that he is to be excluded today,' Sir Alistair said. 'He waits his turn at the glass door, like any other member of staff.'

'The point is,' Maurice said, 'the whole organization of the bank is his. He makes it work.'

'But we are the ones who animate it, who bring in the business,' Sir Alistair said. 'Simeon's realm does not even extend to the trading floor. That is full of eager young men who are overpaid and easy enough to replace.'

'They expect to be replaced,' Maurice said, complacently. 'They understand competition.'

'I have worried about Ryder for some time,' Sir Alistair said. 'He has been most unhelpful about our new association with Jude Klein. He has been talking privately to John Brown, who is hardly our friend – Brown drove him down to Easterford that day, he admitted it. He keeps warning everyone to be careful, that we have some unnamed enemy who springs fearful traps.' Sir Alistair tapped the blue leather top of the partners' desk with his pen, as though he had made a decision or a discovery. 'Of course,' he said, 'if there is such an enemy, perhaps we need look no further than Simeon Ryder himself.' He laughed, unconvincingly.

Rupert Griffier said: 'Ryder's always been a good chap.'

'He's clearly become fanciful,' Sir Alistair said. 'This tear-jerking story of a woman driven to poverty in the East End by a wicked Griffier – it hardly makes sense.'

'It could be his motive,' Maurice said. 'Like a deep cover agent, all these years inside the bank, but harbouring a terrible grudge against us all. Waiting his time to destroy all that Griffier Ltd stands for.'

'Certainly,' Sir Alistair said, 'he has been trying to destroy the family's position.'

'Dilute it,' Rupert said. 'He simply wanted us to think about the future. He's right. If you want to continue in this dull, slow business, you'll need hundreds of millions, and the best place to get them is the Japanese or the Americans. Sell now, or get bought later. It makes perfect sense.'

'I gather,' Maurice said, 'you have liquidity problems again.'

'I could use some capital myself, yes. I don't like everything locked up in a bank which I can't even influence, let alone control.'

'Of course,' Maurice said, 'you wouldn't think of selling at this stage, would you?' If there was irony in what he said, it was heavy and pointed as a stake. 'There'll be the problem of who gets Uncle Edward's shares, too. Did anyone see a will?'

'I reserve my rights,' Rupert said.

'This is not the point,' Sir Alistair insisted. 'At the very core of our organization we have someone who fancies himself to have a grievance against all our family, who is trying to diminish the family's importance, who – '

'Perhaps,' Rupert said, because he was a frank, if dishonest man, 'he wants to save us from ourselves. We've been rather bad at that recently.'

'I think,' Sir Alistair said, 'nobody will disagree that Ryder should be given leave for a while. Perhaps six weeks would be sufficient. In that time, we take a look at his operations here, and decide if he should return.'

'That's fifty per cent off the share price, when the news gets out,' Rupert said. 'Six gins in Coates, and it's bank managing director goes mad, suspended from board – or Griffier family bid to seize control of own bank.' He stretched. 'But do it as you like,' he said. 'I am only the junior partner here.'

Maurice said. 'You simply own shares.'

'I was never arrested,' Rupert said, indolently, 'and there was never a proper warrant for my arrest. How long will you be able to say as much?'

'Really,' Sir Alistair said. 'Naturally, I shall speak to Ryder. We'll tell the rest of the staff that he is taking a break on medical advice – he could have glandular fever, something like that.'

'You'll start rumours the length of the City,' Rupert said. 'The only person here who truly understands how things look in the City is Ryder, and he's the only one you can't consult.'

'This bank operated without Ryder once, and it will again. I do not think hurrying the process will ruin us,' Sir Alistair said.

The three men rose from their chairs.

'We have to look to the future,' Sir Alistair said. 'The future, not the past. The future of Griffier Ltd.'

'Yes,' Rupert said, in a tone that made the other two furious.

In the morning, Adam Heller came back. He walked Miss Aston's driveway, scrubbed and chastened, as the hearse pulled softly away.

He found Emma in a slew of memoranda in the drawing room, her mind fixed on studio business to save it from running like a terrified cat around the horror of the night before. She tried not to let him break her concentration, but he stood in the doorway, still, as though he was waiting for judgement.

'I have to work,' she said.

'I saw the hearse. What happened?'

'You really don't know?'

'How could I know? I was away last night.'

'Edward died of a heart attack,' she said. 'You killed him.'

'I don't understand.'

'Avalon burned down last night. Someone torched it.'

'That's terrible.'

'There's no point in playing innocent.'

'You assume too much,' Adam said.

'I use common sense. In thirty years, nobody did Edward any harm on this island. The only thing that was different yesterday was you.' She had a sheaf of coloured papers, yellow copies, pink copies, white originals and she searched for the notes she needed.

'But if you think that,' Adam said, 'we can't get to know each other.'

'New clothes?' Emma said, looking him up and down. 'Did you buy new clothes in Bridgetown because your old ones were full of smoke and petrol?'

'I had a change of clothes, of course.'

'I'm being polite because I am a guest here and I don't want to disturb Miss Aston. We brought the body back here last night. She had a terrible shock.'

'But yesterday morning, by the pool – '

' – was yesterday, whatever it was. It's over.'

'You are not fair to me.'

'I don't have to make sense of you,' Emma said. 'Get out.'

'I took the seat next to yours on the New York flight. I thought we could talk.'

'There will be other seats.'

'But I do not understand.' He was too close to her, as though he knew her; she was shadowed and bothered. 'I am still the only way you find your enemy,' he said.

'I know the enemy,' Emma said.

'Oh,' Adam said. He stepped back. For a moment, Emma wondered if he could kill her, too. But his eyes were busy with cheap cunning. 'How do I know you are telling the truth? And if you know the name, how will you find him? You can't find him without me.'

'I want you to stay away from me.'

'I know how to find you.' He did not understand why she did not see what was so obvious and ordained. 'I'll see you this afternoon.'

She looked down at the papers spread around her. It mattered whether a declining line of action pictures should move from Britain to the slow, but cheaper exile of a Mexican studio. There was a certain madness which came over film crews so far from home, so far from accountants; she thought she would agree to the change. She never did like the series.

A maid came with a telephone. She was happy, for a moment, that Simeon Ryder had called.

But: 'I'm clearing out my desk,' he said. 'I'm on leave of absence, but I'm not expected to return.'

She had thought of calling him. His advice was always cool and sound, even in a war; and she was of a generation which thought wars were on TV news, and could always be turned off or down. Not being able to escape frayed the nerves.

'They caught you fiddling?' she said, and regretted her tone immediately.

'We had a disagreement, your father and I,' Simeon said. 'And I made a rather curious discovery.' He told her the story that John Brown had offered him like a gift, and all the things he had imagined or found out later. She knew no proper answer; she was embarrassed. It was like finding a schoolteacher in tears.

'John Brown didn't tell me that story casually. He went to great efforts to make the worst scene possible – dropped me at the gates of Easterford so I could only go and confront someone in your family. He's still not sold his shares in Griffier Ltd, and he's trying to buy Rupert's stake.'

'Rupert must have mortgaged those shares a hundred times over.'

'We said there was an enemy,' Simeon said. 'John Brown could have set up Maurice's problem. He might know people in the penny market, to accuse Rupert. He might – '

'Do you know what happened here last night?' Emma explained, and she found pathos in the way Simeon said: 'I didn't know.' He had always known everything that could possibly reflect on the bank and its standing, until now.

'That is terrible,' he said. 'And you lost your ally, too. The others don't want to know about history, even when it's killing them.' He sighed. 'Maybe that was John Brown, too – '

It was only kindness to tell Simeon about James Drake.

'There is another possibility,' Emma said. 'More than a possibility. We found out some curious things and the suspect, if you like, is extremely unlikely – out of it, really.'

'I don't understand.'

'Officially, he's not alive.'

'You can't be serious?'

'It seems so. He has help, obviously. We talked to some of them.'

'They're not just telling you a good story?'

'I could turn that round. Are you sure you're not

confounding all the problems of Griffier Ltd with the one man who did you wrong?'

'My theory is more likely.'

'Is it? John Brown is an impatient man, but he's chosen a long, slow, complicated way to get what he wants – if you're right. He got five per cent without shedding blood, he might get Rupert's shares depending on Rupert's troubles, and what else has he got for his trouble?'

'We shouldn't discuss this on the phone.'

'Besides,' Emma said, 'there are all these ingenious traps for Griffiers, and then there are all these brutal solutions – a trap that involves the whole penny market, and a solution which just means knocking out a man and putting him in a lift shaft. It doesn't sound like one man having all his orders obeyed, does it?'

'I could help,' Simeon said. 'I don't have to be in the bank every day now. I'm quite free.'

'That's kind,' Emma said. In her mind, she was tapping his story as you tap a girder of metal, checking for hollow parts.

'I don't want Brown to win,' Simeon said.

'I don't think he's the problem,' Emma said.

She was grateful to lie back among the overpowering chintz of Miss Aston's drawing room and stare at the pale ceiling, far from home. It would be wonderful to believe Simeon, she thought; at least John Brown was alive, warm, ambitious, greedy. He traded on a reputation for being not quite scrupulous; it made people nervous. But he liked to win cleanly, and as the architect of a campaign of criminal harassment, he was not credible. It simply took too long.

She had been so sure Simeon would take her point, and be able to do something with it; but he had been invalided out.

As for James Drake, he was cold, dead and therefore impossible. He had the kind of motive which might begin such a long and bitter process; he had slipped around the edges of the law, by being dead.

But he was dead.

It was the kind of argument which starts to hurt behind the eyes. She needed new facts, any new facts, to help her decide what best to do, and in the meantime, the only new and surprising fact was that Adam Heller had come back.

He repelled her. Very briefly, he had attracted her and she felt like a traitor to David's memory for that; and that feeling, in turn, infuriated her; and all that was a distraction and a trap. But he was the easiest way to discover information. Miss Aston knew no more. Simeon Ryder was in no position to help.

She could at least be civil on the plane.

'They fired you,' Rupert Griffier said. 'They don't want that leave of absence to end.'

'They're paying me as though I was sick,' Simeon said.

Rupert was genuinely puzzled. He lived from deal to deal, with the security of a comfortable store of shares in Griffier Ltd which the bank would take in any one of his emergencies; he never thought of wages. Perhaps Simeon Ryder had not been generously paid; perhaps, like upper servants, he worked for glory and out of habit. He might be hurting.

'I don't know why John Brown produced the information. It seems to be true, by the way.'

'Maurice and my father don't want to think so. They're like peasants in the Dordogne, afraid there'll be another heir to share the six hectares and the two goats.'

Simeon said: 'I suppose there are legal consequences.'

'Difficult to prove,' Rupert said. 'Not a lot of blood cr sperm left in great-grandfather.'

'We have the parish registers for the christening. He knew he would be recognized anyway, and so he took a chance on giving his name. In a way, it hid him. Anyone who said he was a Griffier and was registering some bastard child obviously couldn't be the Griffier everyone knows.'

'Talk to a lawyer. Get them to pay you off.'

'I was thinking about something else.'

Rupert drew his chair in more closely under the sharp white linen of the table. The ladies of the Fortnum and Mason's Soda Fountain were netted in their small talk, and paid no attention.

'John Brown is trying to shake some more shares loose,' Simeon said. 'That has to be it. I imagine he has called you already.'

'I wouldn't deny it. I wouldn't deny it to my father, either. He still can't grasp the idea that we're vulnerable.'

'It isn't going to work,' Simeon said. 'Brown won't pay for those shares because the Bank of England will never say he is a fit person to run a merchant bank. I don't care how honest and clever and open he is; he's one of the usual suspects.'

'You mean he's the wrong kind of Jew,' Rupert said. 'The new kind.'

'That really wasn't what I was thinking,' Simeon said. 'But perhaps that still doesn't help. Listen,' he waved away an offer of more coffee, 'we'll find an American buyer, Brown will scent a disputed bid and sell to the same Americans, there'll be a smooth deal. Everyone makes money.'

Rupert said: 'And you'd be suggesting this even if you were still sitting in your office at the bank? Would you?'

'I made my whole life at the bank,' Simeon said. 'I don't think your family expect me to be loyal any more, but I'm entitled to save the bank from the Griffiers.'

'Will anyone listen now you're out?'

'Officially, I'm not out.'

Rupert said: 'If you can make me money – '

'Trust me,' Simeon said. He had a quite new sense of trader's blood; he would do what the boys on the trading floor did, without scruple, just like them.

'Just don't get emotional,' Rupert said. 'Emotion gets in the way of everything.'

Simeon paid the bill. Outside, Piccadilly was splashed with rain and bright litter. Simeon needed the office; he had no practice for life outside the office. He did not know weekday mornings, their shape, what other people did. He was lost until he reached his club, which was only a few hundred yards away.

He had been in the habit of lunching in the early week, quite often, with a financial editor – to discuss the state of the City and its current gossip. He was not quite sure the invitation would stand now he had been expelled from the privilege of the bank.

But it did, and the two men sat down to a mess of haddock, followed by cabinet pudding; nursery food for two impeccable, but oddly self-contained men, with glassed-in passions and sharp minds.

Before, it had always been obvious what needed discretion, and what did not; there was no scandal to reveal at Griffier Ltd. Besides, the lunches were a most professional friendship; neither man burdened the other with anything inessential. But Simeon was angry still, and flustered; he wanted others to know what had happened to him, and why.

'Bizarre story,' his City Editor said, dubiously. 'Nobody could use it, of course. It's not the sort of thing that's supposed to happen in banks. As far as we're concerned, it's all slide rules and computer projections and good or bad decisions; no passion, no background. Of course,' he drank a little port, 'it does raise an obvious question. What on earth is John Brown up to? General troublemaking, or specific? Is this phase two of his campaign to make sure everyone thinks Griffier Ltd is funding his movie plans?'

'John Brown,' Simeon said, 'wants Griffier Ltd.'

The City Editor swallowed very suddenly; his quite ascetic face resembled a startled frog. 'You can't be serious,' he said.

'He'll stop at nothing,' Simeon said.

The City Editor was bothered by the melodrama in the air. 'He'll stop at the wrong price, or the wrong p/e, I presume? Or if someone tries to buy him out for billions?'

'Nothing,' Simeon said.

'But the Bank of England can't possibly accept him as a proper person to be engaged in the business of banking.'

'Can't they?'

The City Editor usually sipped his port; now, he gulped it. 'Tell me,' he said, when the drink was out of the way, 'how much of this can I write?'

Simeon sat back. The full story would only detract from the edited, credible version. For the time being, it was enough to start talk about John Brown and a major bank, his real intentions; the City columns would unite in shocked disapproval.

'I suppose,' the City Editor said, 'you are sure about all this? I mean, now you're not at the heart of things?'

Simeon Ryder crossed his fingers to be believed.

He paraded her as though he was proud of her, and Emma could do nothing about it, yet. She had to listen to his court, like a contract she was obliged to read; there was nothing personal in it.

'We have seats on the left of the plane,' he said, 'for the view of the islands. It can be quite spectacular.'

'When I was a child we used to come here most winters.'

‘When I was a child,’ Adam Heller said, ‘we went into the Alps. We went to the places the Swiss went to, not the grand places like Gstaad. We were on the slopes all day.’

Since she needed him to talk, she needed to listen; but his words were infected. He sat between her and the aisle; she could never quite stop noticing such things.

‘The light is always wonderful, even in the summer,’ he was saying. ‘The föhn comes and everything is clear. You think you can see through a window across the valley.’

She took a glass of champagne. The crew had decided Emma and Adam were very much together; he was so attentive, so concerned to amuse her. They decided, in a whisper, she was cold and difficult, an executive bitch. His solicitousness trapped her as well as any threats could, and everyone collaborated.

‘My father was in America, of course, or he was always travelling. Sometimes, he would come to Switzerland; he did a lot of business there in the 1970s. He was always flying in and out to talk to banks. He used to come with great suitcases, and go back with them empty.’ Adam wanted her to want to know. ‘I’m not a fool,’ he said. ‘I suppose he was making arrangements about the money he could not afford to lose.’

It was a fearful childhood: to be visited only as often as the bank required. Every trip, his father flew out again, and so, every time, Adam knew he must have done something wrong. He learned to calculate his way into people’s attention, and their affections. If they would only stay, they might learn to love him.

‘Tell me about your father,’ Emma said.

He had a child’s cunning. ‘You want to know, don’t you? Then why should I tell you?’ But he said it with such warmth and concern that the crew assumed he was wooing her.

'He's the one thing we have in common,' Emma said.

'He was a big man. He was very foreign. My mother was Swiss and she wasn't – exuberant. He would arrive with huge dreams and go away again quickly. They weren't married, of course. She was going to marry another man, but somehow he had a talent for coming back just when everything was fixed, and changing it. He liked that.'

'He had another family in America?'

'No,' Adam said. 'He had a wife, maybe he had married before, but I was his only son, I think. At least, he always told me that. I was the one who owed him duty, who had to live up to what he wanted. I felt like a soldier on a foreign posting, in his army.' Emma had a brief, hellish vision of life for Adam's mother, trying to make a life without James Drake, with this spy in the house always keeping her to just the standards that his father wanted. After a while, Adam had been the worst kind of ghost.

'I knew he could find oil,' Adam said. 'That was what he was famous for.' The steward passed with wine; Adam leaned across and asked Emma if, darling, she wanted a glass. When the wine was poured, she said to Adam: 'Don't even think of calling me darling again. Don't bloody dare!'

'I thought we were getting on,' Adam said, whining.

She stared out of the window. Unreasonable bitch, the crew thought; he was doing all he could.

She was thinking of poor Edward Griffier, and the way his suit of flesh seemed terribly rumpled when they laid him on the floor. She thought of David, and the job of identifying his smashed face. She thought of Maurice in Bayreuth, Rupert in Denver. On two out of four occasions, at least, Adam Heller had been there; but why had he been there?

She thought of him carrying out orders, but then she

knew that was too comforting a theory. Suppose this sour infatuation of his was not so new; suppose he had been following her. Then perhaps he created disasters wherever her path crossed that of her family. Avalon had burned, Edward had died, because she was there. She shivered. David had died because Adam knew her, not because of James Drake's orders. It made far too much sense.

'I had no family,' he was saying, 'not to say family. I expect you had a fine family?'

She did not want to understand him. She wanted to stop him. Nothing less would do.

She couldn't be rid of him. She couldn't ignore him; she needed his slips of the tongue. She tried to think of him as Adam Heller: agreeable, attractive, bright. He had a certain energy she could like very much, except for the chorus of the dead that slipped between the margins of her mind. Their soft reminders made her alarmed when she simply liked the shape of his body, or sometimes, his smile.

'Then,' Adam said, 'he went back to Denver – '

She realized she was struggling to pay attention because she was struggling to keep awake. The night before was full of smoke and horror. She had to concentrate; she could not. She was afraid of sleep. She imagined him covering her tenderly with a blanket, marking her as his property.

The reality of loss crammed in upon her, but she must not acknowledge it.

' – he wanted to save the mutual fund business. He wanted to be the man who did what the Griffiers could not do, and helped them out. He, James Drake, would save all the people's money. He had a bit of politician in him – '

She fought, but she felt herself rolling into sleep helplessly; she wrenched herself awake and for a while she could turn the pages of the in-flight magazine, and then the magazine fell from her fingers.

Adam Heller whispered to her: 'You should have stayed awake. I would have told you where to find him.' She half heard him, with resentment; it was a trick to spoil even her sleep, which was her only certain luxury.

The crew brought him blankets, and he covered her.

It was not the time for visitors. There was a pack of reporters clinging to the railings on Chester Square, like foul birds, Maurice thought. Going out to dinner meant evading them, trying not to make grotesque faces at their brilliant flashlights. He kept hoping they would get tired of his downfall.

'Ryder came to see me,' Rupert was saying. 'He was being very odd. He said John Brown was behind everything that had happened to us all, and I was on no account to sell my shares to him. He said he'd find an American buyer.'

'You won't sell to Brown,' Maurice said.

'Nothing's certain,' Rupert said.

'I want to be certain of that. Brown has done quite enough mischief.'

Rupert smiled. 'That brings us to the issue of your shares, brother. When the polizei come roaring up in their nice black Mercedes, you're not going to be quite such an ornament to the board. Are you?'

'This unfortunate incident – '

'I know you. And I gather your constituents gave you a tiny vote of confidence, and now they're looking for someone new.'

'They would not do anything like that.'

'They don't like losing. They won't tell you until Central Office comes up with a new candidate, I suppose. They must be combing their files.'

'I shall be in the House at the next election, and after.'

'The House has a lower threshold of shock than the bank, then. Because you can't run Griffier Ltd from a German jail. And the bank can't afford to have you there. Perhaps it would be better if you disposed of your shares – '

'I do not bail out at the first sign of trouble.'

'If you have the shares, you have the influence. Criminal influence.'

'I do not intend giving up my role.'

'I think it just gave you up, brother. The queue for lunch with Maurice Griffier is shorter every day. I gathered even poor Patience was bumped from a couple of her charity ball committees – no hard feelings, just had to be done, you understand.'

'Patience is concerned about my welfare. She – '

'The fact is,' and Rupert was now enjoying himself shamelessly, 'that I am the senior member of our generation. I'm the only one outside jail or Hollywood. Unless, that is, you have a quite brilliant lawyer.'

Maurice snorted.

'So we have to discuss what happens to your shares, what attitude we take to Mr Brown and whether or not we take the good Ryder's advice and look around for a white knight to rescue us.'

'White knights are expensive when you don't even have a dragon in sight.'

'We have a dragon,' Rupert said. 'Think what happened to Uncle Edward, as well.'

'A terrible business. Probably one of his boyfriends – '

'The question,' Rupert said, 'is when you ought to give me your proxy.'

'Absolutely not. Out of the question. Your record over the years – '

'At least I've never been indicted. Mentioned in *Private Eye*, perhaps, but never thrown out of the House of Commons.'

'I have not been thrown out of the House.'

'And how long do you think you can survive? Kidnapping is what terrorists and gangsters do. It's not even white-collar crime. It's déclassé.'

'I have nothing to discuss.'

'Even if I sell my shares, and John Brown follows me, and we make damn sure you have a dragon to worry about? You really think Father is fly enough to beat off an American raider?'

'I shall not say you would never do such a thing,' Maurice said. 'I have known you too long.'

'Let me back into the bank, or I start the selling of the bank,' Rupert said. 'If I don't get back, you all go. You don't think a new owner would tolerate the same old family board, do you?'

Maurice said: 'Don't be preposterous.'

After Rupert left, thin-lipped, Maurice sat in the first-floor drawing room, looking out into the square from the shadowed side of the room, so the reporters could not see him. He told himself the troubles were now deep within his family, and nothing was sure. He seemed happy this was so, as though it blunted the cut of his own mistakes.

His lawyers called to say they had arranged for his arrest, discreetly at an office in Gray's Inn. He left the house the back way in his wife's Honda; he took pride in evading the scruffy and patient ratpack at the front. He could find pride in the saddest evasion.

But there was a reporter and a cameraman in Gray's Inn. He came out between two diplomatic policemen, with a face as bleak as February. He knew he should wave and protest his innocence, make it seem as if this was some trivial misunderstanding.

His first public life had died in his lawyers' rooms. Now he had to live a second, of court testimony and tabloid headlines and mocking cartoons. He could not even lie; if he lied, he lost his chance to seem a hero. The policemen told him the extradition hearings would have to be in Horseferry Road, close to the Ministries, close to Parliament.

He thought he knew what went wrong. Somewhere in that great adventure on the border, he had stopped believing. For a moment, he was not quite convinced that he was the man to live such things.

He watched the girls in the street rather than listen to the cops. He would have liked to pray like his father, to an orderly God.

She heard the screening room, down the corridor, spilling at last; there was the awful quiet which comes when friends have seen a bad movie, not respectful but dulled. The security man came to check who was still working, the projectionist came to cadge a Diet Coke from the last of the secretaries, who was only there because Emma was there. Very soon, Emma would have to go.

There was nobody in the company apartment; she had checked. She asked for a car, and she gathered her papers together.

'You can go, Sandra,' she said to the secretary. 'I'm sorry I kept you this late.'

'No problem,' Sandra said. 'I got a date with a guy from Rio and their digestions don't even kick in until midnight.'

She called security to lock the studio offices behind her, and she waited beyond the glass doors for the lift. She was tired, and she could make out in the shine of the corridor chrome that she looked tired. She tried to avoid the elevator mirrors.

At the fourteenth floor, the doors flew open on the dark. There was a corridor, and there was no movement. She stood warily at the back of the cage. She felt very alone. She thought she could hear someone moving but it was only the machinery of the elevator settling in the shaft above, snake after snake of coiled cable. After a minute, the doors slipped together and the cage went down. It was quite long enough for her to remember.

The doors opened on the grand ground-floor atrium; she hardly wanted to leave the cage. She imagined David waiting there, big and warm; the touch of him would make sense of her. But he could not be there, and it was her fault; she was stung red and hot with the memory. She could have saved his life, she was sure. There was something she should have noticed, or seen or done.

She stopped the doors from bouncing shut, and she walked out into the atrium. The ficus trees dappled the floors with shadows, and it seemed a terrible distance to where the doorman sat in a pale pond of light.

She did not look back until she came to the fresh, kind air of the night. She knew she was close to exhaustion, and she let the limo driver hold open the door with his ten-dollar manners. Everyone was civil; she felt protected by their manners, almost safe enough to sleep.

She walked down the corridor of the building on Central Park West, where the carpet spread around her on the floor and walls, like beige moss. She turned left.

She thought at first she had stumbled on a new grave. There were day lilies and white lilies and piles of red and pink roses, still bundled and wet from the florist, smelling cheaply, heaped up against the door of the apartment in high, promiscuous colour. They might have delighted her, from a lover; but there were far too many of them. They were too lovely to kick aside. They imposed.

She put down her bags and she made a path through the flowers; she slammed the door shut behind her. She closed the Yale, the Medeco, the police lock.

He knows where I am, she thought. He's been here,

in the past half-hour; the stems on the flowers are still wet.

She opened each room of the apartment cautiously. The air had settled like dust since the maid left that morning. There was the inevitable message from LA on the answering machine, but it did not need an answer until the next morning. She sat down with a glass of seltzer.

There was a note that had been pushed under the door, and very nearly under the rug. 'I shall see you later,' it said.

She had to stay awake despite the pain behind her eyes. She used to be grateful when David called on nights like these, and the sound of his voice connected her to feeling again, and saved her from the dry thoughts of a business night. Tonight, she was afraid the phone would ring; it would be Adam. And he was the only one who knew how things really stood. He, the enemy, had become the only one with whom she could be honest, like a lover.

She ordered dinner from the building's restaurant, and, in time, it came on a trolley. She picked open all the locks to let the waiter in. He lifted the silvery cover from the platter, and there were roses and lilies.

'They are for you,' Adam Heller said, filling the door. 'You must accept them, please.'

The waiter took his tip, smiled, and changed the flowers for a platter of fish and a salad. He set a table, and withdrew; but Adam Heller settled himself in an armchair.

'I just wanted to be here,' he said.

Emma pulled apart a piece of swordfish with a fork. She lacked a dictionary mind, but she remembered the root of the word 'obsessed': from the Latin, meaning to besiege or be besieged. A siege trapped both sides, Adam and Emma equally.

'How did you get this address?'

He said: 'Your receptionist told me who was the company florist, and the company florist thought it was most romantic. You had such a terrible loss, and now there was a new young man.'

There were thin beans bound in a bundle on her plate, and a little boat of sweet potato puree. She paid them careful attention. She thought it was blasphemy that he mentioned losing David.

'They like you,' Adam said.

'Would you rather I had no friends?'

'I want to be your friend.'

'You could call me tomorrow morning, we could have breakfast somewhere. I need sleep, now.'

He seemed interested by this idea. He said, brightly: 'But you did not like the flowers?'

'There were too many.'

'Would you have liked the flowers if there was only a bunch or two?'

She said nothing.

Very loudly, he said: 'Would you have liked them? Would you?'

'It's very late,' she said.

'If I go, you never will find James Drake. I just walk out of that door.'

'Walk,' she said. 'Walk now.'

'You promise about tomorrow?'

When he had gone, she called the doorman. Nobody was to be admitted; if anyone came calling, the doorman was to call the police. She went to bed and lay there, turning, always rolling out of balance or lying on an arm. Her body seemed as full of spasms as her thoughts.

She killed David. She killed Edward. They died because she was there, because this creature Adam Heller had a lickerish fascination for her. And she must be kind enough to Heller to catch his father and his master. She had no bed in which to rest, no easy thoughts to think.

The damn phone rang. Because it was only midnight, she took the call: it was possible, just possible, that some Los Angeles maven was calling at nine in their evening, Pacific time. She was still on the studio team.

But the voice was Rupert, from London, thick with early morning and the consequences of the clubs. 'I'm getting out,' he said. 'I'm not waiting to be attacked. Maurice won't have me in the bank, and Maurice has been arrested and it makes no damn sense any more.'

'It's very late in London,' Emma said.

'You ought to do the same. Simeon wants us to sell to some big American bank.'

She closed her eyes. 'It's the wrong timing,' she said. She was sensible, like a mother, sister, wife. 'If we sell now, with all this news, we're the losers.'

'I don't care what I lose. I've lost money before.' He had panic like a cancer, and he wanted a knife of an answer.

'We can't get out,' she said, sweetly, reasonably. 'You'd still be a Griffier. You wouldn't be safe.'

'I don't know who we're fighting. I don't know what to do. The man is in Denver and Barbados and Germany. He fakes a bank in the Caribbean and a kidnapping in Bayreuth.'

'He has nothing else to do.'

'It could be bloody anybody,' Rupert said.

He rang off before she could answer. The call had shocked her awake, like iced water. She rummaged in sponge bags for some kind of chemical peace, a Mogadon from months ago. She sat in the drawing room, looking at the movie posters ranked neutrally on the walls.

The door bell rang.

The waiter, perhaps, or security checking.

The bell sounded out again.

She went very quietly to the door, and she slipped the spyhole cover. The hallway was a ruin of colour, gaudy like candy and snow. In the middle of it all, Adam stood.

She assumed he had left the building earlier, but he could have waited on any of the back stairs. She had a vision of his sheer patience, hunkered down on cold concrete, under the greeny white of emergency lights.

'I know where James Drake is,' he said, 'if I can see you.' It was a child's proposition, but a man's threat.

'I can see your shadow,' he said.

She knew what he had to do next. He had to reach into his pocket and take out a handgun. It was a shock to see that the gun was real: long and dull. It caught on the fabric of his coat, and she had time to throw herself down.

The shot was muffled, like something distant; it lacked the resonance of shots on soundtracks. She fancied he had turned the gun on himself, and was lying among the old blood reds of the roses. But when she looked up at the door, the metal around the Yale lock had been sprung.

She called security.

'Nobody came by me, lady,' the doorman said. 'You can be sure of that. Sleep well.'

'There is a man in the corridor with a gun.'

'Lady, you're tired. Excited. Get some sleep.'

'He shot out one of the locks.'

'Just make sure the door's locked,' security said.

Adam was rattling the door by its handle. The door no longer seemed solid to her. And it lay in a dog-leg of corridor where nobody looked, not even security.

She dialled 911 for the police. She heard a recorded message, and then a live voice. The cops said to call building security and it was after midnight, which was a busy time, but, hell, they'd be there when they could. Keep the doors locked, the man said.

The door bell rang again.

'I only wanted to talk,' Adam said. 'You could talk to me.'

'I want to sleep,' Emma said.

'The door's damaged. You wouldn't be safe,' Adam said. She saw herself in a high-angled shot, the bare-shouldered heroine braced against the doom that was waiting for her. In her reasonable world, this could not happen; there was no carnage of flowers out there, no man with a gun, and the cylinder of the lock did not project uselessly from the door.

'You know who I am. You could let me in.'

He fired a single shot through the centre of the door's top panel, just above the spyhole. It could as easily have made its blunt way into her skull.

She crept to the door. 'I'm opening,' she said.

He had flowers in his hand. The phone began to ring, and he told her to ignore it. He spoke the lines from some romantic scene, carrying a gun.

'It could be LA on the phone,' she said.

'You work too hard.'

He sat on the sofa like an awkward boy. The gun was out of sight, but it was present like another guest.

'I wanted you to have the flowers,' he said. 'I didn't want to leave them in the hallway.'

'Why did you come back?'

'I am looking after you. You see, the cops don't come and the security men don't come, even when I fire a gun in the corridor. That's terrible.'

'What do you want?'

'I like to be close to you.'

'I'd like to find my dressing gown.' He nodded, and she wrapped herself; when she came back to the living room, he had closed the door on to the corridor and chained it.

'You can sleep,' he said. 'I'm here.'

He had taken off his coat. She was exhausted, and she wanted the sweet escape of sleep, but she did not want it as his gift . . .

'You have to sleep,' he said.

She lay under the sheets, wrapped in her dressing gown, curled up as a small animal tries to make itself invisible by closing its eyes. He pushed the bedroom door open, like a chaperon. After half an hour, when she had slept fitfully, she woke to find him sitting on a chair by the bed. Sometimes she could feel his breath when he came close.

He tugged the sheets off her suddenly. She lay in the fine armour of her dressing gown, too tired to fight. She tried to huddle on to the opening of the gown, hiding the tie in the belt, so he would at least have to turn her and wake her before he could make any other move.

He sat, and he waited. He waited for her to admit she was awake. She tried not to squeeze her eyes tight shut, and give herself away. She wanted him to touch her, so she could fight.

He turned on the lights. She blinked for a moment. Her dressing gown had worked open as she turned and her nightdress rode up; he was standing over her. She had not meant to give him any privileges.

He took off his jacket. She understood; with some odd sense of propriety he had stayed at her bedside dressed for the street. Now the propriety was over. He took off his tie. She was dressed enough to spice her body. He could warm her cold body to death.

He held his tie between his fingers, and let it fall between her legs. Her eyes were wide open now, and blank. He wanted to see fear; she would not give him that satisfaction. He moved the silk of the tie to the inside of her legs, very gently. Her mind was no longer wedded to her nerves; she resisted.

He bent over her and pulled her nightdress up. He had a doctor's eyes. He expected no more reaction than a stunned animal might make; he was absorbed by looking. He let his tie swing across her nipples, as though the feather pressure was bound to bring her to life.

'I'm not going to do anything,' he said. He thought that was reassuring. He wondered if his father would approve, at last, and tell him so; he had never been sure about the other girls.

There was a thunder of knocking on the door. Adam looked petulant and silly. A big, raw voice bellowed: 'Open up! Police!'

She lay quite still.

'Are you OK, miss?'

He jabbed a finger painfully into her ribs. 'Tell them you're fine,' he said.

She shook her head.

The pounding on the door stopped. The corridor was awash with dying flowers and there were shot marks on the door. Surely the cops must break down the door.

'Open up!'

The wood began to splinter. A hand followed the axe through the door, slipped the chain and turned the Medeco. Two cops, guns out, nerves raw, saw a dressed man standing by a bed on which was stretched a woman, almost bare. They aimed their guns at the man.

'Down!'

He was on the floor, out of her sight. The younger cop came over and covered her with the sheets; it seemed a gesture for his comfort as much as her shame.

'Did he?' he said. 'I mean, would you like to talk to a woman?'

'He didn't rape me. Not that way.'

'Have you got friends you could go to?'

He held a blanket around her and she shivered helplessly.

'You done good,' the cop said. 'He didn't do no harm.'

She couldn't shower before going to the precinct. She dressed as quickly as she could.

In the precinct station, in a little back room which smelled of yesterday's smoke and burgers, she asked the policewoman: 'Did he give an address?'

'I can't tell you that.'

'I don't know much about him. He just forced his way in. I'm not going to track him down.'

'Yeah,' the woman said. She was kind, knowing what the city did to women daily, but she was sceptical. She wondered if the fancy British lady had got in over her head, and turned proper after the very last minute. 'Still,' she said, 'you have to see the charge sheet.'

It was a hotel address, of course. 'We get the real address from the hotel,' the policewoman said. 'That is, if he gave a real address.'

'Thank you,' Emma said.

She wanted to kill him. She would have to get him out. She wondered why she had ever thought he would tell the truth to the cops.

The morning hurt her eyes.

'We go travelling,' James Drake said. 'A European vacation.'

Helen, the nurse, waited to hear the catch. She looked like a hopeful sparrow.

'We go to Amsterdam for a while,' Drake said. 'Close enough to London, but it doesn't raise any awkward questions.'

'You don't have a passport.'

'Oh yes, I do. I have a passport in the name of Jude Klein, consultant. Not everyone in the State Department is a degenerate Commie bastard.' He did not intend to be ironic.

'I thought you'd let me go skiing for a day or two. Aspen, maybe.'

Drake put back his head and laughed, unkindly. 'You, in Aspen, girl? You'll be better off in Europe. Nobody knows what class you are in Europe.'

'I'm as classy as any of those other girls.'

'That's saying nothing. You be grateful I want you along at all. I could throw you out, you know. I'm a well man.'

'I know things,' Helen said.

'Sure. But do you understand them?'

'You have the Griffier family where you want them. They're falling over each other like pigs in a small sty.'

'Good. And what do you think in your pretty, empty little head is the point of all that?'

'After what they did to you – '

'No, girl. I mean, after what I do to them, what then?'

'I understand that,' the girl said, bravely.

'I wouldn't bet my life on it. I sure as hell wouldn't bet my balls on it.'

The girl scampered to the phone. She hated the moments when he was angry at his static world, frustrated because his sluggish blood could still shut down sectors of his body without warning. He hit out, and he was still so clumsy she didn't know whether to save her ass and get out of range, as she easily could, and risk making his anger serious.

'This is the Drake office,' she said. 'And residence.'

'Give me that!'

She watched telephone calls carefully, for clues to how he would next behave. This time, he was suddenly glassed in and unblinking. He said nothing.

When he put down the phone, he was sombre. 'I had a son once,' he said.

'You have a son called Adam.'

'He got himself put away for rape and assault, and with a handgun. He got put away by goddamn Emma goddamn Griffier. He let them fight back.'

'They still don't know how to find you.'

'He gave the Amsterdam address at his hotel.'

'Then we don't have to go to Amsterdam.' The hope in her eyes was sad. 'We could go to the Rockies. I could go skiing. We could go to some of those fancy eating places. I could – '

'We go to Amsterdam. We put on a show for Miss Emma Griffier, and all the rest of them.'

He found the London number for Griffier Ltd, and he asked for Sir Alistair Griffier. He said it was Jude Klein calling.

'Of course,' Sir Alistair said. 'We would be absolutely delighted to see you here. We could offer you lunch at the bank; it's quite a tradition for our honoured clients and associates. Any day, any day.'

Drake said to his girl, so softly it could have passed for affection: 'The bitch don't win, girl. You see how the bitch don't win.' He stroked her hair; she felt calm and hopeless. 'You see, girl, very soon it won't be personal any more with the Griffiers. I'll have won, and I take my profits. Only Miss Emma Griffier is different.'

The girl smiled up at him.

'So we deal with her,' James Drake said.

Her smile hesitated.

10

Angry, John Brown was pure threat. He hardly moved. He spoke with great clarity, his accent scaling the social register, class by class, as he talked. His staff moved softly, for fear of detonating him.

'We will sue them all,' he said. 'All of them.'

His aide-de-camp drew himself to a polished height. He had once been a Fellow of All Souls, the kind of professor who is consulted, listed once in a major Canadian newspaper among the hundred future leaders of the world, and he had been a junior minister. He was insulated against most shocks.

'I think that might not be productive,' he said, carefully.

The brows of John Brown had the menace of a dark wood. 'They'll pay,' he said.

'They haven't said you are not a fit person to control the affairs of a bank. They've said the Bank of England refuses to say that you are. That's hardly surprising, because the Bank would never make a public statement in advance of a bid.'

'It comes to the same thing.'

'Then demand a correction.'

'The damage is done. The mistake will be made again. I want them to know it's too damned expensive to mention my name.'

'But you are known – '

'Known, and liked, I think. The English understand a man like me.'

'Yes,' the aide said. 'I suspect they do.'

He scuttled quietly from the room and went to his

office, doorless to stop the very thought of conspiracy. He thought for a while about who would get the shares in Griffier Ltd, and whether they were held in any of the trading companies; he wrote some notes, but he had learned the steel secretaries knew what was said on the phone without listening, and what was written without anything so vulgar as steaming open letters or stealing the carbons. He scrumpled the paper, and put it cautiously in his pocket.

He could hear the steel ladies cooing. 'Mr Brown would appreciate a moment or two – ' 'Mr Brown would simply like to clarify the Governor's feelings – ' 'If the Chancellor has a spare moment – '

He had thought John Brown might, this time, buy respectability, and, with it, peace. He had thought of Griffiers a little like an Embassy, something to give substance and protocol to the life of an aide-de-camp. He was going to be disappointed again.

He began a position paper which Brown had not yet asked for. He had the civil servants' faith that longhand is a form of thought, and he took up a pen.

He wrote: 'In Britain today – ' He caught himself chewing the end of the pen.

'It is a poisoned gift,' Simeon Ryder said.

Emma lay on a rigid *chaise-longue* which had been built to perfect a lady's posture. Officially, she was working from home for a week or two. She did not tell Simeon how much they had in common.

'What gift?' she said. It was awkward to hold the telephone at this angle; the receiver slipped.

'I am the executor of Edward's will,' Simeon said, 'which is a little embarrassing in the circumstances. As you can imagine.'

She shifted carefully; her bones against the thin padding on the boards could be most painful. 'You said there was a gift,' she said.

'According to Edward's will, you inherit his entire shareholding in Griffier Ltd. He doesn't explain why, but there are no encumbrances, no entails, none of the Bleak House stuff. You own the shares absolutely.'

'God,' Emma said.

'You realize of course this means you have a greater share of the bank than your father and brother put together?'

'I'm not sure I want that.'

'And I don't suppose the family would want the scandal of trying to upset the will – unless, of course, you decided to sell.'

'I'm not good at decisions just now.'

She tugged at the phone; she turned against the cushions. Nothing seemed more pressing than being comfortable.

'It looks as though John Brown will pull out,' Simeon said. 'The papers have roasted the very idea of his controlling a bank.'

'Fine. Do you have a buyer, Simeon?'

'I might,' Simeon said. 'I could try to place the shares. There are dozens of American and Japanese players who want a piece of London. You know that.'

'And father? I thought you fell out with him over just this?'

'He likes to have things in his gift. He likes to hold territory until he can cede it gracefully. He has good Colonial Office attitudes.'

'I don't have the energy to fight my father.'

'But you have to preserve the value of what you've just inherited. If you won't take the responsibility, take the income.'

'Do I have any choice about taking Edward's gift?'

'Hardly.'

'And selling out immediately seems rather brutal. Rather ungrateful.'

'It's a practical matter.'

'I don't get emotional about money,' Emma said, tartly. 'I've always had it.'

'There may not be a lot of time.'

'Things falling apart without you, Simeon? Is that it?'

'Yes,' he said. 'I'm not an arrogant man, but I know the workings of that place. They have a very good trading floor, but everyone wants good traders just now, and traders are fickle. They'll run to bigger money at a more settled institution. Or else they'll do what the Wall Street traders did: they'll pitch to take the power from the men in suits, the men like your father who play golf with people. Griffier Ltd can't stand desertions, and it can't stand more civil war.'

'I know about war,' Emma said.

'You can't simply sit and wait – '

The *chaise-longue* was cracking her spine, brutal as a doctor. She put down the phone and immediately it rang again. She sat up, business-like.

From the studio, her secretary said: 'God, I'm sorry to disturb you.'

'Nothing can disturb me. Someone just gave me ten per cent of a bank.'

'Well,' her secretary said, 'that might help. You ought to know there's a lot of talk about the Turkey project. This morning's meeting said you didn't pay enough attention to it, and now it's over budget. They seem to have forgotten you didn't want to make the script in the first place.'

'They're good at forgetting.'

'If you went down and read the riot act to the producers – '

'They're down at Fox, aren't they?'

'I don't know the stage number. I just think you ought to be seen down there. I'll make sure everyone knows.'

'You're a wonder.'

'It's my job. Real life did enough to you.'

Emma masked herself for executive talks, bright-eyed and formal, and she drove too fast down to Motor and Pico. The guard beamed at her, but she put that down to a little lust in his afternoon mind: she passed the Public Library and the Astoria Gardens from the standing set for New York City – in her life, cities were horribly interchangeable; the details might as well be fake – and she parked sedately. It was not her studio; her name was not painted here on a prized stretch of tarmac. She watched her manners.

The sound stage doors were slightly open, the red light unlit. Immediately inside the doors the two producers were working the phones, one each; they knew enough about the studio's concern to play busy and unavailable. But she simply stood by them, until they smiled awkwardly, like little boys caught. 'We ought to have a talk,' she said.

There was a gulch of sun between the sound stages, and she knew enough to make them stand looking into the light. She wondered which they would respect more: the largest shareholder of a great bank or the wrath of the studio.

'I know,' said the senior producer, a slight man with clever feet like a boxer, 'you've been under a lot of pressure just recently. We could talk this over later, when it won't upset the crew.'

'The crew know perfectly well what's going on,' Emma said. 'I don't have time to play games. I'm not crazy about the rushes, I wasn't crazy about the script or the property in the first place. But you said you could make the movie seriously cheap, and if that breaks down, there's nothing left. The movie isn't worth making.'

'Everything is under control.'

'And if you can't finish the movie, I presume you have a good story for your investors. Because we're ready to pull the plug from this project and the sooner we do that, the more we save. You don't have a lot of time.'

'I thought you were the one who cares,' said the second producer, a classic Californian looker, polished and tended like a second-hand car on sale. 'I thought you were the nurturer.'

'I don't like being wrong, so I look after myself.'

She could see that the first producer was screwing up his eyes, trying to make out something or someone moving in the alley behind her. He sensed lawyers; he had an instinct for writs.

'We need creative space,' the second producer said.

'Creative space isn't the problem,' Emma said. 'Keep inside the budget and I'll give you Nebraska for creative space – '

The first producer was sure about the lawyer now, although she was a sweet lawyer, fleet and brown. He was not sure about two walls of men with dark glasses, and the slighter man between them. He thought about writs, debts, and the Mob. He grew restive.

'Miss Griffier?' The lawyer bounded up to Emma, like a young deer, and the posse followed.

Emma turned. She knew the desperate effort in the young lawyer's face, the kind you see when reporters feed a microphone to a passing star, or salesmen come to pitch some long-distance phone company. She turned further, and she saw that the lanky man between the muscled guards was Adam Heller. He looked hopeful. The deer said she would like to talk in private.

'In a matter of this delicacy – '

Emma said: 'You can make an appointment.'

The producers caught each other's eye, grateful for an intermission and quite possibly for salvation. 'We could talk later, Emma,' they said. 'We can make just one more shot this afternoon.'

Emma walked down the alley with the deer. A chow

wagon of armoured chrome stood glinting at the corner; she stopped and bought mineral water.

'I can't believe you're here with Heller,' she said.

'I wanted you to see my client,' the deer said. 'He faces very serious charges, on very skimpy evidence. I just wanted to see if you really wanted to go ahead with this.'

Emma frowned. The girl could not possibly know how clever she was, or why Emma needed Adam free.

'You understand,' the lawyer said, 'what happens when we get into court. We lead evidence about you – your character, and anything that's ever happened to you. We talk about your sex life, whether you ever took drugs, your dead lover, whether you pick up men in trains in Germany and then again on planes back from the Caribbean. That kind of thing.'

'I know all that.'

'You put my client in the dock, and we'll turn the whole issue round and put you on trial. I don't think that would be good for the studio, do you? Or for your career?'

'I thought sisterhood was strong.'

'Clienthood is stronger. We're working women.'

'I'm not afraid of anything that might happen in court.'

'With your name, and your job, the headlines could be awesome, really awesome.' The lawyer girl was sweet as a nut in her talk. 'And do you really want Adam to go to jail?'

'You shouldn't have brought him here.' It was true that she felt a rush of bile at the sight of the man.

'You were friends, weren't you? We've developed information that you were friends, close friends, over a period of time.'

'We know each other.'

'So can you look at him and tell me he did anything which justifies – '

'He reminds me what I went through. He reminds me what he did to my family.'

'My client did nothing to your family. You wouldn't be accusing him to make up for some imagined slight, would you? Would you, Miss Griffier?'

'There are two cops to give evidence, and me.'

'You should talk to him.'

'I didn't think they gave bail in cases like this.'

'He travels with court officers, in special circumstances.'

She told herself that Adam had no power over her in the presence of the guards. He seemed lost and shambling, hoping to use charm.

'You wasted a journey,' she said.

'My father was furious,' Adam said. 'He said I'd lost to you, that you'd been too clever.'

'I wasn't clever. I was a victim.'

'But I didn't – '

'I don't want to hear excuses.'

'My father said he wants to see you, face to face. He said he admired what you had done, in a way.'

Emma said: 'If you're serious, leave your father's address at the studio gatehouse.'

'I could give it to you – '

'Nothing in front of your guards and the lawyer. Just leave off a note.'

'And you'll think again about the charges?' He was truly afraid of court and jail, she could see; he reckoned his life in the orderly way of a good Swiss citizen, ashamed of impropriety. He must think killing a lesser thing than shame.

Emma turned to the lawyer. 'We don't have anything to discuss.'

And she stormed back to the producers. Nobody was going to slip out of her professional remit, not even for the most terrible personal hurt. The producers sensed gossip in the incident, perhaps of a useful kind; they were trying to define it. Then, they turned their attention to this clever, furious, meticulous woman who had better things to do than lecture them again.

At the gatehouse, much later, Emma collected a scribbled note. It gave an address among the merchant houses on Herengracht in Amsterdam. She called the New York policewoman who had taken her statement, and asked if Adam left this address at his hotel; the woman said she'd say if the address was wrong, and said nothing.

She looked at the note again. It was signed: 'Respectfully, Adam.'

'It's your choice, Emma,' Garrity was saying, playing the boss with conviction, 'I'm afraid.'

She knew he made up his sincerity out of his taste for drama. He was the psychiatrist who dealt with Eve, Marcus Welby using symptoms for a plot. She noticed how each leaf of the ficus had been washed that morning, so it would look casually healthy.

'I hear talk in the corridors,' the boss was saying. 'People always wondered about a Griffier in the movie business. They thought you'd be an amateur, I suppose, or you got your job by trailing money. People say these things.'

'I know.'

Garrity paced on the drawing-room carpet and between the lush, white chairs; his office was his true home. 'Now I realize you've had – a lot happening over the past year. I realize you've been in a lot of pain. But the trouble is, to the others it just looks like family business and it's taking you away from the studio. You're not available, you're not working – '

'I've handled everything,' Emma said. Quite abruptly, she knew that the boss was accusing, not counselling.

'We've got the Turkey film under control, I'm sure. I've talked – '

'You haven't been here,' the boss said. 'The life of the studio is here. We make decisions together. We develop ideas together. And you – you've been away on family business.'

She said nothing. To put up a defence would be an admission that the charges meant something; she could not afford that.

'This would be a problem,' the boss was saying, 'for anyone. But if your family is the Griffiers, then it looks like you get privileges. People work through burying their fathers here. They work through divorce and finding the bodies of their murdered children. They're starting to ask why you're so different.'

She said: 'Times are rough for rich people, too.'

The boss said: 'Nobody believes that.' He put out a hand. 'I'm hurt,' he said, 'you even suggested going to Europe. I'm truly sorry you don't understand that you really don't have privilege here. You're not some fucking aristocrat, Emma, not here. Mike Ovitz is aristocracy around here. Maybe Ray Stark.'

'There's work for me to do,' Emma said. 'I simply want to get on with my work.'

'As for Miss Nova Aston,' the boss said, his logic bending, 'we can't have studio chiefs begging elderly stars to take a part. And taking a week off in the islands to do it.'

Emma said: 'It was your decision. You gave the order.' But she knew that only the person being fired is ever responsible.

'You decide, Emma. You go to Europe, I can't guarantee what will happen while you're away. Stay here, show yourself, keep working and maybe things will calm down.' He smiled, a beatific and doctorly smile that was quite devoid of feeling. 'I say this is a family, and it is, but it's also a machine. I get to replace the defective part.'

She left his office, shaking. Sometimes, she had let herself be fooled by his amiability; she had respect, even affection for the man. But she knew she had been cut, and she was waiting for the walls of the wound to part and the blood to flow.

She said to her secretary: 'We'd better do lunch. You could order something in.'

And at lunch, she said: 'Book me a flight to London. And, please, start looking for another job.'

She had nothing to say because all her thoughts seemed like lunacy. She was going to kill a dead man. She was cosseting the man who had killed her lover. She was in mourning for everything that had been stripped away from her: love, career, the warm and workable side of her family, the service of Simeon Ryder, and a comfortable position on the fringes of a great tradition. Now she only had money, and herself.

She couldn't spend the night in an apartment where David had once been. He was a shadow on the stairs, waiting to kiss her. He was reading on the couch; she could see the warm hollow where he lay. Dead, he had an absolute command of her emotions, more almost than when he was alive. She hurt from lack of him.

And so she slept in the decorous quiet of the Connaught Hotel, which was enough like a fortress and enough like an island to let her think. Obviously, she had to go to Herengracht, to the house where James Drake could be found; she had no choice. She should go soon, because Drake would move again, tracking his mischief wherever it would do most harm. But she wanted to make a kind of peace with her family. In a year she had gone from their exile to their champion, and they could barely tolerate either.

In the very early morning, she could no longer find the exact divide between dreams and thinking; she began to wake. She stretched her arm out first, and then her body. She moved across the sheets, expecting to find him. She came fully awake, shocked by the cold cotton, and she threw herself out of bed.

She drove early down to Easterford, before full light, when the bare hedgerows were like black lines scribbled on the margins of the road and the shadows were not yet strong enough to define the buildings as she passed. In this ghost of a world, the winter sun began to pick out high trees and church spires; there was a faint, low mist scuttling across the ground. The gates to Easterford, solid as they were, had an impermanent air, like a dream that would fade away with light. She nodded to the non-specific saints in their niches, and she drove furiously between the dark, slick rhododendrons. It was the part of the driveway that always scared her as a child.

The lights in the house gave it a lop-sided look, half alive. She walked directly to the breakfast room, and through it to the kitchen. The housekeeper stood at the stove, tending a skillet of bacon; she was startled, and delighted, and she sat Emma down with a cup of coffee, and she said how well, and how brown she looked and what a pleasure it was.

Emma said: 'I thought my father would be up.'

The housekeeper looked at her watch: seven o'clock.

'He'll be at prayers,' she said.

'It's funny how he keeps religion up in the attic,' Emma said, 'like the Catholics used to keep their priest. It's as though he wanted nobody to know.'

'It's a private matter,' the housekeeper said, in a disapproving tone which suggested she thought it was lucky for him it stayed so.

Emma finished her coffee and went walking. The curtains had been drawn back in the grander rooms of the house, but the light was still meagre. She saw the friendly, doggedly shabby furniture, unpolished so the finer pieces would not glitter and grab attention. Everything had a worn, habitual look; nothing was sharp or new. She knew that was an affectation.

This library was a room for taking tea, not Edward's serious room where the past was kept on shelves to prove a man's identity. This drawing room invited large, blond dogs to wallow on the carpets. On one of the stairs, Florence had hung a hack Victorian canvas called 'The Exchange' in which dealers milled, under implausibly tall ceilings, about their business in a trail of paper, some clutching little ledger books, some hailing and greeting and shaking hands, some shouting across the general fray. It was a little acknowledgement to the source of the money which built this house, but only to the workings of an old institution. She could not imagine a broad canvas of Qotrons and terminals, keyboards and telephones, chaos in a world of wires.

'Didn't expect you,' Sir Alistair said.

He had great authority still. He hugged his daughter and offered breakfast.

'You know about Edward's little joke?' he said, taking an egg.

'I don't know what you mean.'

'I'd have thought Simeon would have rushed to tell you. Edward left you all of his shares in Griffier Ltd. You're my major shareholder now, one way and another.'

'I didn't think that was a joke,' Emma said.

Her father divided the egg neatly. 'He always promised the shares would not be left outside the family. Technically, he kept his word.'

She said: 'I don't quite follow you.' She reached for the coffee pot, and felt the impractical weight of Georgian silver.

Her father said: 'Of course, you'll give me your proxy for Edward's shares. We can't complicate things any more.'

'I might want to vote for myself.'

'Your interests are safe with me. You know that.'

'I don't doubt it,' she said.

'Then you'll sign the papers once Edward's will is through probate?'

'I'm not good at business at this hour.'

'I thought it was all breakfast meetings in California,' her father said.

'You forget I've changed time zones,' Emma said. 'This all seems like a late supper to me.'

'Then you can make decisions,' her father said triumphantly.

She asked: 'Where's mother?'

'She'll be down later. You should come into the City with me; they're taking out the partners' room for some museum, and there'll be a ceremony of sorts for the public relations johnnies. I'd take you to lunch, but I have an appointment already.'

'I'll go up to mother,' she said.

'You could sign the papers at the bank,' her father shouted after her.

She asked herself why the issue was so urgent. He must feel under immediate threat, and since shareholders do not decide which loan to approve, which company to support, the threat must be to his own position. He must want to be sure she could not vote him out.

She crossed the corridor to her mother's room, and slipped inside.

'Thank God!' Lady Florence Griffier was already on the phone, surrounded by a heap of thin novels and some disorganized, out of season roses. She beamed at Emma; she dropped her pince-nez from the bridge of her nose;

she gestured to the chair by the bed and mouthed that Emma should ring for more coffee.

'Thank God!' she said, again. 'Of course, you know I'd do anything, anything at all to help. I mean, I have money in the firm.'

She set the phone down and she paid attention to her daughter. 'If I were you,' she said, 'I'd look a wreck.'

'I look better than I feel,' Emma said. 'What's the point of working in Hollywood if you can't do that?'

'We have plenty of time; the papers don't come for ages. The papers take all my time nowadays. I used to pretend to read *The Times*, and now I have to pretend not to read it, and people practically cross-question you on what's in the *Independent* and the *Guardian* and the *Telegraph* just to see which you read, and how black your soul has grown. It's terribly time-consuming.'

'You sounded as though you had problems of your own.'

'I put thirty thousand into C.R.T. Youngman – the designer, you know? He was starting, it seemed like a good idea. A return on the frocks you wear, you know. Now some silly American boutique hasn't paid him, and he's thousands out and he may need more money and I am beginning to wonder. It's not as though I need to make more money.' She bubbled, but she pitched a shrewd look at Emma, disconcertingly so. 'Or is it?'

'I don't know what you mean.'

'Well, dear, now you're the shareholder Alistair has to reckon with, I thought you'd know. I wondered if I should get my money out of C. R. T. Youngman and be sensible. Think of rainy days, that sort of thing.'

The talk was false naïve, the question beneath it serious as redemption; Florence Griffier would have found it a mortal sin to be poor, although she forgave the fault in others.

'I don't know, Mother,' Emma said.

'That's not very reassuring,' Lady Griffier said. 'I was counting on you for reassurance, too. Alistair is rather – inspirational nowadays. He has a new saviour at the bank every day, and an older saviour upstairs, to whom he talks a lot.' She grimaced. 'I'm sorry, I didn't mean to sound so clever.'

'I guess his position is difficult,' Emma said.

'I guess the same. But he doesn't think he can reason or conspire his way through, and he always used to. This just isn't the man who gave away an Empire with hardly a shot fired.'

'I wanted to see what was happening.'

'I can't tell you. Maurice is going to jail, I think. Rupert has been quiet, which is sinister. I imagine he's equipping some financial souk in some unlikely country, if he hasn't been thrown out of every place with decent phones by now. Edward you know about, I'm afraid; you know all too well.'

'He died in my arms.'

'He was a beautiful man,' Florence said.

'He told the most extraordinary stories.'

She said: 'I would have liked to marry him and not your father. But he lacked – the amenities, you know. An island of a man. Alistair used to call him sometimes, and ask his advice. I think Edward had very good information, always, and he shared it with Alistair. I think Alistair is lost without that.'

'Edward said he was quite separate from the bank.'

'He couldn't be. He had a whole library consecrated to the bank. It was his life. His problem was being too fastidious to cope with an imperfect organization or a woman who ate and breathed. He preferred the orchids and the books.'

'Except when he was working for Intelligence.'

'I'm going to surprise you,' Lady Griffier said, 'and say that I'm not at all surprised. Intelligence is just a way of dealing with the world at one remove – patterns and files and suspicions. You sit in an office and think. It's why they hate intellectuals so much, of course,' she improvised, 'because the intellectuals are just the mirror image of the spies. Except they get the wrong answers, and they must be wicked.' She beamed.

'You do sound clever, ' Emma said.

'Don't go yet,' Lady Griffier said. 'I haven't seen anyone bright for weeks.'

'I think,' Emma said, 'my job today is finding things out.'

'One thing,' her mother said. 'The studio seem very tolerant about your travels. I know about American corporations: I have corporate genes. Why are they being so kind to you?'

'They're not.'

'Then don't worry about London,' her mother said, 'or family honour or anything else. Worry about keeping a life on your own terms.'

Emma saw wear in her mother's face that had not been there before, and which was not tended out of sight.

'I know these things.' Her mother, being a kind woman, smiled and broke the cold in the room. 'But you must go. Call me later, will you? Come to dinner this evening if you can – I could come up to town.'

'Yes,' Emma said. 'Yes, of course.'

She offered to drive her father to London, but he would not even consider the offer. The driver was waiting; they would take a serious car, and talk. She dreaded the inevitable pressure, gentle like a father's pressure is, anticipating no resistance, but she could hardly turn him down.

Sir Alistair said: 'Your mother's restless. I wish I knew what was wrong.'

'She's like a cat,' Emma said. 'She smells trouble and

she gets restive. She knows it's coming from a whole hillside away.'

'Very fanciful.'

'But there is trouble, isn't there?'

'You know that.'

'I know about the family. I don't know so much about the bank.'

'These,' Sir Alistair said, 'are difficult times. Competition, change – '

'But you know what to do?'

'The burden rests on me,' her father said. 'Of course, I had rather share it with Maurice or Rupert – or even you, my dear, perhaps. But it isn't possible.'

'You should bring Simeon back.'

'The man's frankly dotty. And besides, he was only the apparatchik. He made things happen, but he didn't decide what to do.'

In the light the winter landscape was no longer a mystery, only a procession of bare trees and grey sky.

'I don't want to be tedious,' Sir Alistair said, 'but we really should sort out your proxies. Unless, of course, you really want to vote your own shares. But that wouldn't be possible from Los Angeles, would it?'

Emma changed the subject, every time, or rather she ignored what her father said. She had a fine talent for trampolining off another person's talk to see the higher ground.

By the time they had reached the lanes of the City, her father was beginning to pitch the bank to her, like a salesman. She was embarrassed, but at least he knew he had to work to convince her.

She said she was suitably delighted by the look of the new logo, the sheer vacuous modernity of it all; she took in the trading floors as though she had never seen them before, and was impressed; she accepted his invitation to the partners' room.

For years, it had been a sham. In among the busy rooms, and the cables and terminals, there was a fragment of the past, bound in rosewood and pale blue leather like an album. It lay on a shelf, unused for anything beyond ceremony and sometimes family conspiracy. And now, with careful trolleys for the desks and the tantalus and the velvet drapes, and scalpels for the panelling, it was moving. There was a smell of cut wood, a mess of dust and memory.

'It was out of its time,' Sir Alistair said. He showed her the plans for offices that would open on to a common room for the directors; he said it was sensible and realistic. But all the box-like armchairs and the marble tables looked to Emma very sad: like something new and ineffectual to replace the ineffectual past. It was show, not change.

'There'll be photographers and reporters,' Sir Alistair said. He beamed with an awful confidence.

'You don't have to convince me,' she said.

'And at midday,' he said, grandly, 'I have an appointment with the future.'

She could stop this bluster of old man's ambitions, just by giving him her proxy. She could stop him begging for her attention and support. But to do that, to let her father take custody of his dignity once more, she had to break with common sense and her own independence. The only way to reassure him, to comfort him, was to give herself away.

'The future?' she asked politely.

'Jude Klein,' her father said. 'Our line to the best information on Wall Street. Our new product and our new friend.'

'Oh yes,' Emma said. She tried to remember where she had heard the name.

* * *

The name was the easy disguise. Immigration and Customs at Heathrow accepted James Drake at face value, as Jude Klein. But for Sir Alistair Griffier, he would need something more. He was never entirely sure his body would obey him, let alone act out a part. It was true his voice now had a mechanical quality it lacked before; but Griffier still might recall some trick of speech or movement. It was only twenty years, and a death, and he was vain enough to worry that he might not have changed enough.

His girl sat quiet as a rabbit, alarmed by his intensity. She knew it might trigger some sudden failure in a body that was none too secure. She was far too nervous to want to know what great matter was at stake.

'There are always papers,' she said.

He had fashioned the snare, and he was going to see the weasel take it – a tired old weasel, a man isolated and embracing a new world like he might embrace a new mistress, at an age when he would be anxious not to disappoint.

He wanted Griffier to be weaker and slacker than James Drake; he could glory in the man's physical decline. But he also wanted Griffier to be worth defeating.

When the car stopped in front of Griffier Ltd, James Drake was only an old man with a back that was subject to shocks and eyes that were dry. He moved awkwardly and the left side of his face was not perfectly aligned. When he had to sit for any length of time, he shifted from ham to ham, agonizing.

But when he stepped out of the car, and straightened himself, he engaged his will. He walked as though held in a brace of muscle. His face lost expression, rather than give away the lop-sided mind that controlled it. He did not fidget when the blood began to fade in an arm or leg; he ignored the intolerable itching that followed.

His girl Helen watched him shift himself from patient to man. She was not sure she liked the transition. As a man, he had choices, and she might not be one of them. But she was proud, too, that he was mounting the steps like someone strong, his sheer bulk and presence freezing the thought that the body might not be in perfect order. She had seen him cold in a wrap of lifeless flesh, on a white table.

She took the car on to Harrods. She didn't even want to spend money that day, just see.

James Drake waited for Sir Alistair Griffier, just as he had done twenty years before on the day he agreed to salvage the mutual fund business, and agreed to his own ruin. The coffee had improved. The secretaries were less austere. There was the muffled roar of trading below, which he had not heard before.

But Sir Alistair welcomed him, as he had welcomed him before. 'It is a great pleasure to meet you at last,' he said. He added: 'This is my daughter, Emma.'

He had not expected Emma. He appraised her like a jeweller with a glass, and she knew it; but she smiled. 'You have quite a reputation in Hollywood,' he said.

She had blocked him. She had blocked Adam. To him, she had become the last worthy opponent among the Griffiers, and therefore the one that must be crushed.

She said: 'I know your reputation very well.' Apparently, your risk arbitrageur could have charm. It was not all desiccated greed, to be watered into life with good champagne.

His look held her eyes, but his words sounded dismissive. 'I'm sure we'll meet again,' he said.

'Yes,' Emma said, briskly. 'I'm sure we will.'

He wanted no distractions. He had a part to play, and an unreliable body, a sometimes flighty mind with which to play it. He allowed himself to be ushered into Sir Alistair's private room.

Emma stood alone in the comfortable ante-room. She felt cold and confused. She imagined it was one of those moments when she had forgotten briefly to hide her real situation from herself, and the panic came through the breach like the sea. There was no reason, she told herself, for this coldness, like a child's fear of the dark.

In Sir Alistair's room, there was magic, of a chapel kind. Jude Klein was expansive; James Drake was absorbed in his own performance. He did not promise or specify, but still he spun a sermon which offered brilliance and cash. There were proper solutions, known to the elect, which brought forth profit from the mundane business of the stock market. Jude Klein let it be known he understood the soul of the market; he might even have bought it.

Sir Alistair sat before him, ready to believe. He was hungry to be taught by new things.

'You see,' 'Klein' was saying, 'we've gone far past the days when the markets were more or less stable – when the Dow Jones could stay around 800 for years, even when inflation should have taken it to 2,000. There's no more average, no more level playing field.' He paused a moment. 'You do say level playing field in Britain, don't you?'

Sir Alistair nodded, unsure.

'You see your dealing room,' 'Klein' said. 'You see the information pouring in from around the world – more facts, more changes, more prices than anyone ever had to manage before. There is a flood of information. And how do you manage that flood – how do you ride it instead of drowning?' One to one, he still could summon something like the magic of a Pentecostal preacher; he had set Sir Alistair in terror by a foaming river. Jude Klein was the ferryman, the bridge-keeper.

'You think,' 'Klein' said, 'you have technical help. You know about business cycles and market cycles. You have men who read charts of stock prices like the priests used to read the guts of a live bull. They tell you to look for three peaks and a house, and then buy or sell or hold. They ring you up to tell you they've found a head and shoulders on a chart. And do you know what that means? Do you?'

Sir Alistair was a sinner before the pulpit, abject and repentant. 'Chartists have their place,' he said, stuffily, which was his way of declaring for the Lord.

'Nothing. Nada. Shit,' 'Klein' said. God, but once they had suckered him and how he would sucker them, good. They told him the truth with bits left out; he would do the same. They sold him a story. 'Your charts, your cycles – meaningless. Your averages, smoothing everything out so you see the underlying trend – meaningless. The jags, the moves, the hiccups in the charts, they're all more significant than the underlying trend.

'The business cycles never do come round, do they – always a few years off, never quite what's predicted. The charts are often wrong, except that when the chartists speak about a share that's under-priced, and say it's going to go up, the people who pay the chartists feel they have to buy the shares, and so, by God, the prices do go up.' Careful, he thought to himself; a little too close to the inner workings of an arbitrage business. Move on quickly.

'And yet,' 'Klein' said, the flow mesmeric enough to hide his little hesitation, 'we're moving towards one grand, universal, unified market of the world – the bond markets keep us out of recession, so they fuel the stock markets; the credit market feeds the stock market and the bond market and the currency market. There's no significant difference between the buyers or the stocks in New York, London, Tokyo – a different menu, maybe, but the same dynamic and often as not, the same goods. But we don't truly understand our local market, the one where we think we understand the politics, the economics and the prospects. Now we have a world market and -' He remembered so well the honey Sir Alistair applied like poultices when he was the one who needed to be persuaded, who wanted to be persuaded by a power such as the Griffiers. 'Consider,' he said, ominously.

'Very interesting,' Sir Alistair said, because how could he confess his passion to know what Klein had to say, to have the trick of survival handed to him as a creed? 'This is all extremely interesting. It is so useful to know the thinking behind – '

'Consider,' 'Klein' said, with great drama, 'the science of chaos.'

For a moment Sir Alistair feared the conversation had turned from the mathematics he could not grasp to some metaphysics he could not take seriously. 'Indeed,' he said. He wished he had papers to shuffle, a phone call to take.

'Chaos,' 'Klein' said, 'is mathematics, but the higher mathematics. Chaos is what you use when economists can't tell you any longer if news is good or bad and the mavens can't tell why the Federal deficit runs a bull market one month and a bear market the next. Chaos is sense out of the disorder in which we live.' He begged forgiveness from Benoit Mandelbrot and all the mathematicians whose work he took in vain; they were only a means to revenge.

'You see random movements, sudden surges,' 'Klein' said. 'I see a hidden order, a key to what is happening. I see the connections.' Also, he most particularly did not add, I make the phone calls and I know the insiders; but let it all seem magic and the weasel would take the snare without engaging his mind. 'The people who understand the science of chaos,' 'Klein' said, 'aren't surprised when the market suddenly rises or suddenly falls. They know,' he summoned the right words from a memory which sometimes grew hazy; he was grateful that today it worked without delay, 'that systems like the stock market are sensitive to the slightest perturbation.'

'This is a branch of mathematics, I suppose?' Sir Alistair knew he had been offered the Holy Grail, the core and fundamental of Jude Klein's success.

'The tiniest fluctuation,' 'Klein' said, 'can be magnified. The tremor spreads. It grows and builds. Suddenly, out of what nobody noticed, there is boom or bust. They know it's true of your heart, and the weather. Imagine if we had the key to what the markets would do next. Imagine if we understood.'

Sir Alistair lay far back in his chair, as though pressed back by speed and gravity in a fast car. Jude Klein leaned forward, for the first kill.

'That,' he said, 'is the secret. To be open to the newest ideas and take them out into the real world where they can make money. Some people do it with the latest technology. I do it with mathematics. I take fractal geometry and I make a billion.'

Sir Alistair was deliciously out of his depth. The world of uncertain forces ordered itself around him into regular patterns: treaties and parades and rituals that he could grasp and manipulate. Figures became an Empire in which he could rule. He was sure he was suddenly modern.

'For the moment,' 'Klein' said, 'you know the tax problem we have in the United States. An arbitrage fund needs to have fifty-one per cent of its investors overseas to avoid penal taxation. Naturally, we would welcome your clients, even yourself.'

Sir Alistair was breathless. It was better than he had hoped.

'And a closer association, over the years, perhaps? We could sometimes – do each other favours. Naturally, I would be acting quite spontaneously, all on the basis of chaos theory. I might predict which side would win in a bid battle. But I could always take the right side; and so could you.'

For a moment, the direct talk bothered Sir Alistair. There was only a sliver of difference between friends who came to the same idea, and a concert party to swing a bid, which was illegal. The difference was usually who talked.

But the prospect glittered. Not only the key to the markets, but also an association with the most famous wizard, the one who did not preach his magic promiscuously at every thousand-dollar seminar on investment strategy. Glamour, and substance, all at once. A future for Griffier Ltd as a source of expertise, the ones who know.

By the time a butler put a trout before James Drake at lunch, he knew he could relax the magic, even shift his stifled leg when it hurt him. Sir Alistair could see nothing but wonders ahead of him. He would do what Drake wanted, because he had been promised a solution without effort and, best of all, without selling out the family name and independence to some anonymous corporation. He would even break the law, in due course.

It was a dangerous time for Drake. He could see Sir Alistair Griffier in court, and he knew there would be no trace of Jude Klein. And if anyone associated Klein with James Drake, they would stop short. There are easier things for a fraud squad than arraigning a dead man.

As for chaos, it made a fine sermon. It also changed the rules. If it was possible to profit from extreme disorder, from a market where nobody else could see sense or rhythm, then it might be desirable to create extreme disorder. The perfect vehicle would be an influential, noticeable London bank, with a famous name; the kind that had once been supposed to save the mutual fund business and had passed the charge to James Drake. He was not so much answering history, as turning it inside out.

The dead need have no scruples in their thought; they have no more future to believe in, and no obligation to their past. James Drake was a free agent, at last.

The telephone stood on a delicate table by a deep sofa; it wouldn't do. It seemed to Simeon Ryder like a social instrument, designed for manners and not conspiracy; it was not the office.

He had five calls on hold, or not returned; his name noted, but not respected; on one occasion, he suspected, his name not known at all. He had always been Ryder of Griffiers; now he was plain Ryder.

It was worst of all when someone was kind as a sick-bed visitor. The British manager of one huge Japanese securities firm said he was most concerned with Simeon's well-being; he was noncommittal when Simeon pressed for a meeting; when Simeon pushed on, and the man could hardly slam down the phone, he said: 'Look,' and he found it difficult to arrange the words, 'maybe you should take a few weeks off. These calls can't be helping, you know.'

'But I have a proposition – '

The man's patience snapped. 'I will get back to you,' he said.

If Simeon had nothing to sell, he had nothing to do, nobody to be. If doing all he could was spoiling his reputation, he had lost his reputation.

He called Sir Alistair Griffier. He heard the secretary's tiny intake of breath when she recognized his voice; he was told Sir Alistair was not available at the moment. Of course the secretary would pass the message. She broke off for a moment, without muting the phone, to acknowledge Sir Alistair and a Mr Klein. She said Sir Alistair had already left the office, and Mr Ryder would please understand?

He understood very well. He had passed into that limbo where a man can be lied to without care. He also knew the name of Mr Klein. He had warned Sir Alistair that the man would be catastrophe, and now the man was an honoured guest.

All his working life, he had been the one to answer mistakes like that. He could phone the right man, buy the right drink or call in a favour; now he could not even connect to make his point.

But it was his life at stake, all he had ever done. It was reasonable to use shock.

He could not have said which was stronger; his fury with Griffier for daring to snub him, or an instinct to drag the man back to his senses, and save the institution which had moulded and occupied Simeon Ryder's adult life. Either way, he had an answer.

He stood on the terrace of his apartment, looking down at the street. It was cold and bright; people bustled between the cars in heavy coats. He did not feel the cold.

Suppose Jude Klein, king of the arbs, was the one to buy Rupert's shares in Griffier Ltd. Rupert had nothing more to gain from the bank except cash, and Griffiers was a company in play, after all, a classic situation for an arbitrageur. Suppose that now John Brown had been cut out, he, too, sold to Klein to make a substantial bloc. Perhaps Emma, too, now she had time to digest her legacy and realize the problems, would want to realize the cash. Then Sir Alistair would have to live with Jude Klein every working minute of the day, and as a threat, not an ally. Sir Alistair would see how the man operated, be convinced the bank could not do business his way. He would see how right Simeon Ryder had been; and when

Jude Klein sold to some American bank, Simeon Ryder would be vindicated.

It made perfect sense at the time. Klein would listen to a man like Ryder, thinking he was a malcontent with inside knowledge. The only problem was how to reach Klein.

James Drake's girl saw Simeon park by the bank at two-thirty. She sat in a spill of shopping bags, happy and tired. She thought it was odd how he stayed in his car. She fidgeted with the lush layers of tissue paper in the bags, fascinated more by the packing and spending than by the objects she had bought.

Ten minutes later, Simeon was still there. She started to wonder when James Drake would come out from his lunch, not that she had any right to wonder. She put her hand on silks, and stroked them like a cat.

A half-hour later, it was weird that Simeon was still sitting in his car. If you can park that close to a bank, you have business there and if you have business, you go in. There was nothing to watch on the sidewalk, she could tell him that, for free. She was restless now, and afraid that Simeon was some look-out guy, the kind that follows and checks.

She would tell James Drake when finally he appeared. After all, Drake had enemies. She began to worry that they had given the old man too much good drink; he still might fall in a faint, or provoke his weak heart, or simply tell them who he was. She cared more than a nurse, less than a lover. And she began to be annoyed by this neat, strange man who sat at the wheel of his car, checking the door, but not checking her. She put her face close to the window, staring at him.

Simeon Ryder did not notice. He supposed some of the staff might recognize him, but they hardly had time for lunch in the new world of the City, and the messengers were not paid to police the official parking spaces. But he still wanted Jude Klein to appear very soon, before security came round.

The girl shrugged. She was nice to look at, she knew, and if he chose not to look, that was his problem. She asked the driver if he could work out what the guy was doing; the driver couldn't. He wrinkled his kind, smashed face and said if the guy was OK, he'd be looking at Helen. She smiled.

She wasn't waiting with all her heart when James Drake opened the door. He was exuberant, and rough. He said the Griffiers were waiting at the bank steps like a crowd of flunkeys. 'Can you believe that, girl? Can you believe that?'

He lunged for the girl and half-hugged her. 'Heathrow, driver,' he said. 'We came, we saw, we conquered. We won, girl. They begged for my help, they invited me in, they offered me their money – '

She said: 'Last time, it was a trap.'

'This time, I make the rules. This time, they're the ones who won't know what hits them.'

Simeon watched the car pass him like a slow black fish in the city stream. The man looked too old to be king of the arbs, and he looked slightly familiar, but it must be Jude Klein; Sir Alistair was watching him drive away. If Simeon delayed, he would lose the car in the traffic. He could see security, too, coming to see who was in Mr Ryder's parking space. He stamped the car into gear.

Helen looked out of James Drake's car. 'This is dumb,' she said. 'That guy is following us.'

James Drake turned his bull neck, but by the painful stages an old man needs. 'We're being followed by half London,' he said.

'There was a man waiting by the bank.'

'It happens. The Griffiers still have clients.'

'He drove off when we drove off, and he's behind us now.'

'For God's sake,' Drake said. 'They're as subtle as a TV car chase, these people.' He snapped at the driver: 'Do something fancy in case this guy is following. Don't shake him off, just make him do something obvious. Then if you can take him up a one-way street and block it, you get a hundred extra.'

'Dollars or pounds, sir?'

Past the gilded spires of Parliament, along the office bunkers by the river, the driver without warning followed almost the full circle of a roundabout into Horseferry Road. He ran a light that was almost red at Marsham Street.

'Look back now,' he said. 'If he's still there – '

'He's still there.'

And Simeon was grimly on their tail, with the terrible seriousness of a man who is growing more hopeful by the moment.

'Hang on!' the driver said.

The long straight of Horseferry Road ends in branches. Instead of following the main road to the right, the driver veered left, and then very sharply right. He brought the car to rest under a broad, bare chestnut tree. There was a cricket pitch within the square, carefully shielded against the wet; it called for boys in white, as on some village green.

Simeon faltered at the first turn, but he sensed the other car had disappeared too suddenly. Only one turn could explain that, and he took it.

He had hoped to track Jude Klein to a hotel where he could simply ask to see him. But there was no sense in growing cautious now; it was no more risky to talk with Klein on this back street than in a grand hotel. At least it was possible to talk to him.

'I think you'd better ask him,' James Drake said to the driver. And the driver went on light feet to interview the waiting Simeon Ryder.

'I wanted to talk with Jude Klein,' he said.

'What's your name,' the driver said, 'sir?'

When the driver relayed the name, James Drake was no longer the curved, tired man he had seemed for the first part of the journey; he was ready. 'Have him follow,' he said, 'and find some good stopping place. Have him come to the car. You and the girl might like to take a walk.'

The girl was flustered. 'I'd rather be with you,' she said, carefully.

'Take a walk,' Drake said. 'I have work to do.'

She put a travelling rug across his lap and he allowed himself to be warmed like a dowager. He had played the vital trader long enough at Griffiers, and the cold from the open door stung nerves into a shrill pain.

The first free parking spaces were at the back of a nurses' home and police station on Rochester Row. The sheer respectability appealed to Drake: he ordered the car to stop. He saw the girl go off around the square with the driver; he felt generous. He opened the car door to Simeon Ryder.

It is hard to crawl into a limo with dignity, and Simeon failed. He settled himself opposite the man he knew as Jude Klein, and he pulled off his gloves.

'I'll come right to the point,' he said. 'My name is Simeon Ryder. I suppose you know who I am since you agreed to see me.'

'The Griffiers' head clerk,' Drake said, unkindly.

'Managing director,' Ryder said, but he did not insist on the correction. 'Until quite recently.'

'I didn't discuss that with Sir Alistair. But I heard the stories.'

'If you heard the stories,' Ryder said, 'I presume you have more than a passing interest in Griffier Ltd.' The man Klein puzzled him; he seemed too tired to be a miracle of market nerves, and too old to have suddenly become so famously successful. Where had he been for the rest of his life?

'Griffier is a well-known name,' Drake allowed.

'And for some time, there has been the possibility of a bid. John Brown thought he could do it, but he failed because of the publicity. Now the way's open for the Americans who want to buy a big City name, or the Japanese – '

'You wouldn't know these things from inside any more, would you, Mr Ryder?'

'Let me finish,' Ryder said. 'It isn't what I know that is the issue. It's what I have. John Brown is reluctant to admit he's been defeated – he is always reluctant to admit he's been defeated, I don't need inside knowledge for that. He won't sell until there's another bidder. Meanwhile, the big American banks don't want to buy from Brown because they know his ego won't allow him to take a loss, not yet. They're waiting for another parcel of shares.'

'You're selling, aren't you?' Drake said.

'It's too soon. It needs someone who can hold for a few months, take a view on the likely price – make some money.'

'Your client needs cash, I suppose? It is a client, is it?'

'Yes,' Ryder said.

'Talk specifics,' Drake said.

'Griffiers are at 171p this morning,' Ryder said. 'It's not good; everyone knows that. There's too much news and people are waiting for the other shoe to drop. They assume there will be something worse.'

'Can you promise me there won't?'

'No,' Ryder said. 'Not entirely. But luck seems to be running out of victims where the Griffiers are concerned. And the Americans won't be buying the business as it is, so much as the business they can make of it – think of

Griffier Mutual Funds and all the rest of it, an old-world name for anything new they need to push.'

'Figures,' Drake said.

'My client would sell at 195p, for a private placing, cash terms. He particularly doesn't want the market to get wind of what he's done.'

'Because his family would discover, I suppose?'

'That's not a bad guess. Now the bid terms can't possibly start under 240p; the assets alone, the property in Griffier Ltd, is worth that. It's only because the market in the shares is so damnably small that they've gone so far down. At 240p you have a profit, of course, but you're also a player. You decide who gets the bank, or when you take your profit. It's a perfect prospect.'

'Assuming someone bids,' Drake said.

'They will, once they know the shares are loose. For a start, John Brown can sell to you without losing face. The Griffiers can accept you as a shareholder without undue fuss; they want to do business with you. The bids will follow on simple arithmetic – something valuable, going cheap.'

'Sometimes people don't act logically,' said Drake. He remembered Ryder from twenty years back, a starched and clear-eyed man, always watching and considering. It might have been Ryder who decided the mutual funds business needed protection. He made himself hard to notice, but the ideas were born in his slick, deferential head. And now, Ryder came after two decades, in curious circumstances, to offer another chance of playing saviour. Drake wondered if this sweetened his revenge; or if he should be careful.

'There's a story,' Drake said, 'you found out you're a Griffier yourself. You don't plan to take the family to court, I suppose?'

'I built a life on a different assumption,' Ryder said.

'I'm too old to rebuild my life, so I choose not to change the assumption. It's as simple as that.'

'Call me in Amsterdam,' Drake said. 'If the price sticks, I want to talk to your principal. If he's available, that is.'

'He's available,' Ryder said.

'There's nothing else to discuss,' Drake said, and he opened the car door.

'It was pleasant meeting you,' Ryder said.

'Likewise,' said James Drake.

But he was looking across the square to where the driver was standing too close to the girl, and the girl was giggling.

'I can raise 195p cash,' Simeon Ryder said to Rupert Griffier. 'You'd be a fool to miss that price.'

'You know something bad?'

'Quite bad,' Simeon said.

'My father rang. He said you'd been seen hanging about the bank and he wanted to know what that was about. He seemed to think you might tell me. You're not planning a bank heist, are you? A retirement career?'

'Of course not.'

'Pity. My instincts tell me to stay put at Griffiers until someone knows what happens next. I could use some short-term alternative. With guns, maybe.'

'195p, cash down. Paid wherever you want. Klein isn't keen for anyone to know he's buying just at the moment, so he'd leave the shares in your name.'

'He wants an option, in other words.'

'He wants the shares.'

'Tell him if 195p is the option price, what is the real thing worth?'

'I have a number for him in Amsterdam,' Simeon said.' 'If you could call – '

'What do you get out of all this?'

'A finder's fee, if everything goes well. Nothing else.'

'No personal satisfaction, Simeon? You shouldn't work without personal satisfaction, you know.'

'I'm sure,' Simeon said, knowingly, 'you'd get a lot out of selling. Not just the cash.' He had seen Rupert beg and intimidate and whine for a place in the bank; it had always been refused. He had no particular reason to go down with Griffier Ltd.

'You do think you're a clever sod,' Rupert said. 'Give me the number and fuck off.'

Simeon obliged; nothing that Rupert said could surprise or disturb him. He puzzled how to get through to John Brown, who was the kind of man who leaves the scene of his disasters. He gave Jude Klein's name, and then had to apologize for the deception.

'I gather,' Brown said, 'you have been acting rather oddly.'

'I have a buyer for your Griffier stock,' Simeon said. 'At 210p. It's clear profit, and the buyer doesn't want to be announced just yet. It's Jude Klein, as you may have gathered.'

'He's a difficult man to get hold of,' Brown said, impressed despite himself. 'The ghostly Mr Klein. Where do I reach him?'

Simeon gave him the number.

'And who pays you if anything happens? I suppose I'm in for a *pourboire*, am I?'

'We can discuss that later.'

'You've been employed too long,' Brown said. 'Always fix the terms.'

'Who knows what might happen?' Simeon said, with feeling.

James Drake drank Bourbon seriously, which was no small achievement on a short flight. He said to Helen: 'Nothing else to do, that's the wonder. We just have to wait.'

'Yes,' she said. She often wished she knew much more or much less about his plans; she would like to understand what filled his day so as to understand his mood, but she had no wish to share the burden. She was paid help, not a lover.

'You don't realize, do you, girl? We're inside. Very soon, they're going to come crawling to us, begging us to accept ownership of Griffier Ltd.'

'But you don't want – '

'I want influence they can't dispute. I need that. And if I ever change my mind, I want a profit and they're coming to me to offer it, on their knees.'

'All of them?'

'Alistair loves Jude Klein. He worships and adores him. He's the only hope. Rupert will sell; he needs cash. Maurice might sell, but it doesn't matter if he's in a German jail. Edward's dead. That leaves Emma Griffier, and very soon she'll come to Amsterdam just like Adam told her. She'll come to me.'

'When you win, what will you do?' She was seriously concerned. Anger had taught him how to break the casing of coma and apparent death; when anger had been satisfied, there might be no more energy. If so, she would need a new assignment. She was thinking of working some pleasant bar where she could sass the men at night, without responsibility; she was tired of carrying this man, in bed and out of it, like a child.

'Oh then,' James Drake said. The plane lowered itself through cloud towards the wet flatlands of Holland and the tiny cars chasing the evening along plumb straight roads. As they touched ground, he turned to her and shouted: 'Then, we're just starting.'

The outskirts of Amsterdam were slick with freezing rain; they drove slowly. Drake had time to be confidential. 'It's like this,' he said. 'In time, they'll catch up with everything they know can make a market go mad. There are computer programs that mean the Index drops or rises a hundred points on a Friday at 3P.M., because everyone sells at once, for the same reason, and as fast as the electronics let them. The Exchanges will spot that; they'll make the big funds deal by hand and voice, instead of disc and modem. They'll feel safe again. Then they'll look at all the wonderful things the banks do – interest swaps, certificates of deposit tied to the price of gold, acting as middlemen in the futures markets between the people who grow and the people who use. They'll see these things as new and strange, and not as controllable as prime rate; they'll get scared and block them, one by one. They'll think the market is back under control.

'But,' he said, as the car came under the shadow of a great church, 'they're wrong, of course. People trade on information, so they trade fast. They can't afford not to trade, in case that turns out to be the worst mistake of all. So, little girl, there will be one world market and it will be touchy as a sensitive plant. And everyone in the world will think it's in everyone's interest that everything is as stable and steady as possible – except for those of us who understand what will happen when the swings set in and the graphs look like they've been sharpened for a fight. We can profit from the chaos. We can start it.'

'Yes,' the girl said. She vaguely thought he was talking about Apocalypse, like God will stir the armies, and Gog will enter Israel and the faithful will be taken into rapture. Her Apocalypse had no dragons; it came from Sunday morning preachers on TV, and mostly consisted of getting rid of strangers.

'You don't understand, do you?' Drake said. He sounded angry, and she was surprised; usually, she was not expected to understand such things. 'Disorder is business, honey. It's as simple as that.'

'Yes,' she said. She very nearly called him 'dear', like a wife might patronize a talkative husband; she had formed the word with her lips before she stopped herself. No sense in taking unnecessary risks; she needed the air ticket back to America in time, and she wanted to keep what she'd bought that day at Harrods.

But for the first time he frightened her, because she saw, for a cold minute, that his plans might have a meaning in her world, too. It was not just markets and business pages; it was suburban streets and trailer parks, coffee from 7-11s and Chinese food at lacquered restaurants, shade trees and freeways and the clothes for the kids. Everything rested on order, except him.

'He'll piss on us all,' she thought.

11

The lanes around Easterford were hollows of cold black and tangled wood and the gates were a folly, streaked by mist. Across their width was wedged a gaudy motor-coach, a huge dirigible moored to earth, its lights staring blankly at the driveway.

Its door was open, and Emma could hear the amplified chat of the guide. '. . . the Griffiers, ladies and gentlemen, the great banking family of England, one of the richest families in the land. They built this extraordinary house in 1858 . . .'

Emma leaned on the horn, but nobody turned to look. Inside the coach was a closed world; the last tourists of the year, come to see there were actual gates through which passed the actual cars of the actual Griffier family. When they could, as Emma darkly thought.

'. . . despite what you've read in the papers this year,' the guide boomed, 'the Griffiers remain one of the most powerful families . . .'

Row after row of faces, she could see, tasting the anecdotes like scones. Whatever the guide said was enough for them; whatever they were shown was sufficient. They would ask no difficult questions, except to check what was famous and what was not, and a great failure would interest them as much, and as briefly, as a great success. Whole lives, whole dynasties were processed into quaint things, to talk about at home.

A person trying to go home was invisible; home was a case in an old museum, a show in a theme park. In the cold, Emma had bleak thoughts of the whole of England struggling to achieve quaintness, so all human life could have signposts pointing to it. English history was no longer historical enough, the past was too brutish and uncute; so something sterile was put in its place. There would be no life in such a place, not least because there could be no natural change.

She got out of her car and went to the open door of the coach. 'Excuse me,' she said. 'You know you're blocking the way into Easterford?'

The driver looked down at her, and the guide paused. A hundred sallow faces, like potato heads, looked ahead. Emma did not exist until the guide had accounted for her, over the tannoy.

'I would be grateful,' Emma Griffier said, 'if you would move this damn coach.'

The guide turned off the microphone. 'These are foreign tourists,' she said, solemnly. 'You don't want them to get a bad impression of England, do you?'

'You're blocking the driveway to my home,' Emma said.

The guide looked unbelieving from her high throne. 'We'll only be a minute,' she said. The microphone clicked back into life, and the potato heads nodded gratefully.

Emma thought she might summon real fury, but she was interrupted by the car phone.

'I'm glad you didn't change numbers,' Simeon said.

'Talk to me now,' Emma said. 'I'm sitting in a lane behind a coachload who think the Griffiers are a waxworks.'

'If you want to sell any part of your shares from Edward,' Simeon said, 'I really do have a buyer. At 210p.'

'I thought the family wisdom was that we always had 240p in property.'

'But if anything else goes wrong,' Simeon said, 'and it's a forced sale, the question is whether we'd raise any more. This is cash in hand.'

'Whose cash, please?'

'Jude Klein,' Simeon said, 'so I know your father wouldn't mind the deal.'

'But Klein doesn't want a London bank. He'd sell to the first big bidder.'

'By which time,' Simeon said, 'I'm sure your father will see the wisdom of diluting the family holdings, if not selling out.'

'You're very confident.'

'I earned my right to care about the bank,' Simeon said. 'I didn't just inherit it.'

Emma said: 'I'm sorry I only inherited my shares. But I still own them, and you can't sell them for me.'

'Will you at least talk to Jude Klein?'

'You could give me a number. I don't promise anything.'

In the start of twilight she watched the coach turn carefully and head into the open driveway. She noted the number in Amsterdam, put down the phone, and looked in astonishment at this winter posse, chasing the monumental shadow of Easterford. They could see nothing but the dark mass of brick, but, like pilgrims, they wanted to be close to the relics.

She followed them. At the main door of the house, she turned back to see a string of still, dumpy figures, vague against a pale sunset, strung out across the tarmac and even on to the faint scrawls of mist over the lawn. They were an army without purpose, except looking.

'We'll only be here a minute or two,' the guide was saying, 'because the Griffiers do not permit visitors . . .' She sounded reproachful.

'There's a coach in the driveway,' Emma told her mother.

'Out of season,' her mother said. 'I'll send Fraser out. I suppose we'll need gates and guards like everyone else now.'

'You should be careful. People get crazy about names in the paper.'

'They've always known our name,' Lady Griffier said. 'And where to find us.'

'You sound like a pioneer when the wagons are circled.'

'I'm afraid I do. I can hear the damned Indians.'

'Then listen to me,' Emma said. 'I know what's been happening over the past year, and I know who's behind it all and where to find him. I'm going to find him.'

'Yes, darling,' said Lady Griffier, in a distinctly abstracted way.

'Are you listening to me?'

'I don't think this sounds like a pioneer story any more,' Lady Griffier said. 'I think this sounds like a Battle of Britain movie – the kind where the pilot sees his best girl and tells her he's going to dare death on the next day, and will she please wish him well. Sometimes she looks pregnant, sometimes she doesn't.'

'Do you remember a man called James Drake?'

'Big man in oil, for what that's worth. He was going to rebuild Los Angeles, the dreamer. Very sharp, but very bombastic when you saw his ideas in daylight. Didn't something go terribly wrong?'

'Most of the things that have happened in the past few months – Edward, David, Rupert's last troubles, Maurice – they were orchestrated by James Drake.'

'He didn't make poor Simeon dotty. That was John Brown.'

'He didn't put Griffier Ltd in play, either, but he did enough. The point is, he's bound to come after you and Father. It's the next logical step.'

'I expect so, darling.'

'And he has already done these terrible things.'

'I don't think the explanations are very interesting, do you, darling? I mean, it's not like some engineering problem where you can change the equations next time and it will all be all right. There can be no next time. This is our particular life, and it seems, at the moment, fucked. As they say.'

'I'm going to see Drake in Amsterdam. I'm going to – '

'To do what, exactly? Are you taking a gun or a knife or a noose? What will you do with the body? Will you remember to wear the finest leather gloves so as not to leave fingerprints? I'm sure they don't hang murderers in Holland any more; they're far too civilized.'

Emma said, exasperated: 'I'm going to talk with him, for God's sake.'

'And what will you say? Here you are in this wonderful city with its centuries of toleration and patience, and how can you possibly go on with your disagreeable vendetta? Do you think that will convince him?'

'I'm going to leave an address in Amsterdam,' Emma said. 'If there's any trouble, you should have it.'

'Thank you,' Lady Griffier said. 'More responsibility is just what I need. When you're in Amsterdam – '

Like a great, loud dog that is suddenly unleashed, Sir Alistair came bounding into the room. He glinted with triumph; he smiled without meaning to. 'Amsterdam?' he said brightly. 'Everyone's going to Amsterdam. Jude Klein's just gone back.'

'Your meeting obviously went well,' Lady Griffier said.

'I think,' Sir Alistair said, 'in this confused and difficult world we have a true ally. A friend.'

'At the moment,' Emma said, 'I wouldn't trust anyone.'

'We could hardly do any business at all if we listened to you,' Sir Alistair said, reasonably. 'I can't think what you mean.'

She saw him clear for a moment: a man who had

always been put away in faith like fine glass is put away in tissue paper. She had to risk breaking him.

'Your new ally,' she said, 'just offered me 210p a share for everything I own of Griffier Ltd.'

'There!' said Sir Alistair, with wonderful illogic. 'He is a true friend. Rather than have that stock running loose, he buys to help friends. He puts his money where his mouth is.'

'He's an arbitrageur, Father. He buys to sell, not hold.'

'He's an ally, an associate. He understands all these new things, quite wonderfully.'

'Do you think I should sell, then?'

Sir Alistair stopped short, like a cartoon character stopped at the edge of a cliff; his mind was quite painfully concentrated.

'I wouldn't say – '

'If I sold, if you sold, if we all got out – '

'I really don't think that is an issue,' Sir Alistair said.

'If we got out, we could protect ourselves better.'

'Protect ourselves against what, precisely? Against the future?'

'Then you don't mind if I do sell?'

Sir Alistair said: 'You have a very substantial holding. You have real power.'

'You don't want me to have real power, do you? So why shouldn't I simply cash in my power, to the first bidder?'

'Nobody is going to bid,' Sir Alistair said. 'I would not allow that. The institutional shareholders would not allow that.'

'Then I sell to Jude Klein,' Emma said. 'Damn you.'

Lady Griffier said: 'We need some time to think. We need some time to settle our nerves, I think.'

'The day went so well,' Sir Alistair said. And, when Lady Griffier had briefly gone to find more whisky, he said: 'You should stay for a few days. There's no need to do anything in haste.'

'I have a job in Los Angeles, Father.'

He looked at her with innocent surprise. 'But you have Edward's shares,' he said. 'That comes first, doesn't it? You are a part of Griffier Ltd.'

'I can't stay. I have an appointment in Amsterdam.'

'With Mr Klein, no doubt. You can't wait to leave us, can you? And when your mother needs such reassurance.' He was confidential and quiet. 'She took Edward's death very badly, you know.'

'I know.'

'She loved him very much,' Sir Alistair said, 'but he wouldn't do, of course. She needs to be at the heart of things.'

She stared at him. It was as though he wanted to remind her how close a father and daughter are meant to be. He was implicating her.

'After almost thirty-five years of marriage, one knows most things. Even the things one hardly wants to know. She is a very kind woman. She never made me know things.'

Emma had lived through such conspiracy that for a moment she wondered if her father was being only cunning, and not open at all. But he could not bring himself easily to talk about emotions: he found it irrelevant and, if he had ever been pushed to the point, tasteless. His odd, maybe hopeless euphoria had loosened his tongue.

'A day or two,' she said.

He looked out on the cold, last light of day. 'The rain's turned to snow,' he said. 'The lawns look like ghosts.'

She could see he was right. The grass seemed grey and luminous, like a photographic negative.

She said: 'I love you both, very much.' It had never before seemed such an urgent thing to say.

* * *

'But he must speak to me,' Simeon Ryder said.

Mr Brown stayed unavailable. Rupert Griffier hung up when he heard Ryder's voice. Maurice Griffier's lawyers would agree only to send on a message. Emma Griffier was not at her apartment, not in Los Angeles, and by now she must have left her car and gone into Easterford. It was hard to call Easterford.

He became restless in the trap of his flat. All he had to run was his empty day. He had become self-conscious at his own club, with the instinct that keeps the wounded away from places where gentlemen might be embarrassed.

He took to telling himself that he was part of an older guard that understood the long term, the structure of the future. He had not been told who would replace him at the bank; he feared an MBA who knew how to work the figures for the next quarter like new bread, but never saw beyond. His office would be occupied by some puppy dog who talked about cost benefit: benefits which had to be immediate, for costs that had to be kept down. It would work until something changed, and they found they could no longer afford imagination.

They none of them answered his calls now, and he had given away Jude Klein's number. It had become too cold to walk outside with pleasure; a shutter of frost had come down and the sky was winter dark. He was desperate enough to call Easterford.

He asked for Emma. He imagined her walking through the library, a tall, fine woman among the catalogue of fine women that hung in gilt on the walls. He imagined the sound of her heels on the floor.

'I'll talk to Klein in Amsterdam,' she said. 'Do you have an address, or just a number?'

'I think I have an address,' he said. He had called the number the day before, and the girl had told him something about a house on Herengracht. 'I have it here,' he said. He had a sheaf of disordered papers at his side; he brushed through them.

He read out an address she thought she knew. She said nothing; more than one person with money lodges on Herengracht. She went up to her room, and she checked her notes.

James Drake. Jude Klein. They had the same address. They had the same phone number.

Her mind began to race most dangerously, threatening every minute to throw her logic. Klein, older than he ought to be, stiff-backed and with a face that reflected feeling only dimly; he had seemed an unlikely dealer. Dealers needed stamina, and she had the feeling Klein tended his energy because he had to.

But her father had met James Drake. He could not possibly accept Jude Klein if he had even the slightest doubt about his identity; and a memory of Drake, however shadowy, would be doubt. Death had not corrupted James Drake, or sent him to the worms, but it must have changed his look and his manner. The stress of resurrection alone, she thought, and smiled uncomfortably.

But if this was indeed the same man, then her family were selling Griffier Ltd to their worst enemy. Her father's hope was his brother's killer. And she could hardly hope to stop her father; all she could do was to stop James Drake or Jude Klein or whichever identity was now more real to the man.

She scampered down the stairs, like a child mad for a high wind. Simeon Ryder would know. He had observed James Drake, not just done business with him; Simeon's style was to cling to the background as though it could hide him. He had been close to Jude Klein, when Klein was not performing in the bank. She dialled Ryder's number and, when there was no answer, she dialled again and again. He could not simply have disappeared. He had to help her; he was the only one who might.

She should stop Rupert doing business with Klein. She should call John Brown. But all that was inefficient, compared with going to Amsterdam and stopping James Drake short – her revenge, but also a most practical act. Perhaps, she thought, she had the nerve.

She called three airlines. All three said flights from Heathrow were difficult that night. The sudden cold was worse than they had expected; it was tough to keep the runways at Schipol from freezing, and there might be snow in London and in Holland. They were not advising passengers to come to the airport, not yet. Perhaps tomorrow there would be flights, and of course Miss Griffier would have priority. The customer relations office would call.

Cold did not freeze out electronics, and while the data networks moved, money could move. Shares could be bought and sold. Deals between her father and Jude Klein could be consummated on the wing of a satellite, and be irrevocable by the time the signal came back to earth.

She tore into the warmth of the drawing room. Her father sat there, by a high fire of sweet logs. Her mother sat across from him, supporting a huge, cheap novel on her lap. They gave a perfect illusion of serenity.

'Was there anything familiar about Jude Klein?' she asked her father. He stared at her, trying to corral a wandering mind.

'Familiar?' her father said. 'I should say "no". His picture very rarely appears in a paper. I would have nothing to recognize him by.'

'I mean, did he remind you of anyone else?'

'Successful men,' Sir Alistair said, 'sometimes do resemble each other. I suppose one notices the success.

Klein did seem a little like John Brown in build, since you mention it.'

'I don't mean this to be a guessing game. I just want to know if there is any possibility you had ever met Jude Klein before.'

'Oh, no,' Sir Alistair said.

'I have to go to London,' Emma said.

'The weather is atrocious,' her mother said. 'Can't it wait until the morning?'

'No,' Emma said, grimly.

'Some affair of the studio, no doubt,' her father said.

'I have to go,' Emma said.

She turned the car into the channel of the dark lanes, letting it find its own slow way through the bitter night and the subtle black ice on the road. She was thinking about insurance: what could help if there was a trap in Amsterdam set as brutally as those for David or Edward or Maurice. If her shares in Griffier Ltd were in safe hands, that would be a start. She could strike a deal that would be ratified on the Exchange at 9.30 tomorrow morning; if, that is, she could find anyone prepared to pay out of kindness to save her from trouble. She would need a very good and very rich friend.

Simeon would know. Someone must have an instinct for loyalty, the right resources and a connection to the Griffiers that was bright as gold and far less malleable. Simeon was bound to know, she comforted herself, in the blind misery of the snow, edging towards London when she most needed to rush.

After Chelmsford, she stopped at a phone box. It was out of order, inevitably; the snow melted at the back of her neck, a river of reminder that she must stay alert. On the road, the cars drudged forward, dipping into the dark and foundering there. She stopped at a petrol station and asked to use the phone.

Simeon answered, but not with his full attention. She could tell that.

'I need a phone number for a bank client,' she said. 'You did take your Roladex with you, didn't you?'

'I have a memory.'

'I need someone who has too much money, and loves the Griffiers.'

'There must be someone, I suppose.'

'You could help me, for God's sake. One of father's clients, one that trusts him from colonial days and thinks of him as a gentleman.'

'There's one who has the money, certainly. In fact, he might be the richest man in the world, and he's got nothing to spend it on. No taste, no time, no population.'

'Then tell me.'

'The Emir of Timor. Oil money, small country, and he always trusted Sir Alistair. Sir Alistair is like a father to him at times. He even rations the pocket money and the Emir accepts it. He wouldn't do anything without the Griffiers, so far.'

'Please,' Emma said, 'I need the number.'

'You have to understand he buys hotels and sometimes small villages with his pocket money. He's most likely to be at his gaming club. Rowlandson's. He has to play for very high stakes just to feel the slightest sensation of risk.'

'I can call him there.'

'Have you ever called anyone at a gaming club? Nobody is ever there, officially.'

'Then I'll go there.'

'Would you tell me what all this is about?'

'Very simple,' Emma said. 'Your first instincts about Jude Klein were exactly right, I think. I have the same Amsterdam address and phone number for James Drake.'

'That must be an old number.'

'James Drake is alive,' Emma said. 'You met him yourself. You talked to him. You offered him other people's shares in Griffier Ltd.'

Simeon was very quiet. But Emma's change was running out, and she could not wait for him to recover his nerve. 'Good luck,' she said. Only when the line went dead did she realize; she had said what he should have said.

He knew that. It was a tiny thing, but she had stolen away even his words, because he did not have the nerve to speak. His words, like his name and his identity and his day, were losing shape and substance.

He put on an overcoat, and took up his umbrella. He might have been dressed for the office, except that he wore the wrong sort of tie; he noticed that in the mirror. He was so very nearly Simeon Ryder of Griffiers.

The cold cut into him. He pulled up the collar of his coat, and stepped out into the street. He could go to his club and find a late game of bridge; he had been a famous player. But he knew they would not know how to welcome him; he brought defeat with him, like a shadow. He went to the doors of the club, and asked the doorman if there were messages.

The doorman passed him an envelope. It contained a brief note from the club secretary, suggesting that he might care to resolve his bar bill. It was not a grand bill, built on late nights and wild generosity; it was barely overdue. He had no more credit, he supposed.

'I will write a cheque, ' he said to the doorman, who looked embarrassed. 'You have a cheque form, don't you?'

Three men in plump middle age passed by, the snow caught in their hair and on their shoulders, laughing. They looked at Simeon Ryder as though they recognized him well. But they did not need to acknowledge him.

'I'm afraid, sir – '

'Get me a cheque form. Get the secretary to find one.'

'Sir, the secretary is not here so late. I am very sorry.'

But even the doorman knew the meaning of one of those brown envelopes. Gentlemen who, most unfortunately, could no longer afford to be gentlemen received them sometimes. It was sad. But Mr Ryder had no special grace in the doorman's eyes.

'I'm sure you could settle this in the morning,' the doorman said, sweetly reasonable.

'I have until the morning, do I?'

The doorman wanted him to go, now. He wondered if Mr Ryder had been drinking. Often as not, it was the drink bills that did for the gentlemen, in the end.

'Do I?' Simeon said.

His friend the City Editor saw him at the door.

'You look as if you need a drink,' he said.

Simeon said: 'I don't belong here any more.'

'Come now,' the City Editor said. 'You can't believe – '

The doorman said, firmly: 'I called a cab for Mr Ryder.'

'Oh,' the City Editor said. 'Oh, I see.' He passed on into the club. At the foot of the grand stairs, he turned back. Simeon stood there, and his whole slack body was begging a friend to turn back and honour him. It was too pathetic. The City Editor walked on.

'I don't need a cab,' Simeon said.

He walked in the snow to a public phone. He called the usual woman. She was free that evening, if he could be there immediately. He took a taxi to a basement in Earls Court. He stood on the pavement for a moment, between the drab stucco and the rusted railings and the sense of neglected appearances. The street was shabby as though homeless.

It was all he had. Everything in his career had been process; now all he had was the moment. Nothing followed, nothing that mattered went before. The momentum had gone.

She was a red-head, in middle years, with a voice that had shifted a few social classes in its time; now she sounded like a very proper, faintly nasal lady, able to make her orders billow like a sail when she needed to. She had no great intelligence, only an appreciation of men's lack. He was dependent on her because, when he was here, he was not responsible. Like mother, like nanny, like the schoolteachers he had known, she was making the world within which he had to behave. He liked to behave. If he behaved, he did not have to ask awkward questions about who and why he was.

She came to the door in a robe, a little floury around the jowls and not entirely clean. He liked the various acts to be surgical; he was not interested in being reminded about the clients who had been there before. For once, he did not simply go into the green-walled room, undress and surrender. He worried where she had been before.

'Naughty, naughty boy,' she said, with mechanical conviction.

'Who the hell are you?' he said.

She was startled. She was a big woman, but not tall; she suggested muscle. She said: 'I am Madame.'

'Like hell,' he said. But he had the force of habit; his trousers were down, and his shirt undone. She carried the usual leather strap and she flicked it, hard, against his under-used thighs. The pain was a habit; he associated it with pleasure. He was confused.

'On the bed,' she said. 'Like you always do.'

Like he always did. That was what he resented, more than anything. He was predictable, usual, used and past. He lay down because he had lain down before. He felt her putting the ropes around him, the ropes that had kindly taken him out of the world for which he was answerable. Once she tied the knots, with a vicious expertise, he was not answerable any more; he was absolved.

When his week was full of decision, he needed this moment. Now his week was full of nothing, and he was being bound and hurt. He was restive; he was unwilling to surrender. He had so many doubts and questions, and to have mind and body shackled in this foolish way was intolerable.

'Naughty boy,' she said, with a swish of the strap. It connected with nerve and blood. It gave him no peace.

'Get off me, bitch!' he said.

'Naughty boy. Bad language. Naughty boys should say only what Madame says. Naughty boys think only what Madame thinks. Otherwise – '

He felt the switch again. His wrists and ankles tensed against the ropes. He thought as he thought, believed as he believed, was different in the ways he was different, and he was shameless about all of it. He was a hero to himself, at last. After a lifetime of compromising with power, deferring to the Griffiers, he had no more need to compromise. It was possible he would discover he had nothing more, that power had left him utterly, but he did not care. He did not have to play this game. He did not have to bear this woman's bullying, screeching, vulgar, thoughtless abuse.

'Get off me,' he said. He tried to say it seriously.

'Oooh,' Madame said. 'Slave revolt. That's extra, dear, and you know it.'

'Get off me,' he said.

He could smell the ordinary sweetness of her body, which had gone stale with use. He was hot and furious, all at once. She was make-up and artifice, the false teeth too gleaming, the hair stiffened into place because no client would dare muss it; she was certainty, in a world which had murdered for certainty. She was an old force: the sure thing, the wrong thing.

He was angry enough to kill her. He bunched his hands that were held in the ropes; he could make them small enough to pass through the loops.

'I'll get the towels,' Madame said.

At that moment, he knew he had to kill her. In his mind and body was passing something serious, something terrible; he had come to understand. And she looked down at another middle-aged body, not much distinguished from any other. Pain was something she gave for money, love was what she mocked; he had come to visit a whore and was furious, in the end, that a whore was all she was.

'Get me out of here,' he said.

She decided, for her own best reasons, that he was serious at last; although she thought her clients serious enough when they struggled for escape and she most particularly did not allow it. It was a very minor tussle of conflicting powers, as long as she got paid.

But he was not happy to go. She stood there in her uniform of sex, in bits of leather and lace. He was naked, and, most unusually, he made his bareness into a kind of authenticity and not a cause for shame. She was abusing power; he was playing with it. She had led him to pervert power, to misunderstand it by surrendering it.

He put two clerkly hands around her neck with startling strength. He waited until her eyes were full of blood and fear. He pitched her down on the mercenary bed, where her principles allowed her to feel utterly safe, where no man dared disagree. He pushed the life out of her with his thumbs.

When he saw her dead, he was disappointed. In his mind, he had killed some kind of dragon which, living, she could easily remain. Dead, she was a soft thing, only human. He had not killed his fears at all.

He dressed himself quickly. He went to her phone, and turned off the answering machine which made sure she was not interrupted when servicing a client. He could see the soft, clean snow coming down to gentle the street with white. He went to the bathroom and washed his hands, several times.

He called the police. By the time Emma Griffier reached London, he was in a cell. He was grateful he would never have a choice to make again.

In the city, the snow had turned into slush, and the cold had turned the slush into steel. The evening radio news shows were talking about a historic drop in temperature; they described, with headline emphasis, a great storm passing over Europe. Emma fought and dragged her way through the barred streets, snorting at the vulgar way the weather conspired with her feelings.

The heart of London was chill and lifeless. Around Rowlandson's, a grand house on Berkeley Square, the absences were most noticeable: no cars parked close, no stick-figure walkers struggling through the snow. Everybody who meant to be here had organized their arrivals; everyone else had no chance. And once through the doors of Rowlandson's, nobody needed to remember the slow, cruel blanket coming down upon the city. Here, there were grand chandeliers and pillars of veined marble, a sense of gilt and comfort. Here, you were at your ease, win or lose.

A woman coming in from the storm was not usual. The members of Rowlandson's mostly liked women, and they liked taking risks; but they did not confuse either with serious play. That was a matter of nerve against nerve and, by definition, man against man.

Emma asked for the Emir, and she gave her name.

'I can't say if the gentleman is in the club or not. We don't say if the gentleman is in the club or not.' The doorman was not entirely disapproving; the Griffier name could be important, even here. But he was sure that the Emir was far too rich to be rescued.

'If Madam will wait,' the doorman said, and slipped through tall doors into the body of the club. Emma sat in a side room lush with glass and red; like a movie brothel, she thought, with some surprise. She imagined the customers waiting through the mirror, choosing their pleasure.

'Miss Griffier,' the Emir said. His dinner jacket sat neatly on a short, impeccable body; he had the stillness which comes from knowing you will never be contradicted. His talk was like an English public schoolboy who knew he would spend his life, without effort, as a prefect.

Emma paid her respects. 'I have a very great favour to ask,' she said. 'One I ask in order to help my father.'

'A remarkable man, your father,' the Emir said. 'Won't you sit down? Perhaps the man could bring you a drink?'

Water came, set on silver and drunk from crystal with exaggerated respect. 'I am,' Emma said, 'a shareholder in Griffier Ltd. Since my Uncle Edward died recently, I am the largest single shareholder. Now there are various parties who want to take control of the bank – to take it away from my father.'

'We, too, follow the stock markets,' the Emir said. 'Of course we do not move them quite as obviously as the Kuwaitis. But then, we have the money, so we can take our time.'

'You know about John Brown's interest.'

'I gathered the Bank of England had been finessed into disposing of that.'

'But it begins a game that won't stop, not of itself. The bank is in play. And because of some curious circumstances, there might be pressure on me to sell to the wrong people. I'm not sure I could resist.'

The Emir said: 'You surprise me. I thought you were good at resistance. I was always pestering your father for an introduction, and you would never co-operate.'

She smiled. 'I have a certain talent,' she said, 'but not enough of it.'

'So what do you want? That I should buy your shares? Then why don't you speak to me tomorrow, or go to my brokers through Sir Alistair? What makes it so urgent?'

Emma said: 'It's not a story I would expect you to believe.'

'I think I should have a story,' the Emir said. 'Otherwise it might seem you want to rush me into buying shares that maybe nobody else desires.' He looked at her most directly.

'That is not the problem,' Emma said. 'The problem is that I am at risk, as other members of my family have been at risk. I can't afford to keep the shares in my name.'

'Perhaps Sir Alistair – '

'Sir Alistair is at greater risk than I am.'

The Emir stood up. 'I really think I should have a story,' he said. 'I respect your father very much and I am a client of his bank. He does not mention risk to me. He does not suggest the bank is in any kind of trouble. The bank is not in trouble, is it?'

'Please,' Emma said.

'You understand how to make up a story, I understand,' the Emir said. 'Make me up a story that is good enough, only good enough.'

'I ask you as a favour to my father.'

'He does not ask the favour himself.'

'It is my problem,' Emma said. 'But if anything goes wrong, it could be enough to destroy him. It could put my shares into the hands of his enemies.'

'But nobody can compel you to sell them.'

Emma was infuriated. He was right to be suspicious, and she was quite unable to find a formula to explain the real and melodramatic issue: that she might not live to make a decision on whether or not to sell. Besides, that only raised the issue of why she would not simply pass the shares to her father in the meantime, so he alone could vote them. She could hardly tell the Emir that she did not trust her father, not at present.

'This is most interesting, Miss Griffier. But if you will forgive me, I have a game in progress.'

'I would like to make one call,' Emma said.

A servant, in livery, appeared with a telephone. Emma dialled Easterford, and asked for her father.

'I need your help, Father,' she said. 'I'm in London.'

Her father said: 'We weren't sure if you would get there.'

'I'm quite safe. I need to talk with you.' She turned to the Emir and said: 'Forgive me for a moment.'

The Emir stood at the window looking out on to the square. It was a night for waifs to come begging shelter; the green of the park had turned a sallow white, and the wind was beginning to shape a new, wrapped world out of the backs of benches and the bones of trees. He tried not to hear what Emma was saying.

'I don't say they are the same man. They have the same address and the same phone number. They have to be connected.'

Her father said: 'I absolutely forbid you to take unnecessary risks.'

'Then ask the Emir to take my shares.'

'Nothing is going to happen to you in Amsterdam,' her father said. 'You can't go to Amsterdam.'

'It's what I want, Father. The alternative is to sell out to someone who doesn't value your independence.'

'The alternative is not to sell at all.'

'Not for me, Father.'

'I see.' Her father, too, was watching the night fill up with white. There were paws of snow climbing across the windowsills, and every solid outline had become soft and unsure. 'Then I'll talk to him. If you don't want to be part of us any more – '

She was hurt and furious; it was a kind of blackmail she had never quite resisted. This once, she would be strong enough.

'I want to be rid of those shares,' Emma said.

Her father spoke to the Emir. He talked of the suddenness of women's desires, their changes of mind, the thought that such a large parcel of shares should be in more responsible hands; he believed it, in part, and in part he manufactured what he was sure his client would want to hear. He said it would be a great personal favour to Sir Alistair Griffier, his other father, if only the Emir would consider a deal.

'You can tell me your terms,' the Emir said.

'I've suggested market price,' Emma said.

'That would be wrong,' the Emir said. 'The price is quite artificially low.'

'But you are doing a favour. You may not find it easy to sell, if you want to.'

'I shall say,' the Emir said, 'the asset value at least. 240p a share.'

She was suitably impressed. In the middle of *chemin-de-fer* he had a clear idea of the asset value of his merchant bank.

She put out her hand to shake on the deal. He kissed her hand. 'I wish we had met in some other way,' he said. 'Not just by way of business.'

And, when they had arranged to leave messages with the same grand broker to pass the deal through the market, as quietly as possible, the Emir passed back into the gaming rooms and Emma went down to the square. The snow skirled and spangled in the street lights. She was the only other movement on the square, a dark body in the middle of all the refracted light.

She walked to her own apartment. There was a message from Simeon Ryder, which could wait; she had done what she needed to do, without his help. There were several messages from charity committee workers, with their unfailing social instinct for knowing when the real money is in town, and one from the studio.

She dreamed that each time she went to talk to someone, their head went up in sudden, brilliant flames.

It mattered to be anonymous; she might need an alibi. She took the airport train to Haarlem, not to Amsterdam; she would wait there until she could make an evening appointment with James Drake.

In the dull morning light there were men who cut holes in the canal to fish, and by each one stood a white heron, respectful as a duty, slight in the mists like a memory.

She found a small hotel and she bought maps.

She lay on the narrow bed. Outside, the water in the canals was like old glass, frozen deep; any move she made seemed to fracture the city quiet. It was hard to plan a secret act in such a breathless cold.

She did not actually know that James Drake and Jude Klein were the same man. It bothered her not to have proof; they might be accomplices. She went downstairs to the phone to try the Amsterdam number. She struggled with the small coins in the plastic case.

The girl Helen answered. Emma gave her true name; the girl said Mr Drake was away for the day. Emma said she would like to see Mr Drake that evening. The girl said that would possibly be fine; he would be back before dinner. She could have put the phone down then.

The girl said: 'Miss Griffier?'

'Yes.'

'You know anything about chaos – something called chaos?'

'I know what the word means.'

'I can't explain it on the phone,' the girl said. 'You're a Griffier; you might understand. I could tell you.'

'Can I meet you in Amsterdam?'

'I don't think so,' the girl said. 'It's a small town. We could meet somewhere else, where tourists go.'

Like lovers, they plotted a rendezvous that would be safe enough and unremarkable. The girl would take the train to Haarlem. She would take a taxi to the Teylers Museum on the Spaarne waterfront; Emma knew from past visits that Teylers was usually quiet. Emma would wait there until two in the afternoon.

'I've seen your picture in the papers,' the girl said. 'I'll know you when I see you.'

A public place, in the wrong town, and her own suggestion; Emma felt safe with the idea. If it was more trickery from James Drake, he would need to be monstrously ingenious.

At one, she walked down to the waterfront. The last boat through had left ridges and floes of pack-ice that had frozen back into place. It had long been too cold for snow, but old snow persisted. She found the grand façade of Teylers, like a church with columns and a winged Victory at the top; she walked up the steps, paid her three guilders to the man at the door, and walked into the first rooms.

There were row after row of tall dressers, stacked with skeletons and fossils, in a room which had been varnished brown with age; a great fish left a mark in rock like piano wires; a horned creature looked like the mud from which it had been prised; curls of ammonites, like stone snakes, rose up the height of the windows. There was man, at the time of the flood, and the unorchestrated wings of a primeval bird and a gigantic lizard of which she had never heard; and an organ with a thirty-one-note system and a collection of postage stamps and scientific machines with huge polished spheres and pendulums slicing at the air. She was in the heart of all an eighteenth-century man would need by way of knowledge. She imagined intense men studying the stones until they could will the secrets out of them, men who must be a little mad; and in the burnished beauty of the scientific instruments, there was a sense of obsession.

The galleries opened out into an oval room, under a high dome, with a balcony around it and a glassed table laid with crystals and stone in the centre. Emma walked around it, slowly. The jags and cuts of colour caught her eye. There seemed to be no guards, but there were too many doors to be sure what was happening behind her back.

'Lady,' she heard. She turned and walked towards the sound. 'Up by the balcony,' the girl was saying. There were signs saying flatly: NO ENTRANCE. She ignored them. It crossed her mind the museum guards would hear her heels on the wood slats of the stairs; she took off her shoes and crept up.

She felt a hand on her shoulder.

'Shit,' she said. 'You startled me.'

The girl looked lean like skeletons, worn thin by fretting; she would have made a death's head in a moral picture.

'Don't go further,' she said. 'We can't be seen from here.'

Emma sat down on the stairs. 'What did you want to tell me?' she said.

'I don't know I should tell anyone anything,' the girl said.

'You want money?'

The girl played the remark like an insult.

'Then tell me,' Emma said. 'We don't have a lot of time.'

'James talks a lot about chaos,' the girl said, 'and how

he's going to get your bank and stir up chaos round the world. He says he understands what will happen. He can make money while everyone else is confused.'

'He's a brave man.'

'Yes,' the girl said. 'Yes, he is a very brave man. But you can't argue with him. He does what he wants to do. When he had his accident and his stroke and he was in a coma, he wanted to live, so he did.'

'We thought,' Emma said, carefully, 'he was dead.'

'Oh,' the girl said. 'I never thought of that. They did have the death certificate ready to file. They got him away from the hospital and took him to an apartment and they treated him there. I guess nobody countermanded the certificate. He lost his wife, and he wanted to lose her, and he wasn't bankrupt any more because he wasn't alive and his friends brought back the money he gave them to keep – or some of it.'

'He wasn't buried, then. Somehow I imagined he was buried and came back.'

'Don't be dumb,' she said. 'He went to the cemetery sometimes, though. I thought he went visiting, but maybe it was his own gravestone. Creepy, huh? He'd have the best marble. Very tasteful.'

'I guess you nursed him.'

'I helped him,' the girl said, primly. 'I was his companion.'

'And now you're tired of the job?'

'No,' the girl said, carefully. 'No, not tired. Scared. He keeps talking about this chaos thing. I don't like it when there's no law and order' – the phrase came out as a single word – 'because I don't eat where there are no rules. I got to get paid. I got to eat. If there aren't rules, nobody respects a girl because they don't have to.'

'I understand.'

'No, you don't,' the girl said, tartly. 'You break down order and the worst off are the women who depend on men. We're the ones who suffer. The men can go fight for their bread, and the rich women know how to buy it anyway, and the wives – look at it this way. If there weren't rules about what is proper, nobody would want to break them, would they? And they certainly wouldn't pay.'

'You understand this chaos he talks about?'

'He has a theory about what happens when things go wild in a market. He thinks he can predict it well enough to make money. He'd take Griffier Ltd and he'd work the market, quite deliberately, so everyone would be terrified and he would be making money.'

'It's a theory,' Emma said, 'like a lot of other theories. He should write a book about it.'

'He doesn't talk about it to everyone.'

'I can understand that,' Emma said. 'It sounds like criminal conspiracy.'

'I wouldn't know. I just know that if he can do what he says he can do, I'm in trouble. And he does very well. When I knew him first, he was just James Drake and legally he was dead. Now he's Jude Klein as well, and he's brought Jude Klein to life. Jude Klein can go to dinner and give a lecture when a year ago he was only a thought in James Drake's mind.'

Emma had wanted the proof; it had been handed to her. 'I'm very grateful,' she said.

'It was weird, seeing Jude Klein come to life,' the girl said.

'I'll buy you a coffee,' Emma said.

The girl said: 'I'd like that.' Wrapped in felt and wool, she was like some little animal saved from drowning; she was grateful for any kindness. She must be easy for a man like Drake to run, Emma thought, and she hated him for it.

She stepped carefully down the stairs. It seemed absurd now to have no shoes; she dressed her feet. The sound was not much more than the cold wind in the glass of the dome above, but it was something new and rhythmic. It attracted attention.

At the foot of the stairs, by the NO ENTRANCE sign, there was a tall man wrapped in black. He shook his dark hair, dog-fashion, to spill the last of the melting snow. Emma remembered him all too well: she remembered him on the Rhinegold train, and in a New York bedroom. She remembered the black doctor's bags he had carried the first time she saw him.

'It is not allowed up there,' he said. She remembered the voice, exact as a set-square and as graceless. 'You should know that.'

She wanted to tell the girl to stay back, but she was trusting now that she felt saved, and she came too quickly after Emma.

'You have met my father's girl,' Adam Heller said.

'She has a name,' Emma said, but she realized she did not know it.

'She has several,' Adam said. 'She likes to be called Helen.'

'Then you could use her name.'

For a moment, she had the slight advantage of the stairs.

'You haven't asked how I come to be here,' he said.

'You had a good lawyer, I expect.'

'They couldn't find you when they wanted you to give evidence, so they had to let me go. They suggested quite forcibly that I go back to Europe. That was very helpful, in the circumstances.'

'I imagine the American authorities were glad.'

'They couldn't make sense of your story,' Adam said. 'They decided there was something peculiar but not something indictable. That was because the studio said you were on indefinite leave; that made them worry.'

Emma said to the girl, softly: 'Get up to the balcony.

Find another way out, there has to be one.' She turned back to Adam. 'I'm not going to congratulate you,' she said.

'The girl shouldn't be here. She's not supposed to leave the house.'

'She's a prisoner, is she?' Emma could hear the faint creaking as the girl shifted, foot to cautious foot, along the balcony. She was only the height of two men above the oval room, but she seemed to feel vertigo, and Emma thought of Adam's handgun.

'My father likes his people to be available.'

'He likes you to be available, too?'

Out of a side room full of pictures came a guard. He stood looking at their conversation, finding it curious; he was not minded to interfere unless he had to. Something in the stance of the two told him it would not be welcome, and there was nobody in the museum for them to disturb. But then he heard a board sounding out from the balcony above his head, like the note of an untuned organ, and he heard a sharp hiss of breath.

'Is there anyone up there?' he said, reasonably.

Adam Heller turned towards the sound. 'I think you have a trespasser,' he said. The guard nodded. 'You take that stair, I'll take this,' Adam said. The two men quartered off the corner where the sound had been.

Emma imagined the girl up there, crouched and still. She would not know to go back or to go forward; and she could not hide. She knew only that Adam Heller was waiting for her, and she must not come down to him, not unless she was made to.

'I must ask you,' the guard said, with patience and with firmness, 'to show yourself and come down. The gallery is not for the public.'

The girl edged into view. She could have been walking on a rope above a snakepit.

'I'll go and fetch her,' Adam said. 'I know her.'

The guard was embarrassed. Among the bones and machines and crystals, he rarely had to challenge or prohibit; he did not have the trick for it. 'I'll ask her again,' he said.

But the girl was walking with such care she might have been on ice and not on iron; she wanted to find some escape. Adam Heller watched her, and she backed against the wood of the panelled walls. He could hurt her by watching.

'If you get out, Adam,' Emma said, 'I'll bring her down.' She turned to the guard. 'The woman is afraid of this man, can't you see?'

'Yes,' said the guard. 'But it is not allowed – '

'Get out of the room, Adam. I'll bring her down.'

Adam raised his voice very deliberately. 'She's told you whatever you wanted to know, I suppose? So now you don't have to worry what happens to her.'

The girl looked down at Emma. She had no practice in trust. She looked insubstantial, veins pulsing under a thin skin.

'I'll get her out safely,' Emma said. And then she bluffed. 'James Drake sent her. He should have told you.'

The guard stood foursquare in his lovely panelled room, with the light brightened by the snow and the sparks of colour from the crystals on the central table.

'Get out, Adam,' Emma said. 'James Drake sent her here. It's none of your business.'

She could see the possibility being born inside Adam Heller's mind: that his father had gone away again, had failed to say what needed to be said as he so often had. Adam should have been told. He had a henchman's resentment at looking a fool and a son's fury at being excluded after being included in so much conspiracy, so much killing. The old man did not have the right to cut him out again.

He pulled himself together. 'I will wait outside. I'm sorry the girl has been so silly,' he said to the guard.

He strode out through the broad galleries full of bones and machines. The light, like a church, closed round him.

'Come down,' Emma said, briskly, and the girl obeyed. She stood by the crystals, like a child who does not want for a moment to confront what she has done. 'They're pretty,' she said.

The guard shrugged. His job was done; he assumed the women would leave. He watched them walk through the rooms of fossils. Once, the girl stopped and looked at some dead thing in a case and shuddered. It was a museum of mortality, of ideas and creatures that had long ago exhausted life, and she was nervous.

Close to the high entrance hall and its stacks of books, there were two tiny rooms, lit only by their cases. In one, there were crystals lit in ultra-violet light. The girl wanted to see what was there; she was reluctant to face the cold, real world outside. She stepped into the tiny room. Emma went on, impatiently. She stood on the steps of the museum, and the wind bit into her face like something abrasive, and she thought of simply leaving. The girl was fine; Adam had gone.

She could not walk away, but the cold was hurting her. She walked into the museum bookshop for a moment. She wondered where Helen had gone, and what she was doing, and whether she had to be responsible for the girl.

She heard a bell, insistent as a sad child, in the quiet of the frozen town. It was too early for the Teylers to close. Emma walked to where the doorkeeper stood, bothered and alert. He picked up a torch and a huge bunch of keys; he was looking left and right among the tall dressers, looking for the new evidence among the old. The alarm rang furiously, a real bell and not some electronic simulacrum, beaten by a clapper until the sound shone like worked metal.

The guard was stock still by one of the tiny rooms. Emma came up to him, and he motioned her to stay away; but it was no longer so easy. She had no right to step back.

The room had no air. Its light was the soft blue of ultra-violet, meant to make crystals show their natural luminescence, but suggestive as a fairground horror; it bathed now the body of the girl. Her head had smashed back through the glass of the case, and lodged on the raw edges of the rocks; the glass had cut jaggedly through her throat.

Emma said: 'She was American.'

The doorman said: 'Could you name her? They'll want witnesses.'

'No,' Emma said, almost truthfully, 'I'm not sure of her name. I talked to her for a little while in the oval room.'

'I'd go, if I was you. They'll want witnesses.'

She was ashamed to step back into the bluster of the wind, but there was nothing she could do for the girl. She wrapped herself carefully, against the cold and other things.

Adam Heller was somewhere near. And this time, she knew that he had killed someone; no ambiguity, no guesses. She had to be with people immediately; other people were the best protection she had. She turned the corner into a street without walkers, with no shop windows that she could use as a refuge.

She knew the town a little, enough to make her way back to the church in the main square. She would be safe enough there, in its wide white spaces, until the building closed; and then she could hope that Adam had gone, and take a taxi to the station. At nine, she was meeting

James Drake on the Herengracht in Amsterdam, and she must not miss her time.

She wondered if the girl had efficiently left a message for him. She saw the cut in the girl's neck, a piece of butchery, like a wire caught in the throat of a deer.

The street was narrow now. A trio of schoolboys came cantering down, sliding and diving for scoops of snow. She could hear their laughter echoing as they passed, and faded. She passed antique shops that might have made refuges, but their doors were locked, and nobody looked out from behind the stacks of decoy ducks and tall chairs and inlaid cupboards. She wanted coffee, but she chose instead to walk into the church.

She remembered it as a huge tabernacle of light and air. She kept herself, nervously, in the body of the church, between the pulpits and their sounding boards, and the model ships that hung in gilt splendour and the lights of the chancel. The great organ that filled the whole west wall was being tuned; sometimes there was a spill of sound, like water or thunder.

She found the small memorial tablet she remembered. It commemorated a man called Griffier, some seventeenth-century merchant who was dreaming of a fortune in Amsterdam. It announced his virtues, and it was capped by a weeping widow, and six children, ordered in bulk from the usual quarry in Flanders. She touched it like a talisman: that being a Griffier could be something else than the past months' horror. There could be the continuity she needed, and the future she longed for.

She sat down, where she could sense shadows coming from any direction. She thought of Adam Heller, and how the boy must wonder now if his father ever meant to include him in this second life. His father told Adam nothing, and told Helen what had to be done. She tried to weigh Adam's anger.

This Drake was an infection that could not be stopped

by ordinary means; he had to be cut out, with a blade. But there were things she had to know, know for sure, before he was dead.

Blade and ice; she thought of skates. She thought of the canals of Amsterdam blocked solid by the cold, played on in the mornings by a Brueghel feast of girls in red and blue and matrons amusing themselves on the way to market; she thought how skates do not leave marks like footprints.

She bought skates at a shop close to the church; she carried them in a plastic bag. She thought of wake nights when a hero knight sits vigil to dedicate himself to what must next be done, bloodily. She, too, was sitting out a wake.

She wondered what murder would mean.

The cold hurt his eyes, or so he told himself. He was afraid to cry in case the tears froze. But little Helen had betrayed his father, he was sure now. He was almost sure enough to think she deserved to die.

But only almost, and it pained him. His father demanded, and he performed, and he was never sure if it was enough. The girls never matched what he knew his father expected of him, but he was disappointed in his father's girl. Emma Griffier was going to see his father and he hardly knew whether to protect the old man or the faint, dumb hope that Emma represented.

He kicked the cap of his boot against stone. If his father were gone, then he would not have to plot and work against Emma and her family. If his father were gone, his life would have no more shape, and he would have no more aspirations.

He dreamed of finding her, and then being able to act: to make love, to kill, to quit. He was stifling in the small gap between her will and his father's will.

He climbed into his car and he thought very hard about his father's death, and who would bring it about.

12

On Haarlem Station, high above the street, she waited for the train to Amsterdam. The waiting room was full of other people's breath and smoke, like cattle on a cold night. She felt almost secure. She was nameless here, a woman in a warm coat carrying a plastic shopping bag.

She had to walk out for the train and she felt exposed again in the open. She could not predict what Adam would do. She thought he might be watching, between the fine Art Nouveau rooms on the platforms. She promised herself that all the men were more blond, and bulky than Adam, but she still stooped her spine, and she particularly caught nobody's eye. She wondered what the police had made of that thin girl's body, smashed on to sensational rocks.

At Amsterdam Centraal, the train stopped almost in the open. She ran for the subway under the platforms and, in her hurry, she turned the wrong way, away from the crowd, and found herself on the bleak shores of the Ij. A truck rolled by at a stately speed. She backed away, turned and controlled herself; she walked briskly towards the light and the people. The crowd in the station hall jostled companionably. She covered her face with a scarf against the cold and she marched out of the station, into the winter stillness.

The cold had smothered the breath out of the city. She could hear the brakes of a tram from streets away, like metal shearing. When she stood for too long, thinking, the cold began to seep into her, like water on sand, and shocked her into movement.

There was no more Helen to say she had made an

appointment. James Drake himself might not know she was coming. But she still had thoughts of an alibi, and a taxi driver might remember her. She had to save her name from a dead man, the world from schemed chaos, and she had no doubts about what she would do; but she was not entirely ready to be a heroine. She did not want to be caught.

She had the skates, and there would be no point in taking the tram to a house that must be quite close. She turned to her right, crossed the broad Singel by the lock; the ducks made a sad nest of their own brown feathers on the ice. She walked down to the Milkmaid's Bridge where Herengracht began, a grand canal arching around the city like a finger of water around a glass. She knew the tall gables of the merchant houses; she had been taken here to see where the Griffiers once lived. Their skewed, jumbled look was all practical sense: the houses leaned over the pavements so that goods could be winched into the high storeys, without climbing stairs that were narrow as ladders, and their odd angles meant that mansions could be built behind ordinary façades.

The houseboats were still there, closed against the cold and belching fine smoke. The smell of coffee oil from the coffee shop had died on the cold wind hours before. The ice in the canals had tumbled and broken like a fault line, but the cold had taken it and made it still again. She passed a building settling into the sand, resting on huge trunks of wood.

From now on, she was not just a tourist walking to somewhere warm. She had business. Her shoes left prints in the shallow snow that would freeze as she walked; the skates would let her pass along the frozen canals, unseen, unheard, like a wind in the city.

Along from the bridge was a landing with a shelter, where the boats plied for hire in summer. She could step down over the chains to the wooden deck, and huddle there to put on her skates, hidden from view. She could lower herself on to the ice.

The houses shone with yellow light, but they looked inwards, not out to the dead streets. The city had wrapped itself in whatever warmth it could find – the bars, the beds, the consolation prizes of a bitter night. A solitary man in a raincoat, bulked out with sweaters like a soft pear, walked alongside a dog who lifted old, fastidious paws from the sticky cold of the cobbles.

In the shelter, she put on her skates, and took the guards from the blades. She took her balance and for a moment she felt obvious and vulnerable.

But she felt the blades cut the ice, and she stepped out strongly into the night. There were tracks already, crazily circling and doubling back, in eights and Zs and long, purposeful lines; hers could not be identified among them. She knew to look out for the holes that sentimental people cut for swans; they had frozen again and they were a hazard. Boats had pushed through the Singel, and made pack-ice, but the sides of the Herrengracht were smooth.

No footprints, no sound. All she could hear was the little wind she made as she knifed the air; she fancied for a second it might give her away. She strode out now, glorying in a simple physical skill which gave her an advantage against James Drake at last. She was a woman who worked through her intelligence and her friends, and now it had all come down to blades.

She had directions from the girl that morning: four bridges down; poor Helen had assumed that Emma would walk from the railway station. She kept close to the walls of the canal, where the ice was unbroken and she was unseen in the shadows. At the fourth bridge, she looked around for some way to climb the canal wall. She was by a houseboat; she thought she could hear breath and laughter from within its flanks.

The summer pedal boats had a landing stage exactly where she needed one. She clambered on to the wood. From the bag strung around her neck, she took the guards for her skates. It was surprisingly easy to walk on guarded skates; she had seen the children do it. You left only lines in the ice and snow, and on the pavements the lines had neither length nor depth to give away an identity. She took the steps up to the sidewalk.

The light was wrong. The ice had a metal sheen which was not the usual dance of breeze and lamplight on the water; the city looked like an exhibit under glass. She knew she was the only blood-warm creature in the show.

The house was black and white with a fine gable and steps up to the main door. There were no lights on. She wondered if Drake had flown out of town, or gone to Haarlem to mourn Helen. She knew she should guard against some trick, but she had the comfortable sense that she had come back where her family began, along these canals; from here, they had brought cleverness and concentration into London, and gone from merchants to aristocrats whose opinions could be cashed like cheques. What was defensible about the Griffiers could be defended here.

She stepped up to the door, careful on the packed, rough ice which nobody had thought to wash away. It seemed ironic to take such trouble to come anonymously and silently, and then to ring the door bell like some ordinary visitor, but she could not force the door locks and she could not risk the noise of a breaking window.

The bell jarred like a nightbird. She remembered school manners, that it was rude to look too intent while waiting, or ring again too soon. She looked away, to the stars iced in the bleak sky. She made the bell ring again.

She could not stand here indefinitely in the cold. Someone would notice her from a house opposite, even tell the police. In this city, squatters claim any empty house, and people look after their locks and their neighbours. She tried the door handle, even though there were three stout locks above it.

The door opened. It had been very slightly ajar, she realized, and she could push it wide open. She slipped into the house quickly, and pulled the door shut behind her. She heard the locks tumble into place.

The cold had infiltrated while the door was open; it made the warmth and safety of a house on a cold night seem tenuous. There was enough light in the hallway to make out the shape of a large vase, and an oil painting varnished dark with age; the house could once have been someone's pride, but now it had the characterless smell of a rented place, its life stored away.

All around her, church bells rang nine o'clock. The cold had cleared the air wonderfully. She could hear the scufflings and settlings of an old house set on sand and pilings, like moths in the walls. She took off her skates to be able to move more easily, and slung them around her neck. She opened her coat; the house was growing warm and faintly muggy.

To the left, a door led into the grand rooms of the house. She pushed it open. The street lamps turned ornamental objects into silhouettes; a nymph, a pot-bellied Buddha, a Neptune, some sentimental Lalique glass that glowed like a spectre, tall ficus and the stiff, sharp blades of plants. There was a huge blond wardrobe, like a room, inlaid with dark woods.

She walked to the windows so that the light would be behind her and she could see more clearly. A car came cautiously along the canalside and its lights seemed to shout in the room and make the shadows uneasy.

Along the street stood a little pissoir, made of grey iron lattice. She fancied a man stood there, but it was far too cold. She must be imagining sounds and strangers.

She edged back into the shadows. Beyond the bric-à-brac there was a computer screen, flushed orange; she went to read it. A line of C prompts scrolled up, each one followed by: 'Bad command or file name.' The function keys were labelled for WordPerfect. She typed 'wp' at the C prompt, and when she was in, she hit F5 for List Files. There were three files with the day's date, and one of them had last been touched at 20.52, just after she stepped out of Centraal Station. It was too close for any comfort.

She walked into the hall, and the cold air pressed against her like a cat. She saw stairs going up as steep as a ladder; she began to climb them, the steps whining as she went.

On the landing, she found four ways to go: three doors, and the stairs that led upwards. She chose the front room. She went to the window first and looked down. There was nobody in the pissoir; she must have been mistaken. But now she thought she could see someone in the shadows on the ice, a tall man. He went out of sight behind a houseboat, and then, minutes later, she saw him haul himself on to the boat's deck. He edged gently past the frozen pots of plants, and a summer chair that had been iced into place. She thought she could hear laughter from the boat. The man caught at the chains each side of the gangplank to swing himself off the boat and on to the sidewalk.

She thought of the cold air that stroked her in the hallway, and how she had heard the locks shift into place. She was confused. She knew now it was unlikely that she was alone. She had come to meet a man, and she had nothing more to lose by turning on the lights. She pressed the switch.

The room had a big bed, a pair of comfortable chairs and another of those monstrous, decorated wardrobes: this one had pediments and columns like a temple, and four small rosewood gods on each top corner. She opened the door.

It was the man she knew as Jude Klein, that she knew must also be James Drake. He had been shut in the dark like a child, with his eyes taped and his mouth gagged.

He could hear, she assumed, but he could not nod or shake his head and he could not speak or gesture. He turned in the ropes which held him to a kitchen chair like a fish drowning in air. And something had happened to his bare, blue-veined shanks. He had tensed himself to find the power to escape and a fine bone had proved too brittle. His flesh was blood purple where the stump of bone cut through.

She could not tolerate the enemy as victim. He was her business, nobody else's. She began to untangle the ropes, and he fell forward on to his face. He struggled up, tried to put weight on the broken leg and screamed. He dragged himself to the bed from memory.

She tugged at the tapes which shut his eyes. The tape took the hairs, and left him looking oddly naked.

She could see he was racing his own heart to speak or think. He was saying: 'I come back. I always come back. They put me in bankruptcy, they put me in jail, I come back.'

She slapped him hard across the face and then she was ashamed of herself. He slipped away from pain like a dog does. And then she was furious. He was making her feel pity when she should have known the simplest and most righteous anger.

'You are James Drake,' she said.

He tried to raise himself up. 'At your service. I know you already.'

'You killed my lover,' she said. 'You killed my uncle. You ruined my brother. You – '

'You do me too much honour,' Drake said. 'I had help.'

'You don't justify yourself? Or defend yourself?'

'Why should I? You know my story, I'm sure. You also know that your brother Rupert did what he wanted, and so did your brother Maurice, and your father. They trapped themselves.'

'David Taylor was murdered. Avalon was burned.'

'I'm not responsible for the details.'

'The details?' Emma said, very low. 'You think a man's death is a detail – '

He tried to ease the deadness in his limbs; he tried to stretch and keep the blood in motion.

'Did you think your girl Helen was a detail, too? And her death?'

Drake opened his eyes very wide. They were stained eyes, full of blood and yellow.

'Adam killed her, too. This afternoon in Haarlem.'

'He didn't tell me. The poor little cunt.' She could not quite be sure if he meant his son, or his girl.

'He smashed her head through a glass case,' Emma said. 'He left her to bleed to death.' She was fascinated by the pain in the man's face where she had expected only certainty. She had imagined him sitting like a demon at the heart of chaos, laughing and glorying, but what he was showing looked like regret.

'A little nurse,' Drake said. 'Nobody in particular. She didn't deserve to die.'

She remembered the sudden cold in the hall. She fancied she heard movement on the ground floor.

'He never knew the limits of things,' Drake said. 'His mother said that. He was determined to be noticed.' He shook his head. 'I only thought he would be useful. Like my hands, now I could no longer use my hands, and like my eyes. What a son is for.'

'A son you didn't know.'

'Not well enough,' Drake said.

She said: 'We haven't much time.' She was sure now

that something had been dragged across a lower floor: a chair, perhaps, or a box.

'What do you want me to say?' Drake said. 'I can say anything you want.'

'It wasn't just about us, was it?'

'Your family ruined me. They suckered me into a deal where it was glorious to be suckered, but the jail hurt just the same, and the end of things. Now they have the same problems. I'm clear – an eye for an eye.'

'Why David? Why Edward?'

'They were close to the Griffiers. But then I had a very simple idea, which was to have my revenge and make a new fortune. The refinements all belong to Adam. He would do anything for me, anything.'

'I thought you were giving orders.'

'My friends helped, and my old contacts, but only Adam used his own initiative. He has enthusiasm.'

She could imagine it all too well. The grand, ambitious James Drake, prepared to set his name on a city as the Rockefellers did on New York, with a world of oil and contacts and political prospects; such a man was hampered by a son, not able to tolerate a foreign son who was different. He could easily leave the boy in Switzerland, deny him his name; his rare visits would seem more than enough. If the boy loved him, or at least the idea of a father, too much, then James Drake need not even feel it was his fault. So the boy grew desperate.

'He tied you up?' Emma asked.

'Sons do worse things to dead fathers,' Drake said. 'Even living ones.'

She did not have to turn to know that Adam Heller was in the doorway, cold tangled in the folds of his heavy coat. His father looked up.

'You tell her things,' Adam Heller said. He was shaking. He knew now that his father's world was a treasury of secrets to which he would always be denied access. He was furious to find their family's enemy inside that secret garden.

'You told Helen too much, ' Adam said. 'She went and talked to Emma Griffier. She probably didn't want to know so much. And you,' Adam said to Emma. 'You shouldn't have untied him. You don't know what he'll do.'

Emma said: 'He's an old man.'

'You think he's so human now?'

'He's my business,' Emma said.

Adam moved to her side of the bed. They looked absurdly like colleague doctors at a patient's side, in consultation.

'I put him back in the dark,' Adam said. 'I put him back where he began, where I found him – in the dark, where he could not speak and he could not see and he could not move. He was safe there. He should never have come back.'

He was strong, of course. He must have been strong to engineer David's death. She was marooned between a soft bed and a wall. She had the skates for a weapon, and their long, fine blades, but she could see no way to use them.

'I have something to say,' Drake said from the bed. He seemed very calm.

'Why don't you kill him, the man that killed your lover?' Adam said. 'You have to kill him so he can't come back, ever again.'

'He's a living man,' Emma said. She would have been grateful for anything which proved this weak old man was the monster of the past few months. 'He is your father.'

'Oh,' Adam said, 'but not a good father.' He looked down at Drake with eyes like stone tablets.

'Listen to me,' Drake said. 'This woman thinks we did everything because of her and her damn family. She can't think that. She has to know better. The damn Griffiers don't matter that much.'

'Say what you want,' Adam said. 'For now.'

'You see,' Drake said, and he struggled to prop his back against the ornate bedboard, 'once we have control of Griffier Ltd, we begin to play a game. A game of chaos.' He would buy a little time by fascinating her, as he did to her father. 'We have no interest in the smooth, the ordinary or the average day. We do those small, insignificant things that in days or weeks create terrible storms. We seek out chaos, and because we can predict it, we profit from it. And do the authorities respond?' He began to cough. 'No,' he said, with difficulty, 'no they do not. Oh, they will stop computer trading so the crashes take longer, and maybe they will stop people buying shares and the future of a whole index at the same time. They will clean things up. The investor will be confident. The banks will be happy.'

Emma saw he was coughing blood.

'That is when it starts,' Drake said, 'not when it is finished. When everyone thinks the stock markets have been reformed just enough. When the brokers are hungry for business, and need buyers and sellers. When everyone is terrified of a world in which stock prices stop climbing and climbing. That is when chaos begins.' He settled back on the cushions. 'I never make deathbed confessions,' he said. 'I never made one last time.'

'He didn't do it because you mattered to him, or because I mattered to him,' Adam said. 'It was for money, as usual.' He was waiting for Emma to grow angry.

But Drake's body was now far behind the intent of his mind. He stared directly into Adam Heller's eyes. He had no more excuses or pleas.

'You could be merciful,' Emma said.

'Mercy is not the point,' Adam said. He was inspecting

his father as a butcher might inspect a bull; he saw no more life.

'He came back, he said things would be different. But even when I met you, things were exactly the same. He came and he went. He never talked, except when he wanted something. Nothing changes for me, not until he is gone.'

She saw how eminently reasonable the next bloody act must seem to Adam, and her faith in reason faltered. In his world, everything was consistent, welded and patched into one by sheer will.

'I have some things to fetch,' Adam said. 'You could help me.'

She knew she must not be an accomplice. She watched over Drake as Adam Heller carried two boxes into the room. Each was marked Johnson and Johnson. She wanted to laugh, but she knew the sound would be like retching.

'He has to go back,' Adam said.

His father pressed himself against the headboard. He watched his son as some patient naturalist will observe a fact of feral brutality, and seem quite detached. He was not afraid of death, because he had died. He knew there was only blankness to follow. He had lived on stolen time, and now the theft was called and punished.

Adam tipped out rolls of surgical gauze on to the bed. He teased Drake, touching his leg. It was the broken leg with the stump of bone close to the skin. Drake screamed, and the sound seemed to rise and fill the sky above the city.

'I found a knife in the kitchen,' Adam said.

'Help me!' James Drake said.

Adam shook the knife from the sleeve of his overcoat; it was a well-weighted carving knife, sharpened until it was almost a scalpel. He forced the knife into his father's open mouth.

It was too late to look away.

Soundless, voiceless, James Drake's jaw fell in a dottle of blood.

'Be quiet,' Adam said. 'You know how to be quiet. You were quiet so long.'

His father's eyes were full of terror now. He remembered fighting for life; he could not be resigned because he knew it was possible to fight death. He remembered the months when the body was a casing of dry leaves, and he could only briefly force his memory into focus, and his will clawed at life for a toehold. He thought: 'Dear God, do not let him put me back.'

'This has nothing to do with me,' Emma said.

'Really?'

Adam slammed the knife into the quilt and dragged it out; in the low light, the feathers came in spurts like blood.

'People get scared of being buried alive,' Adam said. He took the gauze and wrapped Drake's arms to his body, turning him easy as a doll; he wrapped the legs together, ignoring the fury in Drake's eyes when he touched the broken leg. Drake made a sound that was pain shut up in a bottle.

'You could stop me,' Adam said to Emma. 'Why don't you stop me?'

She could not answer.

'The hands, the feet, the eyes, the mind,' Adam said. 'The first to come back, the last to go. I know about these things. He keeps his mind until the last.' It was such a careful commentary, lucid as a textbook.

James Drake remembered when his fingers first moved as he wanted. He remembered the long blank waiting before that.

Adam Heller took the knife and cut open first his father's left wrist and then the right. The fingers were in brief spasm, and then they were unconnected to mind or instinct.

'The eyes,' Adam Heller said.

She felt the weight of the skates around her neck. She saw Adam's back as he carried the knife up to his father's eyes. The skates were sharp enough, she thought, and they had weight enough. She thought where to strike. She would get only one chance; he would not be distracted. Against the spine, she might not do enough damage. Around the rib cage, she would be deflected by the bone; he would be no worse than bruised.

Adam pushed and gouged. It was hard to force an eye.

James Drake remembered life going out like a tide over broad, low sands, and then the birds coming down. He was trapped in the ruin of a body. He tried to remember a poem by Tennyson he used to like. He knew, from experience, he was dying.

'They severed the head,' Adam was saying, breathing with effort, 'to make the dead stay dead. They struck through the heart.' He had taken the knife and now he sawed at the resistant, jowly flesh around the old man's neck. When he cut the first artery, blood flew in the chamber like a storm.

It was not a story any more. She took the two skates and held them out, blade up, at the full stretch of her arms. She called to Adam. He finished his cutting; he turned round. He saw her crouched there, and he stood up to come towards her. As he rose she drove the skates up into his groin, as hard and as straight as she could.

He stared at her. He was doing what needed to be done, and she had dared to strike him. It was a moment before he felt pain as well as shock and, when he did, he doubled over. She pulled away the skates.

There was no pride in it, only necessity. She raised herself up from the blood and dust on the floor, and she went to the stairs. She was filthy with blood on both her coat and her clothes beneath it. She did not dare go to the shower, but she found a bathroom, and she washed her face. She washed her hands, again and again. She would be fine if only she had another coat.

She was startled at how rational a woman can be when her mind can encompass no more horror. She walked into a second bedroom, an ordinary and clean bedroom, without blood, and she checked the wardrobe. She found a trenchcoat, warmly lined; she bundled up her own coat and dressed again.

The lights burned in the front bedroom. The window seemed huge, an invitation to spy on the blood and detritus inside. She tried not to look at the bed.

Adam Heller looked up at her, his face suggesting nothing but immense relief.

13

It was the baby that filled her life for a while, the milky, irrational calm of him, brown as caramel, with pale blue eyes. She nursed him in the tower room at Easterford, like the memory of David.

At night, she wondered what he had heard from inside her body in those months, when she thought it was only terror which had made her body slip its usual rhythms; and how he could dare to see clearly from his cornflower eyes, after all he must know.

She could tell him things, as she could never tell David. He was Griffier, after all, and he should care that the bank had been sold to the Swiss, who paid high for the name; the burden had gone. Sir Alistair Griffier was there as non-executive chairman, a decorative fixture like the marble; he had made himself proud of the job.

The baby would be short of uncles. Maurice Griffier had started two years in a German penitentiary, where he seemed to embarrass his jailers; they liked to punish wickedness, not stupidity. Rupert Griffier was away, but not in jail. And as for Easterford itself, the castle in the marshes, Lady Griffier was preparing it to be given away to the National Trust.

'I don't like monuments,' she said. 'Like gravestones, I always think, and Easterford is a monument now. Silly.'

Emma said: 'I have to get back to work.'

'Take time,' her mother said. 'It doesn't heal anything, but it stops the wounds tearing open. You never took time after David died.'